The Wrekening
An Ancient Mirrors Tale

Jayel Gibson

THE WREKENING: AN ANCIENT MIRRORS TALE
PUBLISHED BY SYNERGY BOOKS
2100 Kramer Lane, Suite 300
Austin, Texas 78758

For more information about our books, please write to us, call 512.478.2028, or visit our website at www.bookpros.com.

ISBN-10: 1-933538-30-9
ISBN-13: 978-1-933538-30-3

Publisher's Cataloging-in-Publication
(Provided by Quality Books, Inc.)

Gibson, Jayel, 1949-
The wrekening : an ancient mirrors tale / Jayel Gibson.
p. cm.
LCCN 2005910611
ISBN-13: 978-1-933538-30-3
ISBN-10: 1-933538-30-9

1. Mythology, Celtic--Fiction. 2. Magic--Fiction. 3. Science fiction. 4. Fantasy fiction. I. Title.

PS3607.I268W74 2006 813'.6
QBI05-600211

This is a work of fiction. All of the characters and events portrayed in this book are fictional, and any resemblance to real people or incidents is purely coincidental.

Praise for the Ancient Mirrors Tales

… powerful storytelling. The characters leap from the page, grab you and don't let go. Finally, a new writer has come, one who tells an original tale and revives your desire to read fantasy.

In New York Times Sunday Book Review

The Wrekening will transport you to the world of Ancients, Guardians and Men; a world where you will savor the thoughts, feelings and adventures of many magical beings, totally forgetting everything else around you. Jayel Gibson weaves magic with words.

In The Bloomsbury Review

Ms. Gibson's magical tales have all the elements that make a great fantasy – a quest, life and death stakes, romantic tensions, magic, suspect loyalties, and an overwhelmingly powerful villain.

Andrew Eather, Editor, Independent Reviewer
London, UK

The Wrekening continues the Ancient Mirrors journey. Ms. Gibson delivers on the promise made by the exceptional storytelling in her debut novel *The Dragon Queen.*

Gina Halston, Editor, Independent Reviewer
Florida, USA

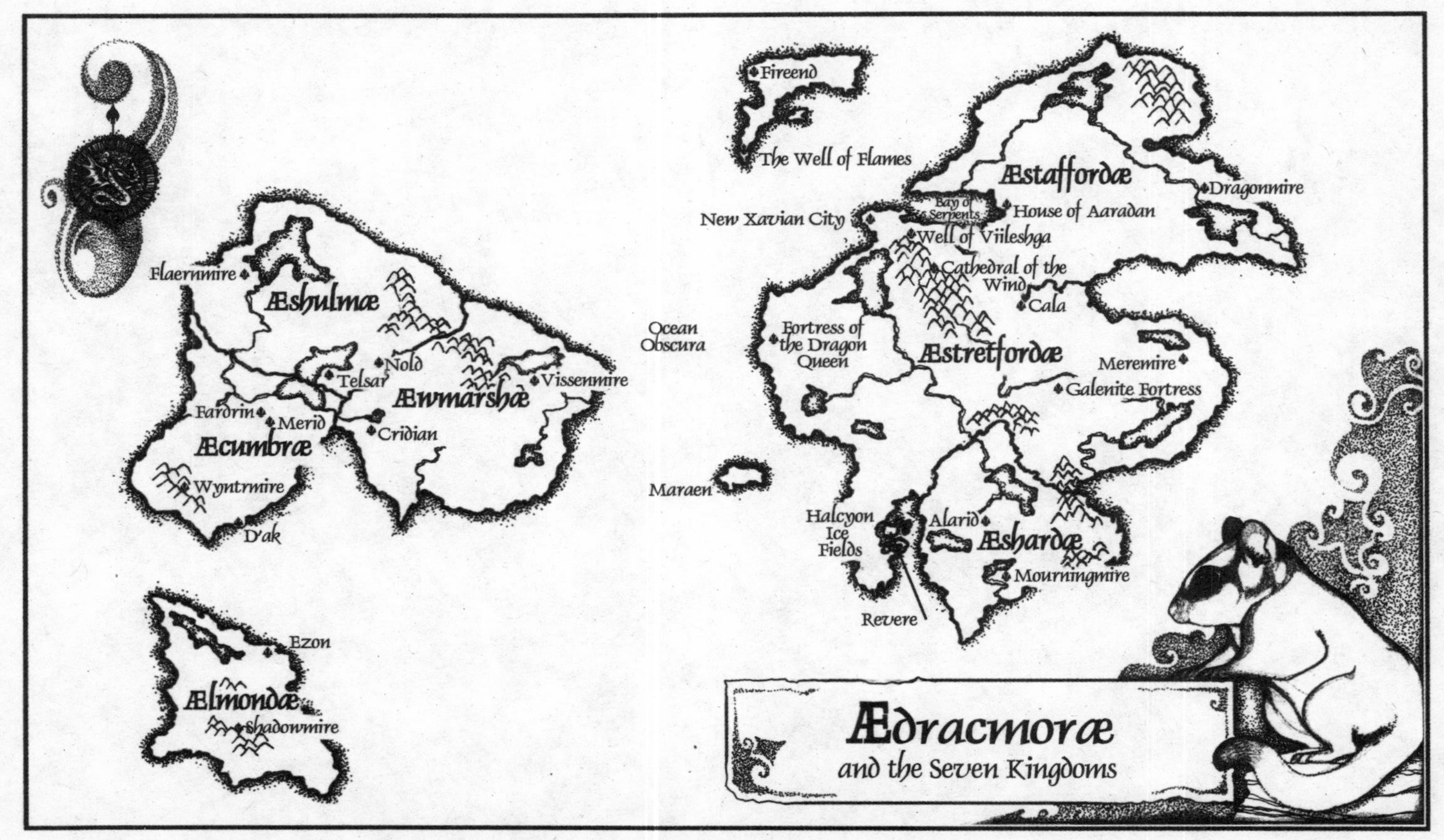

Ædracmoræ
and the Seven Kingdoms
Fireend
The Well of Flames
Æstaffordæ
Dragonmire
New Xavian City
Bay of Serpents
House of Aaradan
Well of Viileshga
Cathedral of the Wind
Cala
Ocean Obscura
Fortress of the Dragon Queen
Æstretfordæ
Meremire
Galenite Fortress
Maraen
Halcyon Ice Fields
Alarid
Æshardæ
Mourningmire
Revere
Flaernmire
Æshulmæ
Nold
Telsar
Æwmarshæ
Vissenmire
Fardrin
Merid
Cridian
Æcumbræ
Wyntrmire
D'ak
Ezon
Ælmondæ
Shadowmire

Verdant Forest
Northern Mountains
Lake of Lost Memories
Meremire
Trembling Sea
Malochian City
Ebony Plains
Fortress of the Dragon Queen
Maelstrom's Lair
Xavian City
Plains of Crimson Grass
Sea of Sorrows
The Wasteland
Galenite Fortress
Azure Sea
Dobbinwort's Furnace
Ruby Sea
Halcyon Ice Fields
Æstretfordæ

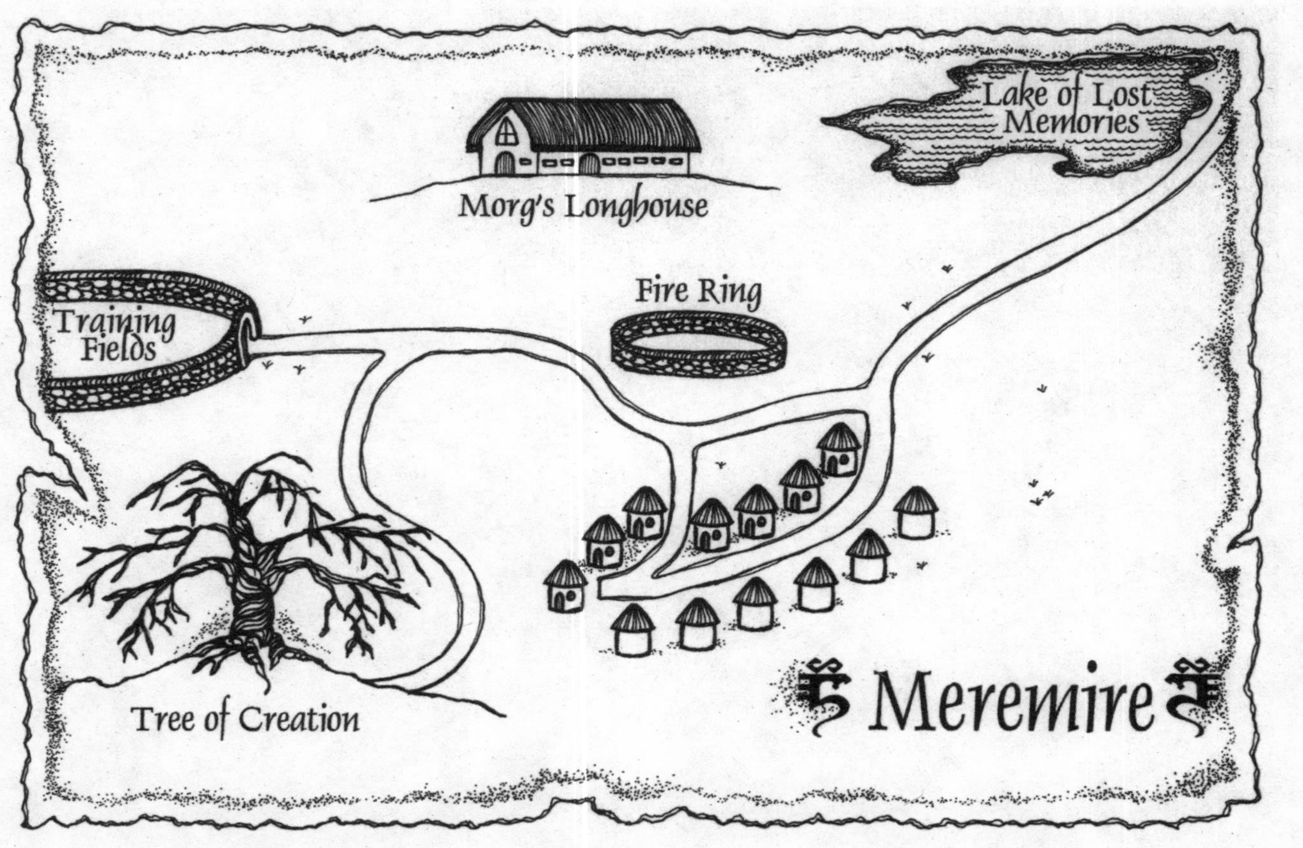
Meremire
Lake of Lost Memories
Morg's Longhouse
Fire Ring
Training Fields
Tree of Creation

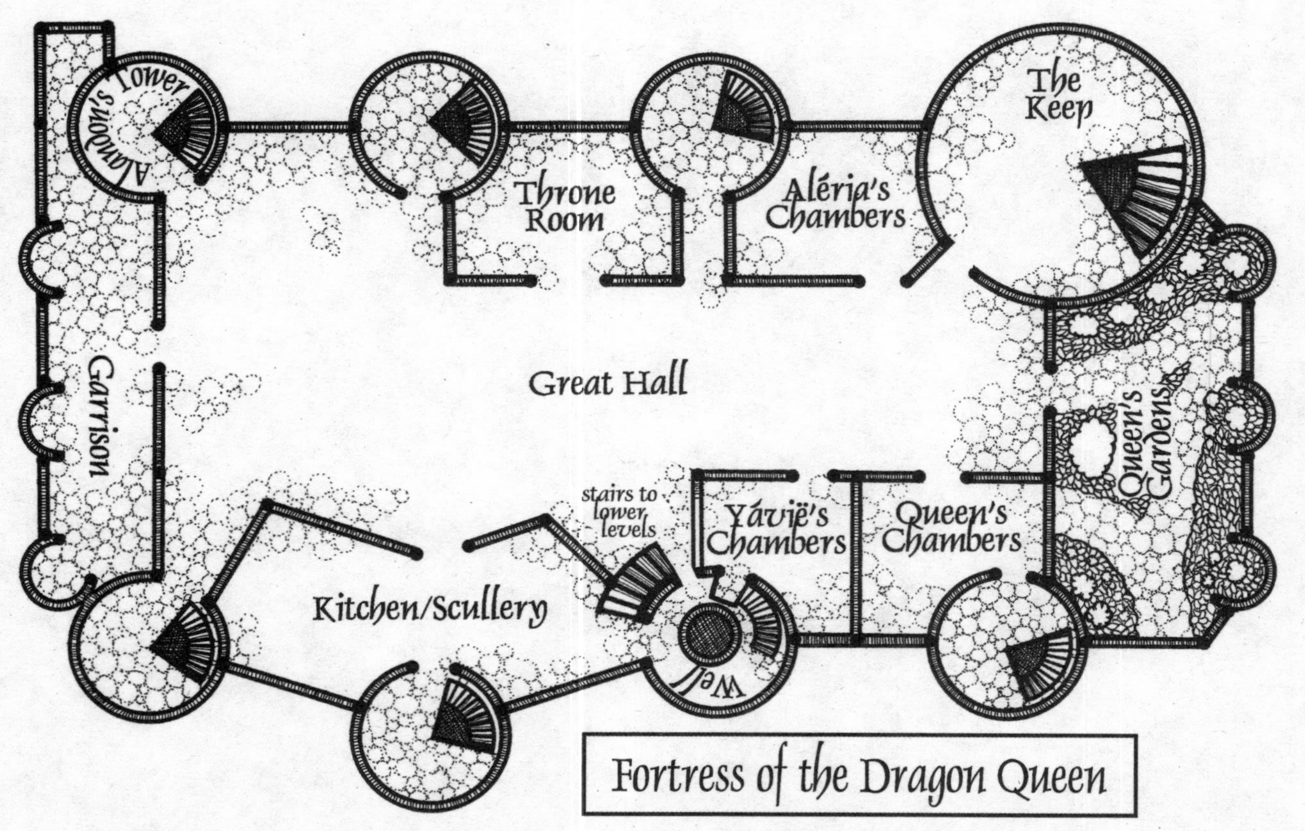

Fortress of the Dragon Queen

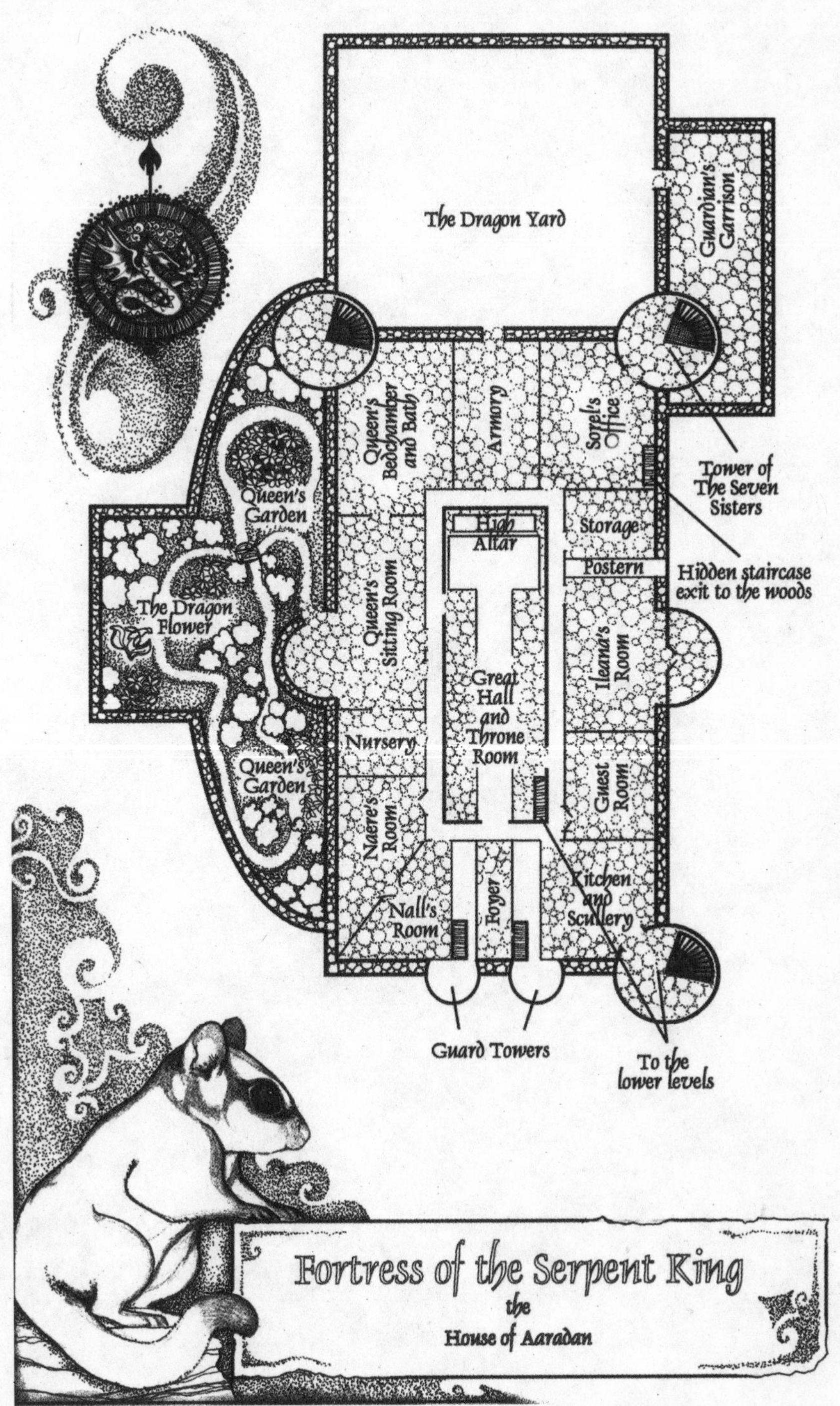
The Dragon Yard
Guardian's Garrison
Queen's Bedchamber and Bath
Armory
Sorel's Office
Tower of The Seven Sisters
Queen's Garden
High Altar
Storage
Postern
Hidden staircase exit to the woods
The Dragon Flower
Queen's Sitting Room
Great Hall and Throne Room
Ileana's Room
Nursery
Queen's Garden
Guest Room
Naere's Room
Foyer
Kitchen and Scullery
Nall's Room
Guard Towers
To the lower levels
Fortress of the Serpent King
the
House of Aaradan

Dedication

In loving memory of Joni Anderson

And to:
Ken Gibson
Sarah Gibson
Peggy Brewer
Jeff Shockey
Dan Bargess
Chris Overcash

For their friendship, support and encouragement

Acknowledgements

Any work of fantasy is a union of magic and madness that includes golden grains of potent sorcery from those who are sometimes totally unaware that their enchantment has rubbed off on the author. My gratitude to these and all my friends for their encouragement and touches of thaumaturgy:

Michele-lee Phelan, my artist and friend, for the inspiration of her artworks. They grace my books, website and walls and continue to fill my mind with magic.

The City of Port Orford, Oregon, my home, for her beauty, tranquility and people – truly a writer's paradise.

Gold Beach Books (the coffeehouse bookstore) in Gold Beach, Oregon for the wonderful inspiration of the rare book room, a quiet table and lots of café brevés.

The South Coast Writers Conference for the encouragement they provide all writers and Southwestern Oregon Community College for their sponsorship of this annual event.

My editors, Andrew Eather and Gina Halston, they are true members of the Errant Comma Enclave. It is with tongue in cheek that I assure you any errors you may find belong to them.

Collaboration

Sean W. Anderson has collaborated with Ms. Gibson in the development of ideas and storyline as well as created a number of characters used in the Ancient Mirrors novels. The characters Nall and Talin are based on role play characters originally created by Mr. Anderson for online gaming.

Mr. Anderson lives with his family in southern California.

Illustration

Fantasy artist Michele-lee Phelan is the official illustrator for the Ancient Mirrors series. Her artwork appears on the covers, as internal illustrations and website graphics for this series. Works are created using traditional and digital media. Ms. Phelan is featured as one of Epilogue's New Masters of Fantasy 2005.

The artist lives with her family in New South Wales, Australia.

Table of Contents

Chapter 1 Discovery

Humming to himself, the little man climbed among the rocks looking for a grosshare to put in his evening pot. Taller than the diminutive Ancients, but not nearly as tall as a Man, he wore a wrinkled cap above a ruddy face. His hair and whiskers were a fiery red and on either side of a bulbous nose sat his muddy brown eyes clouded with the visions of yesterday and tomorrow. The coat and trousers he wore were covered with fine dust, as if he had been traveling along a dry and windswept road.

Seeing a fine fat hare bound forward then scoot down a hole, the man shouted and jumped after it, slipping beneath the earth as easily as a small reptilian bloodren. Landing lightly on his feet, he struck a waffle root match and gave a startled cry at the sight that lay ahead.

The hare was forgotten as he gazed in wonder at a hundred stone figures - an earthen army. Row upon row of demon soldiers stood as if prepared to stride away, though none so much as twitched or drew a breath. Each held a sword and shield that looked to have been carved from stone by a clever artisan. They were the G'lm, the dark horde, the soulless army used against the Dragon Queen by the Sojourners Alandon and Abaddon. The little man had heard the tales. But in the tales the G'lm had been destroyed during the drawing together of the seven kingdoms long, long ago.

Stepping forward, he walked around the closest form and gazed into its empty eyes. A chill gripped him as an image filled his mind, an image of many other caverns filled with soldiers of the damned waiting to be called from their timeless inactivity by some unknown master.

Squealing, he turned away and scampered up the wall and out the hole through which he had entered. As he emerged he whispered an incantation, creating a rift between the sacred land of Réverē and the world of Ædracmoræ.

The air shimmered briefly and left Brengven the Feie stationed before the fortress of the House of Aaradan. Racing forward through the gates he shouted his name and begged the Guardians to let him see the Queen.

Three pair of solemn eyes stared back at Brengven as he told of his discovery.

Shaking her head, Yáviē, Queen of Ædracmoræ and the seven kingdoms, looked toward the Sojourner Ileana.

"Is this possible?"

"I have never known the Feie to err." Ileana's soft voice carried the weight of truth.

"It was believed that the army of the horde was driven away with the rebirth of Ædracmoræ by the binding of the roots of the willow and verdant trees and the restored flow of the waters of life, but now it seems they merely lie in wait."

"I have summoned…" Sōrél began.

"Nall and Näeré," the tall, amber eyed Guardian completed, gripping Sōrél's shoulder and bending to kiss Yáviē's cheek.

"What new crisis has reared its ugly head?" Nall's eyebrows rose as he noticed Brengven.

"This is Brengven the Feie. He arrives from Réverē with news of a rather disturbing discovery. A large group of demon soldiers cast in stone stands within a cavern there and he has had a vision of many other such armies hidden within the earth of Ædracmoræ," Sōrél shared. "I thought it best if we examined them ourselves. Perhaps there is no threat."

Ileana touched her son's sleeve. "Sōrél, if the horde lies beneath us there is a threat. Evil will sense the opportunity and seek to use them against us. No word of this must reach beyond the fortress walls."

"Brengven, do you understand my concern?"

"Madam, as they lie beneath Réverē, the threat is not to you alone," sniffed the Feie.

Shimmering, Ileana soothed Brengven's mind.

"I mention it only that you will be mindful when you speak outside Réverē, for there are many who would like to wield the power of the dark horde."

"In my dreams the netheraven warned against the rebirth of Ædracmoræ. He called it 'the queen's folly,'" Näeré murmured, recollecting the giant bird of legend from her night visions. "I did not think it important at the time, but now it appears his warning may have had merit."

"What exactly did the netheraven say?" Yáviё asked.

"He said, 'Your queen quests for the rebirth of Ædracmoræ even though she knows it will open doorways that should remain closed.'"

All eyes turned to Yáviё, Queen of Ædracmoræ.

"I did not know. How could I have known?" she whispered.

Ileana held up her hand for peace among her children and their partners.

"It is too late to concern ourselves with yesterday. Our only task is to make the wrong right. Brengven, will you open a rift to Réverē and show us what you have found?"

Bobbing his head, the little man stood and created the doorway allowing them to pass into his enchanted kingdom.

Return to Révere̅

Révere̅ is a tiny island of enchantment lying at the southern tip of the Halcyon Ice Fields. Hidden within a land locked in the icy breath of continual winter, it is accessible to very few Ædracmoreans. In the company of Brengven they stepped through the rift to stand before the soldiers of the horde.

Yáviё gasped, memories of the horde's power as it had pursued the Guardians every step of their past quests flooding her thoughts. Each deathshade and demon looked as if it had simply paused mid-stride on its way into battle. Even the tattered, rotting fabric hung captured in stone. It was with cautious unease that she wandered among her old enemies.

A sudden clap of thunder caused them to recoil until they realized it was merely Nall attempting to slay the unmoving enemy. As he struck the figure a second time, a shudder passed up the blade and through his arm, leaving it numb, although it had no affect on the lifeless soldier. Not even dust crumbled from the snarling face where Nall's double-bladed sword had struck.

"I guess simply reducing them to dust where they stand is not an option," Nall shrugged, "but it was worth a try."

Sōrél beckoned the others to him and gestured toward an odd altar-shaped fixture at the back of the cavern. At its center a deep channel had been carved, a resting place for something missing.

"It is the resting place of the heart shard of one of the Wyrms of Ædracmoræ. They are known to provide great magickal powers to those who possess them," Ileana filled their minds with the dreaded knowledge.

Touching her son's arm she looked directly into his eyes as she spoke the words of doom: "Any willing to quest for a shard to fit this altar will control this army. It must be stopped before it begins if Ædracmoræ is to be preserved. While it will be difficult for any to pass into Réverē and place a shard here, it will not be difficult at all within the seven kingdoms. Somehow the shards must all be gathered and destroyed without attracting the attention of those who would harm us."

"I shall go," Nall stated without hesitation.

Näeré kissed her husband and watched his aura pulse brightly.

"How would we hide the glow of your goodness?"

"Näeré speaks truly," Sōrél agreed. "Sending Guardians on a quest to recover the shards would be far too obvious. We shall have to find another way."

"We will return to New Xavian City and speak with Sōviē and Xalín. This is a decision for the entire Council," Yáviē said, receiving 'ayes' of acceptance from all present.

"I should like the Feie to accompany us," Ileana spoke, indicating Brengven, "if he will agree."

Brengven looked at each of them in turn, assessing their strength and honor, before finally giving his approval.

"Though I refuse to bed in the same room with mortals, for I find them offensive," he warned as he opened the rift that would lead them to New Xavian City.

The Council

"Mother!" Sōvië hugged Yávië before turning to her father.

"You look more like your mother each time I see you," Sōrél laughed, hugging his daughter and accepting Xalín's grip.

"Whatever it is you have found here agrees with you both," Ileana said to Sōvië and Xalín.

"Oh Granddame, do you not know? It is Xalín I have found," Sōvië teased, watching the tiny frown appear between Xalín's eyes at the unwanted attention.

Reaching up she touched the frown with her fingertips, causing him to relax.

"Welcome home," Sōvië whispered to Nall and Näeré.

"Come, we shall meet within the council chambers to ensure the privacy of our discussion." Xalín spoke in the soft voice of his Xavian heritage and extended his 'welcome home' to Nall and Näeré.

As they walked along the illuminated pathway they discussed the new city and its radiant beauty. Built among the tangled roots of the verdant forest, the city was one of shimmering illusion created and maintained by the minds of its Xavian citizens. No building ever fell into ruin, for when its usefulness had ended the Xavians simply allowed it to fade from their thoughts. Xalín and Sōvië, both Sojourner halflings, served as the Xavian leaders and Nall and Näeré acted as the treasured city's Guardians. Among the citizenry dwelled the remaining Sojourners, ancient travelers who had come to rest on Ædracmoræ before the time of remembering. Nearby the Emeraldflyte of accordant dragons kept a watchful eye on the comings and goings within the forests surrounding the giant verdant tree that had sprung from the Well of Viileshga. There was probably no safer city within all the kingdoms… and no safer kingdom, save Réverē.

Within the council chambers Yáviё explained what they had seen to Xalín and Sōviё.

"What does it mean?" Sōviё asked.

"Ileana says it means we must locate and collect the shards that belong within each of the receptacles, though I am not sure where we shall begin. It must be done with great secrecy lest we raise the curiosity of those who would use the G'lm against us."

"Xalín and I shall do it," Sōviё offered, ignoring Xalín's raised eyebrow.

"Indeed, I would be willing to quest for the shards if it pleases the Queen;" Xalín agreed, "however, I would not be willing to risk Sōviё's safety. I would require her to remain here with Nall and Näeré. "

"You would not be willing to risk my safety?" Sōviё fumed.

"It is already decided that no Guardian will go. There is no way to hide our presence. A group of Guardians questing would be far too obvious and lead to the exposure of the quest. Its concealment must be maintained," Sōrél explained to soothe his daughter's irritation.

"Who? Who can you send on a quest of this importance if it is not one of us?" Sōviё continued, glaring at Xalín as she saw a smile tug at the corners of his mouth.

"When last I checked, you were not a Guardian, Sōviё," Xalín whispered in her ear.

"Good, then I shall go alone," she said, thinking she had won.

"You are my charge and I forbid it."

Ileana signaled an end to the argument.

"As your father has said, none of you will be on this quest. Sōviё, you and Xalín belong here. The Xavians need your guidance. Nall and Näeré also belong here and your parents must remain visible at the fortress in Æstaffordæ if the quest is to stay hidden from the eyes of those who would betray us."

"But who, Granddame? Who could be trusted?" Sōviё questioned with grave concern, her own interests forgotten.

"Perhaps Galen?" Xalín suggested, knowing the man he called

'father' could certainly be trusted.

"I do not believe he would want to leave the Galenites again, and I would not like to ask it of him," Yáviё said.

"Send the daughter of Nall," Ileana spoke in a barely audible voice, causing all eyes to focus on her.

"No!" Nall stared with disbelief.

Näeré laid her hand on his shoulder, but he shrugged it off.

"She has already betrayed us!" His eyes burned with hurt and frustration.

"She is trained as a Guardian and travels with another who bears the same skills, but they do not bear the aura of Guardianship. She also reads the language of the Sojourners and will be able to translate the scrolls of Alandon and Abaddon. Also a third, Caen, who has both the skills of a thief and the connections of a rogue tracks them; his talents will also be needed," Ileana continued, ignoring Nall's outburst.

Frowning, Sōrél looked at Nall. "What my mother says make sense. Do you truly believe, Nall, that this girl would betray Ædracmoræ?"

Näeré whispered, "Say her name. Her name is Cwen. She is our daughter."

"She does not wish to be my daughter." Nall raised his shoulders in a gesture of indifference and looked away.

Looking back at Sōrél, Nall shook his head. "Nay, she would not betray Ædracmoræ if she pledged to keep it safe, but she will not give her pledge, Sōrél, and she will not willingly offer her allegiance. She has no honor and is bound to nothing."

"She is bound to the Equus and she calls Talin friend," Näeré reminded.

Yáviё leaned across the table and took Nall's hand.

"If we can get her to agree to the quest and if we can win her pledge, do you think she could accomplish the quest with Talin at her side?"

Grudgingly, Nall nodded. "Aye, both are well trained and highly skilled. Cwen is as good a sorceress as Näeré, though she refuses to use her magick. Talin is smart and thoughtful and I have never seen anyone wield the axe any better. But, there will be no way to control her."

"I believe that Talin will serve to guide her hand," Näeré offered. "She trusts him above all others. And he knows how to make 'suggestions' she will accept."

"Well they are certainly scruffy enough - none would suspect them of being pawns for the Queen," Nall admitted.

Ileana looked at Brengven, who had remained silent and watchful.

"Surely you do not expect *me* to quest with these scruffy mortals?" he asked with a horrified look on his face.

Her look told him that she did indeed.

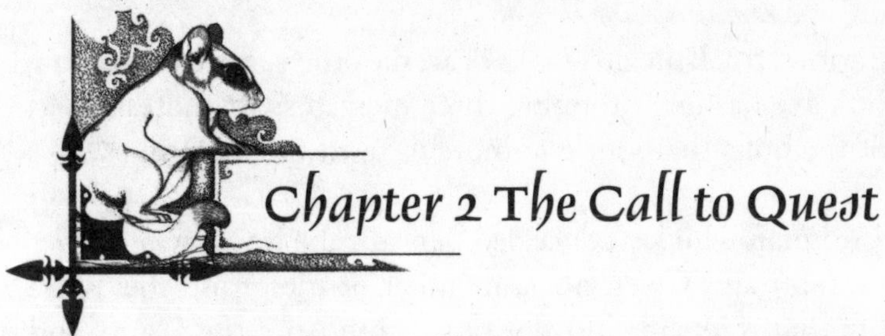

Chapter 2 The Call to Quest

Rogue, Charlatan and Thief

Within the glen the three lay hidden. The first was a young woman of little over twenty summers, long and lithe and deceptively delicate. Her long hair was glistening copper and her skin a pale ivory, but it was her eyes that often drew stares, for they were as golden as the topaz star and their depth and brilliance called to mind those of a hunting cat. In a scabbard across her back rested a long sword and on the ground beside her lay a slender walking stick.

She heard her companion call inside her mind and rolled her eyes at his warning. He lay to her right, a little over half a dragon's length away. He was just under nine spans and broad in chest and shoulders with muscles well defined from practice with the double-headed battle axe he now held lightly in his hands. His skin was tanned, as if from long hours in the sun, and his fair hair gave him a rather rakish look as it fell across his forehead. The woman often teased that he had cut it with a dull dagger. He watched the approaching threat with a set of mismatched eyes, one the dark turquoise of the pools within the ice fields, the other deep green, as if stolen from the forests.

Both wore the soft tanned leathers that spoke of better days and nobler nights than this campsite in the glen.

As the woman rose and stood among the trees watching the strangers approach, she checked her weapons and drew the crossbow from her belt, nocking a bolt and raising it to meet the chest of the first of the trespassers. Just before she dropped the veil and let the arrow fly she sent Talin a silent request.

"*Be sure one remains alive.*"

As the arrow struck the first man's heart the others scattered, seeking cover. Talin's axe flashed, dropping three men in swift succession as Cwen shot the bolts that sent two more to meet their death.

The third man who lay concealed beneath the leaves was neither a friend to Talin and Cwen nor a member of the group they were rapidly thinning. He slid into position behind the trespassers and sent his lance through the back of the man closest to him. Drawing his short sword he dispatched another two before retrieving the lance and dropping back amid the trees. His eyes were the pale green of a new leaf and his face angular and handsome. His dark hair lay bound at his neck and fell between his shoulders. His leathers were old and worn, though not soiled or frayed.

"Talin, does one live?" Cwen called from where she collected her walking stick.

"Aye, but with no thanks to you. Why must you kill everything?"

"Did not my father ever tell you? I am a very angry young woman," Cwen said, using her most convincing impression of her father's voice and laughing at Talin's look of irritation.

"If you wish to question him you had best do it quickly before he bleeds out. His arm hangs by a thread, which means my axe requires sharpening." Looking at his axe, he rubbed his thumb across the blades.

"Next time if you want one alive, save him yourself." Talin raised an eyebrow and looked down at the dying man. "You will soon wish I had killed you sir, for she does not take kindly to those who poach in her woods, even though they are not really her woods."

"You know I never miss, Talin. It is not possible for me to save one." Cwen knelt by the man who bled onto the ground and touched her staff against his wound.

"Did you kill the Equus?" Cwen asked, pushing harder against the wound.

"Aye," the man gasped in pain, "We did not know you owned the woods."

"I do not own the woods, but I do call the Equus kin. Are there others near, others of your creed?"

But the man was dead and of no further use, which brought a flash of anger as Cwen looked up at Talin.

"Do not look at me! I kept him alive."

"Not long enough," Cwen snapped.

Reaching out, Talin touched her arm, sending his thoughts, "*The one called Caen lies in the woods a dragon's length to the south, and do not...*"

Cwen whirled and looked in the direction he had indicated, causing him to give a deep sigh.

"What good does it do me to speak it silently when you always give away the advantage?" he added aloud.

Striding with angry purpose toward the trees that lay to the south Cwen held her crossbow ready and swung her stick in a large arc before her. As the stick struck Caen through the leaves he howled and she released the bolt, catching him as he rolled away, pinning him to the ground.

"I thought you never missed," Talin said behind her.

Lowering her eyes to the man who lay with the arrow clasped in his fist as he tried to pull it out, she replied, "I did not miss. But he did move very quickly for a dead man."

She knelt beside the injured man and stared at him with confused curiosity.

"Have I not instructed you not to track me, Caen?"

"Aye, many times," he answered through gritted teeth.

"Then why do you insist on doing it?"

Examining the damage the arrow had done, she slapped Caen's hand away from the shaft and quickly broke off the quills.

"Hold him," she directed Talin and watched as he grabbed Caen's shoulders and forced them against the ground.

Grabbing the shaft, she leaned her weight on it, causing Caen to bellow in pain. Her eyes met Talin's and she watched as he jerked Caen up off the ground, leaving the arrow behind and a neat hole through Caen's shoulder.

"I should fill the wound with earthen fungus and watch it turn black and secrete foul smelling pus," Cwen muttered.

"But you will not because...?" Talin asked with wry amusement.

Her lips twitched and she admitted, "Because he avoided death by my bow."

"Ah, so you admit you missed."

"Nay, 'twas a maladjustment in the quills, that is all. I never miss."

Drawing a willow bark poultice from her satchel she lifted Caen's vest and placed it on the wound.

"It will heal. If you do not follow me again you may live."

Reaching out with his good hand Caen grabbed Cwen's arm and pulled her close, causing Talin to raise his axe.

Shaking his head, Caen whispered, "It is good to know I shall live, Cwen."

Jerking her arm away, she hissed as she rose, "If you ever touch me again I shall cut off your hands."

Spinning, she strode off toward her camp, knowing Talin would be close behind her.

Refusal

Brengven stepped from the rift just beyond the glen where Cwen and Talin camped. He had been warned against approaching the mortals in darkness, for they were swift to react to intruders; so, he settled down among the trees to await the day star's light.

As the little man quieted and lay back against the soft moss-covered ground, he became aware of another not far away. A low moan told him this one was injured and he rose to investigate. Seeking the heat of the other, Brengven found a man racked with the chills of fever lying beneath the leaf litter.

The Feie knelt to examine the man's wound. A healer had sloppily applied a willow bark poultice unaccompanied by the magick of the healing words or the spell to end the pain.

"Whoever placed this poultice did not like you very much."

Shaking his head and muttering, the Feie removed the poultice and replaced it with a new one from his knapsack.

"I shall heal you so that you can die a different day, mortal."

With another moan the injured man opened his eyes and looked into the muddy brown ones of the small man who spoke to him.

Brengven sat back on his heels as a vision swept into his mind. It was an image of the woman who had loosed the arrow that had pinned this one to the ground. Fuming in silent consternation, Brengven cursed Ileana for sending him into this pit of swamp leeches.

As the magick of the healing took affect, Caen drifted into a restless sleep, battling the demons that lie within his soul.

Scuttling off, Brengven placed a comfortable distance between himself and the offending mortals, then, shadowed by invisibility, napped until the daylight arrived.

He heard their voices as they prepared a breakfast of day doves and bannock and smelled the floral odor of the prickleberry jam and tea. His belly growled and urged him forward in hopes of a meal to start the day.

"H'lo!" he called and they turned toward his voice, hands on their weapons.

Unveiling himself, he stepped from the shadows.

"I am Brengven the Feie of Réverē. I am sent by the Sojourner called Ileana, Granddame of the one called Cwen."

"I must caution you, little man; the names of Sojourners, Guardians and Queens hold little value where you stand," the young woman called back. "So unless you can think of the name of another, you had best be on your way."

"Would you not feed a weary traveler before sending him away?" Brengven asked, continuing his approach and mulling over her rudeness.

"Feed the little wizard, Cwen. What can be the harm? Perhaps the tale he brings will entertain us over tea." Talin gestured the man forward, indicating that he might sit beside the fire.

Cwen dropped the heavy scowl that had been darkening her fine features.

"It is a trick. Some deception of my father's," she flung back over her shoulder. "And I shall not listen to a word of it, for I have heard it all before."

"The one you left lying in pain could use a cup of tea while you are choosing not to listen," Brengven called back to her while accepting tea and a bannock from the tall young man.

Cwen glanced toward the south where they had left Caen lying. She had half hoped he would be dead. Returning to the fire she glared at the flame haired man as she tossed away her tea, refilling the cup from the boiling pot.

Approaching Caen with her staff held in readiness to strike him, Cwen was surprised to find him sitting up, back against a tree, eating what appeared to be some very old bannock.

"You need not strike me, Cwen."

"I have never seen green jam before," she said, her lips curled at the sight of his moldy bread.

"'Tis all I have and I do not beg," Caen stared back at her.

"If you promise not to touch me I shall hand you this cup of tea to go with your moldy bannock." She swung the stick lightly in warning against whatever offense he planned.

"I promise it." He watched her boldly as she stooped to hand him the cup.

"I find your gaze a transgression."

"Cwen, you find everything offensive." Caen gave a low laugh, causing her angry look to deepen.

"Return my cup before you leave the glen this morning," she instructed as she pivoted back toward her campsite.

Caen's eyes followed her and came to rest upon the stranger by her fire. The healer, he recalled from his fevered dreams. What would a healer seek from Cwen and Talin? Perhaps he would learn the answer when he returned the cup.

"He brings a demand from the Queen's council," Talin offered as Cwen rejoined them.

"I do not respond well to demands. And the Queen's council is just another…"

"Sit and listen girl, for I would not come among mortals if the threat were not exceptional. I find you offensive and rude and would rather be among the Feie in Réverē than trapped between you and the one beneath the trees. The breeze mingles your scents in a most unpleasant manner.

"The message I bear has naught to do with you or your family squabbles. It involves a threat to all of Ædracmoræ: the horde of the damned. The Sojourner sent me to ask for your help. Some members of the council were in disagreement over this decision so I doubt that what you decide will matter much."

"I am not interested," Cwen snapped with finality. "Finish your ill-gotten bread and leave this place."

Grabbing her bow she headed off through the trees to the north.

"Tell me just what it is they ask of us and I shall approach her when her head has cleared and her fury has abated," Talin encouraged Brengven.

"The stone soldiers of the dark horde have been found in a cavern below Réverē. I saw a vision of many more such caverns within the earth of Ædracmoræ. These armies wait to be called by any who locate the artifacts required. The council wishes to find the artifacts and crush them before evil discovers them and uses them against us. It is simple. Recover the artifacts. Ileana believes them to be heart shards of some ancient dragons. Return them to the council so that they may be destroyed."

"Tell the one called Cwen. I shall return for your answer three days hence." Brengven stood, bowed his thanks for the morning meal and faded away, leaving Talin staring at emptiness.

"Simple, my eye. They send us because we are strong but without importance and do not shine with the goodness that attracts the wicked like the flame draws the buttermoth," Talin muttered, setting off after Cwen with a final glance toward the closest trees where he knew Caen lurked.

"No, Talin; I shall not be used. Tell them to send Guardians. They revel in the quest. It is all they live for."

She shook her head so violently that her hair flew, sending a sparkle of red as the day star's light struck it.

"Cwen, they cannot send Guardians. This search must be silent and remain hidden. Once it is exposed, every wizard, witch and thief will attempt to recover those shards in the hope of earning a few lule or ruling the world. What the Feie said makes sense. Anyway, we have nothing else to do. We wander aimlessly."

"Do you tire of my lack of purpose, Talin?"

He shrugged, squinting to consider it.

"A little adventure could provide a bit of a diversion," he finally acknowledged.

"No."

Setting off at a quick pace she returned in the direction of their camp.

As she approached, she saw Caen seated next to the fire and drew her staff.

He raised his hands; one contained the cup she had given him.

"I return your cup."

He held it out, waiting for her to take it.

"You did not need to give it to me personally," she said, reaching out to snatch it from his hand.

"What did the stranger want?" Caen asked conversationally.

"Nothing that concerns you. He was just passing through."

Laughing his disbelief, Caen offered an opinion. "I doubt that, for I have seen the remains of those passing through. I believe I am the only living enemy you have."

Glaring at him, she spat, "And it is not wise of you to remind me of my shortcomings."

Talin entered the glen and glanced toward Caen.

"Gather our things. I wish to leave," Cwen directed, dumping water on the small fire and stirring the embers to make sure it was out.

"Brengven the Feie will return for an answer," Talin stated.

"Then he shall return to find me gone. You can come or stay here with him." She gestured toward Caen. "I do not care."

Her movements were efficient and quick, the way of a Guardian, the way of her father. She was soon ready and stood before Talin looking up into his questioning gaze.

"I said no," she whispered.

"Where are we going?" Caen's voice drew her eyes.

"You are not going anywhere. Be grateful I leave you alive and in my camp. I have warned you for the last time, Caen. If you follow me again Talin will test the sharpness of his axe against your throat."

Caen gazed over her shoulder at Talin, who simply shrugged.

"I think you should accept the healer's offer of the quest. What do you have to lose, except your worthless life?" Caen offered.

Her quickly drawn sword drew a drop of blood at the center of his chest.

"How do you know what the Feie said?" her jaw was stone-like with tension and her voice trembled with anger.

"I crept close enough to hear when he spoke to Talin."

"And you allowed it?" she looked incredulously at her traveling companion.

"I did not see the harm, since we refused the quest. Perhaps they will offer it to Caen."

"Offer it to him? Offer the quest to a brute and thief, one without honor?" she sputtered.

"Is that not what your father says of you?" Talin asked, raising an eyebrow.

Her sword dropped from Caen's chest.

"Take back your words." Her eyes glittered with golden fire.

"I take them back. I do not believe he ever called you a brute – disheveled and a charlatan, but not a brute."

Without a backward glance at either of them Cwen headed east toward the port city of Ezon.

To Ælmondæ and Back Again

Ælmondæ is an island kingdom of great tropical beauty. Its largest city lies toward the eastern border two day's journey from the glen where Talin and Cwen had camped. A city of poachers and thieves, Ezon is an excellent place to buy or sell items of questionable origin, like the Gaianite crystals Cwen now carried. Entering the small shop where she often traded she scanned the interior for any threat. Finding it empty save the shopkeeper, she approached his counter.

"I bring you fine crystals, Drell."

"How many men died?"

"A few," she admitted. Dumping the crystals before him Cwen fixed her gaze on Drell's hands, for he was known for sleight of hand.

"Six lule," he offered, looking up for her response.

"Make it seven to include the four you stole and you have a deal, Drell."

Laughing aloud he passed the coins, watching her tuck them into her shirt.

"Where is the axe man?"

"He chose another path," Cwen replied, feeling a prick in her heart at the loss of her companion.

"Well, you do not need protecting, Cwen. I have seen the evidence of your passing often enough."

"Nay, I need no one." Lifting her hand to indicate their business was finished Cwen exited the shop into the bright golden light of midday. At a vendor she purchased willow bark for tea, a pot of prickleberry jam, dried stag and several flat loaves of bannock sufficient for a fortnight's journey.

Leaving Ælmondæ meant hiring a boat and crossing into Æwmarshæ — several days journey depending on the prevailing winds.

Along the road to the harbor on the northeastern tip of the island the air glittered and pulsed, leaving the small man named Brengven standing in Cwen's path.

"It is quite rude to leave when you know you have an appointment," Brengven sputtered.

"I believe your appointment was made with another," Cwen said, brushing past to continue on her way.

"Do you not wish to have the opportunity to adventure, to fight against insurmountable odds, to reign victorious over evil?"

"Are you mad?" she asked, swinging back toward the little man.

"Nay, but your refusal will reflect badly on my kind. We are known for being quite convincing."

"I thought your kind simply foretold the future." Cwen could not help but smile.

"Yes, that is so. But we are also supposed to hold sway over the decisions of mortals."

"My answer is no."

Sighing deeply, Brengven fell into step beside her, hurrying to keep up against her longer stride.

"Following me will not cause me to change my mind. Ask the one whose shoulder you healed," she added.

"Do you care nothing for Ædracmoræ?" His voice held deep disbelief. "Nothing for the Réverē of your childhood? You would kill a man to save a single Equus, but not quest to save our home?"

Frowning, she stopped and looked down at him.

"It is not my battle. Guardians quest for the Queen and protect the Seven Kingdoms. I am no Guardian."

"Nay, but you are trained as one."

A bitter laugh escaped her.

"Obviously you have been speaking to the Guardian Nall. Ask him to save the world."

"Cwen."

The use of her name drew her back to him.

"Without you there is no hope. It will simply be a matter of time before someone uses the army to destroy us. I do not believe the world will survive the darkness a second time. You, Cwen, have the strength and skill to perform the task."

A turn of his hand created a rift; the fiery-haired Feie tilted his head and looked at the golden-eyed girl expectantly. With an angry shake of her head she stepped through into the glen where Talin and Caen waited.

Reconsideration

Why are you still here?" she snapped at Caen.

"I have suffered an injury and require rest before I can continue my travels."

"Did you send him after me?" She swung on Talin.

"Nay, he made the decision. Said he considered you rude and wanted to tell you so himself."

"Are we questing then?" Caen asked, casting a disarming smile at Cwen.

"We are not doing anything. You are not part of we. Remain here and heal. I do not care, but you may not follow me anywhere."

"I was concerned for your safety. A beautiful woman, unattended, wandering alone in a city that is known for its dangers," Caen's voice caressed.

"It is more likely the city holds danger for those who cross her path," Talin whispered under his breath, drawing irritated looks from both of them.

Brengven looked at the three of them with great apprehension and wondered at the Sojourner Ileana's sudden lack of wisdom in choosing them to quest.

"I require your pledge." Brengven the Feie spoke just above a whisper, cringing under Cwen's contemptuous glare.

"Pledge? I knew it!" She shouted, her hands balled into fists. "Look at him! He knew we would not pledge to the Queen and her

Guardians. You can see it in his eyes."

"I do not see anything in his eyes," Talin said, staring openly at Brengven. "They are far too clouded to see anything within them."

"Do you not see? It is a trick. Pledge to them for this and soon they will have bound all that you hold dear!" Cwen shouted at the top of her voice.

"Nay, I do not wish you to pledge to the Queen and the Guardians. I wish only your oath that you will protect Ædracmoræ and Réverē and hold this quest in confidence. Promise it to me." Brengven spoke without guile. "Would you truly not even promise that?"

Cwen walked away, her heart pounding. She felt near tears but she could not allow the others to see. Shaking her head and blinking away unshed tears she turned to face them.

"I shall not swear it."

"And you, Talin? Can you swear it?" the Feie asked.

"Aye, I would never betray Ædracmoræ or Réverē."

"And Caen, have you any honor?"

"Nay, there is not a noble bone in my body. I can lend the strength of my arm, but I do it not for Ædracmoræ. I do it for myself."

Looking at Brengven, Cwen asked, "You would trust a man who tells you himself he has no honor?"

"Aye, I trust his honesty more than your fear and anger."

"I am not afraid."

"Cwen." Talin's voice was calm and quiet. "Just once stand for something. Stand for Ædracmoræ."

She looked away and stared into her past, remembering her childhood and the solemn boy who had long ago come to be her friend. Her nod was almost imperceptible and her voice was low and tense. "For you. I shall do it for you, Talin."

Brengven's sigh of relief went unnoticed. "I must return to the Queen to announce your acceptance of the quest. I shall be back in a single passing of the day star. Be ready to travel then. We shall begin our search within the chamber below Réverē. Caen will require a change of his poultice." Brengven looked at Cwen.

"I shall change it once."

"And speak the healing words?"
"And speak the healing words," she agreed with a glare for Caen.
They watched as Brengven stepped from sight within the rift.

Acceptance

Once again Brengven sat at the council table with the Queen and her council. A diminutive wizard had joined them, an Ancient named Grumblton who had served the House of Aaradan since the time long before the Feie's remembering.

"Do we have their pledge?" Queen Yávië demanded.

"More or less," Brengven shrugged.

"And that would mean?" Sōrél asked.

"They will protect Ædracmoræ and the quest… just not for the reasons you had hoped."

"How shall we control the quest? Who will tell us of their progress?" Nall asked, concern and disapproval etching his brow.

Ileana's voice left no room for doubt, "They will not betray their quest and Talin will send the birds and beasts with word of their progress. He has promised it to Brengven without Cwen's knowledge. Caen seeks only glory for himself, but his arm is strong and he desires Cwen. He will fight to win her acceptance. Cwen is fearless and great strength is buried within her. Together they can do this. And none will look twice at the three of them as they pass among the shadows."

Grumblton spoke, "I will gives them each a gift and the skill to use it."

Rolling a small black pebble across the table toward Brengven he said, "For Cwen, the 'bility to shift. She only has to touch and think to use it; even a girl as stubborn as her oughts to be able to do that."

"For Talin the shield. To protects them in the moment of death."

A small red pebble was rolled toward the Feie man from Réverē.

"Last, for the black heart known as Caen, the touch of sleep."

The small white pebble rolled across the table and Brengven placed it in his pocket with the others.

"More than anything, Brengven, they need your guidance and your visions. Be their eyes on tomorrow," Ileana whispered. "May the grace of the Ancients be with you on your quest."

Näeré touched the little man's hand.

"Cwen is well?"

"Aye, she is as angry as a grass cat whose tail has been tread upon by a wandering dragon."

Nall pretended not to listen but could not help smiling at the image.

Worried eyes watched as Brengven slipped through the small rift he had called to return him to the glen on Ælmondæ.

Brengven's sudden appearance in the glen startled the Equus near the tree line. The shimmering arrival of the small man had caused the elegant beast to glimmer and fade from sight for a moment before Cwen's silent calls assured it of its safety.

The Equus were ancient, luminous white beasts supported on four slender legs that belied their strength and uncanny ability to change direction at a full gallop; they were bound exclusively to the House of Aaradan. Often they were hunted for the magickal quality of their coats. A man wearing an Equus cloak was given the gift of veiling, something coveted by thieves and road agents.

Brengven watched as the golden-eyed daughter of the Guardian Nall stroked the great animal's neck, calming its unease at the arrival of a stranger.

The animal blew and made a soft nickering sound as it nudged Cwen, arching its regal neck and shaking its long mane. Short pointed ears swiveled and sapphire eyes searched, always alert for the danger that would send it fleeing. It was old, for the tail of coarse, heavy hair hung nearly to the ground—a sure sign of age in an Equus.

Staring at Brengven, Cwen leapt to the back of the Equus and urged it away through the trees.

"Did I not tell her to be ready to travel on my arrival?" the Feie asked of Talin.

"Aye, and so she is not," Talin shrugged. "It is always more efficient to allow her to believe she has given the order."

"She has the gift of magick," Brengven stated.

"She does, but do not call on her to use it; she will simply refuse."

"What makes her hide the light that burns within her? I do not understand," the small Feie said, tilting his head in curiosity.

Talin quoted Cwen's statement of belief. "Rules, trials, orders, and oaths are all chains that bind one's freedom and force one's path. She has thrown them off and walked away from the offered Guardianship in pursuit of independence."

"I sense that you do not necessarily agree with her creed, and yet you choose to travel with her, giving up the ease of life in New Xavian City." Brengven seemed confused by the contradiction.

Talin sought the Feie's eyes and spoke the truth, "She is my friend."

"Yet you forced the quest upon her. Not an act of friendship," Brengven pushed.

"It is what is best for her. And I spoke truly when I said a little adventure would be a welcome change," Talin answered with a grin.

The crashing of a man returning through the underbrush brought Caen into sight. With a nod of acknowledgement to Brengven he searched the camp for Cwen.

"Where is she?"

"Unlike you, I do not plague her footsteps," Talin answered.

"So you do not know?"

"She does not welcome your presence," Talin ignored the question.

"She soon will. Does that bother you?"

"Nay, just be certain that the choice is hers." Talin's gaze warned of the consequences if it were not.

"She returns."

Talin's sensitive hearing had alerted him to her distant approach.

As the Equus slid to a stop in front of them Cwen dropped from its back. Looking around the campsite she asked, "Why is it you are not prepared to travel?"

Shaking their heads, both Talin and Caen began to gather their belongings under Brengven's incredulous stare. When the three of them finally stood before him, the Feie wasted no time slipping them through the rift and into the cavern below Réverē.

Army of Darkness

They wandered with mouths agape among the army of the darkness, each lost in thoughts of amazement, fear and uncertainty. The thought that these soldiers had once before flooded the world, leading to its shattering separation, leaving seven solitary fragments orbiting the Topaz Star like a disassembled puzzle until Yávië's quest for the world's rebirth had finally drawn them back together was beyond their imagining.

Cwen rose to her tiptoes and drew her finger along the jaw line of the deathshade before her, drawn by the ugliness of the misshapen face and jagged teeth. She touched the remnants of what appeared to be rotting cloth turned to stone and stroked the ancient symbols cast across the shield. The danger from such a creature, should it live, sent a chill along her spine.

Talin stood stunned at the ferocious expressions frozen on the faces of the demons before him. The stories he had heard of the fall of the House of Aaradan and the destruction of Ædracmoræ came flooding back. Life? Someone would actually offer creatures such as these life? Should a large army of the demon horde be released upon the world nothing could stop it. He could not fathom such evil and his determination to prevent such an act became a weight within his soul.

Caen attempted to remove the sword from the soldier before him. Using his dagger he tried to loosen it, but not as much as a scratch appeared on the stone figure. Might be worth a fortune if there was a way to haul it out of here, he thought to himself and began to look about for smaller, less resistant items he might be able to trade in Ælmondæ. An army of stone hidden beneath the earth did not seem to pose much of a threat to the citizens above.

Brengven sensed Talin and Cwen's unease as he watched them. Calling to Caen, he warned against the removal of any artifact he found.

"To take an item found within this cavern into the world above would be much like shouting the discovery from the rooftops."

Talin and Cwen spun to look at Caen, who simply smiled and shrugged.

"Always looking for a way to make an easy lule? Is that all that you are? Nothing more than a thief?" Cwen accused.

"Cretin," Talin muttered.

"Oh, I am much more than just a thief, Cwen. I consider myself a rather accomplished warrior and an ardent lover. As far as cretin goes, perhaps on occasion I have shown signs of the idiocy of this affliction, but only when a beautiful woman is involved."

Racing forward, staff drawn, Cwen struck him hard against the side of his head as he tried to roll away, splitting his scalp and sending blood across his face and into his eyes.

"I told you your eyes offended me. But your words offend me even more."

As she raised the staff again, Talin gripped her arm.

"We need him, Cwen. If we are to accomplish this quest we shall need a thief and ruffian. He can enter where even we cannot."

Her cry was guttural and angry as she jerked her staff away and strode toward the back of the cavern.

"Show me the receptacle of which you spoke," she ordered Brengven, who was more than happy to oblige.

"He may require healing," Brengven mentioned as they stood before the stone altar.

"Nay, I did no real harm. It merely bleeds freely because of its nearness to his brain. What little he has. I hate his constant pursuit," she confessed. "It is exhausting."

Brengven gave her an odd look.

"I have sensed that he actually likes you."

Laughing aloud, Cwen shook her head, "Do not be deceived, little man. What he seeks I do not wish to give."

Her hand stroked the altar and her fingers slipped into the channel that awaited some crystal or shard to give it the elemental power required to animate the soldiers.

"Who do you think placed them here?"

Then, as though she had not expected an answer, she looked behind them at the sheer rock wall. Raising her torch, she made her way toward it, passing the torch back and forth over the words she discovered carved beneath the dust. Rubbing the wall with her hand and blowing the dust into the air, causing Brengven to launch into a fit of sneezing, she called to Talin.

"Bring me water."

Talin brought a flask and watched as she wet a small section of the wall. Drawing a piece of cloth from her bag she wiped the wall and once again held the torch close.

"Symbols." Talin shrugged. "They have no meaning to me."

"Aye, there is meaning here. It is the language of my… Ileana," Cwen whispered.

"Can you read it?" Caen asked, holding a rag against his head.

Her look was one of loathing, "Of course I can read it."

His attempt to raise an eyebrow led to a wince of pain.

"These are the writings of the Sojourner Alandon. He speaks of a scroll, the Scroll of the G'lm. There is some reference to the Spire Canyon and the Bull of the Woods. It is all very vague and, if I recall correctly, there are no woods in the Spire Canyon and probably no bullrams either. It has been long since I was there." Her voice broke and she breathed a ragged breath.

Talin knew she was recalling the dragon trials.

She rubbed a hand over her eyes as if to brush away the unwanted memories and then looked down at Brengven.

"I would like to go to Meremire and consult with the Ancients there before we make any plans."

"Do they have a tavern?" Caen asked.

"That is wise," Talin agreed, once again finding it best to overlook Caen's apparent lack of sense.

Bobbing his agreement Brengven called the rift.

Meremire

"I shall remain beyond the wall of the training field," Brengven stated. "I am not comfortable within the hovels of the mire."

"He is certainly an odd little man," Cwen said, shaking her head after Brengven.

"I do not believe the Feie are comfortable anywhere beyond Réverē. I wonder what it was that actually forced him into this quest," Talin pondered before shrugging and following Cwen toward the hovels of Meremire.

"Cwen!" squealed Rosie, the tiny Ancient, when she looked up and saw Nall's daughter.

"How's your parents?" Rosie beamed, hugging Cwen tightly and ignoring the fact that she knew the girl would not answer such a question.

"I believe they are well," Talin answered to cover Cwen's silence.

Peering behind them the tiny old woman examined Caen.

"What's he?"

"He has a head wound and requires your 'special' healing Rosie. The kind reserved for ruffians and rogues."

Approaching Caen, Rosie tapped his knees with her staff.

"Down boy, for you is too tall for me to sees the wound if you don't kneel."

Looking toward Cwen he watched her wink as he felt the sudden pain of Rosie's staff against his knees.

"I said down!" Rosie sputtered, earning another look from the young man before her.

"I would kneel if I were you," Cwen laughed. "Rosie does not like to ask twice. Asking a third time may result in a broken bone—yours, not hers."

Scowling at Cwen and again at Rosie, causing her staff to twitch, Caen dropped to his knees before her and allowed her to poke at his scalp.

"Whoever dids this to you did not like you much," Rosie said, giving him a hard poke that caused him to cringe.

"Come. I will heals it in my hovel." She hustled off knowing that he would follow.

"She is mean," Caen said, looking toward Cwen and Talin before he quickly followed the little Ancient as she disappeared around the corner to her hovel.

Talin and Cwen followed after him at a more leisurely pace, looking forward to the hollers produced by his healing.

"Do you have to be so rough, old woman?" Caen asked as Rosie applied the healing salve to his head wound.

"Aye, you cause Cwen worry," she fumed. "Don't give that girl worries; she gots enough."

Caen gave his most charming grin.

"It is not my intent to worry her. I only seek to look after her."

Rosie thumped him on the shoulder.

"Don't lie, boy. I can tells when you lie and no amount of grinning will make it different."

Shrugging, Caen sat silently as the woman finished the incantation to heal the wound.

"How is your shoulder?" Cwen asked sweetly from the doorway.

"You got another wound, boy? Who you been fighting with, grass cats?"

Rosie gestured for him to remove his vest and he did so without argument.

She poked at the healing wound a bit more gently and swiveled toward Cwen.

"You did this?"

"Aye, I asked him not to track me, but he would not stop," she admitted without regret. "He should have died, but he did not."

Rosie added a bit of herbal salve to the partially healed wound in his shoulder and looked into his pale green eyes. "Don't track her no more. Next time she will kill you."

Patting him on the arm she watched him replace his vest, his eyes still focused on the doorway where he had last seen Cwen.

As he left the hovel he looked for Cwen but found no sign of her. Walking from hovel to hovel he peered inside until he came across a wizened little man who stood no taller than Caen's mid-thigh.

"H'lo," Caen spoke.

"You're Caen? I am Morgwort. Let me sees your blade."

Pulling the short sword he handed it to the Ancient and watched him heft it and feel its balance.

"Not bad for one Dobbin didn't make," Morg mumbled grudgingly.

Caen leaned back against the workbench and palmed the veiling stone which lay there.

"Caen, we shall be leaving now… in case you care to join us." Cwen's voice was saccharine.

He sheathed his sword and stepped out behind her to be met by a well-aimed kick to the groin.

Cwen watched him drop to the ground, clutching himself and writhing in pain, tears welling in his eyes as he gasped for breath.

"Do not ever steal in the mire again," she hissed through clenched teeth as she reached down to take the veiling stone before sweeping past him and back into Morg's hovel, slamming the door behind her.

Inside she dropped to her knees to receive Morg's hug.

"You wants to see the sword?" he asked, knowing it was what she had come for.

Leaning down he pulled the weapon from beneath his cot. It remained wrapped in a silken coverlet, just as she had left it two summers ago.

Placing it on the bed he stepped back and left the hovel.

Cwen rolled the coverlet back and stared at the beautiful double-bladed sword her father had given her. Forged by Dobbinwort and infused with the Ancient's magick it had never seen the blood of battle. The blades gleamed in the lingering twilight, each end carrying a wicked hook. Very gently she lifted it, running her fingers lightly across the surface of the blades.

Shaking her head at the pain in her heart, she wrapped it once again and returned it to its resting place beneath Morgwort's bed. As she stood, Morg returned and indicated she should sit.

"You quest against the rise of the dark horde…" His eyes held concern.

"Aye, I do it for Talin. It is his wish. The words within the cavern where the army stands tell of a bull that lives within Spire Canyon. Have you heard of such an animal?"

"Nay, but deep within the canyon lies the lair of the thralax. Be cautious as you seeks your bull, Cwen. The thralax is deadly and its main source of food is the flesh of men. Beware the firedrakes, too; they aren't big but they is nasty."

As Cwen turned to go, Morg added, "And let the boy keeps the veiling stone."

When she exited the hovel she saw that Caen had managed to stand and was leaning against the wall, though still pale and breathing heavily. Talin stood next to him trying not to grin.

"I hope you did not help him stand," she quipped, heading away from the hovels and back toward the training field where Brengven waited.

Talin started after her, slowing his pace to allow for Caen's stiff-legged walk.

"Though there is no healing salve for that, I believe sitting in a glacial pool has been known to help," he offered.

"I am grateful for your concern," Caen muttered through his pain.

Grumblton's Gifts

Finding that Brengven had set up camp several dragon lengths beyond the training field, Cwen decided it was acceptable to remain in Meremire for the night.

"We shall leave at daybreak on the morrow," she stated to the Feie, receiving his cross glare in return.

"Morg has provided us with information regarding the trouble we may encounter on the ground in Spire Canyon. Even the Guardians do not walk the paths among the spires, for it is considered a foolish risk. The canyons are inhabited by firedrake and something called a thralax, if Morg is to be believed."

"The wizard Grumblton has sent gifts for each of you to help you on your quest," Brengven said, digging in his pocket for the pebbles and tossing Cwen the black one.

"For you he sends the magick of the shift. He says you need simply keep the pebble in the pouch around your neck. When you think of the surface you touch, you shall be one with it."

He swung toward Talin and Caen, who had finally arrived within the camp.

"To Talin he gives the gift of shielding." He handed Talin the small red stone. "To use it you must touch those you wish to shield and simply cast the thought to make it so. The shielding will hold no longer than one mark upon the shadow clock, so use it wisely.

"And for Caen," Brengven began, noticing the man's apparent discomfort and deciding not to ask the source of it, "the touch of sleep. You must touch the flesh of another to bring about this magick."

Tossing the white pebble to Caen, Brengven added, "The sleep will last long enough to search a body well."

As Cwen stepped close to Caen she saw him flinch, and took great satisfaction from it. Pulling the veiling stone from her pocket she held it out in the palm of her hand.

"Morg said to let you keep this." Her eyes were hard with disagreement. "Keep it in your pouch with the stone to cast the sleep. You need only think the shadow spell to bring on the veil."

"I do not know the shadow spell," Caen admitted, drawing a sharp look from Cwen.

"Talin will teach you," she answered impatiently before gesturing back toward the mire. "We shall stay the night in the mire. Ask Rosie which hovel to use."

His eyes remained fixed on her as she walked away. A small furrow of wonder creased his brow.

"What makes her so hard?" he asked of Talin.

"She is not," Talin answered, setting off toward the hovels.

Cwen lay upon her cot and called to the Equus – Valckyr, Nevin, and Bruudwyg of Æcumbræ – who would carry them as far as the Spire Canyon. Brengven had told her he preferred to carry himself.

She would not ask the Equus to sacrifice themselves among the massive stones. Her father's warnings were loud within her mind. Always enter the canyon on the back of a dragon; never walk among the spires. Shaking her head to clear away his foolish fears she stood, put on her cloak, and stepped out into the night.

The sky was filled with the luminous light of souls waiting to be called from their slumber. The twinkle of their life lights was brilliant and cast a warm glow across the land. She noticed the twin moons lay low on the horizon, creating a glowing path across the training field.

Walking toward the path that would lead through the woods to the Lake of Lost Memories she heard a soft groan and glanced toward the hovel that she passed.

Looking around to make sure no one saw, she slipped inside.

Within the dream Talin held his father's hand and watched the waterfall plummeting into the azure pool at the base of the Xavian gardens. His eyes were wide with wonder as he looked at his mother.

He thought her more beautiful than all the flowers that surrounded them.

The sound of a crash caused them to look around. A funny man dropped a large dark crystal from which streamed the nightmare.

The crystal struck the stones and shattered, allowing the odor of decay to pour forth into the city of peace and tranquility. The stench caused those nearest to gag and retch. But their discomfort did not last long, for an enormous dragon emerged from a gaseous cloud, quickly taking form and snapping its hungry jaws onto the closest victim.

Snarling with anger pent up by years of confinement, the monster quickly gulped down those closest to it. As they poured forth, blackening the beautiful city and its gardens, the dragons grabbed Xavians and those visiting from the Galenite fortress. Ancients and Guardians were torn apart by battling death dragons free to feast after the ages of imprisonment.

The bellowing and thunder of the dragons' flight and landings deafened the inhabitants of the magnificent city as they ran searching for an escape from the feeding frenzy of the freed flyte of dragons.

A man called out urging them to run for the Galenite fortress, but for most it was too late and too far. The dragons simply picked them off as they ran; men, women and children died as they were ripped apart and eaten as the first meal of the dragons' freedom.

Talin's father raced from the city carrying his small son and leading his wife. Beyond the city lay a great tumble of stones and it was there he hid Talin, ordering him to cover his head and remain until they returned for him.

Talin's mother's scream caused him to cry out and look for her. She stood less than half a bullram's length away when the dragon ripped her apart, covering Talin with her blood. Within the rocky outcropping he cried and begged for her return.

His face was wet with tears as the nightmare began again.

Cwen stepped to the cot and lay down beside him, holding him tightly in her arms; she used the magick taught by her mother to pull away his pain and grant him dreamless sleep.

Rocking him she whispered over and over as she had when they were very young, "Don't cry, Talin. I shall be your friend."

When she felt the shudder of his sigh as he relaxed within the peace she had provided, she rose and slipped away, the weight of his nightmares still heavy on her heart.

Caen considered an evening of theft, but, recalling his earlier punishment and the lingering ache, decided against it. Instead, he closed his eyes and dreamed of a more compliant Cwen.

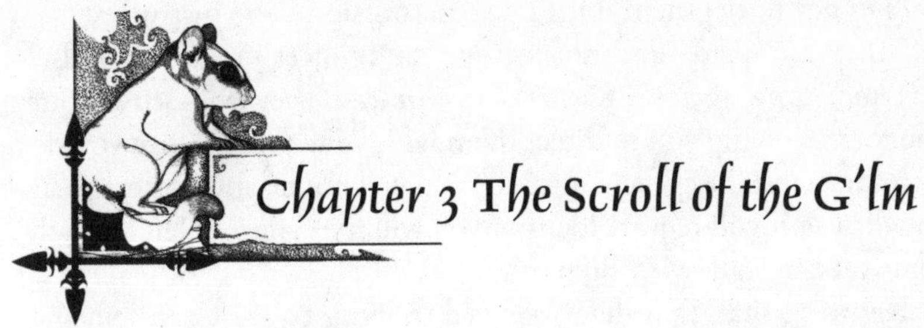

Chapter 3 The Scroll of the G'lm

Camped outside the mire on Æcumbræ, Cwen chewed her bannock and watched Talin instruct Caen in the art of veiling. She was surprised to see that the annoying lout actually paid attention and seemed to catch on quickly. The spell was not a complicated one, but for someone without any knowledge of magick it could be tricky.

A sudden shift in the air told her Caen had settled next to her. Soundlessly she drew her dagger and placed it beneath his unseen chin, forcing his head back.

"If you touch me I will kill you and no one here can stop it," she whispered. "I can sense you even when you are veiled, Caen."

He appeared beside her as he released the veil. A small drop of blood formed and ran down her blade.

"It was his idea," he said, indicating Talin, who maintained an air of innocence that Cwen had learned long ago not to believe.

"He does not like you and would like to see me kill you." Withdrawing the dagger, Cwen jumped up and went to Talin.

"True?"

"Aye, I would not mind it," Talin smirked.

"However…" she glanced back at Caen, "you are safe, at least temporarily; since he says we need your talents."

"Come and I shall introduce you to the Equus. Have you at least ridden a bullram?" she asked without much hope.

"Nay. Poor men walk," he answered, causing her to shake her head.

"Do not touch them until I give permission," she instructed.

"They are gentle and do not like loud voices or harsh hands." Her voice grew softer. "Rather like women. They will sense your thoughts, allowing you to direct them with your mind. Since you do not understand the speech of beasts, you will not be able to hear their thoughts, so it will require focus or you will find yourself left behind. Then you can walk with Brengven."

Knowing that Talin had followed, hoping to see Caen fail, she called to him, "Nevin will carry you, Talin."

Approaching the grazing Equus she gave a low whistle and was rewarded by their calls. They shook their heads and trotted forward, necks extended to catch her scent.

Caen watched the transformation in Cwen's face as she whispered soothing words to the Equus of her bond.

"I thought you didn't make pledges?" he asked, waiting for the flare of her anger.

Without looking at him she answered honestly, "I am bound to them by the blood of my mother. There was no pledge. They demand nothing of me and it is by my own choice that I defend them.

"Extend your hand palm upward that he may acquaint himself with your scent," she directed, watching as Caen complied.

"His name is Bruudwyg." She scratched the animal's neck as he breathed deeply of Caen's scent.

"Watch."

She gave a quick rub to the Equus before her and, grabbing a fistful of his mane in her left hand, leaped lightly to his broad back. Sliding off she did it again, looking to see if Caen understood.

Stepping back, she called to the Equus Valckyr, who trotted forward and swung his side to her, allowing her to catch his mane and swing lightly to his back.

"Try it," she said, watching as Caen mimicked her motion and landed heavily in the middle of Bruudwyg's back, causing the Equus to exhale loudly in distress.

"Tell him you are sorry and that you are a clumsy oaf, but will try to do better."

Caen looked at her in disbelief.

"Tell him."

She watched as Caen obeyed.

"I am a clumsy oaf…" He glanced at Cwen, suddenly feeling foolish and awkward. "… but I shall try to do better."

"Just sit. You need do nothing more. Bruudwyg will follow Valckyr. You may want to hold on with both hands to begin with, though. I do not intend to slow my pace to accommodate your lack of skill."

Talin flew by mounted on Nevin.

"Race me to the trees at the end of the field!" he called to Cwen.

"Stay," she ordered Caen, sending the same silent message to Bruudwyg, who promptly dropped his head to graze on the flowers at his feet.

Caen watched as Valckyr spun effortlessly, raising his forelegs off the ground a bit before surging forward after Talin. The larger animal quickly covered the ground separating them and raced past and into the far trees before swinging around in front of Talin's mount and trotting back toward Caen. Caen felt a lump form in his throat as he heard Cwen's laughter drift across the field, for he knew it was intended only for Talin. Her hair flew out behind her and she suddenly seemed so at ease, almost joyous. Talin galloped up beside her and together they returned to stop before Caen. Looking up, Cwen waved at Brengven, who approached at a steady run.

"Let us go," the Feie called, continuing off in the direction of the road.

Trotting back to camp they gathered their packs and headed off after Brengven.

The Wizard's Staff

They passed no one as they continued in the direction of Spire Canyon. The closer they came the more desolate the land around them appeared. Over the course of their travels they had become separated from Brengven and it was agreed that they would camp in the grasslands that lay before the canyon.

Arriving at midday they set up camp, building a large fire that would be visible to Brengven as he neared. Cwen spent time with the Equus before releasing them to return to the herd that remained deep within the forested lands of Æcumbræ.

Valckyr nuzzled her and whispered in her mind, "*Keep watch among the hoodoo, for they can serve to hide enemies.*"

"Hoodoo?" Cwen questioned.

"*Hoodoos, the earth pillars… mushroom rocks,*" he tried to explain.

"The spires?" she asked.

"*Yes, the spires,*" The Equus nodded his agreement. "*Careful among the spires.*"

She watched as the Equus raced away toward their home and felt loneliness settle over her.

Returning to the camp she found Brengven present and telling a tale of a party of salt mercs on the road.

"Bad element," he shuddered.

"Salt is a bad element?" Caen asked.

"Nay, the salt traders are a bad element. I do not trust them," Brengven stated.

"We shall post guards tonight," Cwen said, looking up at them for signs of disagreement.

Seeing none, she continued. "Split three ways. It will not burden us too heavily. Caen, you can stand first, Talin second, and I shall stand from then until dawn."

"Cwen," Talin started to protest. But thinking better of it, simply shrugged. It would be easier simply to watch the suspect than to argue with Cwen. The land lay flat around them and would make it difficult for any to approach unseen.

Brengven pulled a brace of hare from his knapsack, earning approval from all of them. As the meat boiled and the day star fell toward the horizon, the first of the spires became visible against the golden sky.

"Hoodoos," Cwen whispered, drawing looks from Caen and Talin. "Valckyr said to be careful among them."

Cwen woke suddenly, trying to rise as a hand clamped over her mouth.

Talin's voice whispered hoarsely in her thoughts, "Someone creeps along the ground toward the camp. There are several, perhaps six or seven of them, about four dragon lengths to the west."

Nodding that she understood, she rose into a crouch, looking for Caen. He lay to her left, eyes open and finger to his lips. Quickly she rolled her blanket to give it bulk.

Scanning the horizon she saw the movement of the grass and gestured that she had located the ones approaching.

They crept backward away from the firelight that would give them away as surely as daylight and prepared their weapons. Caen and Cwen nocked bolts in their crossbows and Talin drew his axe.

Across the fire the first of their visitors arrived, creeping forward on all fours toward the blankets they had rolled to look like bodies.

Cwen watched the enemy raise a dagger and plunge it into the blanket that had covered her moments before.

Swearing loudly, she loosed the first bolt, striking the man beneath the arm and dropping him dead. His companions rose and raced toward them as Caen and Cwen brought down the three furthest away. Talin waded into the two that were unfortunate enough to be closest. The axe left their entrails trailing on its forehand pass and decapitated them on the backhand.

Facing Cwen, Talin advised, "None live. I hope you did not have questions."

"Salters," she said, looking at the clothing they wore. "Why would salters attack us?"

"They are not salters," Caen said, kneeling near one of the bodies. "Have you ever known salters to carry a wizard's staff?" he asked, holding up a short staff fitted with a well-cut crystal.

Brengven appeared, panting, having been awakened in his camp by the noise of their voices.

"I knew I did not trust the salters," he muttered to himself.

"You are lucky they did not slay you while you slept," Talin mumbled at the Feie's foolishness.

Pointing, Brengven challenged him, "I am safer away from you than with you. Whose camp was attacked? Not mine. I left no fire burning to announce my presence."

Holding up her hand, Cwen said, "Stop."

"Brengven is right. We are fools. He warned us of the danger and we took no precautions beyond posting a watch. From here forward, the camps remain cold. I have dried stag and bannock and when we leave the canyon we will provision in the city for a longer journey. We are ill-prepared for what we do, but we will not be fools again. Sleep. I shall watch until the dawn."

She walked away from the camp and its death, leaving Talin and Caen looking after her. Brengven headed back toward his camp.

As they covered the fire with earth and dragged the bodies away from the camp, Caen gave a great sigh.

"Why does she like you? What is it you do?" he asked Talin.

"I do nothing," Talin shrugged. "I have known her many summers; we are friends."

Caen laughed. "Friends?"

"Aye." Talin grew serious. "When you look at her your vision is shallow. You see only that she is a woman. I see more. I see a friend." "Not that I have not noticed that she is a woman," he added, knowing it would irritate Caen.

Distrust

Cwen sat away from the others, cross-legged on the grass and looking toward the horizon where the day star would first show its face. For the first time in her life she felt afraid.

Talin arrived before her with the last of the lukewarm tea. Squatting next to her, he handed her a cup.

Sipping it, she looked up at him, brushing back a strand of hair from her face.

"You have blood on your face."

"Not nearly so much as the salters," Talin grinned.

"We shall ask in the city about the staff of the wizard. It should bring a good price," Cwen thought aloud. "Why do you think they came for us, Talin?"

He shrugged, "I do not know. We have nothing and we did not pass them on our way."

"Perhaps we have something but we are not aware of it," she spoke in low tones looking toward Caen. "After all, he is a thief."

"If you will distract him I shall search his knapsack and bedroll." Talin offered.

Sighing, Cwen gave a low laugh, "Could you not distract him while I search?"

"He finds you much more distracting, Cwen." Seeing her nod her agreement, Talin added, "I shall send him to you."

Caen approached Cwen warily and sat down across from her beyond striking distance.

"You look tired," he said without thinking.

"I am, but not so tired I shall fall for your lies."

"I have never lied to you, Cwen."

"I am too tired to parry words. Do you carry something from the cavern, Caen?" She sighed.

He frowned, looking over his shoulder to see Talin walking toward them.

Talin tossed the small symbol-covered disc to Cwen. She turned it over in her hand, fingering the raised signs.

"We could have been killed." Her words were glacial, but the look she gave him was hot enough to melt stone.

"Brengven!" she shouted repeatedly until the small man finally appeared, rubbing his sleep-worn face.

"Will you return this to the cavern below Révere̅?"

Taking the disc he examined it carefully before looking at each of them in turn.

"It is not from the cavern below Révere̅, but from another."

Cwen looked surprised. "Then what is it?"

Brengven shrugged. "I do not know? Ask the thief."

Shifting her gaze to Caen she asked again, "What is it?"

"I took it from the dead man, along with the staff. I do not know what it is."

Caen looked at her, his eyes shadowed with disappointment. "I did not take anything from the cavern on Révere̅, Cwen, and I have never lied to you."

Standing, he glanced at Talin.

"Next time simply ask if you feel a search is necessary. I have nothing to hide."

They watched as he wrapped himself in his blanket and lay down with his back to them.

"*Perhaps I misjudged him,*" Cwen spoke silently to Talin's mind.

"*I do not think so,*" Talin replied with a shake of his head.

Eyeing Talin and Cwen, Brengven suggested, "Since you have called me and I am here you may wish to rest as I stand waiting for the dawn. You both have the look of a fallowass too long on the road and you will need alertness and strength to face the danger of the canyon."

Talin looked to Cwen, anticipating her refusal.

"Aye." She nodded her acceptance of Brengven's offer.

Talin sensed the clutter of confusion in her mind.

The smell of cooking lonely larks woke the three.

Cwen rose, frowning at the fire and at Brengven, who stirred herbs into a pot of thick black tea.

"Smokeless fire by day and darkness by night." Brengven pointed at her. "You know it is the way of the Guardian."

"I am not a Guardian." She rubbed her eyes of sleep and looked for her flask.

"Guardian or no, it is still the way of wisdom, is it not?" Brengven looked to Talin for support.

"Is it not?" Talin asked Cwen, who scowled more deeply and muttered, "I would not use the word wise and Guardian in the same day."

She allowed her eyes to shift to Caen. He stood, his blanket neatly rolled and tied before him and pulled his cloak from his knapsack against the morning chill. He remained turned away from her, staring toward the distant road. As he twisted around he gave her a cursory glance and a nod of acknowledgement before heading to the fire. Sitting on his heels, he held out his hands to warm them.

Talin observed as Cwen stepped toward Caen and spoke his name.

"Caen?"

"It is done and forgotten," Caen answered without looking up.

Talin grinned as he saw Cwen's fists clench at the abrupt dismissal.

Brengven chuckled under his breath.

"It will be much more peaceful if they remain at odds."

Talin snorted, his grin widening, for he doubted it would remain peaceful very long.

Spire Canyon

With its desolate landscape, interrupted only by the towering formations rising several dragon lengths into the air, Spire Canyon was a wonder when seen from the back of a dragon. Cwen knew that those who entered the canyon along its floor were generally sought for crimes against the Queen – thieves and rogues, most of whom simply disappeared.

Brengven sat upon the last grass before the sands of the canyon surrounded by packs and bedrolls, for he had been chosen to stay behind. In the event they did not return, he would report their loss to the council.

"Remember your gifts," he admonished, handing each of them a full flask and some bannock. "And do not argue among yourselves."

Looking from Cwen to Caen he knew his words fell on deaf ears and hoped that Talin would be able to exercise some control over their foolish bickering.

"Five passings of the day star. No more. If we have not returned by nightfall on the fifth day, let my… the council know."

Brengven watched the three most unlikely heroes he had ever seen walk away into the shadowed canyon.

They gazed up at the first of the massive monolithic forms. Rough and misshapen, it rose more than two dragon lengths from base to pinnacle. At its top rested a large flat slab of stone unworn by the eerie winds that swirled within the canyon.

"I hope the resting stones do not topple," Talin whispered to Cwen.

Jabbing him with her elbow she laughed without humor.

"I believe they have rested there since before the memories of Man. It is not likely they will choose today to fall."

From the back of a dragon the distance between the great columns did not see so vast, but here upon the canyon floor the landscape seemed immense.

A giant shadow flowed over them. Looking up, they saw it was simply a klenzingkyte flying far above, searching for the dead or dying. While no one spoke it aloud, each hoped that it would not be him who provided the filthy scavenger a meal.

Odd sounds caused by wind and the cries of unknown beasts echoed within the canyon walls. The sound of sharp claws on rock drifted down from above. It became obvious that the canyon did not lie as empty as it looked.

By mid-afternoon they were deep within the gorge surrounded by the baking sand and brilliant light and shadow cast by the spires. Grotesque animal-like shapes fell across the walls, leaving the travelers with an uneasy feeling.

A sudden call brought out their weapons and they drew in back to back, forming a triangle of protection.

Four men stepped from the shadows, weapons at the ready. Each wore a cloak the color of the earth and heavy leather boots. All were dark skinned and wore their hair long and drawn back, just as Caen wore his.

"You are Caen?" the tallest of them asked.

"Aye, and companions," Caen admitted freely.

One of the men gave a gruff laugh. "I did not know you traveled with a woman, Caen."

"I travel with Talin; the woman is for sale." Caen's eyes shifted to Cwen, cautioning her against denial.

"It is good to see you alive, Fa'ell. Rumor spoke that you were dead."

Stepping forward, Caen offered his grip to each of them and introduced Talin. He did not speak Cwen's name.

Talin nodded to each of the men, offering his hand in friendship as his thoughts sought Cwen's mind.

"*Do not look at them and do not speak. If you do we may not be able to keep you safe.*"

He felt her tension and unobtrusively touched her sleeve.

"*Cwen, by all that is holy do not get us killed the first day in the canyons. These men accept Caen; they will not accept you as an equal. Eyes down, mouth shut—if not for yourself then do it to save my life.*"

"*I shall kill them as they sleep.*" Her angry words hissed in his mind and he sighed with relief.

Two of the men led off up a narrow trail leading back into the cavern wall and the others fell in behind them. Talin pushed Cwen ahead of him, keeping her safely between him and Caen.

The path led to an opening among the rocks where a rudimentary camp had been set. Several more evil looking men sharpened weapons and oiled leathers.

"Sit. Make yourselves comfortable. We have some rather fine ale stolen from the cellars within the Galenite fortress if you would care to sample it." Fa'ell gestured toward the fire.

Talin sat, keeping his eyes on Cwen as she sat beside him and lowered her head to her knees.

Caen moved from man to man, greeting them as long lost friends and offering his hand to each of them in turn before returning to the fire and accepting a mug of ale from Fa'ell.

"The woman is very fine. I could offer a good price for her," Fa'ell said, leaning around to finger Cwen's hair.

"She will fetch a better price within the city," Caen said, grinning. "You know that it is true, Fa'ell."

The man shrugged and grinned, showing missing front teeth and blackened gums.

"There is no denying that truth, friend, but we have not had a woman here in quite some time. Perhaps you would be willing to share her—for a price of course."

"Of course," Caen answered, "I would be more than willing to share; however, she is unsullied and worth a fortune to the wizard Laoghaire."

Roaring his laughter, Fa'ell slapped his thigh and agreed, "We would not wish to spoil such a fine sale. Laoghaire does pay well, even for those who are not so pure."

Talin watched as the man suddenly folded forward and collapsed in a heap. Around them each of the outcasts did the same, bringing a look of amazement to Caen's face.

"It worked! The sleeping spell worked!" he laughed.

Cwen leapt to her feet and slapped him hard across the face.

"You sell women!" She raised her hand again, but he grabbed her wrist.

"I have never sold one. You would have been my first."

"If you two are finished with the courtship, perhaps we could dispatch these men before the spell ends and they wake to kill us."

Talin swung his axe, relieving Fa'ell of his head.

As they dragged the last man from the camp and rolled him over the cliff to the canyon floor below, klenzingkytes and deathawks were already gathering in anticipation of the feast.

"How did you know them?" Cwen asked with a look of revulsion marring her pale face.

"Cwen, I did not grow up as a relative of the Queen. There have been no crystal palaces or beautiful gardens in my life. These were..." He paused, searching for the words. "... business associates."

"You travel the roads as if you were a thief and a ruffian but you are truly just a woman of refinement whose father chooses her suitors, offended by those who lead less noble lives and have desires that are more... fundamental."

She stepped back as if he had slapped her.

"It is not so. I choose who I..."

"Who you what?" asked Talin pretending he had not heard.

Holding out a flask of ale he offered it to Cwen.

Slapping it away she glared at him.

"I have done nothing, Cwen, but drink a dead man's ale."

Her breathing had grown heavy, her pupils were dilated, and her skin was flushed. What most men would mistake as passion Talin knew was merely raw fury held in check by a very slender thread of reason.

"He is mistaken," Talin nodded to indicate Caen.

Keeping his voice calm and even he continued, "You are no lady, Cwen, and no one will ever choose who can and cannot escort you."

He saw her relax slightly and gave Caen a look of annoyance above her head. Offering her the ale once more he gave a sigh of relief as she accepted it.

Talin tossed Cwen's cloak over her and grinned at her drunken snoring.

Walking to the fire he sat across from Caen.

"Do you truly have a death wish?" he chuckled.

"I only spoke the truth. She does not belong here." Caen looked across at Cwen and shook his head.

"She is not what she seems," Talin said.

"A drunken wench?" Caen asked.

"Do not judge her too harshly, for it is not often she drinks heavy ale. I only hoped to make her sleep. It is the best thing for her rage."

The Life Debt

In the brilliant light of morning Cwen held her head and moaned.

Caen stepped before her with a steaming cup.

"I know you do not like me, but I have suffered your ailment often enough to know the cure. If you drink this you will feel better. If you throw it on the ground you will not." He kept his voice low in deference to her aching head.

Lowering her hand from her eyes she stared at him.

"Why do you bait me?"

"In the past I would have said anything to gain your look or have you speak to me, but we have moved beyond that, Cwen. I have seen you stumbling drunk, fall face first into your broth, and heard you snore. From now on I shall consider you one of the men."

"Talin," she called, cringing at the sound of her own voice, "did I snore?"

"I did not hear it," Talin called back grinning.

"Give me the cup," she ordered Caen, who promptly complied.

"What is it?" she asked, sipping it and making a face.

"A recipe given to me by an old whor... woman and it has saved me more than once. You also need food." He added handing her a piece of bannock.

"Why are you being nice to me?" she asked, her voice carrying the sharp edge of suspicion.

"Because every drunk deserves his day," Caen said.

As they reached the canyon floor they noticed the silence. The deathawks and klenzingkytes had flown away and no evidence of last night's death remained beyond the blood-stained earth.

"It would appear that something larger and hungrier than the birds feasts here," Talin said, looking around for drag marks that would indicate the direction in which the bodies had been taken. Finding none, a flicker of unease crossed his face.

From above, sand drifted toward them, dusting their clothes. A sudden grinding sound caused them to look up just in time to see the large stone that had been balanced on the short spire topple forward. Talin shoved Cwen and leapt after her as Caen threw himself backward. The stone struck the ground, sending up a cloud of dust as the pieces settled to the ground.

"Did you see that?" Cwen asked. "The firedrake?"

She pointed above, but it was gone.

"It leapt to the other stone and sent this one tumbling down. I saw it. It was the color of the stones with a red underbelly about as long as you are tall," she said, indicating Talin.

Beyond them another slab of stone fell crashing to the sand below and then they saw the reptilian form of the firedrake slipping back toward them. Its body was elongated and the head wedge-shaped. Short legs carried it quickly over the sand and its forked tongue flickered as it sought the scent of its prey.

Talin drew his axe but Cwen cautioned him with a shake of her head.

"Do not get close, for they have the gift of fire. The crossbow will end its life swiftly and without danger to us if you will lift me to that ledge and offer yourselves as bait." She laughed at their expressions. "I shall not let you die today, and you know I never miss."

Talin lifted her up until she could reach the ledge and pull herself up. Then, as she slowly walked along its length, he and Caen started up the canyon toward the firedrake.

Cwen heard its low growl and saw it in the shadow of a tall, monolithic column. With the swift nocking of a bolt, she aimed just behind its front left foreleg and whistled. As the creature looked up, she sent the arrow straight into its heart and watched it collapse with nothing but a twitch before death. Nocking another bolt, she glanced down toward Caen and Talin.

"Cwen, above you!" Talin's voice cracked with urgency. As she looked up, a second firedrake launched itself across the void from the top of the pillar in front of her. Falling back, she let the arrow loose, catching the animal in the throat and dropping it to the canyon floor where it lay thrashing and exhaling its fiery breath in its death throes.

"Well done," Talin called up to her. "Now I suppose you want me to get you down?"

Without warning the rocks of the canyon wall behind her gave way and Cwen was jerked backward into the dark.

Racing to the ledge, Talin tried to leap up and grab the lip but it was just out of his reach. Caen interlaced his fingers and created a step to boost Talin up to the ledge. Reaching down, Talin pulled Caen up behind him and they charged into the opening. Rock and dust still sifted down, but there was no sign of Cwen.

Cwen regained consciousness in dim torchlight and reached for weapons that were no longer there. Her captor sat across from her, an immense man-shaped creature covered in fine, pale hair. Its eyes glittered as it raised its face to gaze across the wide cavern at its newly acquired meal. The face was hideous, flattened and slightly blue; the flesh of its forehead was loose and fell in folds across the heavy brow. Two large openings served as a nose, the surrounding area moist and glistening in the flickering firelight. A gaping mouth held large canines that extended beyond loose and flabby lips.

"I'll not eat you until the morrow, for I am full from feasting on the dead. Most men wish to spend their last hours talking to their gods," the deep voice explained in a matter of fact manner.

"I have no gods," Cwen responded, examining the creature more closely.

The muscular arms ended in three fingered hands with opposing thumbs. The digits ended in blunt black nails, not claws that could rip and tear.

The creature licked blood from its lips and tossed the slender forearm bone it had used to clean between its teeth into the pile at the edge of the room. Cwen's eyes rested on the pile of clean white bones bare of any flesh.

"Have you no soul?" the beast asked, the flesh of its brow forming a 'v' as it frowned.

"Of course I have a soul, but it is not burdened by the superstitions of the timid," Cwen answered, looking around for an exit.

The only openings were in the walls near the ceiling—large enough for a man's passage but far too high to reach.

Along the walls rested piles of bones and treasures carefully separated by kind. Long bones, skulls, vertebrae, and short bones—all carefully sorted and stacked. Rings, cups, medallions, books, staffs, lule, and weapons rested in their individual lots.

The creature cocked its head as Cwen eyed the stock of weapons.

"While I prefer my meat fresh I can also eat it slightly ripened. The choice is yours."

Cwen laughed in spite of her growing fear, "I shall choose life until the morrow and then I shall make you work for your meal."

A coarse laugh came from deep within the beast's gullet.

"You are not like most men. They cower and beg, offering great riches if I will only spare their lives."

"I am not a man," Cwen spoke truthfully. "And my life is not of sufficient value that I would be forced to beg to save it."

Again the beast gave a low laugh. "And you hope that the two men creeping through my tunnels will reach you before you become my excrement."

Cwen grimaced at the unpleasant thought.

"They will wander in search of you for days, lost among the passageways. Eventually I will prey upon them as I hunger, for I have found that men offer little challenge to a hunting thralax."

"It is obvious that you are thoughtful, and aware that men are as well. How is it that you eat others…"

"Who are self-aware?" The thralax finished her thought before roaring with laughter.

"I learned from men. Are they not the ones who hunt the dragons, the Equus, and the Great Wyrms who live below the earth? Do they not kill and skin us for our scales and hides and shards? They even defile their own kind, for I have seen it in their camps. At least there is purpose to my killing. Are you not the one who killed Fa'ell and his soldiers as they slept?"

"We kill to avoid being killed or to defend the defenseless. We are not murderers."

"No, you are merely food," replied the thralax with a sigh. "If you do not wish to pray to the gods of men, perhaps you could remain silent so that I might rest."

The great creature gave her one last look before closing its eyes as if in sleep.

Cwen stood and wandered around the large cavern, examining the treasures that lay against the walls. She ran her finger along the blade of a long sword, glancing over her shoulder to see the thralax watching her with one open eye. Shrugging, she moved on to a pile of rings, lifting them and placing them one by one on her fingers. At least she would die well adorned. The pile of lauds was quickly pilfered and she filled her pockets with the coins. At the small pile of books she sat down and pulled one onto her lap. It was a book of tallies, sales, and purchases from some bookkeeper who had become excrement. The thought brought a shudder. Next was a journal kept by a poacher, a list of Equus and dragon deaths so long she was grateful to know he was dead. A tightly rolled scroll caught her eye and she untied the leather binding. Carefully unrolling the parchment she frowned at the long rows of symbols—symbols she had seen before on the surface of the G'lm's shields in the cavern below Réverē.

Looking toward her captor she saw that he was wide awake and watchful.

"Property of one who escaped my digestion," the thralax said quietly, pointing to the scroll she held. "A good tale if you should choose to hear it."

"I have nothing else to fill the hours until my death," Cwen said, turning to face the storyteller.

"I knocked him from the back of a dark dragon—a tall man, pale and nearly hairless. He wore the cloak of a wizard and attempted to kill me with bolts of fiery lightning. Obviously, he failed." The beast laughed at his own cleverness.

"I dragged him here and tied him with the wizard binding chains because he would not abide by the rule regarding weapons.

He struggled and fought until he was covered in blood. The scent of it brought me great pangs of hunger even though I had recently fed. As I removed his chains and drew him forward to be devoured, he screamed words I could not understand and disappeared in a flash of blue light. The heat of his magick left me this."

The thralax turned his face to the light showing a deep scar running from the corner of his mouth to his left ear.

"I have promised myself if I ever catch him again, I will eat him while he is still chained."

Drawing the small disc retrieved from Caen, Cwen held it up.

"I also possess the unknown words."

Moving swiftly for one so large, the thralax leapt across the distance that separated them and grabbed Cwen's wrists in one great hand, quickly wrapping her in the coils of the wizard's chain he kept on his belt. Drawing a hefty lock he snapped the ends of the chain together and dropped her to the ground.

With the grimace that passed for a smile he reminded her, "Then I will eat you while you are still chained."

Cwen lay silent, awaiting the sleep of her captor. As she saw his head fall forward onto his chest and heard the deep snores of his slumber, she touched the small pouch that rested against her heart and with her thoughts used her gift to meld into the links of the wizard's chain, leaving nothing visible but empty coils.

Talin and Caen were covered in sweat and dust after hours of searching the long and seemingly endless corridors within the canyon walls. They had come upon huge piles of feces containing remnants of hair and bone and malodorous urine covered walls, an indication that what they sought was large and flesh eating. The only life they had encountered were the swarms of flies that covered the filthy waste.

"It is useless," Caen muttered. "We have seen the same tunnels again and again. Why does she not scream to guide us?"

"Perhaps because in silence she is safe," Talin offered.

"Or because she is already dead," Caen whispered, feeling his stomach churn at the thought of Cwen's death.

"If she is dead we can only hope that it was swift, for no death is painless," Talin mumbled, staring at the ground.

The sudden roaring of laughter sent them racing forward toward the sound, veiling as they went to silence their footsteps.

Openings far too high for a man's reach were cut in the wall before them. The low murmur of an inhuman voice reached them from inside. The tone was low and the words unintelligible, but the voice was calm and did not appear to pose an immediate threat.

Grabbing Caen and pulling him back down the passageway and out of earshot of those within the hidden chamber, Talin whispered, "She lies within, I can hear her voice. If you stand on my shoulders you may be able to reach the opening."

Pulling a thick rope from his belt, he continued, "Once within the opening you can anchor the rope to your waist and allow me to follow. Together we shall disable Cwen's captor by dropping down from above. If we do this while we remain veiled, we shall be silent."

Caen gave his agreement and Talin cast the veil and slowly walked back to the wall and stood below the largest of the openings. Bracing one hand against the wall, he arched his back to give Caen a surface for his foot and reached his other hand over his shoulder to grasp Caen's hand, pulling him up onto his shoulders. As soon as he felt Caen's weight leave him, he looked up and saw the rope drop toward him. Testing it, he pulled himself up, feeling Caen's strength hold his weight. Soon a hand reached down and grabbed his wrist, hauling him up and placing his hand on the sill of the opening.

Together they looked into the room. Cwen was no longer there and the beast below appeared to sleep. Unveiling, Talin dropped into the room with a shout of anguish and fury. Caen leapt down behind him with a warrior's cry of rage and as one they swung to face the beast.

Talin's axe struck the giant's shoulder sending a spray of blood across his face. Six quick arrows entered the thralax's chest as it bellowed in anger and pain, trying to rise. The second blow of the axe crippled the creature, ripping through the muscles of its thigh and causing it to collapse on its side, its blood soaking the ground.

Talin lifted the bloodied axe above his head to deliver the fatal blow, but the words within his mind stayed his arms and caused the axe to fall harmlessly to his side.

Caen's eyes followed Talin's as they sought Cwen's voice.

"Do not kill the thralax," she commanded in a strong clear voice.

They watched her flow from the chain where she had lain hidden. Ignoring them both, she went to the fallen thralax and knelt beside it.

"If I let you live will you allow me to take the scroll of the unknown words and give me my freedom?" She sought the eyes of her captor.

"I am dying." The thralax gave a choking laugh. "Take what you wish."

"It is within my power to heal you." Her voice was soft with the promise of her magick.

"Then you are a sorceress?" asked the dying beast.

"Nay, I am a woman. I require your pledge that you will not harm me or my companions," Cwen said, placing a hand near the arrows within her enemy's chest.

"It requires a life debt." The thralax issued a shuddering breath. "I offer you my bond if you will spare my life."

As the life light began to fade from him, Cwen spoke the healing words to end the process of his death.

Talin and Caen watched as the bleeding stopped and the wounds began to close. Slowly each of the arrows withdrew and dropped to the ground before the beast.

Touching the thralax one last time, Cwen stood and spun toward Talin, laughing and hugging him tightly.

"Did I tell you how glad I was to see you?" she asked, looking up into his oddly mismatched eyes.

A grin crept slowly across his face as his eyes passed to Caen's above Cwen's head.

"Nay, but your gratitude is accepted."

"And you…" She turned to Caen. "I am even glad to see you."

"Woman?" the thralax whispered behind them.

Spinning with weapons at the ready, Talin and Caen drew back, pushing Cwen behind them.

As the beast rose to a sitting position it held up its hand in peace.

"Woman, I am Ock. It is my honor to serve you."

Reaching into the bag at his side, Ock drew out a slender medallion on a gold chain. Beckoning Cwen forward, he watched as her companions tensed, ready to protect her.

With a shake of her head at Talin and Caen, Cwen stepped forward and stood before Ock. He lifted the medallion, slipping the chain over her head and watched as a bright white stone began to pulse slowly within the metal that surrounded it.

"It binds my heart to yours and will tell me of your death and the release of the bond. It can be used along with my name to summon me should you require the strength of the thralax. It also advises others of my kind that I am bound to you and will free you from their threat. I cannot guarantee their safety," he ended, pointing towards Talin and Caen.

"There are others?" Talin questioned under his breath, receiving Caen's snort of approval for the thought.

With a sharp barking sound, Ock caused a door to open in the chamber, allowing them their freedom.

As Cwen tucked the scroll into her shirt, the thralax called to her one last time.

"By the gift of your name, the bond will be sealed."

"Cwen," she said, exiting the door into the starlight of the canyon behind her companions.

Caen held out her crossbow and her sword wrapped within its scabbard.

"Your bow and sword."

"And your staff and dagger," added Talin holding out her walking stick and dagger.

Pausing, she hung the bow at her waist and adjusted the sword across her back with the hilt within easy reach of her right hand. She accepted the staff from Talin and slipped the dagger into her boot before giving them a glance of acknowledgement.

Seeing their eyes fastened on her chest, she looked down to see the pulsing white stone within the medallion.

"It is fortunate for both of you that the medallion rests there. Did it not I would be looking at blind men. And Talin, there is blood on your face."

Sweeping past them at a steady run, she headed back down the canyon toward the grasslands where Brengven waited.

Swinging back suddenly, she held up her hands, wiggling her beautifully adorned fingers.

"I am now a wealthy woman, so I suggest you treat me well."

Once again she was off, leaving them behind.

Talin Tells a Tale

As dawn broke, Brengven rose in the chill air to build a fire and cook them breakfast as he had each day they were gone. He hoped they would return soon, for each day he had eaten the rations of four and his waistcoat was becoming tight across the middle.

He dreaded telling the Queen they had failed and watching the faces of the girl's parents when they realized she was gone without a good-bye. Sighing deeply, he admitted that perhaps they would return in spite of their youth and foolishness.

As the pot began to boil he crushed the willow bark and herbs, adding a few petals of the prickleberry flower to give the sweetness he desired. Setting out four cups, he tossed the ingredients into the pot to steep.

Pulling out bannock and poking at the birds on the spit he pronounced breakfast nearly ready and stood gazing into the enormity of the canyon. The shimmer of movement set him back and he used the power of far sight to catch another glimpse of whatever had been moving across the sand.

The flash of red as the light glinted off her hair told him it was Cwen, and she was followed closely by the two men. Somehow they had survived and were returning to share the breakfast that awaited them.

"H'lo!" Brengven shouted, jumping up as far as his short stature would allow.

Stumbling exhausted into the campsite they threw themselves

upon the ground laughing and rolling about like grass cat kits.

"The desert has driven you mad," Brengven laughed, "but you are not dead!"

Sitting up, Cwen grinned.

"Nay, we are not dead—and we carry the Scroll of the G'lm!" she shouted, pulling the scroll from her shirt and waving it above her head before returning it to safety.

"Gather your breakfast and then you must tell me of all your adventures," Brengven said with shining eyes.

He poured tea for each of them and watched as they gulped it down, shoving great chunks of fowl and bannock into their mouths as if they had not eaten in their absence.

"Cwen got drunk and snored," Caen shared.

"I did not snore," she tossed back good naturedly, "but Talin did force heavy ale on me until I collapsed from drunkenness."

"There was no force involved. She drank it willingly," Talin said with a wink.

"And it was in this drunken state that you stumbled on the scroll?" Brengven asked in disbelief.

"Nay, the drunkenness occurred when Caen offered to sell me to a motley group of poachers. I discovered the scroll in the lair of the thralax, Ock," Cwen said, nodding as if it was perfectly clear.

"You tried to sell her?" Brengven whispered, appalled.

"Aye, but I was unable to get the price I asked. She was not worth much because of her drunkenness." Caen shook his head as if in disappointment.

"But I was paid handsomely," Cwen said softly, pulling the coins from her pockets and tossing them about.

Brengven's look changed to one of horror.

"For what were you paid?" he asked, wondering if he wanted to know.

"Saving the life of the thralax," she responded with a tired yawn.

Swinging toward Talin, Brengven pled, "What really happened?"

Clearing his throat and holding up his hand that he might speak without interruption, Talin told the tale.

"We slipped into the canyon and were accosted by a band of thugs. We offered to sell Cwen to save ourselves, but we received no offers of purchase. She is far too sour to be acceptable to men of such discerning taste. Seeing that the sale of Cwen would not do the trick, Caen befriended one and all and cast his sleeping spell upon them. Once they dropped we killed every one and stole their ill-gotten ale, which Cwen drank before passing out in a stupor. Caen besmirches her reputation with the tale of snoring, for I never heard it."

On the heels of that tale began another.

"We were attacked by falling stones and firedrakes. Cwen used us as bait and killed them all before being invited to dinner at the home of the thralax. Caen and I were not invited, but decided to follow along anyway. We killed the thralax only to see its life restored by the lovely Cwen. The grateful beast swore an eternal debt of gratitude and gave Cwen a medallion to seal his promise. The ungrateful woman stole all his jewels and coin, as well as the scroll she hides within her bodice. Then we headed back straightaway. And that is the true tale of the search for the Scroll of the G'lm as far as I know it."

Cwen gasped with great hiccoughing laughter and Caen shook his head and grinned.

When she finally recovered, Cwen looked up at Talin and shook her head in wonder.

"I have never heard you speak so many words at one time."

She clasped her hand over her mouth to still a new bout of laughter.

Taking a deep breath, Talin shrugged.

"An epic tale requires more than a few words, Cwen, and who could have told it any better?" he asked, raising an eyebrow and challenging her to say differently.

"It was a perfect account of the quest," she agreed, looking up at a disgruntled Brengven.

"It was brief," Brengven stated, looking at Talin crossly. "A tale should be told slowly over a good meal shared among companions."

"Perhaps when we share our next good meal I shall recall more." Talin looked at his bannock grimly.

"Shall we break camp and head for the city?" Talin asked, looking at Cwen. His face softened when he saw her sleeping soundly beside the remains of her breakfast.

"Let her sleep until we are ready to travel," he whispered to Caen and Brengven.

Breaking camp with as little sound as possible, they stowed the remaining items within their packs, dividing them evenly to distribute the weight.

Talin started to pick up Cwen's pack, but Caen lifted it and shouldered it, pointing to Cwen.

"Perhaps you would better serve if you carried our lady. She is far too tired for the long day ahead."

Talin looked at Caen curiously before nodding his agreement and lifting Cwen. Her eyelids fluttered and she laid her cheek against his shoulder and lifted her arm around his neck before her eyes flew open and she glared at him, demanding he put her down.

Shrugging, Talin dropped her.

"We only wished to let you sleep," he said, looking down at her.

"I shall sleep when you do," she said, looking for her pack.

Caen held it out to her and she jerked it away.

"I carry my own weight."

"Cwen, no one said you did not," Caen said.

"It is implied when I am carried like a child," she snapped back.

Whirling on Talin she asked, "Would you carry Caen if he fell asleep? Or Brengven?"

Seeing the look on his face she cursed, "Nay, I did not think so," before storming off toward the road.

Brengven stood with his mouth open, shaking his head at the woman's unreasonableness.

"Does she not realize that she is a woman?" Brengven asked, drawing warning looks from both Caen and Talin.

They made camp early in the afternoon, receiving warning glares from Cwen.

"Cwen, we do not stop for you. There is water here and trees to offer shade and privacy. By stopping early we can have a hot meal before turning the camp cold for the night," Talin assured her.

He watched her drop her knapsack and walk toward the stream. She removed her boots and sat with her feet in the water, cooling the ache of the road. Lifting her hair, she shook it out to cool her neck.

Scooping water in her hands she bathed her face and looked back toward the camp and upstream toward the deep pool. Grabbing her boots she returned to the camp. Brengven had the fire started and Talin and Caen were off hunting grosshare. Opening her bedroll she pulled out a blanket and headed back toward the pool and its shallow falls.

She washed her clothes and hung them wet upon the rocks before scrubbing her hair with a bane boar brush and the small piece of soap she carried. Washing away the sweat and dirt of the quest and the road she began to feel almost human. She rinsed the soap from her body and wrung out her hair and wrapped herself tightly in the blanket. Gathering her clothes, she walked barefoot back to camp.

The hunters had returned and were cleaning the hares and making fun of Brengven's serious nature when they first noticed her.

She pointed a warning finger, causing them to close their mouths.

"Do not say a word," she cautioned, slipping her cloak over her blanket clad figure and hanging her wet clothes on the lowest branches of the tree.

"Tomorrow while you are both still filthy and covered in blood I shall be clean and comfortable; indeed, almost presentable when I talk to Horsfal about the wizard's staff."

"Cook, I am hungry and want a night's sleep," she prompted them. "Again we shall split the watch. Caen the first; Talin, you take the middle; and I shall stand until dawn."

"What is she doing?" Caen asked.

"She gets this way whenever we are around water. I usually wash the blood off my face to keep her happy," Talin shrugged. "I would suggest you do the same," he added, pointing to the blood smeared across Caen's forehead.

"Who is Horsfal?" Caen asked, rubbing at his forehead.

"Her contact in the city. He knows everyone and everything."

During his watch Talin called a sleepy deathawk to him.

"I must ask a favor of you, my friend," he spoke in the speech of the beasts. "Take my message to the Sojourner Ileana within the fortress of the House of Aaradan. Tell her the Scroll of the G'lm is in the hands of Cwen."

With a rustle of feathers and a shrill cry of agreement, the deathawk lifted into the sky and circled toward Æstaffordæ and its fortress.

Cwen woke from a sound sleep with her dagger drawn and pointed at Talin.

"Your watch," he pushed her dagger out of his face.

She reached up and touched his wet hair.

"Did it rain while you were on watch, Talin?"

"Aye, a bit." He winked and pulled his cloak around him as he prepared to nap.

Cwen wandered half a dragon's length from Caen and Talin and drew her long sword; then, as taught by her mother, she began her morning sword play.

With her head held high, she swung the sword rhythmically through the upstroke, backstroke, parry center, and thrust. Her arms strong and smooth, her motions fluid. She had never been more her mother's daughter.

Caen watched her by the light of the moons. Her long hair fell free and swung with the rhythm of her sword. He had never seen anything more beautiful. Feeling Talin's gaze, Caen turned and found him grinning.

"She is rather amazing," Talin said before settling down to sleep until Cwen woke him.

Horsfal's Tavern

Breakfast was quick and cold and eaten an hour before dawn. Cwen noticed the cleanliness of both Talin and Caen. They had a scrubbed appearance and had at least tried to brush the dust of travel from their clothing.

By the time the day star finally rose above the horizon the travelers were entering the city of Merid in the kingdom of Æcumbræ. The streets were empty of the traders and patrons who would arrive later in the day and many shops were still closed. Horsfal's tavern, however, was always open and the rowdy laughter could be heard far down the street.

As they entered the tavern, the patrons grew quiet and watchful, curious to see what the road had brought so early in the day.

"Lady Cwen, savior of my soul and love of my loins!" came a loud, harsh voice as a mountainous man rushed toward them.

Caen placed his hand on the hilt of his sword, drawing a shake of the head from Talin.

The huge man swept Cwen off her feet, crushing her to him and spinning her around as if she weighed no more than a loaf of bannock. He slobbered kisses all over her face and neck.

"I love you, Cwen. When will you marry me and end my agony?" Horsfal asked, laughing at the top of his voice and slapping Talin on the back.

"I fear your agony must be felt a little longer, Horsfal," Cwen said, reaching as far around the man as she could to give him a hug.

"I am far too busy killing and plundering to settle down and raise your babies."

Caen looked on with disbelief.

"Come, bring your friends to my table and let me fondle your hair."

Leading off, Horsfal called to the bar wench to bring a round of ale.

Sitting in the massive chair at the head of the table he smacked his thigh and beckoned to Cwen. She raised an eyebrow and sat in the chair on his right.

He roared with laughter, sending his many chins quivering and reached out to pull her close and kiss the top of her head.

"Let it be known to all that Lady Cwen of Aaradan is promised to Horsfal of Æcumbræ," he shouted to all within hearing and looked to Talin for confirmation.

Talin nodded his approval, sending Horsfal into further gales of gut-busting laughter.

Suddenly, as if day had turned to night, he grew sober and gulped down the ale the wench had set before him.

"What is it you bring me?" his eyes glowed in anticipation of Cwen's treasures.

Drawing the wizard's staff from beneath her cloak Cwen laid it on the table before Horsfal, watching his reaction closely.

As the shadow of recognition crossed his face she leaned over and pinched his ample cheek.

"Tell me friend. Who is it I seek?"

"You seek Domangart who runs the troll mines on Æwmarshæ," Horsfal stated without hesitation. "Though I cannot imagine how he lost his staff."

"You are sure it is his?" Cwen asked, "For I would not want to visit trolls without a good reason."

"Aye, it is his."

"Cwen, why do you seek the owner of this staff?" Horsfal asked her.

"We were attacked by a band of men pretending to be salt mercs. They carried this staff."

"It is possible they had stolen it," the fat man suggested.

“Then I shall return it to its rightful owner and earn his indebtedness,” she responded as she stood to leave.

Reaching out, he grabbed her hands and examined her fingers.

“You wear the rings of many dead, Cwen.”

“Aye, and each died horribly; but not by my hand.”

Kissing the man’s cheek again, she whispered, “I did not kill to get a one of them Horsfal. You see? I am trying to change my ways.”

“Talin, care for her while she is away from me,” Horsfal called after them as they headed for the door.

Raising his hand in acknowledgement, Talin held open the door for Horsfal’s Lady Cwen.

A few paces behind Cwen, Caen whispered to Talin.

“Who, how…?”

“You stutter, Caen.” Talin grinned at his companion’s dismay. “They are friends, Caen. I am beginning to believe you do not understand the concept.”

“I have had friends, but none of them were women,” Caen answered shaking his head. “And he called her Lady Cwen?”

“To Horsfal she will always be Lady Cwen by her permission. If you wish details you must ask Cwen, for I do not tell her secrets.” Talin extended his stride to catch Cwen.

“Cwen, we do not have time to satisfy your desire for revenge against those who sent the salters. We must decipher the scroll and begin our search for the shards that control the armies,” Talin spoke.

“It is not personal revenge I seek this time, Talin. The salt mercs also carried the disc… if Caen is to be believed. Perhaps the staff’s owner also has knowledge of the disc.”

“What is it I have lied about now?” Caen asked.

Cwen swung on him and poked him hard in the chest with her staff.

“I do not trust you, Caen. Your companions of the past have been poachers and slavers, you steal from those who attempt to befriend you and I just do not…”

Caen held up his hand. “Guilt by association. I understand it well and there is naught I can do to sway your distrust. The disc was on the dead man though I cannot force you to believe it. I shall be in the tavern if you choose to collect me on your way out of town."

Taking two of the rings from her fingers she handed them to Talin.

"Call on Casal and get what you can for these. I shall purchase provisions and meet you at the city gates at midday."

Talin headed toward the trader's shop, leaving Cwen to re-provision.

Cwen wandered off toward the vendor's stalls that lay along the dusty side streets of the city. While Merid was not quite the den of thieves and poachers that Ezon in Ælmondæ had become, it still had a rather unsavory reputation.

She purchased salt from a merchant who charged her too much and tea and bannock from a blind man. Slabs of dried stag and boar were wrapped, tied and stowed within her pack after a visit to the butcher. Provisioned sufficiently to reach the city in Æshulmæ that lay midway between Æcumbræ and their destination of Æwmarshæ, she headed back to the tavern for another drink with Horsfal.

Entering the pub, she noticed that the crowd had thinned, leaving only a few serious drinkers at the tables. Standing at the bar, she ordered ale and looked around for Horsfal.

"In the back," the bar wench indicated with a tilt of her head.

Waving her thanks Cwen headed toward the back of the tavern and Horsfal's private rooms.

"Fal!" she called, pounding on the door.

The door cracked open and she laughed as Horsfal's women slipped out past her and he gestured her inside.

"Did I interrupt again, Fal?"

"You, Lady Cwen, are never an interruption but always a pleasant interlude."

She chuckled at his nonsense and sat down, crossing her feet upon the table. Reaching within her shirt she pulled out a small piece of spider's cloth on which she had traced a single symbol from the disc.

"Have you ever seen anything like this before?" she asked, handing it to him and searching his black eyes for the truth.

He touched the charcoal drawing, staring down at it, his eyes lingering there far too long before he sought her face.

"Cwen, where did you see this image?"

She shrugged. "That is not important at the moment. You are obviously familiar with it. What language is it and what is the significance of my seeing it?"

He shook his head and she saw a shiver pass over him causing his jowls to quiver.

"Cwen…" He shook his head again.

She leaned back, tilting the chair onto its rear legs.

"It would not do for me to ask it again, Horsfal. Our friendship might not be great enough to save you."

Her eyes pierced him and held him like a rainbow fish upon a spear.

"Wreken. It is a symbol of the power of the Wreken. Magick from the days when Wreken ruled and men were fodder. The writers of these symbols had no form and inhabited the bodies of the Wyrms. Cwen, I do not know where you have stumbled, but this knowledge is sufficient to earn us grim torture by those who would seek it." He took the cloth and pushed it into his cup of ale, watching as the charcoal outline dissolved away.

He stroked her cheek with his large hand.

"I never saw it and you never showed it to me."

Allowing the chair to fall forward she dropped her feet to the floor and stood.

"I shall not return for a long time, Fal. You will be missed while I travel."

His smile was somber.

"You are the daughter no woman has ever given me," Horsfal stated truthfully, his eyes growing moist. "Far better than all the sons they have."

As her hand grasped the handle of the door she heard him whisper a last thought.

"Protect what you hold precious, for the thief intends to steal it."

She nodded and stepped through the door.

Dropping into a chair next to Caen, who sat before several empty draughts of ale, she rested her elbows on his table and stared at him.

His eyes remained fixed on the table as he pretended to ignore her.

"I have been told I have something you want," she whispered, leaning toward him.

"Have you come to make an offer?" he asked without looking up.

"If you will complete this quest without betraying us I shall give it to you freely."

His eyes rose until they met hers.

"Why do you offer this, Cwen?"

"Because it is all I have to give," she said, "except for your life, and I do not think you hold that as dear."

Pushing back his chair and standing he gave her a lazy grin.

"Cwen, I am surprised at your deceit."

He watched as color rose to her cheeks and he knew he had caught her in a lie.

"I can honestly say I have never lied to you, but you cannot say the same. Though I bear you no grudge, for you seek only to protect Talin and the quest. Shall we go? I am sure he waits for us."

He held out his hand and was surprised when she took it.

Talin entered Casal's to find the man deeply involved in an argument with a customer.

"It is worth far more, Casal!" an angry thief shouted.

"Then take it elsewhere and get what you ask. I shall not pay it. Get out!" Casal shouted back and watched with a heavy scowl on his face as the thief gathered his goods and stormed out the door.

"How may I help you, Talin?" Casal's voice was smooth and unruffled.

Talin placed the rings on the counter and saw Casal's surprise as he recognized them.

"Did she kill them?"

"Nay, not this time; they were a gift for healing." Talin spoke a half-truth.

"It must have been a resurrection," Casal said shaking his head.

"It nearly was," Talin agreed.

"What do you ask for them, Talin?"

Recalling the last patron's plight, Talin responded, "What is it you will offer, Casal?"

"Three lule each and it is a generous offer, for not many will wish to wear the band of a dead man," Casal chuckled.

"Agreed," Talin said, watching as Casal opened his lock box and withdrew the six week's wages.

Sliding the coins into his pocket, Talin bade the shop owner farewell and went to meet Cwen.

As Caen and Cwen arrived at the gates they found Talin lounging against the wall sharpening the blades of his axe.

"Was Casal generous?" Cwen's words were sharp.

Talin's eyebrow rose at the strain in her voice. Pulling the coins from his pocket and handing them to Cwen he let his gaze settle on Caen.

"Did you have trouble in the tavern?" his eyes searched Caen's face for evidence of misconduct.

"Nay," Cwen snapped. "I spoke to Fal again. What we know frightens him and therefore should frighten us."

Without further discussion she set off down the road at a quick pace. Her back was rigid with tension.

"What did you say to her?" Talin prodded Caen.

"I merely declined a contract that she had no intention of fulfilling. Had I accepted, it would have ended in my death."

Talin grinned, imagining what Caen had declined and silently agreeing that to have accepted such an offer would have been very foolish indeed.

Talin dropped down on Cwen's right as she warmed her hands before the fire.

"You have been very quiet," he said without looking at her.

"Caen denied me." Her voice was filled with disbelief.

Talin laughed, drawing a frown from her.

"Cwen, he is not the fool I believed him to be. He did not deny you. He denied your offer. There is a great difference. And what exactly was your intent? Had you even thought about it?"

"I would just have killed him when the quest was completed," she shrugged. “But how did he know?”

Talin laughed out loud.

“Cwen, he has pursued you relentlessly and your answer has always been a threat. Why should he suddenly believe…?”

“The laughter is at my expense, I assume,” Caen interrupted as he joined them, sitting to Cwen’s left.

“Aye,” Talin admitted.

Brengven appeared and put out the fire, pouring the last of the tea into cups and passing them around.

“Where is the scroll, Cwen?” he asked as he dropped cross-legged before her.

She withdrew it from her shirt and handed it to him.

“Horsfal says it is written in the symbols of those called Wreken. At least according to legend.”

Brengven nodded. “We have also heard the legends in Réverē. They speak of a time long before Man rose to build cities, a time before the world was given a name.”

“Can you read the scroll, Brengven?” Cwen asked.

“Nay, not yet. But you have part of the key. When you find the second part I shall be able to decipher the symbols.”

“What key?” Cwen and Caen spoke at the same time, causing Talin to shake his head and roll his eyes.

“The disc; it is one half of a cipher stone.”

“And you truly found it on the dead man?” Cwen’s eyes probed Caen’s face for the truth.

His gaze was direct, with no hint of deceitfulness.

“It was within a small bag around his neck hidden beneath his clothing.”

“Perhaps the other half lies within the wizard’s lair. Horsfal said the wizard’s staff is definitely the property of one called Domangart of Æwmarshæ,” Cwen noted.

“Dealing with Domangart will be difficult. He is powerful and will sense any treachery. He cannot be approached without great caution. Cwen, you are the most accomplished liar so I recommend that you seek him out alone.”

Cwen flushed.

“The statement was not meant to offend,” Brengven continued.

"It is merely the truth. And because you are a woman you hold the advantage. He will not see you as a threat."

With a sideways glance at Caen, Cwen muttered, "It is good to know I have some advantage."

Talin turned away to hide his smirk.

"Fight with me," Cwen demanded, motioning to Talin.

Talin shook his head.

"You know I do not like the sword."

Swinging to Caen she said, "Then you fight with me."

"Very well, but we shall use only our staffs. This will prepare you for Domangart, for he will not allow the bow or sword to enter his lair, not even in the hands of a woman."

"You know Domangart?" Cwen asked, wondering why she felt surprised.

"Nay, but I know of him, and the stories say that those who faced him with weapons were rarely seen again. He is a powerful sorcerer, Cwen, and cannot be met head on. You do not have the skill," he baited.

Her eyes flashed and her chin rose.

"I am quite skilled with the staff. Do you believe you can best me?"

"I do not know, but we shall soon find out."

Grabbing her staff, Cwen leapt to her feet, backing away and beckoning Caen toward her she winked bewitchingly.

She heard Talin's warning in her mind: *"Do not kill him, Cwen,"* and her smile widened.

Lifting his lance, Caen stood and followed her as she backed across the open meadow away from the others.

Gripping the staff with two hands he blocked her first strike easily. He then struck her twice in quick succession, watching as her eyes grew brighter.

She pushed forcefully against him and swiftly spun away to strike hard across his back. Spinning, he knocked her feet out from under her and watched her recover with a leap. He nodded his approval and caught her fleeting look of irritation.

He met her blow for blow as she attacked aggressively, feeling for his weakness. Finding none, she withdrew and dropped her double-handed stance, shifting her staff to her strong left hand and tapping it across her thigh, drawing his eyes away from her face.

Her assault was fast and wicked and she drove him to the ground, straddling him and placing her staff against his throat. Their eyes locked and he dropped his lance, raising his hands toward her.

Her warning look was deadly.

"If you touch me I shall be forced to break your neck," she whispered, lowering her head and allowing her hair to brush his face.

He allowed his arms to drop to his sides.

"Soon, Cwen, you will no longer be able to resist my charm."

Laughing, she rolled off him and leapt to her feet. Without a backward glance she headed back to the camp where Talin watched with amusement.

The Informants

Telsar City in the kingdom of Æshulmæ was small and dirty. Its residents were poor and eagerly sought the ill-gotten wealth of their neighboring kingdom.

The three arrived in the bright midday heat, leaving Brengven camped among the trees on the outskirts of civilization, a place he much preferred.

As they stood before the inn, Cwen drew her dagger from her boot and slid it up her sleeve, the hilt in the palm of her hand.

Cwen gave quick instructions.

"We seek information on the location of Domangart's mines. Talin, you can talk to Soderby. She likes you."

Talin's face held a look of extreme revulsion causing Cwen to grin.

"Well, she does."

"I shall make conversation with Zak." Her smile grew even wider. "He likes me. And Caen, if you have contacts here, see what you can find out. We shall meet in the tavern for a draught before dusk."

Speaking their agreement, Caen and Talin headed off in opposite directions, leaving Cwen to enter the inn.

The innkeeper allowed his eyes to travel over Cwen, making her want to kill him, but instead she simply asked if Zak was still residing in the man's fine establishment.

Nodding, the man pointed down a dark corridor and coughed

out, "On the right at the back."

Stating her gratitude, Cwen stepped over the litter in the hallway and banged on the door he had indicated.

It opened a crack and pale blue eyes looked out from under a mop of dirty brown hair. A muscular arm reached out and dragged her inside.

"Zak, gentlemanly as always," Cwen remarked, pushing his hands away and straightening her clothes.

"If you were more willing we would not have to wrestle." He reached for her again and received her dagger at his throat for his trouble.

"Sit down, Zak." Using her foot she pulled a chair from his table and pushed him toward it good-naturedly.

"I need information and I shall pay handsomely for it."

Seeing his look, she shook her head.

"Nay Zak, only in coin. But I shall give you a full lule if your information is useful."

With a deep sigh of disappointment he mumbled his agreement and asked, "Who is it you seek?"

"A wizard named Domangart."

"He will kill you, or sell you to Laoghaire. It would be a shame to lose you to one of them."

"Your concern is touching, but as I only seek to return something that belongs to him I doubt that he will wish to kill me. But that is the second time someone has suggested I might be sold to one called Laoghaire; frankly, I am growing tired of it. I imagine Domangart will be overcome with gratitude at the return of his property. So just tell me where to find him, Zak."

"He mines beneath the plains of Æwmarshæ. If you make it known in the city that you seek him he will send a troll to escort you to the mines."

Zak leaned forward and grabbed her arm.

"I do not jest, Cwen. He will surely kill you… or worse."

"Many have tried, as you well know, Zak, and it has not happened yet."

Withdrawing his hand he simply shrugged.

"Until the next time, Zak," Cwen whispered, placing the coins upon his table.

Soderby wore a sickly sweet scent that made Talin feel nauseous and he cursed Cwen for sending him to the woman. He had tried keeping furniture between them, but had finally given up in the hope of getting the information quickly and leaving.

"Talin," she simpered, rubbing her hand up his arm, "how long has it been since you last came to see me?"

"It has been quite some time, Soderby. Cwen sends me. She needs information you might have."

Talin breathed a sigh of relief at the look on the woman's face and watched as she withdrew her hand.

"You still travel with her?" Soderby asked, lifting her heavy black hair from her neck and adjusting her neckline to provide him with a better view of her ample bosom.

"Cwen is such a skinny little thing. No meat on her bones. So… unwomanly."

"Aye, she is a warrior," Talin gulped and looked away, "and she waits for my return."

With a snort of displeasure, Soderby said with feigned hurt, "You merely use me, Talin, without any real affection."

Talin cringed at the thought and shook his head in denial.

"Domangart, a wizard; this is who she seeks."

Soderby laughed loudly and her lardaceous flesh fluttered like the leaves of the chale tree in a stiff breeze.

"In the mines of the trolls on Æwmarshæ, but tell her she is not woman enough to satisfy Domangart."

Talin stood, backing toward the door and expressing gratitude for the information.

"Next time do not bring Cwen's name into our conversation, Talin, it dampens my passion," Soderby warned.

Talin fled, promising himself there would not be a next time.

Cwen entered the tavern and scanned the room for Talin. Seeing him, she headed for the table in anticipation of the tale he would tell about his visit with Soderby.

Her pleasure faded as she saw Caen and the woman with him. She was beautiful. Her pale gold hair cascaded over her bare shoulders and rounded arms and across her back. Her bright blue eyes looked up at Caen and her hands rested upon his chest as she gazed up at him while he whispered, causing a lilting laughter to bubble forth from her pouting mouth.

Talin stood and went to Cwen.

"Come and sit down before you do something foolish."

Cwen allowed him to lead her to the table and accepted the draught he placed before her, draining it swiftly and looking up for another.

"That is his contact?" she hissed under her breath. Talin shrugged and filled her cup with ale, watching as she drank it without thinking, wiping her mouth with the back of her hand.

"He was with her when I arrived. I did not intrude, hoping that the information he gained would be useful."

"Information?" Cwen snorted. "A man does not go to a woman like that for information."

"A woman like what, Cwen?" Talin urged, enjoying her discomfort.

"Well she is obviously…"

"Very beautiful?" Talin supplied in an offhand manner.

Cwen stared at him and then glanced over her shoulder at the woman with Caen. "You think she is beautiful?" Cwen asked, looking back toward Talin.

"Isn't she?"

"She is fat," she answered with a shrug. "I would not like to be so fat."

"Collect Caen when he finishes… gathering information," she said, rolling her eyes and standing. "I shall meet you at the campsite before nightfall."

Talin frowned as he watched her leave the tavern.

Domangart's Mines

Their faces flooded with relief as they saw Cwen approaching the campsite. She carried a large parcel wrapped in several layers of spider's cloth and tied with green ribbon. Ignoring the three of them she went to her knapsack and stuffed the package inside as Talin tried to reach around her to grab it.

"It is not for you," she laughed, slapping his hand. "It is a weapon for me."

"What kind of weapon is wrapped in spider's cloth and tied with ribbon?"

Cwen glared past him at Caen.

"A woman's weapon. One that works on men like Caen, and perhaps the wizard Domangart."

Talin frowned and mumbled, "The meal is ready if you wish to eat before we douse the fire for the night."

Following Talin, she sat down next to Caen and looked up at him, her eyes wide and innocent.

"Did your tart provide you with much information?"

"Aye, she gave the name of a man called Walthor in the Æwmarshian city of Cridian that can contact Domangart for us and get you an invitation to the mines. So that you can return the wizard's staff and win his undying gratitude," Caen answered, looking pleased.

"And just how does she know this man?"

"He is her business partner," Caen responded, pouring another cup of tea and handing it to Cwen. "They deal in the crystals that

Domangart mines."

Cwen searched his eyes to see if he was teasing, but he seemed quite serious.

"Were you jealous, Cwen?" Caen gazed into the flames.

"I? Jealous? Of course not. What would I have to be jealous of? You are nothing to me."

"Then why did you buy a dress?" he asked, holding her gaze.

"You bought a dress?" Talin asked in disbelief.

"I thought I could wear it to visit Domangart. I thought that I would look less threatening… in a dress."

Both Caen and Talin stared at her.

Talin burst out laughing.

"A weapon!" he laughed, shaking his head.

Suddenly an odd look came across his face.

"How did you know she bought a dress? You were with me," he asked Caen.

"I have purchased dresses for women, Talin. I know what they look like."

"Are you going to show it to us?" Brengven asked from the other side of the camp.

"Nay, I am not going to show it to you. It was a foolish idea."

"Not so foolish, Cwen. You are right. A dress can be a powerful distraction and I am sure a dress is perfect for a visit to Domangart," Caen admitted.

"Now can we see it?" asked Talin.

Cwen rose to her feet.

"If you laugh I shall kill you," she said, looking at each of them in turn. "I mean it."

As she went to get the dress, Caen grinned at Talin.

"She was jealous. She may not care for me yet, but she would not like anyone else to care for me either. It is a good sign."

Talin raised an eyebrow and shook his head.

Returning with the dress over her arm Cwen shook it out and held it up.

It was made of silk, soft and delicate and the color of the deep forest in shadow. Against its color her hair seemed redder, her skin more fair.

"You will indeed look less threatening," Caen said, receiving Talin and Brengven's nods of agreement and Cwen's shy smile.

"I have never had a dress," she whispered as she folded it carefully and carried it back to her satchel.

Then she went to practice with the sword.

They received a warm welcome in Vissenmire on Æwmarshæ. Borrolon, the elder Ancient, insisted they stay in the mire at least one night to "rest in proper beds."

They were fed and hovels were assigned and then they were left at the fire to discuss a plan for getting Cwen into the mines to return Domangart's staff.

Brengven sat with them at the fire, though he had insisted on camping beyond the mire for the night.

"We shall have Walthor contact Domangart. He needs only tell him that a woman comes returning a staff she believes he has lost. That should draw his attention," Caen said.

Brengven gave a scowl. "Who will you be?"

"Why I shall simply be Lady Cwen, daughter of Horsfal. If anyone should question it, Horsfal will say it is so."

Talin added, "And do not try to search the mines, Cwen. They are filled with trolls."

She laughed at his warning and gave her agreement.

As they headed for their hovels Caen's voice stopped her.

"Be very careful, Cwen. I would not like to lose you."

"You cannot lose what you do not have, Caen. But I shall be cautious. I do not wish to die at the hands of trolls."

She left him looking after her.

The Ancient Lilli giggled as she tied the last of the laces on Cwen's dress.

"You is beautiful!" The old woman clapped her hands together. "Those boys will just faints when they see you."

"Come," she pulled on Cwen's hand, "looks in the mirror!"

Cwen looked into the polished brass. It was as if she were looking at a stranger. Her hair was washed and brushed until it sparkled with brilliant red highlights where the day star's glow touched it through the window. Her eyes shined with excitement. Unable to believe that the woman in the mirror was really her, she reached up and touched her hair to see the reflection doing the same. The dress fit her snugly, hugging her trim figure as far as her hips before flowing outward to just below her ankles.

Lilli patted her arm.

"Sit, so I can fix the sleeves."

Lilli straightened the sleeves, pulling and pushing until the small points rested perfectly on the backs of Cwen's hands.

Cwen pulled on her boots and went out to face Talin and Caen.

Talin's back was to her so she simply whispered in his mind.

"Please do not laugh, Talin."

He spun around and started to say something facetious but the words never came. Cwen's face was radiant and she looked like the ladies he remembered from the Xavian gardens.

"Domangart doesn't stand a chance," he finally said with a lopsided grin, "and neither does Caen."

"Did someone say my name?" Caen said, rounding the side of his hovel.

He stopped mid-stride and stared.

Talin nudged Cwen with his elbow.

"See? I told you," he laughed out loud.

Caen seemed rooted to the spot. He blinked twice and then whispered her name. A shadow of a smile broke across his face as he spoke in a hushed voice.

"There is no doubt that the dress is a weapon."

"Let us hope it works as well on Domangart," Cwen mumbled.

Brengven was quite impressed with the new Lady Cwen.

"When you talk to Domangart, lie only when you must. If the truth will do, use it."

"He will not be looking at your eyes though, and the distraction your dress provides will give you a strong advantage," Caen added.

"And try to act like a lady. Do not kill anyone or strike anything with your staff."

Cwen curtsied and answered in the demure voice of a noblewoman, "I do know how to behave; I simply choose not to do it. I shall enchant

Domangart and locate the second half of the cipher stone as well."

"Cwen..." Talin and Caen spoke together.

Caen deferred to Talin.

"Do not risk a search for the cipher stone within the mines. Trolls will not be distracted by your dress."

"I do not believe the stone will be hidden in the mines. I believe it more likely he will carry something so important on his person. I shall steal it and he will never know. I am a very good thief." Her eyes dared them to argue.

"Aye, Cwen you are," Talin admitted. "I have seen her steal a man's money pouch while he was looking at..."

Her look served to silence him momentarily, before he added, "Well I have."

Caen laughed. "I do not doubt that it is so."

"But Domangart is no ordinary man, Cwen. Use caution and do not allow him to anger you," Brengven warned.

Yávië, the Queen of Ædracmoræ had done Domangart a great favor by reuniting the Seven Kingdoms. When the kingdoms had been shattered the trolls were forced to remain below Æshardæ's southern sands, but once the kingdoms had reformed the sphere, the trolls had unlimited access beneath the planet's surface.

Following the Æshardians' massacre by the death dragons just after the world's rebirth, the trolls had been left with a short supply of slaves and meat. Domangart was forced to move the trolls to another kingdom, easily done using the underground caverns of the reunited Ædracmoræ.

Now deep beneath Æwmarshæ the trolls mined the exquisite Gaianite crystals that Domangart sold to the wizards and jewelers of the world. The crystals contained elemental energy and were valued highly, by some as fine gemstones and by others for their light.

Trolls were difficult to keep and required a regular supply of flesh, something readily available in the form of men and their offspring. Men never seemed to grow wise regarding the disappearance of the odd drunkard wandering home late, or the sudden change in a child's behavior when the firstborn was replaced with a changeling. Although there had been a few whispers of suspicion from the Galenites over the odd bones found among the dead on Æshardæ.

The human kin served as slaves to the trolls and a ready source of food when time did not permit a hunt. Domangart did find the occasional halfling offspring to be a bit distasteful, but it seemed to be the price one paid for keeping human slaves among the trolls. Trolls were not known for their discretion or restraint.

A sudden scuffle drew Domangart's attention. His halfwit apprentice was being shoved aside by an angry troll.

"I have told you not to speak to them," the wizard called. "They simply see you as an appetizer, not an apprentice."

Under his breath, he added, "It probably would be no loss if they actually did eat you since you are such a fool."

"I bring news," the apprentice mumbled as he stood before his master.

"Do not say, 'I bring news.' Tell me the news, you idiot!" Domangart shouted, striking his underling with a staff.

"A woman seeks you. She wishes to return your staff; it seems that she found it."

"Indeed?" Domangart considered the possibility of replacing the fool before him with a more becoming guest.

"Is she fine-looking?"

"I have not seen her, master. She waits at Walthor the crystal trader's shop."

"Perhaps I shall send a troll to fetch her and invite her to dinner. It has been long since I entertained a woman and it will provide a pleasant interlude."

Walthor proved gracious and helpful. He examined the staff they had found on the dead man and agreed that it did indeed look like Domangart's. He sent one of his crystal carvers off with a note for the wizard and treated them to lunch while they awaited the answer.

"Lady Cwen, you are the daughter of Horsfal of Æcumbræ? I have not had the pleasure of a visit to his establishment for some time. Perhaps when next we travel to Æcumbræ we shall stop in for a draught," Walthor said.

"It is also good to see that he does not allow you to travel unaccompanied. Caen is a very capable guardian and has escorted my wife on a number of occasions. She was always quite satisfied with his services."

Caen chuckled at the glare he received from Lady Cwen. Talin shook his head and wondered silently if Caen had purchased the woman a dress.

"Once I realized the staff I had found belonged to such an important wizard nothing could stop me from returning it." Cwen smiled sweetly at Walthor and was rewarded by a pat on the hand.

"It is refreshing to see such honesty. Many would just have sold it."

A knock interrupted their discussion. A troll was waiting to escort the Lady Cwen to the mines of Domangart.

"Just follow the troll," Walthor instructed. "They are well-trained and obedient. Domangart manages them very capably. You will be escorted back as well, and your guardians can wait here for you if they wish."

"There is no need for I have given my guardians some errands to do while I am away."

Talin and Caen watched until Cwen disappeared from view then veiled themselves and set off after her.

Domangart watched the woman approach. She was magnificent, a true beauty, and obviously well-bred. A small frown creased his forehead, for he had been told that she was the daughter of Horsfal of Æcumbræ, a disgustingly fat man who had many women, some of whom were quite fetching. Perhaps he had had the daughter schooled among the Galenites or Xavians. That would explain her grace and posture.

As the troll escort grunted and left them, Cwen extended the staff to Domangart.

"I believe this is yours, sir." Her voice was soft and low and her remarkable eyes were innocent and without evidence of deception.

"Milady, it is most kind of you to have traveled so far to deliver it."

He allowed his fingers to touch her hands as he took the staff. He was pleased that she did not shrink away.

"I would be honored if you would join me for the evening meal. It is prepared and I shall have you escorted back to Walthor before it grows dark. Will you do me this honor?"

Bowing her head with feigned shyness, Cwen blushed and accepted Domangart's invitation.

"The honor is mine, sir. You are well known for your excellence in magick. Perhaps you would be willing to demonstrate a little. I do love magick."

From the safety of the trees Caen and Talin watched open-mouthed.

Domangart offered her his arm and Cwen rested her hand upon it, allowing her hair to brush against the wizard's shoulder. She glanced toward the trees and gave Talin and Caen a playful wink.

Domangart was neither tall nor handsome. He stood little over nine hands in height, not as tall as Cwen, and his blonde hair was coarse and had the appearance of strands of rope. His face was rather pinched looking, as if his features had been placed a little too closely together, and his complexion grew rather splotchy when he was as nervous as he was near the Lady Cwen.

"I was very sheltered as a child. My father was very strict and I spent many years of tutoring with the Xavian artisans. It is wonderful to be away and here with you."

Domangart wondered just how much it would take to buy her from Horsfal. He certainly intended to find out as soon as possible.

"Where is it you are staying, Lady Cwen, while you are visiting Æwmarshæ?" he asked, hoping it was with Walthor, who owed him many favors.

"I am staying with the Ancients in Vissenmire, as my father wished. He did not feel the city safe after dark. I am accompanied by guardians who await me at Walthor's and will escort me to the mire this evening." Her eyes lowered and she allowed herself to blush.

"I wish I did not have to go."

Domangart felt his heart pound against his ribs and called quickly for the dessert to be served.

Cwen clapped her hands and gave a sultry laugh as she watched Domangart create a flock of day doves and then turn them swiftly into flowers that he gave to her.

"You are wonderful, Domangart," she whispered, looking up at him with longing. "Will you promise to come to Æcumbræ and visit me when I must return home?"

"I do promise it, milady, indeed I do. But now I should return you to the city, for dusk fast approaches and I did swear it to Walthor."

He saw her face crumple with sadness and rushed to her, taking both of her hands in his.

"Do not be sad, milady. I shall visit you very soon."

Cwen allowed a tear to slip from beneath her lashes.

Domangart pulled her against him and whispered reassurances that he did not wish to be parted from her either.

"But you must let me make proper arrangements with your father."

Cwen nodded her sad agreement as she slipped the cipher stone from his vest and up her sleeve, all the while pretending to weep into her handkerchief.

Domangart beckoned a troll to escort her home and walked with her as far as the glen where he had first seen her.

"Oh, Domangart!" She clutched him to her and wept. "Please come for me soon."

Wiping away her tears, she waved one last time before turning to follow the troll toward the city.

"Master, the woman is not what she seems." The troll returning growled, his words barely discernable. "Two men joined her at the city gates. They followed us under the cover of the veil."

Touching his pocket Domangart found the cipher stone gone.

"Kill them," Domangart ordered, watching as the troll hurried off to do his master's bidding.

Talin erupted with laughter as Cwen described dinner with Domangart.

"And he kept touching my hand and looking at me so lustfully I thought I would have to kill him. Taking the disc was child's play. And Caen, you were right. I do not believe he looked into my eyes more than once."

Talin heard a heavy footfall, causing him to draw his axe.

There was a sudden roar as the troll flung Caen away and tried to grab Cwen.

Talin pushed her to the ground and swung his axe, slicing off the troll's hand at the wrist. The hand and the heavy axe it held fell to the grass. The troll bellowed and swiped at Talin with its remaining claw, missing by less than a hand's span. Talin struck high on the troll's shoulder as the grasping hand swung across its body, leaving the remaining arm useless. Then he spun, burying his blade in its broad, ugly head, sending blood and bone spraying across the ground as the troll fell lifelessly onto its face.

Whirling on Cwen, Talin asked, "Are you harmed?"

"Nay, but Caen…"

Caen lay bloodied and unconscious almost a dragon's length away. The troll's claws had left bloody gouges in his chest and crashing against the tree had broken some bones.

Cwen knelt beside him and placed her ear against his chest. "His heart beats and his breath does not whistle. He will live."

"You could heal him."

"The Ancients will heal him at the mire," Cwen replied.

"You could ease his pain."

"He is unconscious," Cwen grumbled, staring at Talin. "Why is it you are suddenly concerned for him?"

Talin shrugged. "Because if not for us he would not have been here on this day."

With an exasperated sigh, Cwen knelt again and spoke the words to take away Caen's pain and laid her hands upon him to heal his cracked ribs.

"The gashes need healing salve," she explained and looked up at Talin. "We shall need a pallet if we are to get him to Vissenmire."

She and Talin cut branches and bound them to form the litter and Cwen covered it with the soft leaves of waffle root bushes.

They lifted Caen to the makeshift litter and strapped him down so that he would not be jarred on the way to the mire. He remained unconscious as his healing continued.

Borrolon and Lilli ran to meet them at the sight of the pallet bearing Caen. Brengven and Talin carried the injured man into an empty hovel and Lilli examined him suspiciously.

"You healed him?" she asked, looking at Brengven.

"Nay, I was not there," the Feie answered, backing out the hovel door and returning to the fire.

"Cwen?" Lilli looked surprised.

"Aye, it was our… my fault that he was there. It was the least I could do." She shrugged it off. "When he wakes, tell him you healed him, Lilli. I do not wish him to read things into it that are not there."

"It is too late for that, Cwen." Caen's voice was barely a whisper and his eyes did not open. "I shall try not to take it as the promise of your undying passion."

He gritted his teeth while Lilli applied the healing salve to the deep gouges in his chest.

As Cwen left she heard Lilli speak the words to take away his pain.

Talin followed her out and she looked at him crossly.

"You should not have made me heal him. Now he will think that I care for him."

"I did not make you. And you do care for him," Talin grinned, "at least a little. I can tell because you have not killed him."

"Do I?" Cwen asked. "I do not find him as offensive as I once did, but it is he who has changed, not I."

As the healing fever raged, Caen's dreams were of Cwen. She wore the leathers of a warrior and sat next to his bed holding his hand, and as the chills racked his body she lay beside him and offered her warmth.

When he woke in the dark of the night it was Lilli who sat in the chair beside the bed, but he thought he could still smell the scent of Cwen's hair.

The Cipher Stone

They sat near the fire and looked at the disc that Cwen had stolen from Domangart.

Brengven pulled the first from his pocket and placed the discs together back to back, watching as a fiery light slid from between them and bound them together, making the symbols on either side glow with a golden light.

Cwen handed Brengven the scroll and he spread it out upon the ground, placing the radiant cipher stone in the center of it. They drew back as the air before them sizzled and shone with the language of enchantment—the translation created by the cipher key.

"What does it say?"

"It is merely a list of place names in the universal language of the enchanted. Perhaps the locations of the underground armies or the shards needed to generate the energy for them to live." He shrugged. "It is not clear."

"Speak the names and I shall write them in the language of the Sojourners as protection against their loss," Cwen said, drawing a stick of charcoal and a piece of cloth on which to write the names."

Brengven nodded and recited the list that hung in the air before them.

"Roots of the Willow
Mountain of the Dragon
Cavern of the Moons
Cathedral of the Wind

The House of the Ethereal Equus
The Tempest
The Eternal Flame
Indigo's Inferno
The Embers
Azure Sea
The Torrent
The Flooded Fields
The Ancient Mirror"

"They are locations tied to the elements," Talin spoke with certainty. "Earth, wind, fire, and water. The willow must refer to the Tree of Creation near Meremire in Æstretfordæ; the Azure Sea is also in Æstretfordæ."

Cwen agreed, "Aye, and the Cathedral of the Wind is rumored to be in the Northern Mountains of Æstretfordæ, though I do not know of anyone who has actually seen it. It is merely legend. The House of the Equus lies within Æstaffordæ, near the fortress of the House of Aaradan, and I have heard the falls on Æstaffordæ referred to as the torrent."

"The Crimson Fields of Æstretfordæ are flooded at harvest every season." Talin shrugged. "Perhaps they are the flooded fields?"

Caen spoke up. "The Mountain of the Dragon lies on the southeastern tip of Ælmondæ. Legend says that it is an empty shell, filled with a labyrinth of caverns. The Cavern of the Moons is said to be somewhere in Æcumbræ and can only be located when both moons rise full, creating the path of light that shows the way."

"Indigo's Inferno lies beneath Æshulmæ and is favored by poachers and slavers. Indigo is not a pleasant woman," he added with distaste.

"A woman you find repugnant, Caen? She must be hideous indeed," Cwen quipped.

Caen merely glanced at her without replying, leaving her curious at his failure to rise to her taunt.

Looking back at the list Cwen mused aloud, "There are many ancient mirrors beneath the mires. This reference could be to any one of them. Brengven, do you have any knowledge of these other locations?"

Tilting his head he scrunched up his face and seemed to be thinking very hard.

"Nay, I recall none of them, though the tempest could refer to the never-ending storm that rages within the borders of Æshardæ." He shrugged.

"At least four are most likely in Æstretfordæ, so we may as well begin our search there. It will allow us to remain at Meremire in comfort while we seek whatever lies within these locations. And the Ancient Morgwort may have some knowledge that will be useful."

Cwen received 'ayes' of agreement from the others and stood to leave them, tucking the cloth with the list of names inside her shirt and placing the scroll and cipher stone into her pack.

"Brengven, will you summon the rift to Meremire? It should be safe to do so, since none will see our arrival except the Ancients."

The Feie gave a brief wave of his hand and with a swift incantation opened the way from Vissenmire on Æwmarshæ to Meremire on Æstretfordæ.

Rosie saw them step through into the mire and hastened to greet them. She pointed at Caen, noticing his apparent stiffness.

"Did she strikes you again?"

"Nay, this time it was a troll."

"And the Feie healed you?"

"Nay, Cwen did."

Rosie beamed. "It is good you uses the magick of your mother."

"I owed it as a debt," Cwen shrugged. "Where is Morg?"

"In his workshop," Rosie said, gesturing to Caen and indicating he should follow her.

This time he did not argue with the little Ancient, but simply fell in behind her as she headed to her hovel.

Morgwort's Wisdom

Cwen knocked on Morg's door and entered at his shout.

"Cwen, you founds what you seek?" he asked conversationally, knowing very well that she had.

"Aye, we have the Scroll of the G'lm and the cipher stone as well. And we are not dead," she added.

"Nay, not dead yet," Morg agreed, shaking his head as if he doubted it would remain the case for long.

Pulling the cloth from her shirt she handed it to Morg.

"I seek these places Morg. Do you know of them?"

She laughed as Morg cast the spell to change the words of the Sojourner to the language of the Ancients and watched his eyes narrow as he read the list.

"Takes the sword, Cwen—the one Dobbin made for you. It holds magick and will helps you on your quest. The places you seek is hard ones fraught with danger."

"It is the blade of a Guardian, Morg. I am no Guardian," Cwen frowned.

"It is yours, Guardian or not," Morg snapped. "A gift from those who loves you most, even if you are too hard-headed to see it. Take it. I do not wants it here."

Morg pulled the double-bladed sword from beneath his cot, unwrapped it, and shoved it out to her.

Though she did not want it, she accepted it and turned to leave.

"The Eternal Flame lies within the Halcyon Ice Fields, the Embers will glows hot below Vissenmire, and the mirror you seeks is not within the Seven Kingdoms," Morg spoke with authority. "And you knows the rest."

She swung back to him and kneeled to receive his embrace.

"And do not kills Caen with that hellish weapon!" Morg chastened, stepping back to his workbench with a shrewd look on his face.

Talin expressed approval at the sight of the sword.

"Now I shall not be the only one with a real weapon."

"I am far more skilled with the bow," Cwen fumed.

"Nay, it is not so. You are equally skilled with this sword; you merely choose to deny it." Talin shrugged, then added, "… which is foolish."

"Perhaps you would like to spar with me." She glared.

"I would not challenge you, Cwen, when you wield the double blade."

"You would be even wiser not to challenge me at all." Her voice was sharp as a dagger's point and he raised his hands in surrender.

"Do you seek a challenge, Cwen?" Caen spoke from behind her.

"This is not a staff Caen."

"I can see that it is not, but if you will allow the use of your long sword I shall be happy to spar with you. Your crabby Ancient says the practice will take the stiffness from my healing."

"Or be your death," Talin mumbled as Cwen tossed her single-bladed long sword to Caen.

Drawing his own sword in his other hand, Caen indicated his readiness and followed her toward the practice field.

Cwen swung on Caen, hoping to catch him unawares, but was surprised to find him alert and ready. The blades rang and she shifted slightly to allow a broader stroke. His eyes narrowed, never leaving hers. He raised both swords, striking again and again, never allowing her the advantage.

He slipped his blade from beneath her hooked one as she tried to cast it away. She twisted away from him and came back with a long, low stroke that caused him to leap over her sword lest he lose his legs. Bringing his swords up he met her left hand force with his right, he reached out to quickly snag the back edge of the blade in her right hand, drawing it toward him and throwing her slightly off balance. She leapt forward, rolling over the center hilt of her sword, disengaging it, and drawing the blades separately. Now, with a blade in each hand she attacked him with a fury, driving him back several steps before a well-placed blow brought him to one knee.

He rolled away and sprang forward to meet her again, using his weak hand sword as a shield against her left-handed attack.

She saw a flicker of pain cross his face and backed away from him.

"It is enough. Where is the pain?"

"It is nothing, merely a twinge," he said with a small grimace.

"It is far more that a twinge, Caen. I can see it in your eyes."

"And what else do you see there, Cwen?" he asked, dropping his sword and clutching his chest where the troll's claw had ripped him. Blood had begun to seep through his shirt where the wound had reopened.

He shook his head and sank slowly to his knees.

Cwen stepped forward and knelt beside him, easing him to the ground.

"I should not like to think I won because you were wounded," she whispered as she unfastened his shirt and sought the injury.

Placing her hand on the wound she cast a spell to stop the bleeding and one to ease his pain.

Rosie arrived with her healing salve and asked, "Dids you cut him?"

"Nay, not this time." Cwen glanced up at her.

"When I told you to practice with the sword, I did not tell you to fights with Cwen." Rosie snapped her disapproval.

With a regretful expression Caen explained, "But there is no one I would rather fight with, Rosewort."

Looking up at Cwen, Rosie pointed a finger at her and warned, "No more. It is hard enough to heal wounds caused by trolls without you adding to the problems."

In the depth of the night Talin called a grass cat to him, speaking to it softly in the speech of beasts.

"Go, my friend, and carry my words to the Sojourner Ileana.

Cwen has recovered the second half of the cipher stone from the wizard Domangart and Brengven has found a list of place names written within the scroll. We shall begin our search as soon as Caen recovers from the wounds of a troll. Tell Nall that Cwen has reclaimed her sword."

Purring, the cat acknowledged the task and set off toward the fortress of the House of Aaradan.

Ileana sat in the throne room with Yáviē, Sōrél, Nall, and Näeré.

"They have accomplished much." Ileana's voice revealed approval for those she had chosen to quest for the magick necessary to gain control of the G'lm. "They have recovered the Scroll of the G'lm and both halves of the cipher stone needed to translate it. The task has not been easy for them. They encountered a thralax in Spire Canyon and Cwen has gone up against Domangart with success. But the true quest has not yet begun. Already rumors are spreading of others searching for the scroll and the shards needed for the reanimation. Those questing seem to be mortals, though I expect that they are also merely pawns in an attempt to lessen the risk of discovery. It is of deep concern that Domangart held a piece of the cipher stone, for wherever there is Domangart, Laoghaire is not far behind and he will want Cwen."

Cwen walked around the willow, the Tree of Creation, examining it from every angle. There was no apparent opening that would allow access below the roots.

She had been told that the roots of the willow and the roots of the verdant tree had reached out to draw the seven kingdoms back together during the magick of the rebirth of Ædracmoræ, entwining their roots and binding the world back into its sphere. It must have been amazing to see, she thought. Her parents had been there with Yáviē and Sōrél; together, they had quested to repair the shattered Ædracmoræ. Cwen sighed. This quest did not seem nearly so important, but she knew it was one the Guardians could not accomplish easily, and that brought pleasure.

"My roots travel far," a soft voice spoke inside Cwen's mind, causing

her to look about.

"Beneath the tumbled stones of the Ebony Plains lies a doorway," the same calm voice continued. *"What you seek is there."*

"She don't talks to just anyone," Rosie spoke behind Cwen.

"Who is she?" asked Cwen, frowning her puzzlement.

"The Tree," Rosie said, shrugging her shoulders. "She has talked to not a one since Nall and Yávië."

"Why did she talk to them?"

"About their blood oath."

"My fa… Nall shared a blood oath with the Queen?" Cwen asked with surprise.

"Aye, but she was not the Queen then," Rosie said. "She was a hardheaded girl likes you. You ought to ask your father to tell you sometime."

Cwen grew sullen and her eyes became hard.

"He has told me quite enough," she said, spinning on her heel and heading back toward the mire.

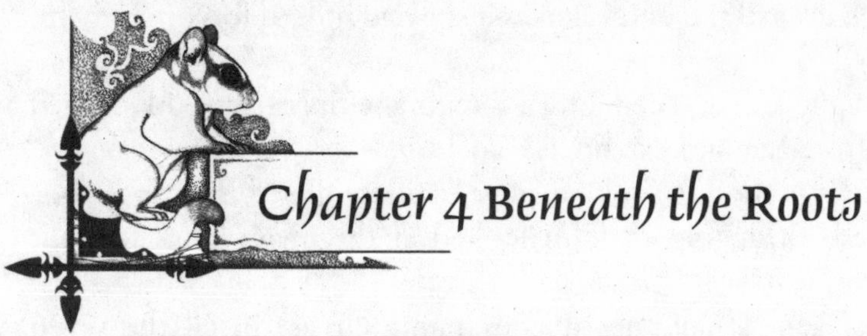

Chapter 4 Beneath the Roots

Old Enemies

When Rosie finally pronounced Caen well enough for travel and "fighting with Cwen," they headed off in search of the door that led beneath the roots of the willow tree.

"Cwen!" called a tall man, dressed in the elegant clothing of his latest victim, as he stepped onto the road before them.

"Aidan." Cwen's voice was brittle; dark suffocating memories flooded her mind at the sound of his voice.

"How dare you cast a shadow across my path?"

From several paces behind, Talin looked at Caen and whispered, "Watch and learn."

Aidan took the two long strides separating him from Cwen and crushed her to him; kissing her hard and feeling her stiffen against him. The threat he whispered in her ear promised death to her companions. Death to Talin. Releasing her abruptly, he smiled the smile that Cwen had found so disarming until she had discovered the cruel intent he kept hidden behind his eyes.

"Who is he?" Caen questioned Talin.

"A direfang disguised as a downy flier." Talin shook his head. "A bigger bastard even than you, Caen. And one who holds some power over her. You will note that she is no longer aware of our presence. He has that affect on her."

"We camp in the woods to the west if you and your companions would care to share our fire," Aidan suggested, resting his hand on Cwen's shoulder, thumb pressing its menace against her collar bone.

Glancing back at Talin and Caen as if she had indeed forgotten them, she pointed.

"Talin and Caen," she said, swallowing with relief as Aidan lifted his hand from her and extended it to Talin.

"Talin, it is good to find you alive." Aidan offered his grip as they approached, shrugging as Talin looked at the man's hand without response.

"And Caen, I have heard your name cursed in all the seven kingdoms."

Caen accepted the man's offered grip, his acceptance belying his displeasure. He nodded his acknowledgement of the compliment. "I am quite good at what I do, leaving behind only pale whispers of suspicion."

"Come, share a draught and warm yourselves by the fire. Surely you have time for that?" Aidan said, seeking Cwen's eyes.

Brengven traveled some distance behind his companions. He had hoped that in the peace away from their foul odor and idle chatter he could gain a glimpse of the doorway they sought.

A sudden image flashed before his eyes causing him to sit beneath the nearest tree. The image was of a woman, fair by the standards of Men. Pale hair fell almost to her knees, covering her as a cloak. Her clothes were scant and silken, hiding her full breasts; her hips were covered in cloth so gossamer thin that it would draw a man's eye. Her eyes were the blue of clouded ice and she whispered to a man within the woods of yesterday as she filled him with her abandon and beguiled him with her beauty.

"Seek the scroll and the stone and bring them to me. If you do I shall give you gifts of pleasure greater than any you have known."

"Faervyn." Brengven whispered the name of the enchantress and leapt to his feet, rushing off to find his companions.

As they reached the campfire, Cwen tried to draw away from Aidan but he held her hand in a painful grip, forcing her thumb upwards toward her wrist.

"Sit with me," he said, his soft voice contradicting the demanding look in his eyes.

Turning to Talin and Caen, he offered them a place near the fire.

Cwen watched as Daedra brought them ale. The other woman's eyes remained focused on the ground and she did not speak to them. Cwen gave a deep shuddering sigh, recalling her own servitude to Aidan and grateful that at least she was no longer forced to travel with him.

"Do not be angry, Cwen," Aidan whispered, fondling her hair. "No real harm was done," he shrugged. "Do not hold it against me."

Cwen looked back toward Daedra, who bit her lip and returned the gaze for only a fleeting moment before her frightened eyes slid away.

As they finished their drinks, Talin placed a hand on Cwen's shoulder and spoke to her silently, "*Brengven comes with disturbing news. It is best we meet him at the road.*" Aloud he offered a different excuse, "It is time we left if we are to reach our campsite before starset."

Standing, Caen stared down at Aidan's grip on Cwen's hand, eyes narrowing as the man reluctantly released his hold. Cwen rose, rubbing her hand and headed off behind her companions.

As Caen and Talin disappeared among the trees, Cwen whirled back, her bow rose and she nocked a bolt, aiming it at Aidan's chest.

"Perhaps if I ended your miserable life I could forget your treachery," Cwen's voice cracked through the ache of clenched teeth.

A sudden shift in the wind brought the scent of a second man's threat, sweat, sharp and foul, bringing with it the paralyzing images from her past. The flash of his remembered face sent Cwen fleeing after Caen and Talin.

Sidon stepped into the camp watching after them as they left.

"She carries the scroll and the stone," he stated. "It is unfortunate you were unable to hold her, Aidan. The task would have been simpler."

Slapping Daedra, he asked, "And why did you not leave camp when you heard them coming? Aidan could have held her here had she not seen your miserable, sniveling face. Then we could have eliminated Talin and the thief as they sat by the fire."

Lifting his shoulders in sudden indifference, he rubbed the woman's cheek where he had struck her. "You will learn, Daedra. Someday, just like Cwen, you will learn."

"A Feie travels behind them," he continued. "We shall need to be alert or he will sense us. Talin's hearing is keen and he will also sense our approach unless he sleeps.

"It is best we give them a few days to forget us before we attempt to retrieve the scroll and stone," Sidon added as he sat down and poured himself a draught.

"That is not necessary. I shall distract Cwen while Daedra collects the artifacts." Aidan's lips twisted into a leering smile sending shivers of revulsion along Daedra's spine.

Brengven was in a flurry of unease, sitting, then standing, then sitting again.

"She is evil. There is naught good about her. She was cast from Révérē for the darkness of her magick. And she seeks us." He shivered at the thought.

"I saw her speaking to a mortal. He was tall and wore his hair long; it was very dark, brown or black, and I saw only his back."

They camped within the crimson fields, a day's journey from the Galenite fortress where Talin had been born. The heavy braid trees offered shelter and hid their camp from those who might wander by along the road. The sight of the wide stream brought a look of peace to Cwen's face and a frown from Talin and Caen, for the air was chill and bathing was not something they anticipated with much pleasure. Brengven settled within shouting distance in a copse of trees upwind of them.

Once the fire had been built they hunted day doves and hares, cleaned them and put them in the pot. Then they settled down to rest.

"How long have you known him?" Caen asked Cwen.

As she answered, her voice held a slight tremor. "I met him my seventeenth summer."

Continuing, her voice became angry as she hid her hurt and fear. "I have *known* him since that day, if that is what you are asking. Not that it is any of your business. I am not a fragile flower to be plucked and saved by you, Caen."

Rising, she glanced at Talin and, seeing his rather disapproving look, pointed her finger at him.

"Nor you, either. I do not require saving, from Aidan or anyone else."

"It is not your rescue that concerns me, Cwen. You have been known to act very foolishly in Aidan's presence. He stole our crystals last time we came in contact with him. He is expensive company."

Gathering her knapsack she announced, "I am going to bathe. Do not come to the stream."

At the stream she sat on a stone and removed her boots, placing her feet in the icy water.

"I thought you might camp here." Aidan's voice was soft behind her. "Your anger hurts me, Cwen."

She did not move or look at him.

He slipped his arms around her and laughed as she went rigid.

Long ago she had learned what must be done to keep Talin from harm and avoid the worst of Aidan's punishments.

From her hiding place, Daedra watched Aidan touch Cwen and shuddered. Bile rose to her throat at the thought of what he would do if the woman did not obey his demands. Without a sound Daedra opened Cwen's pack and slipped out the scroll and stone, hearing Cwen's sharp gasp of pain as she crept away with the treasures.

Cwen bathed beneath the driving force of the falls, allowing the tears of her shame to fall where no one would see them. The penetrating cold of the water eased the ache and drove away the memory of Aidan's viciousness. As she sought the soap within her bag she saw that the scroll was missing and closed her eyes against the disappointment she would see in Talin's eyes. Disappointment at what he would think was simply her imprudence.

Dressing, she headed back to camp.

Talin stared at her as she approached him, his eyes coming to rest on the shadowed bruises below her jaw.

"He has stolen the scroll and the stone," she said.

Talin's gaze remained steady as he spoke to her. "I think that is not all he has stolen. Why do you let him hurt you, Cwen?"

She sank to the ground and closed her eyes against his scrutiny. Caen fumed. Catching Talin's eyes he rose, heading off in the direction of the stream.

Daedra slipped through the gathering dusk, her footsteps hastening in anticipation of Sidon's approval.

Strong fingers tangled within her hair, jerking her head back and ripping a startled cry from her throat. A dagger blade pierced the flesh beneath her chin and she felt the trickle of hot blood course down her throat toward the collar of her shirt.

"I have nothing," she gasped.

"You have something that belongs to Cwen of Aaradan."

"No, I do not."

The blade dug a bit deeper.

"You can give the scroll and stone to me, or I will cut your throat and take them. I will return them to Cwen one way or the other, which way makes no difference to me."

Sniveling and gasping, Daedra begged, "I shall give them to you. Do not kill me."

"Where are they?"

"In my shirt."

Keeping the knife at her throat, Caen released her hair and stepped in front of her, his eyes gleaming as she recognized him. He reached inside her shirt, pulled out the scroll and stone and slipped them inside his vest.

"Go now, tell Aidan not to come back. I would hate to have to kill someone Cwen may care for, but if he touches her again, I will kill him." Caen's gaze left no doubt in Daedra's mind that he spoke the truth. Pulling his dagger away from her throat, Caen wiped the blade on her shirt and pushed her away before turning back toward the camp where Cwen and Talin waited.

As Caen re-entered their camp he went straight to Cwen and knelt beside her. Without a word he pulled the scroll and cipher stone from his shirt and placed them in her hands.

She looked at them and then up into his fierce eyes.

"Is he dead?"

"No," Caen snapped, "but he should be."

Sidon held out his hands to Daedra as she drew near. Seeing the blood on her, he pulled her closer and asked, "Who did this?"

"The one called Caen. He came for the scroll and stone. He said if Aidan touches Cwen again he will kill him." Daedra spoke quickly, the words tumbling over one another.

Aidan's eyebrows rose in surprise. "She told him?"

Lifting her shoulders and letting them fall, Daedra said, "I do not know. But he frightened me; he was very angry."

"Whose anger do you fear more, Daedra? The thief's or ours?"

Daedra closed her eyes and waited for the pain.

Under the Ebony Stones

Cwen and her companions climbed amid the tumbled ebony stones seeking some indication of an opening that would allow them access to the caverns that lay beneath the plains.

"Do you hear anything?" Talin asked the others.

"I hear whispering, but I cannot make out any words," he added, listening again for the hushed whispers.

"Here!" called Brengven. "There is a hole here!"

A jumble of seven glassy ebony stones created a cavern above the ground. Within it lay an opening, a narrow path leading into the earth.

Talin lit a waffle root torch and held it out before him as he entered the mouth of the cavern. Wind whipped up from below, blowing out the torch and leaving him in darkness.

"I do not like wind that blows from within the earth," he muttered, eyes narrowed in suspicion.

Lighting the torch a second time he backed into the cavern, sheltering the flame with his body and examining the walls around him. The walls of the narrow passageway were of ebony stone, glassy and reflective; the ceiling and floor were earthen. Returning to the entrance he urged them all forward except Brengven, who agreed he would remain above ground with their supplies, letting Ileana know if they did not return within three passings of the day star.

Lighting two other torches Talin handed them to Cwen and Caen and explained about the odd wind that seemed to rise from within the cave.

They discovered that if the torches were held low, the wind seemed to flow high enough above them that they remained lit.

"Do you hear that?" Talin asked again. "The whispering?"

"Aye, perhaps it is only the wind as it passes through the tunnels," Cwen suggested.

"Or whatever beings choose to spend their lives far below the earth in total darkness," Caen added, drawing glares from both of them.

The passageway suddenly ended in a deep hole. Talin leaned over and peered into it, but the darkness was so deep he could see nothing.

Cwen stepped forward and tossed her torch into the hole and they watched as it fell, growing dimmer and dimmer until it was nothing but a faint glow far below them.

"Did you see that?" Cwen asked, her eyes seeking Caen and Talin. "The shadow that passed the torch?"

Both shook their heads and peered down more intently. The torch below flickered and went out, leaving them staring into nothingness again.

Caen tossed his torch as Cwen had done and this time all three of them saw the shadow flit by the dim torchlight.

"Great," Talin said, "We must climb down a rope to fight something we cannot see at the bottom."

He gathered the length of knotted rope from over his shoulder and tossed one end into the hole. The other end was tied to a standing stone at the entrance of the cavern where Brengven could keep an eye on it.

"I shall go first. I weigh the least," Cwen said, swinging over the lip of the hole and slowly, knot by knot, climbing down.

"Cwen, stop," Caen called after her. "Do not go too far ahead."

He quickly descended after her, followed closely by Talin and his torch.

"Toss your torch down, Talin," Cwen called. "I think I am very close to the bottom."

"Hold the wall so that the torch can pass," Talin warned before tossing it down past his companions.

The torch hit the floor just below Cwen and the sudden sound of many whispering voices broke the silence of the cavern.

Cwen dropped to the floor, quickly retrieving the torch and holding her long sword ready as she backed against the nearest wall and searched the area before her. Caen dropped beside her and drew his sword as Talin hit the floor and drew his axe.

"I heard them. Whatever or whoever they are, they seem to be many," Cwen said, lifting the torch and holding it out in front of her.

The room opened up below the hole; it seemed to have several tunnels or passageways leading away from it.

"Which way?" Cwen asked, looking to Talin.

"I doubt that it matters, since we shall be lost no matter which road we take." He shrugged and pointed left.

As he stepped forward the torchlight caught movement and the beings of the shadows revealed themselves. They were no taller than Ancients, pale and completely hairless; they appeared to present no threat. Their legs were bent and their feet flat and round. Their arms were terribly foreshortened, as if the hands were attached to the elbows. The hands themselves were small, three-fingered and without nails to protect the tips. Their heads were elongated and resembled futermelons Cwen had seen raised in the mires. Their faces were flat with small round nostrils and dark slits for mouths; they did not seem to have any eyes. The small beings wore no clothing, and there was no indication of their sex, if indeed there were differences they were hidden.

The whispers began again and Cwen tried to distinguish words but found nothing familiar in the language.

Suddenly, the pale beings were flooding the chamber surrounding the three mortals and pulling on their clothing as if trying to draw them forward. Looking at one another Cwen, Caen and Talin shrugged and allowed themselves to be led away.

Stooping to enter the smaller passages, and finally crawling as the way narrowed even more, they crept into a rounded room. This one had a high ceiling supported by some sort of ancient bones bound within the roots of the willow tree. In the center of the room was a circle of white stone, and within the circle lay a brilliant amber shard too large to hold in a one hand. Cwen held the torch near and looked at the shard closely; it seemed to have a darkness within, as if something lay in shadow at the center of the crystal shard.

"Pick it up and put it in your pack, Cwen," Talin whispered in her mind.

The voices suddenly became clear to Cwen. "Take it," whispered the creatures that surrounded them. "Take it away."

Caen placed his sword between Cwen and the nearest group of beings, warning them back.

Handing Caen the torch, Cwen reached forward and lifted the shard, slipped it inside her pack and backed toward the tunnel. One by one the odd creatures began to disappear into the earth. It was as if they were simply liquefying and being absorbed as water would be after a rain.

Dropping to her knees, Cwen turned and crawled back the way she had come, followed by Caen and Talin.

None of the creatures followed and the removal of the shard seemed to have satisfied their purpose.

"It was almost as if they expected us," Cwen whispered to Talin and Caen as they began the climb up the rope.

"What do you think they are?" Caen wondered aloud.

"I think they are the guardians of the shard," Talin stated, "and were just waiting for anyone to take it."

"What kind of bones were those?" Caen asked as he pulled himself over the lip of the hole and back into the surface cavern. "Were they dragon bones?"

"Nay, they were far too large for a dragon. But I am glad that they were bones and not the creature they once supported." Cwen shuddered.

As they stepped into daylight Brengven hurried forward to see what they had found. Cwen held it out to him and saw him grow pale as he lifted it from her hand.

"What is it?" she asked.

"It is the heart shard of a Great Wyrm," Brengven said, shaking his head. "They once lived above the earth, but none live now. They were killed in a war long ago, before Ædracmoræ had a name. The war of the Wreken and the Sojourners. I have never seen a shard. It is beautiful, but it holds the shadow of the Wreken within it."

Cwen reclaimed the shard and handed it to Talin.

"Will you keep it safe? I cannot be trusted as long as Aidan lives."

He accepted the shard and placed it deep within his knapsack next to the scroll and the stone.

Disposal of the Shard

The discussion had become heated and Cwen's words were scorching.

"No! I shall not allow you to give the shard to them. I would rather Aidan steal it."

"Nay, you would not really. Cwen, holding the shard is dangerous. There is more at stake than your personal feud. Simply allow Brengven to carry the shard to Ileana through the rift. We do not know if the shard by itself will activate the stone soldiers; but if even a single cavern of them is released, many lives will be lost. Think, Cwen." Talin spoke, hoping his words would slip through the shield of her rebellion.

"And you, thief; what do you think?"

Cwen's eyes sought Caen's.

"Is the shard not a thing of priceless beauty? Something a thief could sell for sufficient lules that he might never need to steal again?"

Caen answered, "I think your resentment of your father clouds your reason as Aidan's evil clouds your soul."

The fury in her eyes was suddenly replaced with hurt and she swung back toward Talin and Brengven.

"Do as you please. It is obvious I have no allies among you."

Cwen stepped away from them and pretended to busy herself repacking her satchel.

Talin handed the shard to Brengven, who swiftly created a rift in hopes of delivering the shard to safety before Cwen could change her mind.

Cwen turned to scowl at them as Brengven stepped through the rift connecting him to the fortress and Ileana. As the rift closed behind the Feie a resounding thud reached their ears. There on the ground lay the wyrm shard, but Brengven was nowhere to be seen.

A sudden shimmer in the air brought the fussing little man back and he snatched up the shard and stuck it inside his waistcoat. Nodding to them he returned through the doorway he had created. Again they heard the shard hit the ground. This time the striking of the earth was accompanied by a slight pulse of light from the amber artifact.

Brengven returned once again and stood just beyond the flickering rift looking down at the shard. It had ceased to pulse and lay there as dead as stone. The Feie cocked his head to one side and mumbled to himself, "I shall try again."

He picked up the shard and stuffed it into the waist of his pants. Taking a deep breath he once again slipped through into the fortress yard.

Cwen laughed aloud as the shard fell to the ground at Talin's feet a third time. Again it gave several bright pulses before growing dark.

"Looks like I have allies after all. They are just not you."

"It is not funny, Cwen. Why will the shard not pass through the rift? Have you not paused to wonder?" Talin asked.

"Because it does not wish to be controlled by a Guardian or a Sojourner?" she flung back.

Brengven returned and dropped to the ground cross-legged before them.

"Shall I go and explain this development to the council?" he asked, looking up at Talin.

"Aye, I do not think it wise to continue dropping it as I do not like its response. Tell Ileana I shall carry it to the fortress if necessary, just to be rid of it," he added, catching Caen's nod of agreement.

Together they watched Brengven slide through the rift for the fourth time. Talin reached down and retrieved the shard, tucking it back into his pack.

Cwen strode away toward the distant trees.

"This would be a good time to speak to her," Talin said, looking meaningfully at Caen. "Her swords and bow remain here. You need only defend against her dagger and her boot."

Shaking his head, Caen headed off in search of Cwen.

Cwen sat with her back against a great tree with braided trunks, each section as thick as a man's waist, the lofty canopy of leaves soaring far overhead.

She watched as a downy flier chased a buttermoth across the bark and into a hole.

"I did not mean to hurt you." Caen's soft voice startled her.

"I am not hurt and you do not have so much power that you could hurt me anyway." Her words were flippant, but her tone was not.

"I once asked Talin why you were so hard. He said that you were not. I have come to believe that his words were true."

"Talin talks too much," she frowned.

"Actually he rarely speaks, but I have found it wise to listen when he does."

Cwen's smile was genuine as she asked, "And he told you to come here?"

"Aye, he said you were armed only with your dagger and your boot."

"That makes you feel safe?"

"Nay not at all, but my words were harsh and I saw the hurt in your eyes. I thought that since you had no ranged weapons I could at least get close enough to apologize."

"You are jealous." Her voice was soft and knowing.

"Aye, furiously so," Caen confessed, surprising himself.

She turned and looked at him with a new awareness.

"What is it you wish to offer, Caen?"

He exhaled sharply.

Shaking his head he shrugged, "I no longer know, Cwen."

Amused by his sudden discomfort she suggested, "Perhaps we should begin with an attempt at friendship. It is far more difficult than passion, for it requires trust… but it is often more valuable."

"I am not sure I know how to befriend a woman," Caen answered honestly.

"Let us begin simply. If you see that I am cold, offer me a cloak; if you see someone seeks to harm me, give me a word of warning."

She held out her hand and watched as he accepted it.

"I sent word that I would kill him if he came for you again." His eyes were on her small hand.

"And will you?"

Slowly he lifted his eyes to meet hers and he nodded.

"Aye, I shall end his life swiftly without further admonishment."

Talin's casual cough drew their attention. His eyes rested on Cwen's hand in Caen's.

"Brengven returns with news from Ileana," he offered.

Squeezing Cwen's hand lightly, Caen released it and headed back toward their camp, leaving Cwen with Talin.

"He says he is going to kill Aidan," Cwen said.

"Aye, and if he does not, I shall," Talin said. "Either way, the man is dead, so it would be wise if you said your good-byes quickly should he return."

Placing a hand on her shoulder Talin looked at her solemnly.

"You are my friend, Cwen. I will kill Aidan as I would kill any who threatened you."

Dropping his hand he gestured toward camp.

"Now, let us fight about the disposal of the shard."

Cwen laughed as she led the way.

"Ileana asks that Talin deliver the shard to a Guardian who will meet him at the Galenite fortress. It is less than a day's travel from this camp. We can wait for him beyond the fortress and head north toward the Cathedral of the Wind once the delivery is made," Brengven stated.

"Now the Council chooses where we go?" Cwen snarled.

"Nay, it is merely my suggestion," Brengven snapped back, "since you yourself said the cathedral was thought to lie in the Northern Mountains."

"And why should Talin be the one to take the shard? Why should it not be me?"

"Because it is Nall who comes to collect it," Brengven hissed. "Go if you want."

She flushed at the thought of seeing her father. Caen watched and wondered what the man had done to her or what she had done to him.

"They could send another."

"Aye, but they will not," Brengven said with finality. "It has been decided."

"When will he expect to meet me?" Talin asked.

"On the morrow when the day star reaches its zenith, Nall will meet you at the home of Galen and Kayann – if that is acceptable. Ileana thought it would not raise suspicion if you were seen there."

"Aye, it has been long since I have seen them," Talin agreed, catching Cwen's look of concern.

Silently he spoke within her mind in an attempt to reassure her. "*It will be fine. I have not had nightmares for a very long time, Cwen.*"

She shook her head, concern for him clouding her eyes.

As a child, each visit to his mother's sister had brought nightmares, but he was no longer a child.

Galenite Reunion

They broke camp under cover of darkness and traveled swiftly through the night, reaching the fields before the fortress as the day star crept toward its zenith.

Cwen gripped Talin's arm and stared at him.

"I shall go," she said.

Shaking his head, he whispered, "You need not do that, Cwen. It will be all right. It would be harder for you to face your father than for me to face the darkest of my dreams."

"I do not want you to suffer the hurt again, Talin. I could go with you," she insisted.

"Are you afraid to remain alone with Caen?" Talin asked grinning.

"You tease me. Of course I am not. Go then, and be quick about it. We shall be camped to the north in the copse where we stayed last season."

"Tell Galen and Kayann I send my greetings," she shouted after him, watching as he waved back at her.

From the shadow of the fortress wall she watched her father's arrival. The large empathic dragon Ardor landed heavily before the fortress and Nall leapt lightly to the ground. Cwen followed his deliberate stride until he entered the gates and was lost from view. She had not seen him for over three summers, but he had not changed at all.

"We are here if you need to speak to him," Caen spoke at her elbow.

"My father and I do not speak, we scream, and it puts me in an evil temper that causes those around me to suffer greatly." She looked up at him. "It would not be a good idea."

"Let us go. I am in charge of protecting you and Brengven from all manner of harm in Talin's absence," she added, winking at Caen.

"Brengven," she called to the little man, "we are ready."

Together they headed toward the Northern Mountains.

Talin permitted Kayann's embrace and tried not to stiffen, for he knew it hurt her feelings. Galen extended his grip and welcomed him home. Talin noticed that Galen had grown grayer and slower in the time since he had seen them last, though Kayann maintained the long-lived beauty for which the Xavians were famed.

A tap at the door brought Nall. Galen and Kayann greeted him before retiring to their private chambers.

Nall grasped Talin's shoulder and said, "You are missed."

"And is Cwen also missed?"

Talin's bluntness brought a smile that did not reach Nall's eyes.

"Aye, there are some who have asked about her."

Talin reached into his satchel to remove the wyrm shard, scroll and cipher stone.

"These will be safer with Ileana. The shard pulsed with light when it was dropped and there is something lying within it, though I do not know what it is. We have a copy of the list from the scroll; since others have already tried to steal it, it is best left with you."

Nall held up the heart shard. It was larger than those of the dragons, nearly twice the size, and it did seem to have something hidden within it. He placed it inside his knapsack and unrolled the scroll to examine it. Flattening it out on Galen's table, he placed the stone in its center and watched the air shimmer with the language of the enchanted.

After putting the scroll and stone away he allowed his gaze to rest on Talin again.

"She is well?" he asked.

"Who?" Talin asked as he allowed a small, irritating smirk to play around his mouth and his eyebrow rose as if in question.

"My daughter," Nall spoke, frowning at Talin's impudence.

Grinning, Talin said, "Aye, she is well. She has grown strong and beautiful. She carries the sword that you had made for her. She is no longer a child, though she is just as impossible as she has always been. I know that you did not approve, Nall, but the quest is good for her."

"And the thief who travels with you? The one who is now left alone with my daughter? Can he be trusted?"

Talin grew sober. "Aye, he has threatened to kill Aidan."

Nall's gut twisted at the thought of Aidan; blind rage crushed his chest.

"Then he cannot be all bad can he?" he said through clinched teeth.

Talin nodded his silent agreement.

After tolerating a second embrace from Kayann and bidding Galen and Nall farewell, Talin left the fortress and headed north after his companions.

Chapter 5 The Cathedral

Cwen climbed onto a rock and sat breathing in the night air. The camp was cold and Caen lay bundled in his cloak beyond the ashes of the dead fire. She had asked him to stand the first watch, anticipating that Talin would return during the second, allowing her to talk to him privately.

A hand covered her mouth and Aidan's voice whispered in her ear.

"Come with me."

She shook her head and pried at his hand, causing him to grab her around the waist and pull her off the rock. She kicked back against him and caught him in the shins, hearing him grunt in pain as she tried to draw her leg up far enough to reach the dagger in her boot.

Suddenly his hand dropped from her mouth and she heard the hiss of his breath as his grip loosened from her waist.

Spinning, she saw Caen. His eyes were hard as stone and his voice was sharp-edged as he spoke to the dying man.

"I sent you a warning; it seems you did not heed it."

He pulled his dagger from between Aidan's ribs where it had pierced his heart, watching the man bleed out on the ground.

"Caen…" Cwen began.

"Shhh…" he hushed her.

Taking her hand he drew her to the other side of the camp wrapping her in his cloak and lighting the fire that had been laid for the morning. Then he went back and dragged Aidan's body into the woods.

When he returned, Talin was sitting beside Cwen and Brengven was tossing branches onto the fire and bringing tea to the boil.

Caen dropped to the ground in front of Cwen and waited until she looked up at him.

"I could not risk that he would harm you. I am sorry if you cared for him."

Her gaze was firm and her words truthful. "I would have killed him myself if I could have reached my dagger."

"He asked about you, Cwen," Talin shared as they entered the Northern Mountains.

"Did he say my name?" she asked, certain that her father would no more speak her name than she would use his.

"Nay, but he did admit you were his daughter and he did not call you a charlatan," Talin grinned.

Shrugging it off, Cwen said, "He only questioned you because my mother will ask when he returns to her, not because he is interested himself. And Galen and Kayann, how did you find them?"

"Galen grows old and slow and Kayann clings to me as if I were a child."

"To her you will always be a child because she sees you as the small boy with her sister. I am sorry to hear that Galen fails; he has been a trusted friend and a strong leader for his people."

She glanced up to meet Talin's eyes.

"You did not sleep last night. You cannot remain awake forever."

"I did not sleep because I feared Sidon would follow after Aidan and slay us in our sleep," Talin said, ending the conversation as he picked up his pace and joined Brengven and Caen ahead of them.

The Northern Mountains tower above the Crimson Plains; stark and heavily clouded, the summits rarely seen. The forest that covers the lower elevations is dense and shadowed by a tangled mass of broad leaves that create a living canopy. When darkness falls, an impenetrable mist settles in the narrow valleys and deep gorges where the rivers run, making travel at night impossible.

What little light filters through during the daylight hours is insufficient, and torches are required to find the slender, hidden paths leading upwards toward the lofty peaks.

The paths themselves are rarely traveled, for the chilled pinnacles of the Northern Mountains offer little that would benefit men.

A cold camp was not an option in the dank mists of the dell where they chose to rest. The night would bring the hunting direfang and other dark beasts that hunted the woods.

Brengven built a large fire, agreeing that it would be best if he shared their camp while traveling through the mountains.

"I have heard tales of horror from these woods," he muttered, nodding to himself. "Beasts of indescribable ugliness that can tear off a man's arm in a single swipe and eat it in one gulp."

"Is that all you do in Réverē? Tell tales of the hideous creatures that hunt men?" A sullen Cwen asked.

"Nay," the Feie shot back, "we also practice powerful magick to keep the likes of you out."

"And how exactly do you keep out the riffraff, Brengven?" Caen called.

"Unless you travel with a Feie you must enter Réverē upon the back of an accordant or wind dragon, and only the pure of heart may pass. Others are burned away in a flash of fire as they slip into the rift."

"And I thought death at the jaws of a direfang would be hellish," Caen snorted.

"Nay," Cwen responded lightly, "the direfang tear out the throat so that you bleed out very quickly. Burning up in Brengven's evil rift would be far more unpleasant."

"Personally I would prefer to die old and in my bed," Talin shouted from the other side of the fire.

"Not true," Cwen called back, "I happen to know that you wish to die at the hands of a worthy enemy in a grand battle for some excellent cause."

"And you, Cwen, how would you wish to die?" Caen asked.

"In the arms of one who cares for me," she answered without pause as if she had already given it a great deal of thought.

"Then do not die so far away I cannot reach you," Talin's grin was wicked.

"Perhaps I shall replace you," Cwen shot back with a wink at Caen.

"Until you do the solution is not to die," came Talin's grim recommendation.

Caen stood watch in the deep darkness before dawn. The fog was so dense he could not see the trees around them. He thought he heard a cry, but the mist caused sound to fall flat so that one could not tell where it began.

A whimper as if from a child drew him back toward the fire and his sleeping companions, where he watched Cwen rise and go to Talin. She looked up at Caen, holding her finger to her lips as she lay down next to her friend's sleeping form, placing her arms around him, whispering soothing words as a mother would to a son.

The words she spoke were foreign to Caen and the dazzling array of lights that fell around her and over Talin told him it was magick. The shadowy cloud of the dream's dark dragon rose from Talin and seemed to hover a moment before Cwen pulled it away and into herself.

Talin relaxed and his breathing became calm and steady as the deep, dreamless sleep of the spell took hold.

Cwen rose and went to Caen, drawing him away from Talin.

"Never speak of what you saw. He believes the nightmares have left him; he does not know I take them from him."

"How long has he been haunted by the dragons of death?" Caen asked as a shiver ran through him.

"Far too long."

Caen nodded.

"I watched from the tall grass on the hill beyond the city as they burned Æshardæ. They left nothing living, save me. I was too frightened to stand for three days. I was five."

Suddenly smiling, he added, "And I have been a rogue and a thief since that day."

"A thief perhaps, but I do not believe you to be the scoundrel you pretend," Cwen said, staring at him with interest.

"Do not place too much trust in me, Cwen," he warned.

"Oh, I do not trust you, Caen; not yet." Her eyes sparkled with golden fire. "But I no longer have the desire to strangle you with your own steaming entrails. At least, not regularly," she added as she returned to her place near the fire, ending Brengven's snoring with a tap of her foot as she passed.

The Feie would remain with the camp tomorrow as they headed for the summit.

Within the Bones

Serpentine, steep and narrow, winding back and forth amid the trunks of the towering braid trees, the trail drew them upward. Wind whistled down from above, channeled through the constricted valley. The travelers leaned forward against the continued assault of the driving current of chilled air. The mist had been blown from the ground and the heavy clouds above them roiled as if to storm.

The wind howled, pushing them back as if it hoped to drive them away and the sound of pipes battered their ears. High, thin whistles of an ethereal flute were added to the deeper sounds of summoning horns. They were drawn up the gorge by the wailing of the angry storm, calling them to worship the wind.

Sticks and leaves sent by the swirling currents beat against them and they covered their eyes against the onslaught as they continued to make their way forward slow step by slow step. As the forest opened onto a hidden glen, rays of starlight broke through the swirling mass of clouds, illuminating the glistening bone cathedral before them. The walls towered skyward, polished and gleaming in the filtered light. Each of the bones rose a dragon's length before curving outward, ending in a rounded point. Huge thigh bones served to brace the wall and lay as carved and shining steps leading into the earth below.

Wind surged through bones void of marrow, creating the music of the storm. Tendrils of mist reached for the travelers, lashing out and whipping at their clothing and their hair. A stronger gust sent a shard of heavy bone toward them, narrowly missing them as they ducked.

With his hand on Caen's shoulder and Cwen's hand in his, Talin called on the power of the shield, watching as it charged the area before them with brilliant blue light, solidifying the air. A second bone crashed against the shield and fell away, then the wind sent another toward them, slamming into the shimmering barrier.

"Run!" shouted Talin as the shield began to fade away. Pushing Caen before him and dragging Cwen behind, he rushed down the steep bone steps.

The wind roared and a battery of bones cascaded after them, shattering and clattering as they broke up in their descent down the steps.

At the base of the staircase a long, broad corridor ran ahead into the depths of the mountain; to the right and left, narrower passages disappeared into the darkness.

"I hate decisions like this!" Talin snarled, striking the wall with his axe.

"Left!" Cwen said just as Caen shouted, "Right!"

Rolling his eyes, Talin led them down the wide corridor straight ahead.

The wind screamed down the stairway behind them, pushing debris ahead of it and sweeping away their breath as it whirled around them. Choking on dust and grit, they fell into a doorway to the right of the corridor, pushing the heavy wooden door closed behind them.

"It seems we have not expressed the appropriate reverence that would grant us a welcome in the temple," Talin coughed, spitting out dirt and leaves.

Cwen wiped her grit-covered tongue on her sleeve as Caen continued coughing and choking on the dust that had filled his lungs.

The wind continued to wail and scream outside the door.

Wiping grit from his eyes, Talin searched the room they had entered and gestured towards a narrow corridor leading out the back.

"Shall we try here?" he asked, shrugging his indifference. "As if it really matters."

"At least this passageway is calm," Cwen choked out, still deafened by the wailing air stream beyond the windless corridor.

Pulling out a torch, Caen lit it and handed it to Talin, who led off down the dark hall. The flickering light of the torch played in an eerie dance across the polished bone walls.

"Who built this?" Cwen wondered aloud.

"A better question is what killed the beast that bore such bones," Talin said, eyes tracing the bones rising toward the distant ceiling.

The corridor split before them, downward to the left and upward straight ahead.

"We have already seen upward and we did not like it, so we may as well go down," Talin muttered, glancing back at Cwen and Caen. Both nodded their assent and watched as Talin made the face of a man drinking sour bullram's milk.

The passageway began to descend steeply and the angry song of the wind became less shrill.

Ruby light played over the walls before them, flowing across the chamber's ceilings and floors before returning to touch the walls. There before them lay the altar of the wind. It had been built within an enormous gaping skull with canines as long as a man's body protruding from the heavy jaws. The large eye sockets were filled with human skulls.

Within the mouth sat the altar stone, which had been carved of scarlet lightning glass. The artfully carved creatures that coursed around it were dragon-headed, covered with a large bony crest; no evidence of wings or legs was visible. Long and snake-like, they coiled around the altar, each head holding the tail of the beast before it. Great dorsal scales rose the length of their spines, ending in a barb at the tip of each tail. The eyes were Gaianite and glowed from within.

The three stared up at the towering skull. Talin reached out and touched one of the upper fangs. It was longer than he was tall and ended in a sharp point. This beast could swallow a man whole and the open orifice formed the doorway leading to the stone altar. Reluctant to step inside the crushing jaws, he looked back at Cwen and saw a shudder of loathing run through her.

Caen reached up with his lance and poked at the human skulls that filled the beast's eye socket, sending them crashing to the ground and rolling around his feet.

Looking up he shrugged an apology before reaching down and

lifting the skull closest to him. There were no marks of death on the skull, no evidence of crushing or piercing. The skull appeared old and Caen wondered if the beast whose jaws hung open before them had digested the flesh of the man whose skull he held.

"Someone needs to get the shard," Cwen whispered.

Together they leaned in to examine the large crimson shard that lay atop the lightning glass altar.

Talin pulled a length of rope from his pack and held it out to Cwen.

"Tie it around your waist," he prompted, receiving a frown in return.

"I do not wish to die today, Talin. I truly do not."

"Wait," Caen spoke. "Do not step though the jaws. We will lift you through the empty eye socket. You can grasp the shard while suspended from above and will not have to touch the earth before the altar."

Talin helped Cwen secure the rope at her waist. The hair around her face was damp, her eyes wide and glistening.

Talin formed a step with his hands and boosted Cwen until she could reach the rough, bony ridge of the creature's eye. Swinging her leg inside the skull, she looked back at them.

"Do not let me fall." Her voice was hushed.

They both shook their heads, as they held the rope in a death-like grip, ready to support her weight as she slipped inside and released her hold on the bone.

She slid in, releasing her hands one at a time, letting go and leaving them to bear her weight.

"Lower me," she called and felt the rope slip forward, dropping her toward the altar.

"A little more."

"Stop."

She reached out and lifted the shard from the altar.

"I have it; pull me out!" she called and was relieved as the rope drew her back toward the beast's gaping eye.

She flung her leg over the ledge and leapt into Caen's arms.

"Watch," he whispered as he released her. Lifting a human skull from the floor he tossed it into the open jaws, where it landed with a 'thud' before the altar.

Cwen cried out as the jaws snapped together, sending sharp pieces of bone flying toward the altar and sealing off the way to the shard.

"How did you know?" Talin asked.

"It is what I would have built if I did not want anyone to steal my jewels," Caen shrugged. "It was just a suspicion."

Cwen's hand covered her mouth and her face had lost its color. "I could have died today, alone inside those jaws with no one to hold me as I breathed my last breath." Punching Talin on the arm she said, "Next time you get the shard."

When they returned to the surface they met no angry wind. The music of the bones was silenced in the still heavy air and the once roiling clouds delivered a soft misting rain to the Cathedral of the Wind.

Old Friends

Cwen removed two rings from her fingers and handed them to Talin.

"We shall need provisions. You may as well get them from the Xavians. We need bannock, tea and dried stag; also herbs for healing – ask Brengven which are best. I would like soap and prickleberry jam."

Talin took the rings.

"Go to Yadanta. He will give you an honest price," Cwen added.

"You could come and do it yourself," he laughed.

"It is not likely I shall go to New Xavian City in this lifetime. It is filled with members of the Council and more Guardians than I wish to see," she replied, wrinkling her nose at the very idea.

"Idris will carry you swiftly there and back," Cwen said, stroking the neck of the Equus waiting before them.

As Talin spoke with Brengven, Cwen and Caen built the fire in their new camp at the base of the Northern Mountains. They would remain there until Talin returned from delivering the new shard to the Queen's Council.

Watching as Talin leapt to Idris's back and turned him toward the city with a wave of farewell, Cwen felt a chill of unease and called silently, "*Safe journey.*"

The arrow struck Talin high in the right shoulder, its impact driving him from the back of the galloping Equus. Idris halted and trotted back to his fallen rider, nuzzling the unconscious man and shaking his head at the scent of blood. The Equus lowered himself beside Talin and rested his muzzle across the rider's back.

Klaed saw the man fall from the Equus and lie still in the dust of the road. The fact that the rider traveled on an Equus willing to lie down beside him tied him to the House of Aaradan and Näeré, Klaed's mentor in the art of magick.

Quickly casting a barrier against further attack, Klaed dropped beside the man, whispering soothing words to the Equus and receiving its words within his mind.

"He is Talin, sent to the Guardian Nall by Cwen of Aaradan."

Klaed looked up in surprise. Talin and Cwen had trained beside him as Guardian apprentices; three years ago both had declined the offered guardianship, just as he had that very day.

Examining Talin's wound, he found that the arrow had passed through the flesh of the shoulder, leaving no broken bones. The large knot on Talin's head had most likely come from striking the road when he fell.

"You have grown heavy, old friend," Klaed muttered as he lifted Talin and placed him across the back of the Equus. "Let us deliver him to the sorceress Näeré. She will heal him and deal with his need to see Nall."

The Equus bowed its head and answered, *"I shall carry you also."*

Leaping to its back, Klaed urged the steed toward the city at a swift gallop.

"I found him on the road," Klaed answered Näeré's worried question. "The Equus that carried him said he was sent by Cwen."

Näeré applied her healing hands to Talin's wound, examining the arrow she drew from him.

"Sidon," she sighed, drawing a curious look from Klaed.

"Sidon who travels with Aidan?" Klaed asked, a dark frown marring his handsome features.

"Aye, Aidan stalks Cwen as if she were the evening meal." Näeré shook her head in frustration.

The door burst open, banging against the wall as Nall entered.

"What happened?" he asked Näeré, his eyes clouding with

disappointment at the sight of Klaed.

Pointing toward the open door he said, "You are not welcome in my house."

"Nall!" Näeré chastised him. "He found Talin wounded and brought him to us."

"I am grateful. You are still not welcome in my house," Nall repeated through clenched jaws.

Klaed said good-bye to Näeré and went out the way he had come, once again heading away from New Xavian City and its harsh Guardian restrictions.

Talin moaned and held his head, slowly opening his eyes to find Näeré looking down on him, concern radiating from her sapphire eyes.

"Head hurts," he mumbled, licking his lips to ease their dryness.

Näeré's fingers quickly found the bump and her healing incantation took away the pain.

"I had focused on the hole the arrow left in your shoulder," she said, offering a flask to ease Talin's thirst.

"The Equus Idris?"

"He and Klaed brought you to me. Idris waits beyond the city."

"Did they take the shard?"

"It is safe; I found it in your knapsack. Apparently Klaed's presence prevented that – and saved yours and Idris's lives. The arrow was Sidon's."

"Klaed found me? He is a Guardian now?"

"Nay," came Nall's harsh voice. "Like you he has chosen to seek his fortune elsewhere."

"He declined a Guardianship?" Talin asked with surprise, unable to stop the small smile that touched his lips.

He remembered Klaed well; he had been another who wondered if the rules and restrictions placed on Guardians were going to limit his freedom, but Talin had not expected the son of a Xavian councilor to rebel openly.

Rising, Talin spoke his concern. "I must go; Cwen and Caen may be in danger if Sidon dogs our heels."

He placed his hand on Näeré's arm as he spoke the words he knew would ease her mind. "Aidan is dead – at the hands of Caen; though I believe Cwen would have killed him if she could have reached her weapon. She grows wiser, Näeré."

Näeré's eyes glistened with tears as she hugged Talin to her. "Keep her safe, Talin."

"Allow us to provision you," Nall stated gruffly to hide the relief he felt at the death of Aidan. "It will save time."

Talin thanked Näeré for her healing touch and picked up the arrow she had removed from his shoulder.

"I shall keep this. Perhaps an opportunity to return it will present itself."

He winked at Näeré and followed Nall to the garrison for supplies.

As he placed the last of the dried stag in his pack he recalled Cwen's voice.

"I need soap," he said.

"Soap?" Nall's eyebrows rose.

"For Cwen."

"Ask Näeré," Nall snapped, whirling away and walking briskly toward the training field.

Näeré packed several pieces of soap and a number of healing herbs into Talin's pack while he eyed her from his seat at the table.

"Why does he not forgive her?" he asked Näeré.

Näeré shook her head at his youthful naïveté.

"He believes she betrayed him by leaving with Aidan. He cannot see past his hurt pride and his anger. She was just a child," Näeré sighed. "One day he will understand that it was Aidan's doing and not Cwen's, though if she were not so much like Nall it might not have happened as it did."

Again she hugged Talin, causing him to blush.

"You are like a son to us, Talin. Never forget how much we care for you."

Her words were gentle as they had been when he was small and lonely.

"Klaed would make a good traveling companion, if Cwen will allow it. He has a natural talent for magick and uses it with skill."

Talin nodded his agreement, as he had been thinking the same thing.

He rose and hugged Näeré, whispering, "She really misses you."

Idris expressed relief at his rider's uninjured return and pranced impatiently as Talin mounted. The Equus was anxious to end his close proximity to the accordant dragons' lair.

At a hard gallop they quickly caught up to Klaed.

"I probably owe you my life," Talin called to the man ahead of them, causing Klaed to swing around, bow drawn.

"If you decide not to kill me yourself that is."

Klaed laughed and stowed the bow, extending his grip to Talin.

"I do not believe the injury called for a life debt, but a draught with a friend when time allows would be more than gratefully accepted."

He was tall, dark hair and tanned skin mimicking those of his Galenite mother and his startlingly pale blue eyes reflecting his Xavian father. His features were strong and he carried himself with the natural grace of a warrior and a confidence born of nobility, for his father was a member of the Xavian Council.

"And Cwen?" he added, unable to stop himself.

"She is as evil as ever," Talin laughed. "She is swift to strike and slow to admit guilt, and, to hear her tell it, she has never missed a target."

Klaed's face softened as he remembered Cwen in training – a slender girl of seventeen summers, angry and quick to take offense. But his smile faded as he recalled the day she had left with Aidan.

"Does she still travel with Aidan?"

"Aidan is dead,"

Klaed's eyebrows rose in surprise.

"Did she finally kill him?"

"Nay, another we travel with killed him," Talin admitted before adding, "but it was for the right reason."

"Perhaps now she will truly have the freedom she seeks."

"What are your plans?" Talin asked, hoping Klaed had none.

"I head for the city of Telsar in Æshulmæ in hopes of an offer of work. The training should allow me to provide someone with protection."

"Are you still wickedly skillful with that bow?"

"Aye, I am far better than you. I see that you still sever arms and split heads with that brutal axe."

"Näeré says you are also skilled in magick," Talin added thoughtfully.

"I am not a sorcerer, but I have shown some talent, according to Näeré," Klaed answered modestly.

Knowing his offer would incur Cwen's wrath, Talin took a deep breath and explained their quest. "We would welcome you among us if you would like to travel in a different direction."

Klaed gave Talin a solemn look. "She will try to kill me, will she not?"

"Most likely," Talin replied honestly. Then they both burst into laughter.

Chapter 6 The Azure Sea

Cwen jumped up from the fire at the sound of the approaching Equus. Talin had returned far sooner than she anticipated.

Her expression set to welcome him back and prepared to tell of the fat stag that hung on the spit, she strode toward the clearing where the Equus had stopped.

The warmth she felt faded as she saw the second man, a man she recalled well: a clone of her father and a member of the Xavian nobility.

She drew her sword as she raced toward him, eyes blazing and mouth turned into a snarl.

Talin nodded at her approach and whispered to Klaed, "If you cannot defend against her I withdraw my offer."

Holding out his hands to show he was unarmed, Talin backed away leaving Klaed to the woman's fury.

Klaed drew his sword and stepped into Cwen's attack, swinging his blade into hers with both hands. His eyes were warm with affection and his voice was low and unruffled.

"It is good to see you too, Cwen."

She gave a growl as she tried to sweep his sword out of her way so that she could thrust her second shorter sword into his gut. He forced her back and stepped away as her long sword swept past his ear, pulling the air behind it.

"Close," Klaed winked.

Caen and Talin watched as the combatants flew against each other repeatedly until both began to tire.

"He is good," Caen said.

"Aye, I have asked him to travel with us if she does not maim or kill him. He will be a good man to have along. He is skilled in magick and was trained by the same Guardians as Cwen and I."

Brengven finally appeared, drawn by the shouting and clashing swords. "Who does she kill now?" he asked, looking up at Talin and Caen.

"An old friend," Talin stated.

"It is good he is not our enemy," Brengven shrugged, "for he stands well against her wrath."

Caen and Talin nodded their agreement.

They stood apart, swords hanging loosely, as their breath came in great ragged gasps. A wide grin broke Klaed's face and he whispered, "I am tired."

"Good," Cwen returned, "then I can kill you."

"I do not think so, Cwen, though you are very good."

"As are you," she acknowledged his skill. "But you may not remain in my camp. You obviously come to spy on us and I shall not allow it."

"I do not come to spy. What will it take to convince you?"

"Other than your death? Nothing. You are the Guardian's perfect student, the one he said I should follow as my example."

"This very day I refused the Guardianship and was cast from your father's house after finding Talin wounded on the road. I am not your father's spy." Klaed sheathed his sword.

Cwen swung to Talin. "You were hurt?"

"Aye, one of Sidon's arrows ended up in my shoulder. Näeré healed me and sent me back to you."

Glaring once again at Klaed, Cwen said, "I am not finished killing you."

"Could you finish after I am fed? I have had no meal since bannock at breakfast."

Cwen tried to hide a smile, but laughter bubbled up and spoiled her fierce frown.

"We have a fine fat stag over the flames, and if Talin did his job we shall have tea and bannock as well," she said, replacing her swords in their scabbards.

"Do not turn your back on me Klaed, for after your meal I do intend to kill you."

"Perhaps I could sleep first and you could kill me in the morning," he called after her.

She waved her hand to show she had heard him as she looked up at Talin's face.

"Where are you hurt?"

"I am not hurt. Näeré healed me."

"Where were you hurt? Do not test me, Talin, I am irritated enough already." She glared.

He opened his shirt to reveal the angry scar that remained after the healing.

Cwen took in a deep shuddering breath and bit her lip.

"It is good Sidon does not have better aim. Why did you bring my enemy here?"

"He is not your enemy. He is adequate with a sword and skilled with the long bow and in magick. He will be useful."

"He will be another to watch," she snapped, looking at Caen, who raised his eyebrows.

"I have done nothing; do not take your anger out on me," Caen said, frowning back at her.

"But she thinks you might," Talin laughed.

"I told you I did not trust you, Caen; now there are two in my camp I cannot trust. I shall never sleep."

She looked over her shoulder to the fire where Klaed and Brengven spoke with the ease of old friends.

"He always did have an enchanting smile," she murmured, "and while his sword arm was not strong enough to best me he did not allow me to kill him."

Swinging back to Talin she reminded, "But he is the son of a Xavian councilor – nobility, Talin. He is no thief, no rogue. He would not take kindly to our way of life. And there is a gentleness about him that could get us killed."

"Let him stay the night, Cwen. What harm can it do? He adds a pair of well-trained ears and eyes." Talin's look dared her to deny it.

"We shall feed him and offer him a place of rest for this night only. I want him gone after breakfast."

Watching her walk away toward Klaed, Talin said, "She will allow him to stay."

Cwen stood before Klaed and warned him.

"You may stay the night if you wish, but I shall not promise not to kill you in your sleep."

Klaed nodded and said, "I accept the offer and I stand warned. I shall sleep with my dagger in my hand."

"You do not take me seriously, Klaed. Talin should caution you that that is not wise." Her eyes narrowed in annoyance.

"He has already cautioned me, Cwen."

Suddenly his smile grew and he spoke in a whisper only she could hear, "You are not the girl I remember, Cwen of Aaradan."

"I am not a girl at all, nor do I stand for the House of Aaradan. Much has changed since last I saw you."

"When last I saw you, you were crying." His voice was tender with the memory.

She looked away, embarrassed by the truth.

"You were kind to me," she said, meeting his eyes, "and I shall now return the kindness, but I want you gone after the morning meal."

"Perhaps you can finish killing me before I leave. I rather enjoyed your first attempt."

"Now you mock me. I may not be able to let you live until morning," she laughed.

"How is it you always make me laugh?"

"I simply touch you where the laughter dwells, Cwen."

Against Cwen's wishes Klaed shared their watch and when she woke in the morning she realized she had indeed fallen asleep under his watchful eye with no more thought than if it had been Talin's watch.

Talin and Caen laughed at Klaed's recollection of his fall during a dragon flight.

"It was not so high that too many bones were broken, but it was painful and required several weeks of mending."

"Good day, Cwen," he spoke as she poured her tea.

"Do not try to sway my decision with your nonsense." She frowned at him. "And do not think that because Talin and Caen find you amusing I shall agree to let you stay."

"Is she always so talkative before tea?" Klaed asked Talin, causing him to choke on the bannock he was attempting to swallow.

She tossed her cup away and drew her sword, staring at him with unrestrained anger.

Nodding to Talin and Caen, Klaed excused himself, "Excuse me gentlemen for I see that she wishes to continue my killing. Hopefully I shall return shortly, but if not you may divide my weapons among you."

He swept his sword from its sheath and raised it to meet hers as it fell toward him.

"You are supposed to allow your opponent to stand before you strike," he chastened. "There are rules in swordsmanship, Cwen. Have you forgotten?"

Their swords rang against one another as Talin and Caen broke camp. Brengven arrived ready to depart, but settled for a last cup of tea as he watched Cwen attempt to beat Klaed into submission.

Finally, when neither of them could lift a sword high enough to strike the other, they collapsed side by side on the grass.

Without looking at Klaed, Cwen whispered, "You can stay if you will never speak of my parents, or Guardians, or training, or the Queen, or New Xavian City, or the Council, or your parents."

"You have more rules than the vows of guardianship, Cwen," Klaed said, "but I agree that I shall not speak of these."

Turning her head, she looked at him and saw him smile.

"And you will not smile at me," she added, watching as his contagious smile grew wider.

He held out his hand and dragged Cwen to her feet as Talin called to them.

"Whoever travels with us should be ready to do so."

"Brengven grows impatient," he added receiving a cross look from the Feie.

Cwen grabbed her pack where it lay near Talin's feet and said sharply, "I have tested Klaed and I find him acceptable."

Dobbinwort's Supernatural Sword Shop

"We shall camp near Dobbin's furnace and travel to the Azure Sea from there," Cwen called back to them as they approached the little Ancient's sword shop.

"I have heard rumors…" Brengven began, stopping as Talin and Caen glared at him.

"Well I have," he muttered.

"What rumors have you heard, Brengven?" Klaed asked.

"His rumors and tales always involve some hideous way of getting rid of mortals," Caen spoke, frowning at Brengven again.

"Rumors of sea dragons," Brengven said, wrinkling his face up at Caen.

"I have heard the rumor too; a rumor of sea dragons that only eat those who are Feie and hail from Réverē. Very specialized dragons they are," Klaed added.

Talin and Caen whooped with laughter as Brengven grew red.

Ahead of them Cwen shook her head at their foolishness.

Cwen leaned down and banged on Dobbinwort's door, staring up at the large ornamental sign above the portal. 'Dobbinwort's Supernatural Sword Shop' it read. His shop was constructed of the bones and shells of creatures living beneath his feet. Dobbin was the creator of her double-bladed sword and the only metal master with the ability to forge magick.

"Dobbin!" she called loudly, knowing that the Ancient often ignored his visitors. "It is Cwen."

"Cwen of Aaradan," she added, glaring over her shoulder and daring anyone to mention the use of her title. Wisely, they all pretended not to be listening.

As she started to pound on the door again, it opened and the wizened little man squinted out at her through half-closed eyes.

"I heard you was dead."

"Who told you such a thing, Dobbin? As you can see, I am quite alive."

"Maybe you is and maybe you is a spirit." He peered behind her, beaming when he saw Talin.

"Talin! You is not dead?"

"Nay, Dobbin, I live," Talin shouted back laughing.

"Now that you see we are not dead, are you going to let us in?" Cwen asked in exasperation.

"You and you, and you, and that one, but not the Feie," Dobbin said, pointing at Brengven. "He would disturbs my magick."

"Hmph!" Brengven snorted, "As if I would enter your establishment even if I was invited."

"I shall prepare the camp and start the meal," the Feie called back to them as he headed off beyond the forge.

Together the four of them crowded into Dobbin's shop, ducking to avoid banging their heads on the dozens of weapons dangling from the ceiling.

"Do you wants to buy a sword?" Dobbin asked, looking at Caen.

"I have a sword," Caen responded.

"Aye," Dobbin said, poking at it, "but I didn't makes it."

Lifting an eyebrow, Caen looked to Cwen for clarification.

"Dobbin is the maker of the finest swords in all of Ædracmoræ," she explained, taking the double-bladed sword from her back and handing it to Dobbin.

"Swords like this one."

Dobbin hefted it and spun, nearly catching Talin's knee.

"Careful, Dobbin. I would hate to have Cwen heal me so far from Meremire."

"What makes you think I would try?" Cwen asked.

"You must keep me alive so that you can die in my arms,

remember?" he laughed.

Looking from Caen to Klaed she tilted her head and examined Talin. "Do not be so sure that I need you alive any longer."

Dobbin swung the sword again, causing Caen to press back against the wall as the blade swished by in front of him.

Cwen collected the sword from Dobbin's dangerous hands and slid it back over her shoulder.

"May we camp near the forge, Dobbin? We seek something near the shore of the Azure Sea."

"The dragons will eats you," Dobbin said shrugging. "But I do not care if you camps in my woods. Be careful in the caverns."

"There are caverns?" Talin asked, looking dispirited. "I was hoping to find the shard lying above of the ground this time."

"Since the seven kingdoms came together there is lots of caverns."

"Are there really dragons, Dobbin?" Cwen asked, lifting a berry from a bowl on the table and popping it into her mouth.

"Aye. Well, some says so." The Ancient shrugged, leaving them with no more knowledge than Brengven had given.

"There is no need for a cold camp tonight, not with that cantankerous curmudgeon sleeping a stone's throw away," Brengven snapped as they walked into the camp. "Such a rude and unpleasant person," he muttered under his breath.

Cwen hid her smile from Brengven, sharing it with Caen and Klaed, who were trying not to laugh aloud.

"That is a case of the grass cat calling the bloodren sneaky," Klaed whispered.

"I heard that!" Brengven hollered, causing all of them to break into loud laughter.

"Fix your own dinner," the Feie yelled, throwing the pot and stomping off toward his own camp.

"Can you cook?" Klaed asked Cwen, receiving a fiery glare until she realized he was teasing her again.

"I shall make the tea. If the rest of you oafs will drag out the dried stag and bannock we shall have a feast," she said.

"You smiled at me," he called after her. "It is against the rules."

"Nay, it is only against the rules for you to smile at me," she tossed back over her shoulder.

"She called us oafs," Klaed said to Caen.

"And so we are, for we follow her as the moons follow the day star, fools, every one of us," Caen laughed.

"Why do you follow her, Caen?" Klaed asked, suddenly serious.

"I follow her because she is my friend," Caen answered, heading off to unpack the dried stag.

Shaking his head, Klaed looked after him.

"I think you settle for her friendship, but you wish for something more."

Talin laughed at the remark.

"It is most likely that she will kill you both," he told Klaed with a grin, "or you will kill each other."

A Case of Mistaken Identity

They packed camp, leaving Brengven still fuming over the remains of breakfast.

The Azure Sea is not a large sea, but it is surrounded by soft white sands and tall escarpments. A wide waterfall fed by an underground river cascaded from the top of the cliff, filling a large pool before emptying into the sea. The cliff face was filled with ancient caverns and it was among those caverns that they hoped to find the shard listed on the scroll.

Locating a shallow cavern at the foot of the cliff nearest the waterfall they began to set up camp. Grinning, Talin pulled the soap from his pack and tossed it to Cwen.

"Perhaps you would like to keep some for yourself," she said, causing him to frown.

"Cwen, the air is chilled, the water is freezing, I have no blood on me anywhere and I do not wish to smell like a flower. If I need to bathe, plain water will work well enough."

"I shall keep the ruffians here." He winked as she grabbed a blanket and headed for the pool.

Placing her clothes and sword on a ledge behind the falls, she stepped into the icy water and held the soap to her nose. The sudden scent of her mother caused a surge of tears and a sob caught in her throat. As she washed her hair she wept for the loss of the innocent child she had once been.

Hot tea and dried meat was the meal of choice in the absence of

Brengven's cooking skills. Cwen returned and asked Talin where her prickleberry jam was, receiving a lifted eyebrow from him.

"I was wounded and provisioned at the garrison. You were lucky to get soap; they had no jam."

Pouting, she looked up at him. "Very well, I shall forgive you forgetting the jam since you suffered so to get the soap."

She drew a boar's bristle brush from her pack and began to brush the tangles from her wet hair as she warmed herself by the fire.

Klaed walked to her and held out his hand, waiting patiently until she handed him her brush. He knew that she remembered when last he had brushed her hair, before he had taken her home to her father.

Caen observed as Klaed held Cwen's hair and skillfully removed the tangles from its wet strands. When he had finished, he handed her the brush and returned to sit next to Caen.

Seeing Caen's expression, Klaed grinned and offered a whispered word of advice.

"Never forget that her mother is the sister of the king. While it is not wise to speak it aloud, remembering it will help you treat her with the deference she demands. Her heart is fragile and she lies when she says she does not care."

"You have known her long?" Caen asked.

"Aye, since her thirteenth summer. Together with Cwen and Talin, I trained for the Guardianship."

"She seems to trust you in spite of attempting to kill you only yesterday," Caen mumbled.

"I once helped her when she was young and frightened. She has not forgotten it," Klaed said in a hushed voice, looking across at Cwen.

The firelight set the deep red highlights dancing in her hair and gave her golden eyes a fire of their own. She had indeed grown into a beautiful woman.

"You are both staring," she said sternly. "Have you never seen a woman with clean hair before?"

"I am sure neither of us has ever seen one so beautiful," Klaed answered.

Caen's foolish grin told of his agreement.

Pointing, she answered, "And I have never met two men more full of bullram scat."

Talin threw back his head and sent his laughter echoing off the cavern walls.

They prowled along the cliffs, seeking an opening that would provide access to the labyrinth of caverns they knew lay beneath the earth around the Azure Sea.

"There seems to be a tangle of vegetation ahead." Caen spoke in a whisper to avoid the revealing echo.

"What kind of vegetation grows without the light of day?" Cwen asked.

"It covers the ceiling of the cavern ahead and there are long tendrils that hang down from above. There appear to be spiders attached to the vines. It is quite strange."

Cwen stepped forward and held her torch out before her. Talin and Klaed drew in close behind them.

The plants that covered the ceiling and draped themselves down the wall were pale and fleshy, each tendril ending in a spider-like appendage as Caen had described.

As they edged into the cavern, the long tendrils reached out, straining to touch them and causing them to shrink back and out of the cave.

"Perhaps a different entrance is in order," Talin stated, pausing as his companions gave their agreement.

Cwen held Talin's arm and together they watched a gray-furred downy flier scamper past their feet and into the vine-filled chamber. A slender tendril shot forward and seemed to sting the small creature before the spidery, hand-like tip settled over the body and drew its fluids up into the plant. The pale tendril grew a cloudy red as the downy flier's life-blood was drained away, leaving only a desiccated corpse.

Talin's face was grim as Caen voiced the opinion of them all.

"It is good we did not decide to enter here."

Passing into the next cave they found it riddled with passageways leading into the side of the cliff. Lighting fresh torches they entered the corridor that seemed to lead directly downward into the cliff face.

At the first juncture Caen paused and grinned back at Talin.

"Left, right or straight ahead?" he asked.

"I hate this," Talin said, shaking his head.

"Straight ahead," Klaed offered as Cwen said, "Left."

"Then we shall go right," Caen laughed. He led them down the winding corridor until it opened into a wide antechamber that was sunken at its center.

"Perhaps it once held a pool," Cwen shrugged.

"At least there is no hungry garden growing in it," Klaed added. Together they entered the cavern, skirting the walls and looking for exits.

"There are bones," Caen said, stepping toward the center of the room.

With a loud cracking, the brittle ground gave way, dropping Caen into the waist deep water of the cavern below. Before him lay a great dragon resting on a sleeping ledge. It blinked its great eyes and drew back its head to strike.

"Stay," Cwen shouted to Talin and Klaed as she dropped into the water in front of Caen. "No!" She yelled, spreading her arms wide to draw the dragon's attention.

The dragon extended its huge head toward Cwen, squinting in disbelief and breathing in her scent. "Huntress?" It questioned in confusion.

Cwen's eyes widened as she realized it must have mistaken her for her father's sister, Rydén, the copper-haired Huntress of the Sailflyte of sea dragons. The dragon's eyes were clouded with age and it carried the scars of a poacher's lance.

"It is long since we have seen you, Huntress. Honor of the Ancients to you and your human. Do you not know me, Huntress?" the old dragon asked, giving the low "shuff, shuff" of dragon laughter.

"I am Sygarnd, once mate to Sybeth. The flyte has moved on and left me behind to end my days."

"Honor of the Ancients to you, Sygarnd," Cwen said, pushing Caen to his knees beside her and whispering to him, "Do not look at the dragon, Caen."

"It is with great sorrow that I learn your time of passing is near," Cwen continued in the strong steady voice required by dragon diplomacy.

"Might I honor you by claiming your shard?"

"Nay, Huntress, the flyte will send an acolyte to claim it, but your offer speaks of your pledge to the Sailflyte and we shall sing your praise in the songs of our legends."

"What is it you seek from us?" Sygarnd asked Cwen.

"We seek the heart shard of the ancient wyrm, that it may not be used against Ædracmoræ as it was in the time before remembering."

"The other has taken it; he came for it by the appointment of the Queen. He bore her seal."

Cwen's heart sank and her stomach felt suddenly hollow. The sudden remembrance of Aidan pulling the signet from her finger and tossing it to Sidon brought burning bile surging into her throat. It was the ring of her birthright, the symbol of the House of Aaradan, the seal of the Queen. Sidon must have used it to claim the shard without raising the old dragon's suspicions.

Swallowing the gagging bitterness, she lifted her hand toward the hole in the cavern's ceiling she asked, "Would you grant us passage to the surface, Sygarnd?"

Lowering his great head, Sygarnd directed them to the hall that would lead them to the caves above them.

The Signet

What do you mean he has the seal of the Queen?" Talin shouted, face pale, corded muscles rigid along his neck. "Your signet ring? The one Sōrél and Yáviē gave you? That signet? You gave it to Aidan and Sidon?"

Klaed gave Talin a look of warning. "It is done. We shall simply get it back."

"We cannot simply get it back!" Talin continued to glare at Cwen, the heat of his anger flooding his cheeks. "We do not know where Sidon is. How could you be so mindlessly selfish?"

Caen pushed him, causing Talin to wheel on him. "Do not interfere. You do not know what she has done!"

Caen's voice was calm and quiet, "Do not shout at her again."

Throwing up his hands, Talin yelled at them, strings of spittle flying.

"Fine! Let her lead us into ruin. We can watch as the world collapses beneath the chaos of a war with the G'lm led by Sidon or whoever holds his leash." He stormed away, kicking at the fire and sending sparks and embers sailing into the night, causing Cwen to cringe.

"Talin!" she cried after him. She started to follow but Klaed took her arm.

"Let him go, Cwen. He will return when his temper has cooled."

She looked up at Klaed, her eyes wide, brimming with hurt that implored him to believe her.

"I did not give it to Aidan. He took it. I never gave him anything; they simply took what they wanted. He and Sidon."

Klaed's mind was flooded with pain as Cwen released the memories of her lost innocence and brutal betrayal at the hands of Aidan and Sidon. He drew her against him, whispering enchanted words to soothe her shattered heart and folded her into his warm embrace. Looking over her head, he shook his head at Caen and watched as the man headed to the far side of the camp.

"Why did you not say so, Cwen?"

"I could not. They told me Talin would die if I did not… obey them." She sobbed, broken, against his chest.

Klaed held Cwen until she finally slept and then laid her down and covered her with her cloak. Even beneath the spell of deep sleep she still shook with deep shuddering sobs. Tonight he would tell Talin and then they would not speak of it again.

Going to Caen he whispered, "I must speak to Talin. Keep her safe. Hold her if she wakes and tell her that you care for her."

As he stepped away he looked back and added, "Even if you do not."

"Do not kill me, Talin," Klaed called, entering the cavern where he sensed Talin had bedded down for the night.

"You have judged your friend harshly and your words have done great harm," he said, sitting down next to his friend in the blackness.

"She is a fool," Talin whispered.

"Nay, only foolish… and so are you. She carries no blame, Talin. Aidan and Sidon took everything from her. She gave them nothing. Nall is the biggest fool of all for he has lost a daughter because of his own pig-headed pride."

Talin lit a waffle root torch and sought the truth in Klaed's eyes.

His voice was hoarse with anger and guilt. "Where is she?"

"She sleeps. I have cast the spell of deep sleep upon her and still she weeps. I cannot heal the hurt, only you can do that – only you and Nall. Though I am not sure she will ever allow it of him."

"Why did she not tell me?" Talin asked.

"They threatened her with your death. I felt her shame and fear when she shared her thoughts, Talin, and the depth and purity of her love for you. She will never speak it aloud; do not ask it of her. You are her friend; simply tell her what they did does not matter. Even now she agonizes over their threats against you."

Within their camp, Caen watched Cwen sleep and wished he had not killed Aidan so quickly.

Cwen woke and looked up to see Talin standing before her with a cup of steaming tea. He held it out to her and watched as she tried to decide whether to accept it. She did not meet his eyes.

His voice was soft within her mind, "*Come, Cwen. Talk to me.*"

He placed the cup on the ground before her and walked away toward the sea. Taking a deep tremulous breath, she picked up the tea and followed after him.

He stopped and waited, not looking back but staring out to sea and listening to the hiss of her footsteps in the soft sand.

When she finally stood next to him he glanced down at her and realized how small she was and felt as if his heart would break.

She stared at the sea and whispered, "I have never given Aidan anything, Talin."

"I know. Cwen, it does not matter that Sidon has the ring. Klaed is right; we shall simply steal it back. I am a fool; nay, I am a fallowass – worse than that, I am a black-hearted son of a bane boar. I believed you cared for him, how could I…"

"I told him not to take it, but he did," she interrupted, "and my father thought I gave my honor so freely."

"Cwen…"

"Nay, Talin. I no longer care what Nall thinks."

"*I care only what you think of me*," she spoke the trembling truth into his mind.

Talin reached out to rest his hand on her shoulder.

"I think you are the finest friend any man has ever had."

"Indeed I am," she answered, raising tear filled eyes above a fragile smile.

Talin withdrew Sidon's arrow from his pack and handed it to Brengven.

"Perhaps it will tell you something of his whereabouts," he suggested. "We need to find him quickly and end his treachery."

Brengven sat upon the grass and held the arrow across the palms of his hands and closed his fists around the shaft.

An image of Sidon in a stand of trees above a road flooded his mind. Sidon crouched, arrow nocked and ready, waiting for his quarry. As Talin passed below him, the arrow flew, striking him and knocking him from the Equus back. The evil man fled when he saw Klaed cast the sheltering shield over the fallen rider.

Blowing sand covered the next image – sharp, stinging sand. Sidon pulled the hood of his cloak over his head and dragged the dark-haired woman along behind him. Suddenly Brengven saw the image of a great fortress. It was old and pitted from the wars of long ago, its walls crumbling from neglect. He saw an image of Sidon entering the fortress before the scene faded from his mind.

"He has crossed the desert and entered a ruined fortress. I could see the shimmer of the sea and the red haze of a city beyond it," Brengven said, opening his eyes.

Talin sought Cwen's eyes.

"They have gone to the Fortress of the Dragon Queen. It is filled with the rabble of the world now that it has fallen to ruin and it is the gateway to the port city of Bael. It would appear Sidon seeks to leave Æstretfordæ; if he reaches Ælmondæ, there will be many willing to hide him."

Cwen continued with conviction. "When I traveled with Aidan I learned one can quickly disappear in Ælmondæ."

"Then let us not waste time with idle chatter," Klaed suggested. "Let us find the rogue and end his life."

"Brengven?" Talin sought the Feie's thoughts.

"I shall remain here, camped in the shadow of that hateful Dobbinwort until you return. Do not be long, for I cannot bear his company and may turn him into a fallowass in your absence," Brengven said sullenly, rolling his eyes at the thought of conversation with the Ancient.

Cwen warned. "It is more likely that you shall be the ass when we return. I would recommend camping a bit further from his forge."

Grumbling, Brengven nodded at her suggestion and began gathering his pots.

Caen sought Cwen as she packed her knapsack. His eyes were solemn as he spoke her name.

"Cwen."

Turning, she looked up at him and frowned at his serious expression.

"I have no time for deep conversation, Caen." Her words were sharp, but her voice was soft and without anger.

"I should have allowed you to kill Aidan," Caen said, his eyes clouded with regret.

Her eyes softened and she placed her hand on his arm.

"You killed him for what he did and what he would have done again. It is enough that he is dead."

Dropping her hand from his arm she said, "And we shall kill Sidon with great relish and take back my signet."

Talin watched them from across the camp.

"You lose ground, my friend, for today she sees Caen as her hero."

"It is enough she turned to me in sorrow and although I do not entirely trust Caen's intentions, he is quick to learn and may prove a worthy rival yet."

Talin grinned and chuckled at the thought of their rivalry.

"Just remember, she is not above killing either of you in your sleep."

The Fortress of the Dragon Queen

A low fog covered the Wastelands, dampening the sands and making their travel easier.

"I did not know the fortress remained," Klaed said to Cwen.

"Aye, after the rebirth of Ædracmoræ Yávië lifted the veil of invisibility that hid it during their quests. She had hoped it would fall to ruin and return to the sand."

Caen spoke up. "It is now a den of thieves and murderers. Poachers and slavers use it as a holding place for cargo headed for Ælmondæ. I have a contact in the port city of Bael that lies beyond the fortress. He may have knowledge of Sidon."

Cwen said, "Is there a city where you do not have contacts, Caen?"

"Aye, I have none in the New Xavian City and none within the fortresses of the Galenites or the Queen. Unless I count you."

She scowled at Caen and turned to Talin. "How long?"

"We shall be there before the day star rises, but I would prefer we entered with the light. Those residing in the old fortress will not welcome the arrival of strangers under cover of darkness."

The dark decaying fortress loomed before them. The remaining towers held the flickering light of many torches, announcing that the new occupants were on watch.

Caen looked Klaed up and down.

"If you attempt to enter dressed as a dandy they will slay you on sight."

Klaed raised his eyebrows and looked down at the soft blue leathers that covered his legs. His shirt was made of soft, tanned hide dyed a deep black, its laces white and clean. Heavier leather armor guarded the shoulder of his weapon arm.

Talin tilted his head and grinned at his friend.

"He does have a point. You rather look like the spoiled son of a Xavian Councilor."

Cwen picked up a handful of dirt and tossed it across Klaed's shirt.

"If I work at it a bit I can make you look shabby enough to fool anyone. You can simply say you killed the noble and stole his clothes. Talin, give me Sidon's arrow and I shall create the dead man's wounds.

"Take off your shirt, Klaed," she instructed, watching as he did it and pursing her lips at the solid muscles of his chest and arms.

"No wonder resting against you was so uncomfortable it made me cry," she said, making light of her shared tears.

Taking his shirt she threw in on the ground and rubbed it in the dirt, flipping it over to do the same to the other side. Then she drove Sidon's arrow through it several times before returning the arrow to Talin.

As Klaed reached for his shirt, she said, "Nay, not yet; there must be blood."

Drawing her dagger she held out her hand to Caen.

"Why my blood? Why not his?" Caen grimaced.

"Do you not wish to bleed for our cause, Caen? I shall heal it for you when I am done."

"I suppose I should be grateful that you wish to hold my hand," he said, offering his hand to her.

He stood steady and did not flinch as she drew her blade across the palm of his hand. Tilting it, she allowed his blood to drip into the holes she had created in Klaed's shirt. Swinging quickly, she shook Caen's hand hard, throwing droplets of blood across the front of Klaed's expensive blue leathers before pulling out a healing cloth and whispering the words to seal the wound.

Still holding Caen's hand she looked at Klaed.

"Now rub dirt on your leathers and you will be almost presentable," she said. "You will indeed look like you have murdered and robbed a nobleman, which will be considered fine work among the men we are about to meet."

Picking up the ruined shirt, Klaed slipped it over his head, frowning at the grit against his skin. Then he began to rub the earth into his dark blue leathers.

"It is quite costly to pretend to be a murderer. Though I am grateful it was not my blood you chose to spill," he muttered, causing his companions to laugh.

"Now we must do something about you, Cwen," Caen said.

"What do you mean, 'do something about me'?" She jerked her hand from his.

"You cannot enter the fortress with such glowing hair," he said.

"I could braid it and we could throw dirt on it," Klaed grinned.

"Or I could cut it off with a dull dagger," Talin offered.

"Cutting it off would be best," Caen said, drawing his dagger and stepping toward Cwen, watching her recoil in horror.

"You will not touch my hair! None of you will touch my hair! Caen, give me a strip of leather and I shall bind it like yours."

Pulling a slender strap of leather from around his wrist he handed it to her.

"Turn around and I shall do it," Klaed offered.

Glaring at them she handed the strip of leather to Klaed and turned her back to him. He quickly braided and bound her hair and spun her back toward him.

"You would look better with a dose of Caen's blood on you and dirt on your face, but I suppose you will do."

Leaning down, Cwen picked up a handful of earth and rubbed it across her cheeks.

"Definitely an improvement." Talin whooped at the sight of her dirt-streaked face. "No one will ever suspect you carry soap."

Music drifted on the wind and echoing shouts of laughter filtered from the tavern that filled what had once been the Great Hall of the fortress.

Caen stepped ahead, blocking those approaching from any view of Cwen. The man before them was obviously a poacher, his clothing was soiled by the blood and fat of the dragons and Equus he had slain.

Talin felt Cwen tense and whispered in her mind.

"Do not do anything foolish. We can kill him later when he is not surrounded by a hundred others."

Her eyes shifted toward him and she lowered her eyes to indicate her agreement.

"He has several rings we shall soon collect." she thought back to him.

"Aye, indeed," she heard Klaed speak in her mind, startling her, for she had forgotten he could hear her thoughts unless she blocked them from him.

Caen extended his hand in friendship as the tall poacher stepped forward.

"Ezrael, it is good to see you old friend."

"And you, Caen. What do you bring us?" he said, leaning around to look at Cwen.

"Nothing but trouble if you look at my woman again," Caen laughed loudly.

Ezrael grinned and nodded to Cwen before glancing toward Talin and Klaed. Stepping forward he placed a finger in one of the holes in Klaed's shirt.

"I see that you have killed a nobleman. That is a sign of good character indeed. I am Ezrael."

Klaed accepted the man's grip.

"I am Klaed," he responded, "and this is Talin, another rogue and killer of noblemen."

Talin accepted the man's grip while committing his face to memory.

"And your woman, Caen, does she have a name?"

Caen leered and laughed, "Aye, but only I am allowed to speak it."

He reached forward and pulled Cwen close, kissing her roughly. Placing his mouth next to her ear he whispered, "I am sorry," and felt her relax.

"Sit at my table," Ezrael said, slapping Caen on the back and leading the group forward.

Cwen sat crushed between Caen and Klaed; Talin sat across from her sipping ale and grinning at her increasing discomfort.

"*I shall kill you all before the evening meal*," her voice hissed into his mind.

Talin choked on his ale and sputtered with laughter, causing Ezrael and Caen to look at him in confusion.

"I just recalled a three-legged bar wench I once met," Talin covered his unexpected mirth as he continued to laugh at Cwen's infuriated expression.

"Klaed, would you ask the barkeeper if there is a room free upstairs?" Caen asked. Turning to Ezrael, he added, "There is some business I would like to discuss with you."

"Aye, and I with you." Ezrael stared at Cwen's chest.

Pushing through the crowd that had congregated on the stairs to the tower room that Klaed had arranged for them, Caen threw open the door and slammed Ezrael against the far wall.

"Business, Ezrael, and I told you not to look at the woman."

"Cwen, is there anything you would like to say to Ezrael?"

Ezrael looked down into the fiery golden eyes.

"I am no man's woman," Cwen hissed as she drove her boot into his crotch, causing Talin, Caen and Klaed to cringe. She kicked Ezrael again, breaking his teeth and splitting his lip as he huddled on the floor gasping. Then she went to the table and sat down.

Caen dragged Ezrael to his feet.

"We are looking for a man named Sidon. Until recently he traveled with a man named Aidan, now he travels only with a mousy looking woman named Daedra. Have you seen him?" Caen asked in a low voice.

"Do not lie or I shall give you to Cwen. She would very much like to remove your eyes."

Ezrael spat out blood and teeth and glared at Cwen, causing her to stand and step toward him. He held up his hand to ward her off.

"Answer him," she snarled, drawing her dagger, "Or I shall cut out more than your eyes. I am a healer and I can keep you alive for a very long time while you suffer by my hands."

"Sidon has taken his woman and gone to Bael. They seek a vessel to take them to Ælmondæ," Ezrael gulped.

"And just where in Bael might I find him and his woman?" Cwen asked, drawing closer and placing her dagger below Ezrael's right eye, watching a drop of blood form at the blade's tip.

"At the inn near the dock," Ezrael lisped through the spaces where his teeth had been.

Cwen leaned closer to the foul smelling man.

"Did you kill the Equus?" she hissed, dropping her blade to his grease-stained leathers.

"What?" he asked, looking confused.

"Did you kill the Equus?" the tip of her blade sliced through the leather, cutting into his thigh.

"I am a poacher you crazy wench! Of course I killed the beasts!" he screamed.

Her blade cut deeper, severing the artery and allowing his life's blood to pour forth. Caen muffled the sounds of the man's dying and then dropped him to the floor. His gaze slipped to Cwen's pale face and he led her to a chair and pushed her head between her knees.

"Breathe," he said softly with his hand against the back of her neck.

"Why must they kill the Equus and the dragons?" she whispered.

"Because evil men buy their pelts and scales, Cwen," Klaed said, kneeling before her.

"We must go if we are to reach Bael before Sidon leaves for Ælmondæ."

Wiping her eyes, Cwen stood and went to the fallen poacher. She removed his rings and placed them in her bag.

Bael

Twilight brought them to the port city of Bael, a small city hastily thrown together to meet the needs of the black marketeers, a city not found on the crown's maps. It would have little to offer any except poachers, thieves and murderers.

"Where is your contact here?" Talin asked Caen.

Grinning, Caen answered, "In the tavern."

"And she is probably fair-haired and blue-eyed," Cwen said rolling her eyes, causing Klaed to chuckle.

"The best contacts can always be found in a tavern," Caen said by way of justification.

Caen's entrance brought squeals of recognition and delight from several working women, all blonde and blue-eyed. They hung on Caen and he whispered to them, making them laugh.

Cwen wished she had washed the dirt from her face.

"Cwen," Caen said, dragging a woman along with him. "This is Orlia. She will see you upstairs to a bath. I told her we have been hunting poachers for the Queen and have not been in a town for weeks. We will await you down here."

Cwen's lips twitched in a tiny smile.

"You have blood on your chin," he smiled back at her.

"Come with me, milady," Orlia said, curtsying and pushing Caen out of the way. "The tub is deep and the water is hot and none will bother you. I shall see to that."

Cwen followed Orlia toward the stairs, looking back to see Caen still staring after her.

"Why did you call me 'milady'?"

Orlia ducked her head shyly and answered, "Are you not Cwen of Aaradan, milady?"

Cwen frowned and briefly considered killing Caen, but the tub was deep and the water was hot and her soap smelled like flowers, so her wrath was soon forgotten. She scrubbed her hair and brushed it free of tangles before braiding it and wrapping it high upon her head.

Orlia helped Cwen with the laces of her dress and led her back downstairs to her companions. Heads turned as she made her way toward their table.

All three men stood as she approached. Klaed pulled out a chair and so did Caen. Talin grinned at their enthusiasm while Cwen chose the chair that would place her between them.

"I have ordered a feast," Klaed said. "Broiled day doves and fresh bread instead of bannock, several jams, boiled roots and lots of tea and ale. Sidon remains in his room at the inn and will not depart for two days. We may as well enjoy the meal and the company."

"I wish to enter his room in the darkness and wake him with my blade," Cwen said looking at Caen.

"Aye, I shall take you if you like." He agreed, receiving warning glares from Talin and Klaed.

"For all of us to locate and enter his room would cause much commotion; if it is only Cwen and me we will draw no notice," Caen shrugged.

"I do not like it, but it does make some sense," Talin muttered.

"We will retrieve the ring and the shard and return here to collect you within an hour; if we leave straightaway we can be back at the forge camp by midday tomorrow if the mist continues to grip the sands. The flooding of the fields occurs in less than a fortnight. If the crimson fields hide a shard we should be able to discover it then," Cwen spoke in a low conspiratorial voice to her companions.

The meal was served and they ate with the gusto of those who have lived many days on dried stag and old bannock. Cwen served their tea and spread jam upon their bread, making them try each flavor and tell her which was best. Her eyes sparkled, her smile was bright and her laughter was unfettered by fear or anger.

Caen watched her and thought of Klaed's words. She was the daughter of the king's sister, not a woman for a thief and a ruffian, but a woman for a nobleman's son.

With a deep sigh he spoke her name, drawing her attention.

"Cwen, it is time you changed into more appropriate clothing if you wish to kill Sidon."

She froze and looked at each of them. "The festivities end," she said with a reluctant sigh. As they watched her walk toward the stairs, Caen spoke for all of them.

"To Lady Cwen," he raised his glass. "I have never seen a woman make a dress look so fine."

Sidon

Together Caen and Cwen crept up the dim hallway to the room Sidon had rented.

"What if he is not here?" Cwen whispered to Caen.

"If the ring and shard are not in the room then we shall wait for him."

Taking a set of picks from his bag he quickly unlocked the door and slid inside, drawing Cwen in behind him and closing the door with just a whispered click.

Sounds of breathing reached them and Caen turned to Cwen with a look of caution. The victim was present. As their eyes adjusted to the darkness they were able to make out Sidon's form on the small bed in the corner of the room. Daedra did not seem to be there.

Cwen drew her blade and crept toward the bed, pausing just out of arm's reach. She stared at the man's face, remembering the way he had laughed as Aidan held her out like a prize and the stench of his foul breath and body as he had covered her. With a deep breath she slid close and slipped her blade against his throat, watching as his eyes flew open.

"Cwen," he sighed, the word making the knife prick his neck and drawing a line of blood.

"I want my ring, Sidon. I want it now. It was not Aidan's to give."

Sidon's leer grew as his hand slid up and squeezed her breast, causing her to shrink away.

"Everything of yours was Aidan's Cwen – everything – and everything of Aidan's is now mine. Do not make me kill your friend." The foul stench of his breath brought a flood of gagging memories.

She felt tears sting her eyes and watched his look change to something more predatory, causing dark images of misuse to further cloud her mind. Behind her she heard an arrow being nocked and a bowstring drawn back.

"Give the lady her ring, Sidon. I killed Aidan for his transgressions against her and I shall kill you for yours. Cwen, move away from him." Caen's voice pricked the black bubble of Cwen's memories.

She backed away, shuddering, gooseflesh claiming her exposed skin. Handing her his bow, Caen drew a long, slender dagger and approached the cot where Sidon lay. With one hand grasping Sidon's throat, he placed the blade's sharp point against the right side of the man's abdomen and asked again.

"Where is the ring, Sidon?"

Sidon choked out a laugh and Caen drove the blade into his bowels, flipping a feather bolster over the man's face to stifle his high pitched scream. Slowly he withdrew the knife and placed it on the other side of the man's belly.

"They say eventually it begins to feel like a fire inside you, as the fecal matter infects your body and the fever grows ever hotter. I did not hear your answer. Where is the lady's ring?" he asked, removing the suffocating pillow.

"My bag. On the chair," Sidon gasped as his face grew pale.

"Cwen, check his bag."

Cwen opened the bag and rummaged through it, finding not only her ring, but also the necklace her mother had given her. It shimmered with precious metals, the dragon and the coiled serpent of the joined houses.

She held them up to show Caen she had found them.

"And the shard?" Caen asked Sidon.

"I do not have it," the man replied.

Caen drove the slender dagger through the muscles, again stifling the man's cries.

"That was not the answer I seek. Perhaps you would like to try again."

Caen shifted slightly, moving the blade to the center of Sidon's abdomen, turning it slowly and watching as horror finally claimed the man's face.

"The enchantress has already taken it. I do not know where she makes her lair."

"What enchantress?" Caen asked.

"Faervyn of Révérē she calls herself. I merely do her bidding. She asked me to gather the shard from Cwen and one from the old dragon."

Caen drawled, "You should choose your work more carefully."

He drove the dagger in a third time and Sidon's eyes rolled back and his head lolled to the side as he lost consciousness.

Caen went to Cwen and removed the bow from her hands. He saw her tears fall and hated Sidon almost as much as he had hated Aidan.

"Even with my dagger at his throat he saw my weakness and I feared him," she whispered in shame.

Cwen bit her lip and looked at Caen, her eyes bright with uncertainty.

"Cwen," he whispered, and pulled her to him.

He felt her arms slip around him and he whispered her name again.

"Men like this are not real, Cwen," Caen said, gesturing to Sidon. "They are only nightmares. Do not judge the rest of us harshly for the guilty shadows that they cast."

She pulled back and met his eyes.

"I did not like your kiss," she said, wiping her tears away.

"Nay, but Ezrael liked watching it, and that was more important at the time. Someday you will ask me for another and you will like it very much," Caen promised.

He reached up and touched away a final tear as it traveled down her cheek. Then he took her hand and led her out of the room where the nightmare lay and back toward the tavern.

Daedra returned to Sidon's room, jingling the coins in her pocket. She knew he would be pleased with the night's earnings.

His name remained frozen on her lips, for as she entered she saw his soul rising from his body as foul and black as the sludge that bubbled up beneath the swamps on Ælmondæ. Faervyn the enchantress stood beside him. The woman's eyes were closed and her lips murmured the words of some silent incantation. With one delicate hand she reached out and grasped Sidon's soul, causing it to writhe and constrict like some ethereal snake trying to escape her hold.

Little by little, as the enchantress whispered the words of her spell, Sidon's soul settled, resting motionlessly above his ravaged body. With a swift sweep of her hands she forced Sidon's black spirit to slip down and blanket his corpse. Then, with a brilliant flash of light it disappeared into the damaged flesh.

Daedra gasped and drew back as she saw Sidon draw a great heaving breath, the punctures in his abdomen gaping open and thick malodorous blood bubbling forth.

Daedra watched in horror as the enchantress breathed her hateful breath into Sidon's mouth and ran her fingers across his dreadful wounds, sealing them without leaving a scar.

Sidon's eyes opened. They were devoid of life, reflecting a soul of the damned that was ruled not by life, but by the demon of death, condemned to walk the earth and carry out the vile orders of the enchantress.

"Find me an army, Sidon, that I might use my shard," Faervyn whispered into Sidon's mind as she turned toward Daedra.

Beckoning Daedra forward, the enchantress watched with pleasure as the young woman shrank away from the icy flesh of her master.

The desert was not as kind to the travelers on their return to Dobbinwort's furnace. The mist no longer held the fine grains in its blanket. Blowing sand and lightning storms caused them numerous delays as they huddled among the fallen stones.

On his watch Talin called a large klenzingkyte to him.

"Fly, my friend," he instructed the large bird, "take my message to the Sojourner Ileana. We have lost a shard to one called Faervyn of Réverē."

Brengven's Warning

They entered Brengven's camp just before nightfall on the third day after leaving Bael. Smells of cooking stag drew sighs of anticipation. The stag was small and thin, but it was much appreciated after a long day's trek.

Brengven had not been turned into a fallowass and actually smiled at the sight of them, laughing loudly at Klaed's disheveled appearance.

"Looks like you killed someone and stole his clothes," the Feie quipped.

"The enchantress Faervyn has the shard from the Azure Sea," Talin said.

"And Sidon did not know the whereabouts of her lair; I would guarantee that he did not," Caen assured them. "He would have spoken it if he had known."

"Is he dead?" Brengven asked.

"If not today, he soon will be. I left him to die in the filth of his own intestines," Caen said, feeling the anger again.

"Did you bring me something of his?"

"Nay, I did not think of it," Caen shook his head.

"He held my ring and the necklace of the joined houses," Cwen spoke, "perhaps they will be useful?"

She dug into her knapsack and pulled out the necklace and took the signet from her finger, handing both to Brengven.

The little Feie held one in each hand and closed his eyes.

A sudden shudder coursed through his body and he tossed the jewels away. Blinking rapidly, he shook his head.

"She sees us," he whispered.

Within her lair deep beneath the Galenite fortress Faervyn laughed at the fear of the Feie. From the wounds on Sidon's throat and belly she had discovered the whereabouts of Caen and Cwen, watching them in the silver waters of her pool as they joined their companions and traveled through the desert and into the camp of the Feie. Unfortunately, the hateful little man had given the secret away and would soon remove the connection with his nasty little magick.

"Caen," the enchantress whispered, touching his image within the deep water of the divining pool, causing it to waver and distort. "Perhaps you would like to help me in my quest for power? I could give you the lovely Cwen as your prize; make her willing and grateful for your attention."

Sighing, Faervyn sent the images swirling with a touch, "I shall seek you out within the Crimson Plains. We shall decide together which path you will choose."

Her seductive laughter echoed through the halls as Brengven shielded the new objects of her desire from her view.

Faervyn closed her eyes, taking the form of the Xavian woman whose life she had ended and went to join her husband. Kayann, Galen called her.

Brengven cast a cleansing spell, shielding Caen and Cwen from the enchantress.

Shaking his head, he warned, "She has seen you, watched you as you traveled. She was trying to touch your minds. I did not see the location of her lair, but I sensed that she has taken human form to remain undiscovered. Perhaps she is living in one of the cities. I saw her divining pool; it was within a stone room."

Brengven shuddered again.

"She is evil. Do not allow her to touch you. If you see her do not look into her eyes; she can hold your soul and use you to cause great harm to those around you."

"How will we recognize her, Brengven?" Cwen asked.

"She will not come to you, Cwen; but she will hold you out as the prize. To the three of you she will be the most beautiful woman you have ever seen," he said, looking at Caen, Talin and Klaed.

Cwen shrugged at them. "And I suppose she will appear as a blue-eyed temptress."

"She will be whatever they wish to see," Brengven said soberly.

"We shall no longer stand watch alone, but in pairs," Talin said, pacing near the fire. "This woman has a wyrm shard and we cannot afford to be deceived and turned against one another."

"Aye," Cwen whispered, looking at each of them. "And since it appears I am the one at risk, I choose to stand watch with Klaed. Talin can stand with you, Caen. I will kill anyone who threatens me."

Dobbin's voice startled them as he wandered into their camp.

"I brings a gift for the thief." A wide grin brightening his face until he saw Brengven; then he sniffed and scowled as if he had smelled something rotten.

"Vile little man," Brengven fumed, grabbing his bedroll and heading toward the distant trees.

Dobbin clapped his hands in glee.

"Sees? I ran him off!"

"Dobbin, you should try to get along with the Feie. He helps us with our quest for the Queen."

"Bah, he could not helps himself out of a thicket of prickleberry. Stinky little man," Dobbin snorted.

From over his shoulder he pulled a gleaming short sword and held it out for them to see.

The hilt was carved with a spiral of willow leaves and the blade gleamed with the results of Dobbin's skill.

"It holds no magick," Dobbin said, "but it is strong and sharp and a far finer weapon than what you carries now."

"No man should have to quest without a sword from Dobbin." The Ancient winked at Cwen.

"Aye, Dobbin, it is a fine gift and I thank you for it," Caen said, hefting the sword and slicing the air with its swing.

Cwen's eyes grew bright as she drew her own blade.

"Shall we test it, thief?"

"With pleasure," Caen said, "provided you promise to heal me if

I am left bleeding."

Cwen tapped her blade against his as her eyes drew him toward her.

"I shall make no such promise. Klaed can heal you if he chooses. My advice is 'do not get cut'."

Talin and Klaed watched as the new sword flew against Cwen's double blades.

Dobbin chuckled gleefully at the hubbub he had caused.

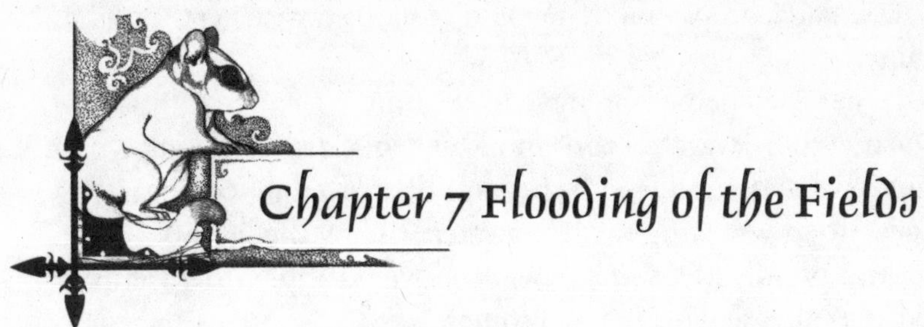

Chapter 7 Flooding of the Fields

The travelers stood on a small hillock overlooking the newly harvested fields of the Crimson Plains. The flood waters of the Arago River had already begun to rise, filling the fields with the rich silt carried by the runoff from the Northern Mountains.

Klaed's hand rested lightly on Cwen's shoulder, causing Caen to scowl and Talin to smile inwardly, as she offered her thoughts on the possible location of the next shard.

"I do not believe it will be within the farmlands, for someone would most likely have already found it there. Perhaps it lies within an abandoned field or orchard."

"Or perhaps someone has already found it," Talin suggested, thinking of Brengven's warning regarding Faervyn the enchantress.

"I have heard tales…" Brengven began, earning warning looks from all of them, "…of slithering creatures given life by the waters of the Arago when it drenches the fields."

"Keep your tales to yourself, Feie, for we do not wish to hear them. I am sure if there are slithering creatures anywhere near we will undoubtedly encounter them – and we will deal with them then." Cwen spoke for them all.

"I do not like things that slither," Talin mumbled, swinging his axe in readiness and catching Klaed's mischievous grin. "Well, I do not."

"We will set up a camp there." Brengven pointed to a nearby

meadow situated atop a hill that would remain above even the highest flood line.

Together they helped Brengven lay camp.

During their watch Talin and Caen divided the camp, each covering several dragon lengths beyond their sleeping companions.

Caen stood watching the floodwaters rise by the light of the full moons and pondered Cwen's newfound friendship with Klaed. She seemed very at ease with the newcomer.

"And you wish she felt at ease in your presence, thief?" a sultry voice asked from the shadows.

Turning, Caen watched a vision of beauty glide toward him from the heavy darkness beneath the trees. The woman wore a scarlet cloak, its hood tossed back to reveal pale, heavy tresses falling far below her waist. Her eyes were the bluest he had ever seen and sparkled like light over a glacial pool.

"I seek an ally, a hero for my cause – and I am willing to pay well for his service." Her silken voice flowed over him.

"What cause is that, milady?" Caen asked, gazing deep into the woman's eyes and finding fire there.

Her smile was lazy and seductive with the promise of her rewards.

"I wish to rule Ædracmoræ. Do you not think I would be a sublime queen, Caen? Perhaps you are interested in becoming one of the nobility so that you might be in a position to compete with the son of the Councilor? Or perhaps you would rather just take what you wish from the girl with golden eyes?"

Caen laughed. "You must be new to Ædracmoræ, milady, if you do not know the Dragon Queen – and I would not make a good nobleman, for I lack the social graces that station requires. As for Cwen…"

The visions blinded Caen's soul and burned him with their heat.

"Yes Caen, Cwen – the one you desire. Long you have suffered to win her. Is it not time for your reward?"

"Caen!"

His name was a curse in his ear.

"I do not know who you think you are talking to, but there is no one here." Talin's eyes were hard and his voice cold.

"Aye, she was here," came Caen's whispered response, "and she wanted my soul in servitude."

Morning dawned damp and stiflingly hot. The floodwaters had risen across the land, leaving it covered beneath the silt-filled water. The crimson grasses were hidden under the dark blanket of the life-giving flood.

Caen saw the suspicious glances Klaed and Cwen cast in his direction and knew that Talin had warned them of the enchantress's visit. He sighed deeply and wondered if it would have been possible to deny her if Talin had not intervened. Probably not. The visions she had sent were burned into his mind and he could not look at Cwen without seeing them again.

"*Caen is weak and cannot be trusted*," Talin spoke into Cwen's mind.

"*I think he is stronger than you believe*." Her unspoken words surprised Talin.

"*Are you willing to risk yourself for your belief in him, Cwen? I am not willing to take the risk, regardless of what you think. I want you to remain with Brengven while we seek the shard.*"

"You do not decide what risk I take. Not today, not ever. I take what risks I choose, Talin. I decide," she snapped loud enough to be heard by all.

"Do you not recall the outcome of risking Aidan's company?" Talin snarled, instantly regretful.

Heat rose to Cwen's face at the harshness of his words.

"I was young and had not learned that most of what men say is lies."

Talin placed his hand on her shoulder, but she shook it off, glaring with an anger he had often seen used against others. She stalked off to her bedroll and began to pack her things.

"*He is angry because he does not know how to protect you from the enchantress's threat*." Klaed's voice was soft within her mind.

She twisted toward him, eyes flashing a warning.

"I am not his to protect. Look at the three of you! All of you want something from me and I cannot give what any of you want. I cannot allow Talin to protect me for I must learn to protect myself, or you or Caen to possess me because I have seen what it does. I am weary of the games of men." She shrugged with finality and threw her knapsack over her shoulder and placed her weapons in their sheaths.

As she walked away, Klaed reached out and grabbed her arm. Her blade swept out swiftly and cut him deeply across the chest.

"Do not ever touch me again!" she spat as he crumpled to the ground clutching the wound.

Brengven watched in horror and sprang forward to stop the bleeding and cast a healing spell.

"Girl!" he called after her, but she did not even glance around at the sound of his shout.

"Go get her!" he shouted at Caen and Talin. Both of them stared at him as if he had gone mad.

They watched her as she slogged through the water and headed south toward Æshardæ and the port where she would hire a boat to take her back to Ælmondæ.

A sudden gaseous bubbling in the water around her caused Cwen to cry out, but the scaly hands that reached for her were strong and drew her into the watery grave before she could call out a second time.

"CWEN!" Talin's shout was hoarse and strangled by shock. He raced forward and leapt into the waist deep water. He swept his arms through the black water, finding nothing but her pack. Standing, he looked back toward his companions in disbelief.

"Get out of the water!" Brengven shouted, pointing to a swiftly moving streak headed toward Talin.

Swinging to face the threat, Talin drew his axe and slammed it into the approaching enemy, slicing through thick scales and muscle, filling the water around him with a froth of bright blood. Reaching down, he hauled up the front half of an unbelievable creature and dragged it up the hillock, tossing it to the ground in front of Brengven.

"What is that and what has it done with Cwen?" Talin growled.

"Naga. I did not believe the tales," Brengven answered, shaking his head.

Before them lay half of a body: the head and face resembled a man's, but it was covered in tight black scales. The black eyes stared blankly from the dead face. A long forked tongue hung from the corner of a mouth still open in a grimace of agony. The rest of the body was serpentine, with the exception of muscular arms and strong hands that appeared human. These too were covered in dark luminous scales. Had the entire body been present it would have extended more than the length of three men and measured the size of an average man's waist at its thickest point.

"I do not know what became of the woman," Brengven added truthfully.

Talin thrust out her pack to the Feie.

"Find her."

A sudden shriek behind them caused them to jump and draw weapons.

Cwen rose from the darkness with both swords drawn, screaming in rage and defiance. Blood boiled in the churning water and pieces of flesh and scale floated around her. She stood, chest heaving as she gasped for breath, swinging in a circle as she sought her enemies.

"Perhaps you would like to return to the safety of the camp?" Brengven called.

"Aye, that was my plan." She glowered at them, brushing the wet hair from her face and staggering from the water.

As she passed Brengven she snatched her bag from his hands.

Talin held a blanket out before him with his arms spread open wide.

"You still trust me enough to hold the blanket while you change your clothes?" His voice held a hint of sarcasm.

"Talin, I trust you as if you were a sister." Cwen's face held only a trace of her previous irritability.

She pulled the blanket from him and stood before him in her dry clothes.

"You know I do not truly wish to be your protector. I am far too busy and you are far too much trouble," he said with a frown, picking a piece of scaly flesh from Cwen's hair and handing it to her.

"What are they?" she asked, looking at the shiny scales before tossing it away.

"Brengven called them naga. They look like some sorcerer's failed attempt to create a new beast." Talin shrugged.

Klaed and Caen approached warily, neither coming within Cwen's reach.

Holding out her hand, she looked directly at Caen.

"I need a strip of leather for my hair," she said, watching as he quickly unwound one from around his wrist and handed it to her.

"Talin thinks you are a threat to me, Caen. Are you?" she asked as she pulled her hair back and bound it.

Caen gave a sharp laugh and shook his head in denial.

"Nay, any hold the enchantress had was driven from me as I watched Klaed bleed."

She shifted her eyes to Klaed.

"And is it clear to you that I will not be touched unless it is at my request?"

Klaed backed away, holding up his hands in surrender, "You made it very clear, Cwen."

She swung away and called to Brengven, "And you, do you have any ideas, Feie?"

"About what?" he called back.

"About how I should behave or what I should do," Cwen shouted.

"Nay, none whatsoever; your behavior is none of my business," he returned.

"Fine. Then I shall stay," she said, heading for the fire and a cup of tea. Behind her three men and a Feie grinned broadly.

Faervyn's Army

Deep beneath the earth, several leagues from the small border city of Calá, Faervyn the enchantress stood gazing out over her new army. She reached out and stroked Sidon as one would a pet flier and smiled at Daedra.

Withdrawing the emerald wyrm shard from her cloak she held it out for them to see.

"It is only the beginning of our reign. We shall test the strength of this small group of soldiers against the citizens of Calá. Then you will bring me many more shards and I shall release many armies of the G'lm upon Ædracmoræ. Soon the Dragon Queen will grovel in the dust at my feet and I shall give her to you as a gift, Sidon."

Sweeping upward to the altar where the shard's receptacle lay, the enchantress held the throbbing crystal above it and whispered an ancient prayer to the ones who had ruled before. Lowering her hands she allowed the shard to settle into its resting place and whirled to watch her army receive new life.

The shard pulsed rapidly, its rhythm growing more insistent with each beat. A sudden flash of deep emerald light shot out across the cavern, seeking the eyes of each soldier. Gently caressing them from the crown of each head to the soles of the feet, the light played over and around each demon and deathshade, changing dusty gray stone to deathly gray flesh and releasing the voices of the horde. They screeched, howled, screamed and roared, eager to be away and doing the bidding of their new mistress.

Raising her hand, Faervyn commanded her army.

"To Calá! Seek out every living thing within the city and along the way. Kill them! Kill every living thing!" she shouted, her eyes glowing with the delight of her success as she watched the army march toward the exit of the cavern – step forward to commit the atrocities she had directed.

As the G'lm strode from beneath the earth they cut a swathe of death before them. It was as if the very thunder of their footsteps drove the life out of everything before them. The grass withered before their feet and the trees and shrubs faded and lost color; beasts and fowl fell dead as they passed, leaving behind a roadway of disease and destruction.

Overhead storm clouds gathered and lightning flashed, followed by the angry voice of thunder. A long narrow tempest of darkness followed the army across the land, bringing with it the chill air of a slowly dying world.

Gazing out across the countryside Yáviё the Dragon Queen watched the narrow strip of storm clouds form and heard the cries of the deathshades as they headed for Calá.

"Sōrél!" she shouted, "Call the Guardians! The G'lm have been released upon the earth."

Together they ran for the garrison, calling for swift action. Within moments a battalion of Guardians was mounted and on the way to defend Ædracmoræ against the coming destruction.

By the time they reached Calá little remained of the small settlement. Bodies littered the road along which the army had traveled and the citizens of Calá were dead or dying. Many had been partially consumed as the voracious G'lm swept over the city.

The Guardians swept in from above, diving down upon the enemy from the backs of their dragons. The acidic breath of the accordant dragons sizzled and released searing gasses as the G'lm fell before them. The war dragons rained fire across the enemy, consuming them in flame.

As the Guardians landed their dragons outside the city's remaining walls they raced forward to fight the demonic soldiers on the ground. The din of death was deafening as Guardians and demons shrieked and roared in battle. When Sōrél's Bow of Ages pinned the last deathshade to a wall, the storm clouds broke overhead and the day star's light shone down on the remnants of the city and its few living inhabitants. The air did not warm, for the chill brought by the G'lm remained.

"We were fortunate," Yávië whispered. "This was only a small band of G'lm and look at the destruction they have caused. Talin must be contacted and they must be urged to move more quickly in the search for the shards that control the dark horde. If they do not find them soon, Ædracmoræ is doomed."

"I will send Nall," Sōrél said brusquely.

Seeing his wife's uneasy look, he added, "Cwen will just have to accept it."

In the cavern where she waited, Faervyn snarled in rage, pushing Sidon away from her and tossing Daedra to the ground before her.

"Go! Bring me more shards and find me more soldiers! I will not have my hand stayed for the lack of an army!"

Nall

Their heads were bowed over Klaed's map of the area when the distant sound of a dragon's flight caught their attention.

Cwen instantly recognized the large brutish dragon as Ardor, her father's chosen mount.

Standing in indecision, she looked to Talin for guidance.

"Just do not get mad, Cwen. Hear him out and let him go."

The large dragon settled noisily onto the hillock near the floodwaters and Nall leapt to the ground and strode purposefully toward Talin and his companions.

"Calá has been destroyed by a small army of the G'lm. The Queen has sent me to urge you to act more swiftly." Nall spoke directly to Talin without looking at Cwen.

"You ungrateful son of a witch's tit! Find the shards yourself! Damn you, Nall!" Cwen's rage flared and her eyes blazed in fury at her father's arrogance.

Talin held up his hand to stop her, but without hesitation she drew her sword, disengaging the hilt and approaching Nall with a blade in each hand.

"Get out of my camp before I kill you and leave Näeré a widow."

Nall's eyes narrowed and he lifted his sword from his back, breaking it at the hilt as his daughter had done, holding a blade in each hand.

"Do you truly wish to die today?" he snapped at Cwen.

"I would rather die than be in your company!" she spat back.

Klaed tackled Cwen from the side, taking a nasty cut to the upper arm before he and Caen finally wrestled the swords away from her.

"Nobody is going to die – at least not today, Cwen. Go, Nall; you are not welcome in the lady's camp. Tell the Queen the message has been delivered and the pawns have rebelled. Only a fool like King Sōrél could have sent you here."

Pulling Cwen to her feet Klaed handed back her swords and examined his injury.

"Twice in as many days you have cut me, Cwen," he said, wearily shaking his head.

She did not hear him and her eyes were fixed on Nall, her hatred so heavy the air hung with it.

"Tell them I will kill you if you come again." Her glare intensified. "Tell them."

"How did I get the spawn of a demon for a daughter?" Nall said, sheathing his sword.

"Because you are a father from the depths of the abyss!" she screamed, drawing her dagger and charging at him again.

This time Talin intervened, grabbing her around the waist and lifting her off her feet as he jerked the blade from her hand.

"Perhaps it would be best if you found others to quest for the shards."

Nall's jaw dropped, his eyes widened with disbelief.

"You would withdraw from the quest because I have a demented daughter?"

Cwen kicked against Talin and tried to bite him.

"Take her," he called to Klaed.

Klaed lifted Cwen and threw her over his shoulder.

"Do not bite me, Cwen," he warned.

"We would withdraw from the quest because we stand with Cwen. You do not know her, Nall." Talin's eyes were cold and his voice edged with anger.

"The shard is near. We will recover it within the next two passings of the day star. I will deliver it to you at the Galenite fortress and you can let me know then whether we are to be given the freedom to recover the others. We are not Guardians, Nall. We do not fly about on thundering dragons, nor do we carry the aura you do, but it does not make us any less valuable for this quest, does it?"

Nall shook his head and backed toward Ardor.

"You have all fallen under the spell of her insanity. I will look for you in two days, Talin."

With that he strode back to Ardor, mounted and urged the dragon to flight.

"Well, Cwen, that could have gone better," Talin said to her as she hung upside down over Klaed's shoulder. "At least we did not let you kill him."

Her eyes still glowed with the fever of her fury, but her breathing had slowed and she was no longer clawing against Klaed's back.

"If I put you down do you promise not to hurt us?" Klaed asked, lifting her from his shoulder.

"I will not hurt you," she mumbled.

As he set her on her feet she swung and viciously kicked Caen in the shins.

"Next time do not help them disarm me," she snapped at him.

She sat down at the fire, drawing her cloak around her as the exhaustion of her fury took hold.

Klaed came bringing a mug of ale.

"Talin said it would help warm you and make you sleep."

"And did he say that I would stumble about in a most unladylike fashion and end up snoring?"

"Nay, he did not."

She reached out and took the mug, sipping the ale and feeling its warmth.

"None for yourself?" she asked.

"Nay, we felt it wise to remain sober and alert, since it took all three of us to best you," he teased.

Brengven arrived from his nearby camp asking, "Who arrived on the dragon?"

He drew quick glares from all but Cwen, who had already given in to the fatigue left by her rage.

Field Sprites

There was no evidence of returning naga. The floodwaters lay calm and the silt had drifted to the bottom, leaving the water slightly brown but clear enough to see the crimson grass that lay beneath.

Talin stepped into it first, his axe raised against unseen enemies that might lurk below. Together they headed for the next hillock about ten dragon lengths away. As they waded through the water the silt rose in swirling patterns around their feet and the vibration of their steps called the naga from their burrows in the earth.

Cwen felt the slithering beast as it passed her leg and sent an arrow through it pinning it to the earth.

"Run, get to the hillock! The water is full of them," she called to her companions.

Blades flashed and arrows flew, killing several of the naga and tainting the churning waters with their blood.

As the four stood upon the mound and gazed out at the water they saw the naga move toward them as a unit, but none left the safety of the flooded field.

"How will we make any progress if we cannot wade through the water of the fields?" Caen asked.

Klaed's captivating smile took in their discouraged faces and he whispered, "The magick of sorcery is at your service."

"Would you care to help, Cwen?" his mischievous voice teased.

"Nay, I do not practice the art of magick."

"Then watch and be amazed at what I learned from the Sorceress Näeré."

"You promised not to speak her name, remember?" Cwen gave him a stern look.

"Then watch and be amazed at what I learned from some unnamed sorceress," he restated, with a wink for Cwen.

Stepping forward to within inches of the water he threw up his hands and began the incantation to call the lightning. Clouds gathered quickly, blacking out the light of the day star as the darkness deepened and the sky fluxed with the assembling storm clouds. The first strike was short and its following thunder muffled, but as the electricity within the clouds built the charges became greater, their blue-white light blinding and the crash of their thunder booming. The lightning touched the surface of the water, running swiftly across the field and leaving in its wake sizzling naga and the stench of burning flesh.

Klaed pushed the storm forward across the valley, striking the earth with its killing bolts over and over until the smoke of the burning beasts was heavy in the air.

Lowering his hands he glanced back at his companions and bowed before them as if he were the jester of the queen concluding a performance.

"She said you were good, but she did not say just how good," Talin laughed. "Thank you for your assistance, old friend. Can you really do that too, Cwen?"

She shrugged and looked at Klaed. "It was child's play."

"Milady, I am no child as I am sure you have noticed," he said, raising his eyebrows.

She burst out laughing and shook her head.

"You may not be a child, but you certainly act like a fool."

"You defame me, milady! It is no act. I am a fool."

Again her laughter bubbled forth and she cautioned him.

"Stop it; you promised not to smile at me."

Turning to Talin he asked, "Am I smiling?"

"Nay, that is just the way you look, fool," Talin chuckled.

"Caen, did you not say we were fools to follow Cwen?"

"Aye, I did indeed. And as I feel the fresh bruises on my shins with every step I take I find that I have not changed my mind," Caen said, glancing at Cwen. "Why did you not kick Klaed and Talin? They helped disarm you too."

Her laugh came slowly and her eyes lowered as she answered. "I expect the two dandies to do such things, but I do not expect it of you."

"I am not a dandy!" Talin refuted. "Klaed yes, but not I."

Pointing at him she laughed again.

"You forget I have seen you in your finery, my Lord Talin."

Talin roared with laughter.

"Lord Talin and Lady Cwen. We should have our own kingdom. We could allow unsavory characters like Caen to become noble and honorable."

"I believe I prefer to remain unsavory, Talin," Caen chuckled.

"Cwen of Aaradan?" a small voice called.

They spun around looking for the speaker, but saw no one.

Weapons drawn, they moved back to back, eyes sharp with suspicion.

Several small sparkles of light drifted past them. Each held a tiny being no more than a few thumbs in height, perfectly formed in the image of male or female. Each was dressed in trousers or a skirt of brilliant scarlet with a matching waistcoat. Upon their heads each wore a crown of delicate emerald flowers over shining black curls.

"Are you Cwen of Aaradan?" one of the small beings asked again.

"Aye, I am Cwen."

"We are the field sprites and have come to show you to that which you seek. The Feie told us you were here," the tiny voice spoke.

"Brengven sent you to us?"

"Aye. He said seek out Cwen of Aaradan and tell her of the shard within the tree. It is there to the north, less than one league. You will come upon an orchard of long dead pappleberry trees. They have mostly turned to stone, and one at the center of the orchard looks like a standing man. At its heart you will find the wyrm shard. It was hidden long ago beneath the earth and as the tree grew it pulled the shard into itself and grew up around it."

"Thank you, sprites; you have saved us much time in hunting for the shard. We are in debt to you," Cwen said as the small sprites pulsed with pleasure at her gratitude.

"You have killed many naga and so saved the lives of many field folk. It is repayment enough," the wee man spoke again.

"Good-bye Cwen of Aaradan. Tell Yáviё our stone brothers ask after her."

With that the tiny sparkles of light flickered and swept off toward the east.

Caen shook his head in wonder.

"I have never seen a sprite before," he whispered.

"Nor have I, thief, but it is apparent our Queen is quite familiar with them," Talin remarked.

"I have seen them among the Giant Stones," Cwen whispered, remembering a visit there with Yáviё and Sōrél.

"Well, now we have all seen them," Klaed said. "And so we should be off after the shard before the dragon rider is forced to return."

Cwen gave him a black look, but it turned to laughter as he grimaced in false despair and begged her not to hurt him.

They crossed the field toward the ancient orchard the sprites had spoken of, pushing dead naga aside as they went.

As they climbed over a small hill they saw the trees ahead. Hundreds of trees, all dead and so old they had simply become stone. The trunks were gnarled and beaten by time and the long branches reached skyward as if in some silent spell casting ceremony.

At the orchard's center they discovered the tree that looked like a man. The main trunk was split and to each side an arm-like branch reached out, ending in hand-like appendages with slender fingers of twigs. At the center a large bulbous growth rose like an ugly head. Indeed it did look very much like a man become a tree.

Talin drew his axe and waved the others back. With a great heave he struck the tree at the center of its 'head,' splitting it right down the middle. As the sides fell away, the beautiful sapphire shard became visible within the remaining fibers of the tree's heart. Taking his dagger, Talin gently removed the shard and handed it to Cwen, watching as she slipped it into her knapsack. He knew she too was thinking of her mother's bright blue eyes.

Brengven's eyes grew large at the sight of the sapphire heart shard.

"You will take it to the fortress, Talin? First thing on the morrow we should leave. We can camp within the woods beyond and await your return."

Brengven looked to Cwen for her approval and received her curt nod.

"Take Klaed with you to the fortress. Caen and I shall stay with Brengven," she instructed Talin, watching as disagreement flickered briefly before he nodded his head and mumbled, "Aye."

Nall strode toward Talin and Klaed as they entered the gates of the Galenite fortress.

"You have the Queen's acceptance of your terms and the freedom to search at your discretion has been granted, though she does still request that you not dally," Nall said tersely. "Follow me."

Klaed and Talin exchanged an uneasy glance and followed Nall.

"She is totally unreasonable," Nall muttered under his breath.

"The Queen?" Talin asked, overhearing his remark.

"Nay, my daughter," Nall said, pausing and turning to stare at Talin and Klaed. "Not only does she betray me herself, but she causes me to lose good men as well."

Shaking his head he turned on his heel and headed back toward the council chambers.

At the large, ornately carved table sat the Council. All examined Talin and Klaed with interest as Talin placed the shard on the table before the Queen.

"I understand that Cwen has threatened one of my Guardians?" the Queen spoke with a quizzical look on her face.

"Aye, and if you have a lick of sense you will not send him to her again," Klaed answered, gazing toward Sōrél and receiving a smile in return.

"But how will they ever come to terms if they never encounter one another, Klaed? Does your father know you address the Queen with such little respect?" Sōrél's grin widened.

"I am sure that he does; however, I do apologize to the Queen." Klaed bowed deeply to Yávië, causing her to chuckle.

"It is good I do not stand on ceremony, or you would have lost your head long ago," she returned.

"Talin, you hold great sway over Cwen. If you cannot control her, I must ask that she leave the quest. Word reached me that you had traveled to the port city of Bael. What could possibly have drawn you there?"

Klaed's fists clenched and Talin shook his head, cautioning him.

"It is time someone spoke the truth," Klaed muttered.

"What truth would that be?" Nall asked belligerently. "That it is my fault she is beyond all reason."

"Aye," Klaed nodded his agreement, receiving a second warning glance from Talin.

Näeré placed her hand on Nall's arm, flooding his mind with her calming thoughts.

"She wanted to kill me," he fumed.

"Nay, she did not, or she would not have allowed us to disarm her," Talin shrugged.

Yávië held up her hand to halt the conversation.

"The devastation of Calá is beyond what you can imagine. If there were time I would send you there and have you smell the stench of death. This was caused by fewer than a hundred soldiers of the G'lm. Do you understand my concern, Talin?"

"Aye, and if you had sent a different emissary, so would Cwen. I will tell her of the urgency. Our next search takes us to the southern ice fields. I shall send word when the shard has been collected."

Nodding to the Council he turned away from them, expecting Klaed to follow.

"You have judged your daughter harshly, Nall. I have seen…"

"Klaed, it is not your place…" Talin cautioned.

With a last glare at Nall, Klaed strode swiftly from the Council chambers, slamming the door behind him.

"What is it you do not wish him to say, Talin?" Nall snarled.

"You will have to ask Cwen," Talin snapped back before storming out the door after Klaed, back toward their camp and Cwen.

"*What is it the Council said that is bothering you so badly?*" Cwen spoke silently to Talin.

"A small group of those stone soldiers totally destroyed Calá, Cwen. What if we fail and many are released?" His eyes were filled with apprehension as they sought hers.

She shook her head and answered aloud. "We will not fail, Talin. We can use the Equus to travel more swiftly, though we will become more obvious if we do."

"Nay, it is wiser to remain hidden, although it is obvious Domangart and the enchantress are aware of the soldiers. One of them must have released them on Calá." Talin hung his head. "A little adventure has unexpectedly become a great burden."

Cwen's eyebrows rose.

"Already you tire of saving the world, Talin?"

"Nay, but I suddenly realize it truly needs saving."

"Cwen?" Caen's voice questioned.

"Aye, Caen?"

"What is it that Klaed is doing?"

Cwen stood and stared toward the field adjacent to the Galenite fortress. Klaed came toward them leading four bullrams. As he grew closer she could see his wide and cocky smile.

"I grow tired of walking," he shouted and, "and after all, I am a dandy."

Cwen, Talin and Caen collapsed with laughter.

Brengven held his nose and made a nasty face.

"Disgusting beasts smell more foul than mortals," he snorted and held his nose.

"Well they will be in your care while we are in the ice fields, so you had best learn to like them quickly," Klaed told the Feie, receiving a look of revulsion in return.

Chapter 8 The Eternal Flame

As they dressed in warmer clothing for the trek onto the glaciers, Klaed settled the bullrams in a grassy field just beyond the ice. Hobbling them, he instructed Brengven in their care as the Feie covered his nose and mouth with his cloak.

"I have belled the oldest female so listen for the sound. If you do not hear it they have wandered too far and you must collect them and bring them in. There are three bags of fodder, sufficient for at least a fortnight. It will supplement the grass they consume. And be sure they get plenty of water."

"Why is it mortals insist on traveling with beasts that require so much care?" Brengven asked, sneezing the foul odor of the beasts from his nostrils.

"Because we are lazy and like to ride."

As the topaz star crested the mountain ridge the travelers set off in search of the fifth shard.

Sensing Cwen's unease, Klaed fell into step beside her as she shivered in the cold morning air. He pulled a pair of heavy mittens from his pocket and handed them to her.

"Put them on over those." He pointed at the ones she already wore.

Looking up at him she shivered again and nodded gratefully, pulling the new mittens over her own.

"Are you not cold?"

"Aye, I am freezing," he admitted, stuffing his hands inside his cloak.

Nothing but great sheets of ice lay before them as day after day they pushed deeper into the Halcyon Ice Fields. Often their eyes were blinded by flurries of snow that blurred their surroundings and left them lost.

Exhaustion plagued them and each night's tiny fire was the highlight of the day.

As Cwen stood watch with Klaed she saw the lines of weariness in his face and wished she could offer him some comfort. Sighing, she poked the fire with a twig. A sudden howling wind swept across the camp, blowing the embers of their fire across the ice and leaving the fire ring empty of flame.

"We shall probably freeze in this white death," Klaed murmured as he attempted to tease the fire back to life.

"I do not want to die here," Cwen whispered.

"Where do you want to die, Cwen?"

"In a place where it is much warmer," she laughed, shaking off the solemn mood.

Squinting into the night she grabbed Klaed's arm and pointed ahead of them.

"A light. I saw a light. There!" she pointed as she caught sight of the glimmer again.

"Did you see it?" She turned to see him nodding.

"Wake Talin; I will get Caen," he said, pushing her toward the huddled form that was the sleeping Talin.

They forged through the deep snow toward the flickering light, finally reaching the remains of two great stone doors. Above them burned an eternal flame. It looked as if someone had crushed the doors and the rubble of their remains lay littered along the passage leading into the gloom before them. Lighting torches they examined the path ahead. It was steep, and glass-like walls of ice lined the way, giving off a deep frosty chill.

They inched forward in wariness, remaining close together. With torches in one hand and weapons in the other, they were ready for what might be hiding within the caverns. Light from the torches sent eerie shadows across the icy walls and the silence was as deafening as the wails of deathshades would have been.

They reached the end of the long passageway and heard Cwen's sharp intake of breath as she caught sight of the great cavern before them.

It was the chamber where many souls had been imprisoned; they had stumbled into Abaddon's Abyss.

Slowly tiptoeing forward in a tight group, the explorers shifted and turned, senses alert to any danger as they stared in awe at the remains of the crystals where hundreds of souls had been imprisoned by Abaddon and tormented for ages until the Guardians had set them free.

"Nall was held here," Cwen whispered.

"Aye, long ago Cwen, very long ago. The soul thief Abaddon remains imprisoned by the Sojourners; there is no danger here now," Talin answered, running his hand over a shattered crystal.

"Here," Cwen said, kneeling before the remains of the crystal that had once held her father's soul.

"He was here."

Her fingers touched the crystal and images charged into her mind with terrifying speed.

Nall in torment so terrible it caused his soul to withdraw from the wickedness that surrounded him. Images of her father with Aléria, of the deaths of his friends, of Sōrél betraying Yávië, images to tear Cwen's father's soul apart and leave him endlessly tormented.

The agony was so fierce it caused Cwen to cry out in anguish, drawing Klaed near.

"He suffered so." Cwen looked up, her eyes wide with disbelief. "Why did they never tell me of his suffering?"

"Some things are too horrible to speak aloud," Klaed said, searching Cwen's eyes. "Perhaps he could not speak of it."

Thinking of her own torment at the hands of Aiden, Cwen gave a brittle smile.

"Who do we have here?" whispered a soft sweet voice, causing Klaed to look around for Yávië the Dragon Queen.

Cwen looked up and met the woman's violet eyes, watching as they deepened in color with the realization that she was Nall's daughter.

"Aléria." Cwen took a deep breath, swallowing her fear.

Nodding as she approached, Yávië's twin cocked her head and answered with a soft laugh so like the Queen's it sent chills across Cwen's skin. "You recognize me? Has your charming father spoken of me often?"

"My father never mentioned your name," Cwen answered honestly, "and he never speaks to me."

"How sad," Aléria said.

Swinging quickly, she caught Talin backhanded, throwing him across the cavern and into a crevasse as he attempted to strike her with his axe.

Cwen's eyes widened and she emitted a strangled cry.

"Talin!" she screamed as she watched his body slide into the darkness of the abyss.

"Why?" her eyes glistened with tears as she sought Aléria's.

Klaed and Caen surged forward, weapons raised.

"Tell them to back away, Cwen, if you do not wish to see them die too," Aléria hissed.

Cwen held out her hand toward Caen who had drawn his sword, eyes glittering, mouth curled into a snarl.

"Go. Klaed, go with him. Go find Talin. I will be fine here with Aléria."

"Yes, little Cwen will be safe with me. I am an old friend of the family. Go; check on the one who fell," Aléria reached out to stroke Cwen's face, her sarcastic laughter echoing off the walls of the vast cavern.

Cwen cast silent terror-ridden thoughts out to her mother.

Näeré suddenly appeared in Yávië's chamber, grabbing the queen's arm and screaming, "Aléria has Cwen in Abaddon's Abyss. I heard Cwen call."

With a quick wave of her hand, Näeré created a rift in front of them and dragged Yávië into Abaddon's Abyss.

Yávië drew the Sword of Domesius as she had once so very long ago when she came to do battle with her twin, Aléria, a time when she had come to free Nall's soul from captivity in Abaddon's Abyss.

She whispered to Näeré, "Let us finally end it here today."

Näeré swore her solemn agreement.

Entering the chamber they saw Aléria standing before Cwen, her back to them. Cwen's eyes widened at the sight of them, alerting

Aléria to the danger, but not quickly enough.

Näeré's staff flashed with brilliant sapphire light, its energy throwing Aléria into the ceiling before dropping her to the cavern floor. Aléria leapt to her feet, sending a wave of force at Näeré, driving her back against the wall.

Rising Näeré called out, "Long you have tormented my family." She spoke through clenched jaws, her eyes flashing. "Never again, Aléria; never again will you rise from slumber."

With a flick of her wrist she launched a heavy block of ice across the cavern, narrowly missing Aléria as she rolled away.

"Yávië," Aléria whispered with hatred, seeing her twin behind Näeré.

Aléria drew her swords and called to her sister, "Yávië, do you now allow the sorceress to fight your battles? Nall's little witch does not have the power to defeat me. Nor do you!"

Motioning Näeré back, Yávië raised the scarlet-bladed Sword of Domesius and moved with determined steps toward her sister as Aléria prepared to defend against her.

Yávië did not rush but kept her eyes locked on Aléria's as she swept the sword back and forth like a serpent seeking a strike; then, suddenly, she slammed against her sister with a wicked backhand swing followed by a quick thrust that narrowly missed Aléria's ribs. Yávië saw Aléria's chin lift and she moved back a step preparing to meet the new aggression. Battering Aléria back, Yávië watched her sister's look of disbelief as she realized her weakness and spun away in an attempt to strike from behind.

As their swords locked and Yávië pressed against Aléria's blade, she looked her sister in the eye and hissed, "I am no longer the weak second sister, Aléria. I am the Queen of Ædracmoræ and the Seven Kingdoms and today I decree no mercy."

With that she swiftly drew back the fiery sword and thrust it deep into Aléria's chest, watching with detachment as her sister slid to the ground, clutching the weeping wound.

Shaking her head, Yávië withdrew a small violet creation crystal from the pouch she carried against her heart.

"Once I spared you, sister; even though your transgressions were great and had left grievous wounds on the souls of many I loved, I spared you. In gratitude you entered my mind and placed deception there, causing me to doubt Sōrél. The harm you have caused is far beyond redemption, Aléria. Today there will be no such mercy."

Extending the crystal toward her sister, Yáviё spoke the words that would imprison Aléria's soul and destroy the body she treasured beyond reclamation. She listened dispassionately to Aléria's final screams as her soul was drawn bit by bit into the void of the tiny crystal. As Aléria's final cries were stilled by the walls of her prison and her remains fell to dust, Yáviё swung toward Näeré and said once again, "By the power of the House of Aaradan, I declare no mercy." With that, she dropped the crystal to the floor of the cavern and crushed it beneath the scarlet blade of her sword. No word of lament was spoken; no tear of regret was shed for Aléria.

"Mother!" Cwen's voice was shrill as she flew into her mother's arms. "Why did you not tell me father suffered so?"

Näeré held her daughter and whispered her questioned truth, "Would it have mattered?"

Klaed and Caen had managed to pull Talin from the crevasse ledge where he had landed and now they stood by silently watching Näeré soothe Cwen.

Klaed knelt before Yáviё and kissed the ring of her authority. "Your majesty," he said with humble gratitude.

Yáviё bid him to rise and said to him, "Perhaps there is hope for you as a nobleman yet, Klaed. Now introduce me to the thief."

"Caen. His name is Caen," Klaed spoke, beckoning Caen forward.

"Kneel before the Queen," Klaed urged Caen, but Yáviё waved his words away.

"You are the thief who quests to protect my kingdoms?" Yáviё asked.

Caen shook his head, "Nay, I am the fool who follows Cwen."

Laughing, Yáviё turned to look at Cwen. "It seems you have a larger entourage than I, Cwen. Many seem anxious to serve you."

"They do not serve me, Yáviё. They are my friends, though they may also be fools." Cwen cast a glance at Caen.

Näeré drew a shimmering rift before her and looked toward Yáviё. "Let us go and ease the minds of those who may miss us."

Drawing Cwen near, she whispered, "I love you, daughter."

Cwen sighed, tears welling in her golden eyes as she watched her mother go, but still she could not return the words.

As the rift closed behind their saviors, Caen shook his head and looked at the tiny shards of crystal on the floor at his feet. All that remained of Aléria's soul was a small black stain upon the ice.

"She would have killed us all." His voice held the awe he felt at Näeré and Yávië's powerful intervention.

"It still does not make me wish to be a Guardian," Cwen said. "And no, I could not have done that," she added, seeing the question on Talin's face.

"That was not what I was going to ask," he laughed. "Where is the wyrm shard we came for? That is the question I was going to ask."

"Liar," Cwen frowned. "I heard you wonder if I could have tossed Aléria into the ceiling."

"Well where is the shard?" asked Klaed.

"In that cathedral," Caen said, pointing to the faint pulsing violet light. Together they approached the cathedral of ice, walking without fear to claim the wyrm shard for the Queen.

"Tell it again!" Brengven said, looking up at Talin. "Tell how the Queen crushed her sister and ended her tyranny!"

Mouth laughing beneath drowsy eyes, Cwen clapped her hands and watched Talin take a deep breath before beginning the tale again. "Is he not the finest storyteller?" she asked of Caen and Klaed. Both shared the 'ayes' of their agreement.

Morning found all wide awake and hungry for the day's first meal. All except Cwen.

"Cwen?" Talin leaned down and shook her, but she still did not respond. "Something is wrong with Cwen," he called, sending the others hurrying toward him. "I cannot awaken her."

Brengven knelt beside her and placed the back of his hand against her face. "She burns with fever," he announced, looking up at them with a frown. "Did the mind witch touch Cwen before she was killed?"

All three men shrugged. Klaed answered, "We were not with them. Cwen sent us away to safety."

Brengven lifted the hair around Cwen's face and neck, looking for scratches. Finding none, he looked up again. "We need to get her to an Ancient," he mumbled grudgingly. "They know how to deal with mind spells."

"Break camp. I will gather her things," Talin instructed as he began gathering Cwen's belongings and packing them into her pack.

Brengven stood next to Talin and spoke urgently. "She cannot travel overland. I will take her through the rift directly to the mire."

Talin's face grew taut and his eyes pierced those of the little Feie.

"How great is the danger?"

"I do not know. It could be grave. Only the Ancients or a wizard can deal with the torment of the mind witch."

Talin knelt and put his hand on Cwen's shoulder and whispered into her mind.

"*Cwen, Brengven will take you to Rosie. I am going to take Klaed and secure the next wyrm crystal, the one on Æshardæ. We will come for you after we deliver the shards to N… the fortress.*"

He called to Klaed, "You and I are going to Æshardæ. Caen, go with Brengven to the mire and watch over Cwen."

Klaed turned to stare at Caen, warning, "If harm comes to her, you will be held responsible."

"And I will not bother to sharpen my axe before I strike you!" Talin called.

Leaping to the backs of their bullrams, Talin and Klaed raced off along the frozen coast toward the border of Æshardæ.

Brengven summoned the rift as Caen lifted Cwen across the back of her bullram and gathered the reins of his own.

"Let us see how well bullrams pass through your rift, Feie."

The Mire

Morg and Rosie stood frozen as the glistening rift released the Feie and two bullrams among the hovels of the mire.

Recognizing Caen, Rosie called to him, "What do you wants, Caen?"

"Cwen is hurt, or ill. She has a fever and we cannot wake her," he said, lifting Cwen onto his shoulder and hurrying toward the little woman who had healed him of the wounds left by the troll.

"Brengven, I will meet you beyond the practice field," he called back over his shoulder.

Muttering, Brengven picked up the leads of the two bullrams and led them toward the field.

"Brings her in here." Rosie pointed to an empty hovel.

Caen placed Cwen on the cot and pulled the coverlet over her.

"What do you think it is?" he asked Rosewort.

"Tell me where you has been," she said in an accusatory tone. "Where's Talin?"

Her bright black eyes pierced Caen with hawk-like intensity.

"Talin has gone with Klaed to Æshardæ on a quest for the Queen. He asked me to bring Cwen to you."

Shaking her head Rosie muttered something Caen could not quite make out, but he knew it had to do with Talin's stupidity and his own unworthiness.

"Well? Where has you been?" Rosie asked again.

"A place in the Halcyon Ice Fields called Abaddon's Abyss," Caen answered, suddenly leaping to his feet as Rosie began to beat him with her staff.

"What kind of fools goes there?" she screeched, striking him again.

Backed up against the wall he held out his hands to ward her off, but she suddenly dropped her staff and climbed up on the cot next to Cwen.

"Poor girl. You travel with fools," Rosie whispered, patting Cwen's arm.

"Who touched her?" Rosie asked, looking back at Caen with trepidation.

"We think it may have been the Queen's sister…"

"Aléria? You let Aléria touch Cwen!" Rosie snatched up her staff and raised it over her head.

Caen jerked it from her hand and glared at her.

"Are you going to help Cwen, or just beat me?"

"Fool," Rosie mumbled, turning back to Cwen.

"Give me my staff and gets out of here so I can look at her," Rosie snapped angrily.

Holding out the staff, Caen backed toward the door.

"I will wait outside."

Rosie undressed Cwen and looked for scratches, as Brengven had done. Finding none, she sighed and whispered, "Aléria puts the fever in your mind, planted a seed of evil, Cwen. I will gets Willow."

As she exited the hovel she glanced down at Caen, who sat with his back against the wall.

Remembering the way Sōrél used to sit and wait for Yáviē, Rosie smiled.

Willow smoothed herb-filled oils over Cwen's feverish body and spoke the silent incantations to drive away the fever. She and Rose took turns sitting with Cwen and watching for signs the fever was breaking or worsening, but neither happened. Cwen simply remained feverish and unconscious; her mind swirling with the dark thoughts Aléria had placed there.

Nearly a fortnight later Cwen's eyelids fluttered and she asked if Talin had returned from Æshardæ.

Rosie helped her bathe and wash her hair.

"Why is there scales in your hair, Cwen?" Rosie asked with some concern.

Chuckling, Cwen answered, "I was attacked by snakemen in the flooded fields and there has been nowhere to bathe since."

She sank into the tub and let the water cover her head, luxuriating beneath the sweet-smelling petals that carpeted the water.

Rosie held out newly made leathers and a shirt with sleeves made from gossamer spider silk of deep brown and gold.

Dressed, Cwen headed out to find her friends.

"Cwen!" Caen jumped up from his seat near the hovel as she passed.

"Where is Talin?" she asked.

"Gone with Klaed to Æshardæ in search of the wyrm shard and then on to the Galenite fortress to deliver that and the one we recovered at the abyss to… the Guardian."

"And he left you to look after me?"

"Aye, but there were a number of threats involved that included words like 'responsible' and 'death by a dull blade'," Caen admitted.

"And have you been responsible?" she asked.

"Nay, but I have been worried, and I would hold you if I did not fear the consequences," he answered.

Her voice grew soft and teasing, "Perhaps you would like to walk with me to see Brengven."

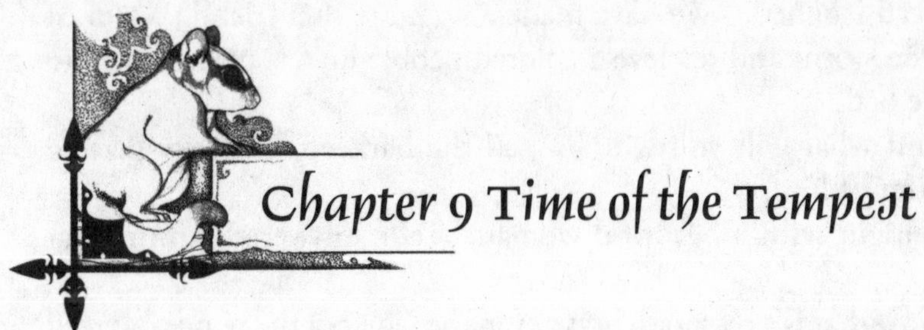

Chapter 9 Time of the Tempest

Klaed and Talin followed the frozen beach toward the Æshardian border, past the great angular boulders carved by the glaciers and spat out along the shore. Towering trees resistant to the freezing snows and howling winds scattered the shoreline.

The bullrams' breath billowed about them like steam as they urged the beasts forward at a steady pace.

"Are you sure it was wise to leave Cwen in Caen's care?" Klaed asked.

"Nay, I am not certain of it at all, but after the destruction of Calá I did not feel that we could wait until she recovered before gathering another shard," Talin answered, his voice tight with doubt.

"And will she recover?" Klaed's eyes met Talin's.

"I do not know. Brengven did not know."

They urged the bullrams ahead more quickly, driving the beasts with the flats of their swords.

Arriving in the border town of Alarid shortly after star set, they proceeded to the tavern in search of information about the never-ending storm Brengven had mentioned.

They ordered heavy ale and asked the barkeep if he had knowledge of such a storm.

"Aye, 'tis a hooricayne of wind, swirling at a speed that will drive a grown man from his feet. Said to contain the razor winds, it is – those that flay the flesh from the body, leaving only bones. Why is it you seek it?"

Klaed laughed. "We have made a wager with a friend. We must enter the storm and retrieve a colored pebble he has placed there to win the bet."

"And what will you win?" asked the barkeep, curiosity getting the better of him.

"A night with a beautiful woman," Talin answered, grinning at Klaed.

"Now that is a reason to brave even the worst of the winds," agreed the barkeep, laughing heartily and slapping Klaed on the shoulder.

"Indeed it would be," Klaed murmured, downing the rest of his draught.

"So where would we find this storm?" asked Talin.

"Toward the center of the kingdom. You canna miss it; it rages day in and day out, year after year – an evil wind left behind by some wizard or other." The barkeep chuckled.

"And where would a slightly drunken man find a room for the night?" Klaed queried, suddenly aware that the room had grown fuzzy.

Pulling a key from beneath the bar, the keep placed it on the counter before Klaed.

"A laud in advance and the room is yours."

"Pay the man, Talin, or I shall have to sleep on the bar," Klaed claimed the key as he slid off his stool and staggered toward the stairs.

"Your friend's not much of a drinker, is he?" the barkeep said, sweeping the coin off the counter and into his apron pocket.

"Nay," Talin laughed, watching Klaed stumble up the stairs. "Not long ago he was merely a nobleman."

"Come upon hard times, did he?"

"Aye, very hard indeed."

"Did we have to leave so early?" Klaed asked, squinting at the rising day star's brightness.

"Aye, I want to get that shard and the other to Nall as quickly as possible. When was the last time you had heavy ale Klaed?" Talin chuckled, causing Klaed to cringe.

"I remember it well," Klaed responded, "It was at Lady Sephilia's wedding – or was it the Queen's coronation?"

Talin roared, "You were not even born."

"Well it must have been the wedding then. Either way, it has been quite some time," he admitted, holding a hand against his pounding brow.

They heard the winds long before they saw them whirling in the distance. The storm was indeed a 'hooricayne', as the barkeep had described it, towering far into the sky and covering several leagues across the salt flats left behind by a dying sea. The bullrams became skittish and threatened to dislodge their riders in an effort to escape the howling blast so they hobbled them and left them on a grassy knoll far enough away to keep them content.

Running toward the storm at a steady jog they stopped to judge the speed and force of the winds of this new trial.

"This is going to sting," Talin said, shaking his head. "I surely hope that what we seek is in the center, otherwise we will have been flayed for naught."

Klaed nodded and raced forward into the wind.

"Klaed, you fool!" Talin laughed, following closely on his heels.

The flying salt did indeed strip great patches of skin where it was exposed, sanding their clothing and blinding them as well. The salt became embedded in the scraped skin, stinging and causing the wounds to throb.

Staggering into the calm center of the storm they fell to the ground, rubbing their eyes and trying to scratch the salt out of their wounds.

Talin pulled his water flask from his waist and poured water across his eyes, dissolving the salt and causing them to sting even more ferociously. He continued to flush them until he finally felt a bit of relief and looked up to see Klaed doing the same.

"Save some water for the return trip or we will arrive at the tavern blind."

"Just which beautiful woman did you say we would win for this endeavor?" Klaed asked, blinking through his burning eyes.

Talin laughed, "Somehow I do not think the beautiful woman we know is going to be terribly impressed."

"I imagine you are right." Klaed stood and looked toward the center of the storm's eye.

There at the heart of the storm stood an altar carved of topaz stone surrounded by the 'razor' winds of which they had been warned. Upon the altar lay a brilliant, rose-colored wyrm shard.

Shaking his head Klaed looked down at Talin.

"You can run through this one first." A cheeky grin flashed across his face.

They approached warily, watching as the winds swept around the altar.

"It does appear there is sufficient room to stand beside the altar inside the winds without them striking us."

"And if you are wrong?" Klaed asked doubtfully.

"One of us will return as a pile of bones," Talin shrugged. "So we might as well go in together."

"I am not sure I agree with your reasoning," Klaed laughed, "but as a dandy and a fool, I will of course follow you into this madness of yours."

"I have a shield," Talin said.

Klaed looked at his friend and shook his head.

"You mean you have one but you do not carry it?"

"Nay, I have the gift of a shield – given by the wizard Grumbl; but the magick does not last long. Of course, we will need to time it so that we get in and out without being stripped of the rest of our flesh," Talin laughed.

Easing even closer to the flesh-stripping wind, they gave each other a last look as Talin grabbed Klaed's arm and called on the shield. As the air shimmered and solidified, they dashed through to stand before the altar as the 'razor' winds tore across the back of their clothing, snatching bits of cloth and leather and sending them swirling into the sky.

"No closer than that on the return if you do not mind," Klaed said, drawing his shirt around to look at the damage.

"It only makes you look more of a ruffian. You should thank me."

"I will thank you when we are reunited with the lovely Cwen and I am resting comfortably next to her near the roaring fire, eating the stag that Brengven has prepared for my supper."

"You truly are a dandy," Talin laughed, lifting the glowing shard from its resting place and putting it safely in his bag next to the other.

Turning with great caution so as not to be caught by the wind tearing past them, Talin once again called on the Grumblton's shield, throwing them to safety as the wind sliced by.

Racing back across the eye of the storm and out through its howling winds, they fell to the ground gasping and moaning at the bruises, cuts and scrapes the brutal wind had inflicted. After picking pieces of salt from their wounds and flushing their eyes again they collected the bullrams and raced away toward the Galenite fortress to deliver the shards.

"Cwen, wait!" Caen called after Cwen as she hurried to one of the bullrams. "Talin said we should remain here until…"

"Talin said! Always Talin said! I do not care what Talin says!" she shot back, jerking the bullram about and racing off in the direction of the Galenite fortress, her fury growing with the darkness of the mind witch's planted visions of deception and betrayal.

Drawing the bullram to a sliding stop, Cwen leapt from its back, swatting its rump and driving it away.

She stood in the middle of the road, swords drawn, ready to deal death to her enemy. She would, as the fever in her mind suggested, "kill him before he killed her."

Klaed pulled up next to Talin, staring at the figure in the path ahead.

"Why is she standing in the middle of the road?"

"A better question is why does she draw swords and stand in the middle of the road. It appears she is expecting trouble."

"You are the trouble," Caen said, stepping from the trees to their left. "She intends to kill you, Talin, though I do not know why."

Cwen's voice carried to them across the dragon's length that separated them.

"Arm yourself, Talin, or die unarmed – the choice is yours. I will not allow your treachery to go without challenge. Klaed and Caen – you need not die unless you interfere."

Talin jumped from his bullram, handing the reins to Caen and holding up his hand indicating they should remain where they were.

"There is no need for us all to die," he said, taking a deep breath. "This is Aléria's doing, I am sure of it." He shook his head and handed Klaed his axe, drawing instead the sword he so rarely used.

"I cannot best her with the sword, but I will not chance harming her with the axe. Make some attempt to heal me if enough of me remains to heal," he grinned up at his friend.

Then he strode off to meet Cwen.

"I have committed no offense against you, Cwen." He spoke as her sword struck his.

"You lie! Your heart is black with deceit," she snarled, bringing an angry forehand stroke against his single sword and slicing a long cut across the back of his unarmed hand with her weak hand sword.

Talin drew his dagger to defend against her with both hands, his blood running freely down its blade.

Driving him away with a furious backhand and sending a thrust across his side, cutting through the leather of his shirt and leaving him staggering, she swung to catch him across the shoulder as he turned away from her.

The swords rang as their blades locked against one another. Talin used his superior strength to push her away. Cwen snarled and drove Talin back forcibly, the threat of her deadly blades sending him to the ground. Talin rolled away and leapt up to attack with a series of fore-hand swings before allowing his strength to lock their swords.

Cwen disengaged with a quick circling of her blade that knocked Talin's sword hand away. Her eyes were filled with hatred and rage as she drove Talin back again.

With a final thrust she forced him back and to the ground with her sword at his chest. As she drew back to deliver the final blow to his heart, strong hands pulled her away and Talin watched in amazement as a stranger saved his life.

The man was tall and dark, his shoulder-length hair swept freely around his shoulders as he twisted Cwen away from her victim.

His voice was soft and calm as he spoke into Cwen's ear, "Drop the swords."

Her hands went limp and the swords fell from her fingers.

"What offense have you committed against this woman that she so strongly wishes to take your life?" the stranger asked, dark eyes piercing Talin as sharply as Cwen's sword.

"None, but it is a very long story." Talin rose on unsteady legs.

"Her thoughts are clouded with the fury of the mind witch Aléria. Why has no one taken it from her?"

The man's familiarity with Aléria brought great unease and his direct, unwavering gaze was unsettling.

"How is it that you know Aléria?"

"I have lived with evil all my life. The mind witch Aléria is low on the ladder of wickedness, though she can do great harm to the weak-minded." His smile was grim and his gaze shifted to Cwen, still hanging limply within the circle of his arms.

"Do you wish her freed of this possession?" he looked up at Talin. "If I take it from her she will not recall it."

"Who are you?" Klaed asked as he approached with Caen. "And why do you believe you can cure her when the Ancients could not."

"The Ancients' incantations sometimes work against the darkness; other times, they do not. They are not well-versed in the spells of dark wizards."

"And you are?" Caen asked flatly, looking at the man's dark leathers and heavy cloak.

Shadowed eyes meeting Caen's, the man drawled, "I am merely a traveler with some knowledge of the dark arts. Do you wish her released? Or shall I allow her to continue her pursuit?"

The question was directed at Talin and while he felt his irritation rise he did not wish to lose the chance to heal Cwen's mind.

"Aye, take it from her if you can."

With a curt nod, the stranger placed one hand upon Cwen's face as he held her against him with the other. He closed his eyes and whispered words that were foreign to Cwen's companions. A dark, smoky shadow rose above Cwen and the man grabbed it quickly, holding it out for them to see before slipping it beneath the folds of his cloak.

"A remnant of darkness; its inscription was clearly your name," he said, indicating Talin.

Cwen gasped. Her eyes opened wide and she pushed against the man who held her. Instantly he released her and backed away, bowing formally.

"Lady Cwen," he acknowledged. "You tripped and I caught you to save you from falling. I apologize for your alarm."

She blinked, looking around her for confirmation. Talin and Caen nodded their agreement. Klaed's eyes remained focused on the dark handsome man who had held her.

"I do not like to be touched," she spoke between quick gasps for breath. "I am grateful you did not allow me to fall."

As he turned to go she asked, "How do you know my name?"

He gazed back at her for a moment before answering, "Your mother was once a guest of my father."

Bowing slightly, he continued toward the south, away from the Galenite fortress.

Scowling up at Talin, Cwen asked suspiciously, "Why are we standing here? Did you go to Æshardæ? Have you delivered the wyrm shards to the fortress? Why are you bleeding? Why are my swords on the ground? Why is it I know nothing?"

Talin shook his head and held up his hand to ward off her words.

Her eyes narrowed and she looked from Klaed to Caen.

"Who would like to tell me the truth?" she asked, reaching down and reclaiming her swords.

"Well?"

Her eyes shifted among them, but none of them met her eyes.

"What did I do?" Her voice was soft, uncertain.

"You tried to kill me," Talin shrugged.

She looked at him with alarm. "Why?"

"You were… bewitched. By Aléria. The stranger was a wizard or a healer of some sort. He took the darkness from your mind. We saw him do it."

"I did not fall?"

"Nay, he pulled you from me as you sought to drive your sword through my heart."

Her hand flew to her mouth as she became aware of his wounds.

He grinned and shrugged, "Most are the result of the storm on

Æshardæ; healing me would be appropriate."

Speaking the words her mother had taught, she laid her hands upon his wounds and healed them one by one.

"I also have wounds," Klaed said.

"And you can heal them yourself," Cwen replied.

A sudden shimmering rift deposited Brengven before them.

"Next time it would be best if someone told me we were leaving," he grumbled, receiving disbelieving laughter from his traveling companions.

"We shall camp to the north of the fortress while you deliver the shards. On the morrow we can head for Æstaffordæ and the falls," Cwen stated. "Klaed and Caen can remain with me."

"And Brengven, of course," she added, receiving a glare from the Feie.

"Talin, tell Nall that I am sorry he suffered." Cwen's look defied any to remark on her decision to send a message to her father, but neither Talin nor Klaed could hide their smiles.

"*Give him this*," she whispered into Talin's mind as she handed him her signet ring. "*Ask that he keep it safe for me*."

She swung away from them and headed off toward the northern edge of the fortress where she would make camp for the night.

Caen and Brengven hurried after her, leaving Klaed to speak with Talin.

"If Nall is not the fool I think he is, he will hold this gesture dear," Klaed sighed. "She is strong and brave, but longs for her father. It is a shame he cannot see it."

"I believe her attempts to butcher him may have clouded the truth," Talin chuckled. "I will pass on her message."

Leaping lightly to the back of his bullram he set off toward the Galenite fortress.

Visions

She asked that I give you this," Talin said as he prepared to leave Nall.

He withdrew the signet ring from his pocket and held it out.

"She asked that you keep it safe for her. And she said to tell you she was sorry for your suffering."

Nall's eyebrows rose in skepticism.

"We have been to Abaddon's Abyss," Talin shrugged. "She was overcome by visions of your capture and torture. If you do not wish to accept her ring I will tell her so."

He started to replace the signet in his pocket, but Nall suddenly held out his hand.

As the ring hit his palm, Nall paled.

Talin called out his name, but Nall did not hear him, for his mind was filled with the image of a young Cwen. She stood with her back to him, facing Aidan in the glen behind the training field at New Xavian City. She shook her head defiantly and Aidan's fist struck her jaw, dropping her as if she were dead. Nall heard Sidon's laughter and watched Aidan throw Cwen over his shoulder as the two men quickly swung about and entered the dense woods beyond, taking Nall's daughter with them.

Nall's breath came in great gasps and he bent forward at the waist, hands on his knees to keep from falling.

"She did not go willingly."

His eyes rose as he searched Talin's face.

"Nay, she did not," Talin answered, walking away and leaving Nall to this new suffering.

As he rounded the corner he saw Galen and Kayann ahead of him.

"Galen," he said, offering his grip.

"Kayann." He leaned forward for her embrace.

He pulled back giving her a hard look. Her fragrance was different, not the suffocating floral scent that made his head ache.

"Are you arriving or leaving?" Galen asked. "I am leaving," Talin said, waving his good-bye. Faervyn watched him walk away from her hiding place within Kayann's body. He would be of no use to her. He was far too suspicious. She would have to be wary not to give her ruse away.

Nall stood before Näeré as defeated as she had ever seen him.

"How could I not have seen it? I knew what Aidan was. I believed she chose him. How could I have believed that of my own daughter?"

"Nall," Näeré drew him to her, "even I did not see the full truth of it. She did not want us to see. Do not blame yourself."

"I should have hunted Aidan down and killed him myself." He shook his head, wiping his face, weeping for his daughter's innocence lost at the hands of someone so cruel.

"Aidan is dead. It does not matter who killed him. It is enough that he is dead." Näeré held Nall tightly and shed her tears with his.

Nall drew back, his eyes suddenly stone-hard. "I will kill Sidon for his part in this."

Näeré soothed, "As Cwen's father it is your right."

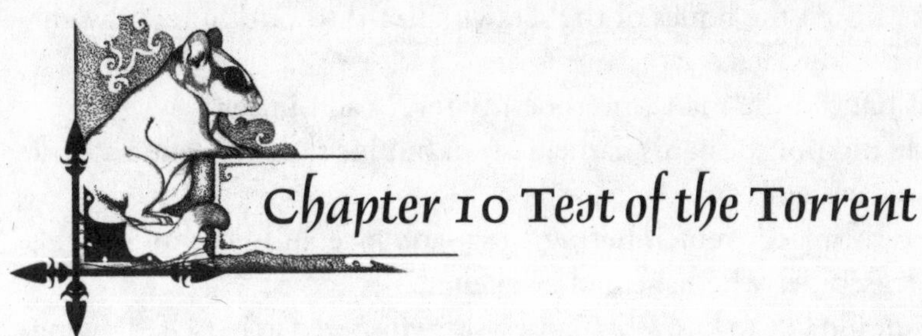

Chapter 10 Test of the Torrent

The destruction of Calá drove the travelers forward, sent them racing across the border into Æstaffordæ on the backs of the exhausted bullrams. They camped at dusk, not far from the sacred falls where their queen had long ago been cleansed of her sorrows as she sought the truth of her past. Brengven built a roaring fire, for the air was chill and damp. He roasted grosshare and several scarlet lizards, drawing looks of distaste from Klaed.

"How can you eat those?" Klaed asked the little Feie.

"You should try them, they are quite tasty. Hot and peppery. Though I do not suppose one would find them on the plate of a nobleman," Brengven answered.

Licking her lips, Cwen lifted one by the tail and bit off the head, chewing with moans of pleasure and winking at Brengven.

"I told Talin you would not approve of us," she laughed at Klaed. Klaed's eyes softened and a smile lit his face.

"Lady Cwen, there is naught that you could do to lose my approval." He bowed and stepped toward the boiling tea. "But I still do not intend to eat lizards."

"Talin!" Cwen called across the camp. "Would you not like a scarlet lizard?"

"Nay, I shall hold out for a grosshare," he called back, laughing. "And I know that you do not like those bony reptilians either. I have heard you call them 'disgusting' out of Brengven's earshot."

She tossed the bones of the scrawny lizard toward him and went to sit next to Klaed.

"What did the man who took my fever call himself?"

"He did not speak his name, Cwen, but his skill at healing a dark fever was extraordinary."

She shrugged, remembering the man's face and how quickly he had released her when she had awakened.

"I should like to know his name," she whispered to herself, drawing a curious look from Klaed.

Caen sat down, handing Cwen a cup of tea.

She accepted it and warmed her hands.

"Did I cause you great trouble while at Meremire?" she asked, glancing sideways at him.

"Nay. Well, Rosie did beat me with her staff, but she was worried – as was I. You slept so long and then you became so angry." He shook his head. "Talin is fortunate the stranger intervened; you are a formidable swordsman."

"As well you should know," she laughed. "I have bested you often enough."

"But still you have not killed me," he replied lazily.

The laughter quickly left her eyes. "Perhaps one day soon I shall."

She stood and stepped to her pack, pulling out her cloak and bedroll. As she settled down to sleep she called back to Klaed, "Wake me for our watch."

Talin watched Cwen across the cold camp. She stood staring into the distance, her swords poised for practice. He wondered where her thoughts lay and smiled at her strength and beauty. As he stepped up behind her, she swung around, her swords thrust forward in threat.

"I would never harm you, Cwen."

Lowering her eyes, she turned away and began to work the swords. Her form was perfect, taught by the Guardians and practiced unfailingly since she had escaped Aidan and joined Talin.

"Your ring is safe in Nall's care. I gave him your message."

"Why is it you take Klaed's watch?" she asked, never faltering with the sword.

"I do not. He stands to the west. Cwen, did you know Nall would see the vision?"

She allowed her swords to lower and looked at him in surprise.

"What vision did he have?"

"I am not certain, for I did not see it; but it nearly brought him to his knees. He asked me if you had gone willingly with Aidan. I did not lie to him for I do not believe you did," Talin admitted.

She grew momentarily somber before shrugging her shoulders as if she did not care and returning to her practice.

"*Perhaps it is time Nall knew the truth*," she spoke silently.

Talin returned to his bedroll but remained sleepless until dawn.

The travelers stood together at the base of the thundering falls, behind which lay the caverns where Yávië the Dragon Queen had been held captive by Ya'vanna's dragon, a demon that had nearly driven her mad. The quest for Ædracmoræ's rebirth had held many challenges and not all had ended well. Cwen recalled again the images of her father's torment at the hands of the soul thief Abaddon and the queen's sister, Aléria.

"Do you believe the shard to be in the caverns?" Talin asked Brengven, who had insisted on accompanying them.

"Nay, I believe it to be there," Brengven said, pointing to the top of the falls.

"Then why did we not go there?" Caen asked with irritation.

"Because there is a cavern just beneath the lip of the cliff where the water begins its cascade. It cannot be reached from above. Someone will have to climb up from below," said the Feie.

Talin gave a shake of his head and began to remove his weapons.

"I will make the climb," Cwen said, "It will be easier to catch me if I fall."

"No one is going to fall; and I am going to make the climb because I am the strongest," he stated, waiting for her argument.

She bit her lip and took a deep breath before giving her agreement.

"It is an easy climb," Talin said, "with many handholds."

Leaning down he dusted his hands with sand and filled a pocket as he stepped to the wall behind the falls.

There were indeed many handholds and plenty of places to rest his feet, at least for the first two thirds of the climb. The last third proved more difficult; he had to traverse far to the right of the falls before returning toward the opening above him. The walls grew damp and slippery as he reached the ledge below the cavern. He braced himself to add sand to his hands.

Without looking down he called to those below, "I am at the opening."

With those words he disappeared from view.

Talin slid into the low opening, finding that he could not rise even to his hands and knees. He hoped Brengven had been correct in assuming the shard was hidden within this narrow cavern.

Lighting a torch, he pushed it in front of him. The walls ahead only seemed to grow narrower and he feared he would have to retreat and send Cwen after all – she might be the only one small enough to reach the wyrm shard.

As the walls grew so close they scraped the skin from his shoulders he discovered an opening on his left. It required a sharp turn, but he finally manipulated his large body until it slid into the new passage.

"I hope I do not become lost in some labyrinth of slender passages," he muttered to himself.

Continuing forward he saw an azure glow ahead. Pulling himself through the small entrance he rose to stand in the chamber of the shard. It did not lie on an altar, but in a shallow willow wood bowl at the center of the room. He crouched and examined its pale blue color. As with the others, it held a shadow at its heart. With a deep breath he lifted it and placed it in the waist of his pants at the small of his back before heading back out through the narrow passages.

Leaning out over the ledge he looked down at his companions and waved.

"I have the shard," he called.

Sliding forward he again dusted his palms with the dry sand and allowed his legs to slip over the edge of the opening and out into space.

With a firm grip on the ledge he felt for a foothold and found one that would take him back to the right of the wall where he would be able to begin the descent toward the sandy floor at the base of the falls.

Easing his weight onto the rocky outcroppings supporting his feet, he reached out for the next handhold, feeling the stone give way beneath his feet and his fingers slip from his handhold. With a harsh cry he cursed himself as he fell to the bottom of the falls.

Crying out, Cwen ran to his side. His body straddled a slab of rough stone, his head in the water and his back across the rock. Cwen raised his head slightly to keep the shifting water from his face and saw him clench his eyes shut in pain.

Her hands flew over his body searching for broken bones and bleeding.

As they reached his abdomen she whispered, "I cannot heal this, Talin. I do not have the power – nor do Klaed or Brengven. The bones of the back are shattered and you bleed within. It will take a wizard's touch."

Klaed placed his hand on Cwen's shoulder, drawing her eyes.

"We will make a litter and bind him tightly so that the injury does not grow worse. We will have to go to the House of Aaradan and seek the healing of Grumblton. I know of no other with this power in Æstaffordæ."

"Talin," Cwen rested her hand on his chest, "I will take your pain."

Closing her eyes she silently spoke the words that would take the pain from Talin, pulling it away and into herself where it would come to her as she slept, adding to the suffering of her already fearful dreams.

Opening her eyes, she watched him relax as the agony left him, but the fear in his eyes was still terrible to see.

"Grumbl will heal you, Talin; he will." She spoke the words she hoped were true before casting the spell of deep sleep over her only friend.

They built the litter that would carry Talin to the fortress of the Queen. Cwen layered it with heavy moss to provide a soft resting place for his broken body.

As Caen and Klaed lifted the unconscious Talin to the litter, the azure shard dropped to the sand at their feet. Its light pulsed and the shadow within squirmed as if looking for an escape. Cwen tossed it into her pack and began binding Talin to the litter. She used long strips of spider silk, sweeping them over and around the litter until there was no way that Talin could move, even if he chanced to wake.

"Klaed." Cwen's voice was sharp and demanding. "Take the shard to the House of Aaradan; we will go through the rift with Brengven."

She held out her knapsack and tried to hide her tears as he took the hateful shard.

He leapt to the back of his bullram and shouted, "I will be there soon."

She waved her acknowledgement and looked toward Caen and Brengven where they stood holding the rails of the litter.

"Go," she said, and watched Brengven call the rift.

The shining rift opened and they stepped through into the interior of the palace of the Queen and the long corridor that held Grumblton's quarters and workshop.

Screaming for Grumbl, Cwen raced ahead to the little Ancient wizard's rooms.

Yáviё heard the screams and raced down the stairs from her chambers, nearly running into Cwen as she turned the corner toward her wizard's rooms.

"What is it, child?" she asked.

Cwen pointed, her voice lost in her fear for Talin.

"Come." Yáviё opened the door and beckoned Caen and Brengven to follow her into the wizard's bedroom.

"Lift the litter and place it on the cot," she directed, silently calling Grumblton from where he worked in Sōrél's chambers.

Heavy footsteps pounded on the stairs and Yáviё knew Sōrél accompanied Grumbl.

Grumblton headed straight for Talin, glancing at Cwen and seeing the despair in her eyes.

"If he lives, I can heal him," the little wizard reassured.

Cwen's lips curled in a tiny smile that said she did not believe him.

"Out!" Grumbl bellowed, "I haves work to do, so out with you all."

Grabbing Sōrél's arm, the little wizard whispered, "You stays.

What I haves to do is going to hurt worse than the Queens' sword and you got to hold him."

Nodding, the king remained behind.

Yáviё led the others to the dining hall where they settled at the table as a servant poured willow bark tea for all.

"I would rather have a mug of ale," Caen grumbled. A gesture from the queen sent a serving wench after it.

"What happened?" the Queen asked, looking at Cwen's pale face.

"He fell collecting your damn shard," Cwen snarled viciously, flinging her tea across the table.

"I will excuse your disrespect because I know you are afraid," Yáviё spoke.

Klaed entered the room, tossing Cwen's pack on the table.

Cwen hung her head. "He fell because I did not make the climb."

Caen pushed his ale in front of Cwen.

"Drink it," He commanded.

Looking at Yáviё, he said, "Have them bring her another."

"His decision to climb was not your fault, Cwen." Klaed laid his hand on her arm, only to have it thrown off.

"He could have caught me!" she cried out, the pain of her guilt causing her gut to cramp and forcing her to gag. "You could have caught me."

The guttural, wordless bellow from the room holding Talin drew Cwen to her feet and sent her racing back toward Grumbl's chambers.

"Stop her," Yáviё directed Klaed, who jumped up and raced off after Cwen.

Looking at Caen, Yáviё added, "She has never been easy. She is too much like her father. Easily angered and often belligerent and unreasonable. Though Nall has become softer with the comfort of Näeré, Cwen has no comfort."

"She wants no one," Caen said.

Yáviё eyes rose to meet his. "I do not believe that is so. Her heart aches with need, but she is too frightened to listen to it."

"She fears no one. You have obviously not seen her fight."

Yáviё slammed her hand onto the table, causing Caen to draw

back. "She fears everyone. She reeks of it. If she does not overcome it soon it will destroy her. Do not let her fear destroy her, thief. She fights out of fear, not out of strength." Yáviё sighed, "I do not want to see her harmed."

"She has already been harmed." Caen's voice was almost inaudible, his eyes shadowed with concern.

"Then she must be healed. You care for her, why do you not tell her?" the Queen asked.

Laughing softly, Caen answered, "Because I am a thief."

Klaed grabbed Cwen as her hand reached for the handle of Grumbl's door.

"No!" she screamed, throwing herself backward against him and trying to free herself from his grasp.

"He is dying, Klaed! Please, please let me go to him." Her cries were heartbreaking and Klaed held her even more tightly as he felt her collapse against him, weeping.

He dropped to the floor and turned her toward him.

"He will not die, Cwen. He will not."

"Did you not hear his screams?" she asked, looking up at him with tears streaming down her pale, haunted face. "I have let him die," she sobbed, closing her eyes and wishing she could die with him.

"Come, drink your tea and let Grumbl work his magick. They will tell us as soon as we can visit Talin." Klaed's voice echoed his certainty and caused Cwen to look up at him.

"I hate the Queen," she mumbled, causing him to chuckle.

"Cwen, you hate everyone. We have all grown accustomed to your anger. I, for one, rather enjoy it," he admitted. He lifted her and placed her on her feet. "It will be more appropriate if you return quietly, rather than kicking and screaming over my shoulder." He looked at her with eyebrows raised. "But the choice is yours."

Sniffing and wiping the back of her hand beneath her nose, Cwen headed back toward the dining hall and her tea.

Yáviё was deep in conversation with Caen as Cwen entered, but drew back quickly, smiling at her niece.

"Tea or ale, Cwen?" Yáviё asked.

"Both." Cwen gave a deep sigh. "Tell me the truth. Will he die?"

"I have seen Grumbl raise the dead," Yávië lied. "Talin will be healed."

"I want to see him." Cwen's chin quivered, but she held back the new flood of tears, blinking them away.

"I will ask Grumbl." Yávië stood, giving Caen a last glance before she left them.

"What lies was she filling your head with?" Cwen asked Caen sullenly.

Caen shrugged. "None that I shall take to heart."

Klaed sensed Caen's confusion and grinned.

"Yávië is good at giving advice she herself would never follow," he chuckled. "She once suggested I ask for Cwen's hand in marriage."

Caen frowned and Cwen coughed, spitting tea across the table, followed by a fit of choking laughter.

"Does she really hate you so much?" she asked Klaed, gasping for breath.

"Aye, I believe she does. I would urge you not to follow her advice," Klaed warned Caen.

"Come, Cwen." Yávië's voice drew the three of them. "Only Cwen. Grumbl does not wish a crowd."

"Is he dead?" Cwen asked, standing, every muscle rigid in preparation for the news she believed Yávië bore.

"Find out for yourself. You will not believe what I say anyway."

Talin lay on the cot covered from head to foot in warm coverlets of soft spider cloth. His face was flushed and damp with pain, but he was not dead.

Cwen looked down at him, her lip held between her teeth, her eyes filling with tears.

"I should have let you climb," Talin whispered, opening his eyes to gaze at her. "I could have caught you."

"I told you so," she wept and smiled, wiping back her tears. "I did tell you so."

He gave a barely perceptible nod.

"Did you get the shard?"

"Aye," she looked away to hide her anger.

"Give it to Sōrél," Talin whispered again as his eyes began to close. "I am very tired."

Cwen wiped her tears again and turned away from him. Grumbl stood behind her, his eyes stern.

"He can't travel," he said harshly. "You will have to go on without him."

"I cannot."

"Then Ædracmoræ will fall to darkness and all of you will die anyway. Do as you please." The Ancient wizard shrugged.

Talin spoke behind her.

"Cwen, take Klaed and Caen. Seek the shard of the Ethereal Equus. It is here within the borders of Æstaffordæ. It will give me time to heal."

Spinning, she looked into his eyes.

"You want this?" she asked.

"Nay, I do not, but it is all that we can do. Trust Klaed."

Cwen said, "And still I should not trust Caen?"

Talin nodded grimly.

"As you wish. Shall I leave Caen with you?"

"Nay, take him with you. He has a good sword arm. And Klaed will not allow him to harm you," he grimaced at the pain the use of his voice caused.

"Really? And have the two of you spoken of this? My protection?"

"Nay, but it will keep you sharp if you must watch out for treachery as well as protection," he winced, allowing his eyes to close. "Go. I will await you here."

"As if you could do anything else," Grumbl muttered behind them. "If you had accepted the gifts of Guardianship you would have been healed by now. Fool."

The wizard fumed and left the room.

When Cwen slipped out the door Sōrél was waiting for her.

"He will be able to travel in a lunar cycle, perhaps sooner. Grumbl will continue the healing while you are gone."

"Sōrēl, what makes you think I will leave Talin?" Cwen glared.

"He told me you would," Sōrél's grim sapphire gaze met Cwen's bright golden eyes.

"Klaed has the shard in my pack," she said, turning her back on the king. "If you want it, get it from him."

"Why did you bring him here?" Sōrél called after her.

"Because he is the only friend I have and I do not have time to train a new one." Flinging over her shoulder, "And whatever I may think of you and your Guardians, your wizard is a superb healer."

Wizards

The wizard Domangart sat at the wizard Laoghaire's table drinking prickleberry wine and eating the pappleberry tarts that his host's most recent consort had made. The woman was stunning and Laoghaire had trained her well. She was silent and very compliant. On the table before them rested the shard of a wyrm.

"I bring news from the border between Æstaffordæ and Æstretfordæ. The city of Calá has been destroyed by an army of the dark horde – the G'lm of the past. The enchantress Faervyn seems to have been in control of them."

"Faervyn," Laoghaire murmured, touching the scar beneath his chin. "She is a formidable opponent, Domangart. Are you sure you wish to challenge her?"

"Alone? No. But together we can best her at her own game," Domangart said with wine inspired confidence. "And there is a greater prize than Ædracmoræ at stake."

"Greater than the Seven Kingdoms and the throne? It must be a grand prize indeed," Laoghaire laughed.

"Indeed it is. Do you recall the sorceress Näeré? The one who escaped you?"

Laoghaire glared. "She did not escape. Her husband came and reclaimed her."

"Well, she has a daughter. A strong and beautiful daughter. One with the golden eyes of her father and rich copper hair. A woman that would please you greatly, Laoghaire," Domangart said as he reached for another tart.

"A daughter? Of the Guardian Nall and the sorceress?" Laoghaire licked his lips, recalling the beauty of Näeré.

"And she seeks the same items as the enchantress. She is on a quest for the Dragon Queen."

"Is this not the woman who stole your cipher stone?" Laoghaire asked, suddenly recalling Domangart's tale of the beautiful golden-eyed woman who had come to him claiming to be the daughter of Horsfal.

"Aye. I was simply going to have her killed. But then I remembered you, old friend, and decided it would be a shame to waste her."

"Undeniably," Laoghaire agreed.

His eyes followed the woman who served him now. She was beginning to grow tiresome and he would soon have to seek new company.

"I shall help you if – and only if – you promise me the daughter of the sorceress and the Guardian Nall. If you break your word I will be forced to deal harshly with you, Domangart, and I do not believe you would want that."

He reached out and grabbed his woman as she passed, pulling her down to him.

"You grow ugly, Questra," he said, pushing her away.

Domangart smiled, knowing he had purchased a strong ally.

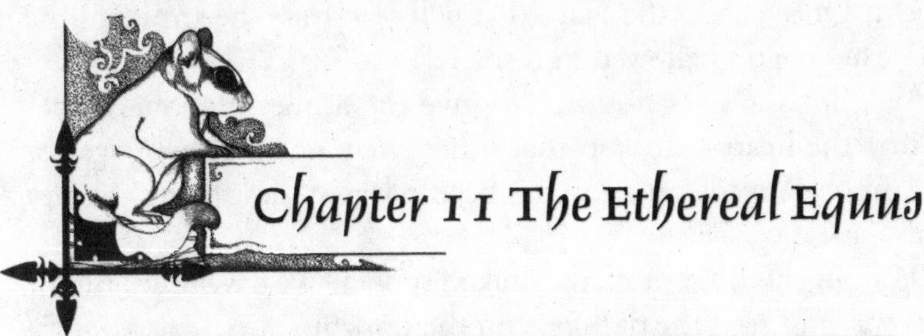

Chapter 11 The Ethereal Equus

Defender of the Equus of Aaradan

The beauty of the Ethereal Woods was second to none in all of the kingdoms. Light filtered through the heavy canopy of leaves, sending motes of dust and pollen dancing like sprites upon a gentle breeze. The ground was covered with soft, dense moss ranging from deep greens to vivid scarlet, and a carpet of fragrant flowers lay beneath their feet in the dell.

Cwen gave a low whistle, summoning the Equus of Æstaffordæ and closed her eyes waiting for the pounding beat of hooves and soft trilling whinnies that would signal their arrival.

With a thunderous roar, the Equus of the House of Aaradan arrived under the protection of a large wind dragon. The dragon landed lightly before Cwen, its shimmering iridescent scales flowing in the still morning air.

Klaed nodded his recognition to the wind dragon. Caen tensed and placed his hand on the hilt of his sword, drawing an offended snort from the dragon, and Brengven fell to the ground, covering his eyes and quaking in terror.

"For what purpose do you summon the Herd of Aaradan, Cwen, daughter of Nall?" the breathy voice of the wind dragon called, a deep frown shifting the scales of his forehead.

"I seek the wyrm shard held by the Ethereal Equus," Cwen replied, bowing in respect to the protector before her. "We are on a quest for the Dragon Queen."

"Our Queen seeks the shard that will reactivate the armies of the G'lm?" the dragon bellowed in disbelief.

"Aye, but she does not seek to give the armies life. She wishes to gather the heart shards so that others may not use them against Ædracmoræ. Already an army has been released, destroying the city of Calá."

Dropping his huge head, the dragon spoke, "We have heard rumor of this war and seen the darkness on the horizon."

"The wyrm shard can be claimed if you are willing to accept my test," the wind dragon continued, receiving a scowl from Cwen.

"What test would that be, Dragon? We are not Guardians and do not quest for a pledge," Cwen answered flatly.

The dragon snorted with laughter.

"I can see clearly that you and your cowering companions are not Guardians. What I ask of you will not gain you the pledge of my flyte, for none of you is worthy." The dragon sniffed his displeasure.

"It is spoken among the Equus that you are bound to them by your bloodline and that you and the man with the axe have acted as their protectors on your travels through the kingdoms. Is there any truth in these tales?" he continued.

"Aye, I do kill the poachers who seek to claim the coats of the Equus for their veiling properties," Cwen admitted. "I have also killed those who seek the bones and scales of young dragons," she added, seeking the eyes of the great dragon.

"So it is spoken."

"This herd is in great danger from the poachers camped beneath the shadow of the Mountain of Merylgoth. Many have already been claimed, their skins now drying upon the racks of these wicked men. I ask that you remove them from Ædracmoræ, sending their souls into the dark abyss. Are you worthy of this simple task?" the wind dragon asked.

Cwen trembled, anger again claiming her soul, and she nodded without speaking.

"And the man who wields the axe? Does he accept the task?"

Cwen's voice vibrated with tension as she spoke. "Talin, the man who carries the axe, lies broken within the fortress of the Queen. He is under the healing care of Grumblton the wizard. I must meet this challenge without his assistance."

The dragon released the low "shuff, shuff" of dragon laughter as his eyes shifted toward her present company.

"I see a Feie shaking in fear, a nobleman whose father is a councilor, and a thief of ill repute. Are these your paladins?"

Cwen smiled at the thought. "They are indeed, Dragon."

"Call my name when this charge has been accomplished, Cwen, daughter of Nall. I am Aerife, son of Aerodorn, Defender of the Equus of Aaradan."

With a final bow of his head and a last windy breath that covered the shuddering Feie, the great protector of the Equus lifted off on airy wings, sweeping away as the herd of Equus spun and followed.

Cwen sank to the ground shaking her head.

"Just what we need. A cranky dragon dictating our movement."

Klaed laughed, pulling Brengven from his cowering position.

"The hideous beast is gone, Feie, and you have not been eaten; though I do not believe your performance instilled any more confidence in the dragon than ours did."

Caen stood silent, watching the dragon in the distance. When he finally lost sight of it he looked down at Cwen and whispered, "Let us hunt the poachers. It is, after all, what we do best."

Cwen's smile was dazzling as she gave her agreement. "That is true. Brengven, think of the tales you will have to tell Talin when we return! This time you shall be the teller of the tale of the quest."

She winked at Klaed and Caen and watched the Feie's face light up with pleasure.

"True. Talin will be sorry he missed the adventure," Brengven beamed.

The Dragon's Test

Seven poachers were in the camp when the travelers found it, a camp so vile it sent their stomachs churning. The bodies of three Equus lay staked to the ground as the poachers gutted them and stole their hides to sell in the markets of Ælmondæ. Racks with drying hides lined the far edge of the camp just as the dragon Aerife had described. A poacher stripped the still moist fat from them with an evil looking blade.

"We could take them as they sleep, avoiding the need for a fight," Klaed suggested.

Cwen gave a violent shake of her head. "Nay, I will look into their eyes as my sword spills their intestines. They are filth and they will not die easily. Caen, make sure one remains alive."

She shifted her gaze to Caen. "If you do not, I will make you regret it."

Caen nodded his acceptance and hoped she did not kill them all without leaving him a chance to save the life of one.

"Brengven, you will remain here, for you are of no use to me in a fight. Be prepared to heal Caen and Klaed if they require it, or a poacher if Caen brings him too close to death to suit me," Cwen snapped her demands.

"And you, milady? Shall I heal you? Or allow you to die so that we can be rid of your harassment?" Brengven spat back.

Cwen's sword swept to the Feie's throat and her eyes were filled with fire.

"I did not ask you to come," she snarled, using the tip of her sword to flick off a button from his waistcoat. "Do not test me, Brengven. I am in no mood for it and your cheekiness is likely to see you join your ancestors in their final resting place."

Brengven gulped and gasped as she spun away. Looking toward Caen and Klaed with great concern for their safety, the Feie wrinkled his brow and wiped the sweat from his face. Talin's loss had made the woman even more hateful and unreasonable.

"*Cwen*," Klaed spoke calmly in her mind. "*We have a common enemy. Should we not focus on the task, rather than waste our time at each other's throats?*"

Fixing him with her gaze, she answered aloud, "I have nothing in common with you. And I do not need your help to slay half a dozen mangy poachers. Perhaps it would be best if you took your friends and left."

Klaed glanced at Brengven.

"Brengven, it appears we are not needed and would best serve Lady Cwen by staying out of her way."

To Cwen he added, "We will await you in the dell where you called the Equus."

With a last glance toward Caen, Klaed gave a nearly imperceptible nod and strode purposely away from Cwen and her anger.

"Two against seven. Not bad odds," Caen grinned. "It seems you are stuck with me, as I do not fall into Klaed's circle of friends."

Cwen glared at him, trying to decide whether she was pleased he had stayed, or if she should just kill him and end his constant banter.

Finally, she simply shared her plan.

"You will approach the camp from the west, from there – beyond the drying racks. Do not forget to use your ill-gotten veiling stone. I will enter from the east and strike the skinners. Remember, I need to question one."

She stared, awaiting his agreement.

Slowly he gave a nod of acknowledgement and pulled the pouch that held the veiling stone from inside his shirt. Together they invoked the veil and slipped silently toward the camp of the enemy.

Cwen stepped up behind the first of the skinners and disengaged her veil, calling softly, "Dead man."

The poacher swung toward her and gagged as the tip of her sword drove into his gut. Jerking upward, she watched with satisfaction as his intestines spilled to the ground.

Swiftly, she drove her weak hand sword upward behind her, impaling the man who stood there foolishly waiting for her to turn. Spinning, she rotated the sword within his body before pulling it out and slitting his throat.

Across the camp, Caen drove his lance through a poacher's heart as he stood before the drying racks scraping a hide. Leaving the lance, Caen drew his crossbow, nocked an arrow and let it fly, striking the approaching poacher in the heart.

"Two dead and none living," he muttered, allowing a sigh to escape his lips.

A third man slammed into Caen from the side, knocking him to the ground and straddling him, blade drawn to cut his throat. A sudden thrust of Cwen's sword dropped the man atop Caen. Kicking the corpse away, Cwen glared, "Where is one who lives?"

"Behind you!" Caen shouted, watching Cwen spin and slit the man's throat, taking a cut to her upper arm as the man fell, dragging his blade behind.

Leaping to his feet, Caen placed a carefully aimed arrow into the shoulder of the remaining poacher as he tried to flee the camp.

Pointing, Caen said to Cwen, "That one lives."

He saw her purse her lips to stop a smile as she strode toward the crawling man and stomped her foot into his back.

"Bind him. And hang him there."

Caen dragged the man to the tree, ran a rope through the bindings around his ankles and hoisted him head down from the branch Cwen had indicated. Seeing the man did not hang quite low enough to meet Cwen's eyes, Caen made an adjustment, leaving the man face to face with her flashing eyes and bloodstained cheeks.

"Is that suitable?" he asked, grinning at her unwavering glare.

"You are going to be one very repentant poacher," he said and slapped the man on the back before sitting down to watch Cwen work.

A sudden commotion at the edge of the camp drew their attention away from the captive. Cwen gasped as she saw Klaed enter from behind a large copse of trees. He dragged two men, both battered and bloodied, and threw them at her feet.

"I thought you might like to ask a variety of questions, milady." He bowed respectfully, receiving a grunt for his trouble.

"They hid within the trees, hoping to kill you once you began the interrogation of their partner. I told them it would be disrespectful to interrupt your work," he said cockily, wiping blood from a cut on his chin.

"Find a place for them to wait," Cwen whispered. "I do not wish to rush the dialogue."

Returning her attention to the matter at hand she drew her dagger and began to cut away the hanging man's shirt.

As she worked she asked, "Have you heard the Equus' screams as they are gutted? They are quite frightful."

Placing her blade at his navel she drew a shallow cut down to his sternum, watching as blood beaded along its length.

"Of course you probably do not care that they are dying in agony at the hands of your blade any more than I care how you will die at mine."

"Milady, spare me, I will change my ways. I will become a shopkeeper or a barkeep. Please, I do not wish to die."

"Really?" Cwen asked. "Who sent you here to butcher the Equus?"

"No one. I came…"

His hoarse scream caused his partners to cry out and swing around toward him. Their faces paled at his exposed entrails.

Cwen pushed him, causing him to swing gently and shook her head as he vomited and gasped as the contents of his stomach ran into his nostrils.

"I wonder how long you can live like this?" Cwen asked, shrugging with indifference.

Leaving him, she squatted before the other two poachers.

"You are going to die today. It is the choice you made when you slaughtered the Equus of Aaradan. Whether you die slowly," she gestured toward the hanging man, "or swiftly is the only choice left for you to make."

"I asked him who sent you here. His answer was not the one I wanted. Perhaps you can do better." She touched the first man's chest with her dagger, causing him to shrink away.

She drew her dagger up the leg of his pants, slitting the leather as if it were no more than soft silk and pulled the sides away to expose his pale, black-haired thigh.

"Here," she poked him with the tip of her blade, "lies a tunnel of blood, coursing through your body, giving you life. My mother taught me that."

She glanced at Klaed.

"Did she teach you this as well?" her eyes blazed with her question.

"Aye, Cwen, she did. She taught me how to make a shallow cut and allow a man to bleed out slowly, or to cut a bit deeper and end his life swiftly and painlessly," Klaed nodded. "I have heard that with the latter method one merely grows cold and drifts off to a never-ending sleep… after he finishes screaming."

Cwen's blade pricked the man's thigh again and she watched his eyes grow wide.

"Who sent you here? I will not ask again." Her eyes were glassy, pupils widely dilated and her face was flushed with the fever of her task.

"Domangart," the man gasped. "The wizard Domangart. He sells the pelts as veiling cloaks to those who can pay handsomely."

Her blade caught the light as it swept across the man's throat, ending his life quickly and painlessly as she had promised.

"Release that one."

"Do not kill me, milady," the poacher whined.

With a swift kick to his stomach she doubled him over, gagging.

"Do not speak to me. Listen, and hear my words. Go to Domangart and tell him that Cwen of Aaradan is coming for him. I will strike from the shadows; he will not know when. His death will be slow and painful. Tell him I swear it will happen. I swear it," she hissed, slicing through the ropes that bound him.

"Cwen." Caen's voice brought her eyes to his. "It is not wise to free him."

She shoved her dagger up under Caen's chin, mingling the blood of poachers with his own. "If I need the wisdom of your counsel I shall let you know."

Withdrawing her blade she walked through the camp touching the softness of the Equus pelts and whispering her promise to avenge them.

Klaed gave Caen a silent signal, looking after him as he headed off in pursuit of the fleeing poacher.

Returning to the glen, Cwen called for Aerife and was rewarded with his rapid arrival.

"The poachers have been dealt with, as you requested. Now tell me how to find the wyrm shard."

Hearing a sound behind her, Cwen looked over her shoulder to see Klaed and Caen entering the field.

"All of the poachers are dead?" the dragon asked, searching Cwen's eyes for deceit.

"Aye, all of them," Klaed called out behind her, saving her the lie.

She spun around searching his face for the betrayal of her command. Her nostrils flared, her fists clenched, nails biting into the palms of her hands.

"Aye, all of them," she repeated the truth to Aerife.

Opening his large claw, the dragon dropped a pale yellow wyrm shard to the earth before Cwen's feet.

"For the Queen of Ædracmoræ," he growled low in his throat. "May she not bring death to us all."

With a brush of great wings the dragon lifted from the earth leaving only a gentle shift in the air around those remaining.

Cwen swung on Klaed and Caen.

"Which one of you killed the poacher I freed?"

"I did," Caen spoke without hesitation.

"At my request," Klaed added.

"I should kill you both."

"But you will not," Klaed whispered, "because you know that we are right."

Slowly she let out her breath and shook her head. "But I shall not because I am too tired and Talin awaits us at the fortress."

Leaning down she grabbed the shard from the ground and placed it in her bag.

Shoving the bag at Klaed she said, "The Feie and I shall return through the rift. The two of you can walk and carry the shard."

Talin awoke to find Cwen sitting at the table. Her feet were propped up and the chair was tilted at an alarming angle. He smiled and wondered if she would topple to the floor if he called her name, startling her from her sleep. Instead he stood and limped across to the chair, gently lifting her feet and placing the chair on all four legs.

Returning to sit on his bed, he called her name.

"Cwen?"

Her eyes flew open and she looked around, disoriented. Then she saw him and grinned.

"We got the shard."

"That is it? Just 'we got the shard'?" he frowned.

"I cannot tell the tale because we promised Brengven he could do it. With some help from Caen and Klaed."

"This should be good," Talin laughed, imagining the tale the Feie would weave.

A tap at the door brought them – Klaed, Caen and Brengven – all beaming at the sight of Talin seated, rather than lying on the bed.

"I hear you have a tale to tell," Talin said, casting a solemn eye at Brengven.

"Indeed I do," the Feie agreed.

"It was horrible; a quest filled with slavering beasts and murdering poachers."

"Truly? Tell me more, Feie," Talin encouraged, receiving a broad grin from the teller of the tale.

"We arrived in a beautiful glen surrounded by a towering wood. Cwen herself called the Equus of Aaradan and they came in a thundering herd, but they were not alone. A hideously vicious dragon accompanied them and drove us to the ground in terror. Then the beast threatened to eat us if we did not do its bidding. We were forced to hunt the murderous poachers, though Cwen sent Klaed and me away for our own safety."

Cwen raised an eyebrow and glanced toward Klaed to see him waggling his head in agreement.

"But," Brengven continued enthusiastically, "we did not follow her orders. Instead, we crept back to the poachers' camp and caught two violent killers and foiled their plans to ambush Cwen and Caen as they interrogated another of the fiends. Cwen wrung all the information she could from them before killing every last one. Later, she confronted the evil dragon again and wrested the wyrm shard from his great claws with her bare hands. She is a hero."

Talin's jaw hung slack as he looked from face to face.

"And all of this happened as I lay here moaning in my bed?" he asked.

"We knew you would be sorry you missed it," Brengven chirped with a clap of his hands.

"And I do not suppose any of you will ever tell me what really happened," Talin added as he saw the astonishment on Cwen's face.

Suddenly laughing, she said, "Actually, I would have killed all three of these remarkable liars if I had not been so exhausted from wrestling the vicious dragon."

"Now that is the first part of this tale that I believe," Talin laughed, adding, "It is good that I have healed. I certainly do not wish to miss your next adventure."

Chapter 12 Darkness

Laoghaire gazed out over the army of the G'lm. Uncovered by Domangart's trolls beneath the mines on Æwmarshæ, it was far greater in number than the group of soldiers Faervyn had discovered. This army not only contained deathshades and demons, but more than a dozen death dragons as well – each with head bowed in submission to whichever new master would bid them to rise.

Domangart wandered among them tracing his fingers over the ancient symbols on the shields and swords.

"Amazing," he whispered breathlessly, looking back toward Laoghaire.

"I estimate three hundred, maybe more," Laoghaire called to him.

"Certainly a large enough army to divide and conquer Æshulmæ, Æcumbræ and Æwmarshæ," he continued.

"We shall send a third of them into each of the three kingdoms, dividing the strength of the Guardians and weakening their forces. I predict great fear within the realm of the Dragon Queen long before dawn."

As Domangart joined him before the altar, Laoghaire slid the smoky crystal wyrm shard into the receptacle and together they watched the evil awake within the cavern.

A dim, shadowy light shot out of the crystal, striking the eyes of the demonic horde and covering each soldier with its life-giving glow, calling them to battle.

The cavern was filled with the din of their battle cries and all eyes were focused on Laoghaire, seeking his direction. As the dragons rose to their feet and unfolded their wings, the smell of death and decay filled the room.

"Chaos, I command you!" Laoghaire raised his arm and pointed to ten rows of ten minions. "Seek the city of Cridian and bring your destruction upon it. Leave no building standing; leave nothing living." As he lowered his arm the first of the ranks began pouring out into the kingdom of Æwmarshæ.

To the second group he commanded, "Go forth to the city of Merid in Æcumbræ. Seek out every living thing and kill it; leave no building standing and no stone unturned."

The center rank of soldiers turned as one and the fearsome force headed toward the kingdom of Æcumbræ.

The last ten columns of ten minions Laoghaire directed toward the city of Telsar within the kingdom of Æshulmæ, watching as they too turned and set forth to do his bidding.

Above them the land had turned to chaos as the wicked soldiers of the darkness marched in waves toward their targets. As they crossed the fertile plains and entered the deep forests, all life fell before them, withering and dying. Overhead the demon storm raged, growing as the army spread out across the three kingdoms. The heavy, dark clouds boiled within the heavens, sending out drumbeats of thunder as the air crackled with electricity. With it came the dread chill that cooled Ædracmoræ's very heart.

Under cover of night the horde swept toward the sleeping cities, pausing only to burn farms and cottages along the way. No human was left alive and the demon horde feasted on the bodies of the dead as they continued toward the cities Laoghaire had marked for destruction.

Cridian fell amidst the cries of its dying citizens as dragons and deathshades tore down its walls and butchered innocents in their beds.

The Guardians of the nearby fortress were mobilized and sent to the neighboring kingdoms for help, only to find that they too were under attack from the armies of the G'lm. Messengers were dispatched to the House of Aaradan seeking assistance from the Queen.

Yávië and Sōrél gathered Xalín, Sōviē, and the Guardians Rydén and Zeth and swiftly turned their dragon mounts toward the three kingdoms that were under attack.

In the pale light of dawn the three death dragons swept toward the darkness of the heavy clouds, racing ahead of the pursuing Guardians. As they reached the dense blanket of cover they bellowed in victory, knowing that the Guardians would withdraw rather than risk death in the blindness of the vapors.

Sōrél's lips twisted upwards as he broke off the attack and called the others back. The death dragons had never before experienced Xalín's uncanny ability to bring a dragon down whether or not he could see it.

Xalín flew past on the rogue dragon Fastolf. The dragon was large, a third larger than any other Sōrél had ever encountered, and although he appeared to be an accordant dragon, Fastolf's evil temper was more in line with that of the death dragons he pursued.

Sōvië raced past her father and received a sharp reprimand, causing her to bring Fëan around in a wide arc. Blowing her father a kiss, she drew her lance and scanned the heavy cloud cover, seeking some sign of Xalín.

A sudden roar followed by a bellow of pain told her a death dragon would soon flee the blindness of the billows. Fëan pushed forward, sensing his Huntress's excitement. As the panicked death dragon shot into sight the young dragon surged ahead, allowing Sōvië to fling her lance into the beast's chest.

Sōvië shouted in triumph, watching as the dragon seized briefly before it spiraled toward the earth.

Yávië watched Sōvië and shook her head at her daughter's enthusiasm for the hunt.

A second dragon bellowed in fear as Zeth's lance struck it just behind the foreleg, shattering the heart shard and sending the limp carcass hurtling toward the ground.

The third dragon dropped from the protection of the dense cloud cover, already dead. Xalín's lance had found its mark even in the darkness.

The city of Merid in the kingdom of Æcumbræ fared no better than Cridian. Its walls were blackened and homes and shops ran thick with dark blood, the ravaged carcasses of its citizens scattered like the unwanted remains of a meal. Yávië strode through the death and devastation, her eyes blazing with the fury of failure. She called three Guardians aside and snarled instructions to locate the one responsible.

"Someone released this army using a wyrm shard in a cavern of the G'lm. It is most likely that they came from beneath the troll mines of Æwmarshæ, since Cridian was attacked first. Take a battalion and find the remnant of this horde where they lie beneath Ædracmoræ and destroy them in their lair. I want the name of the one responsible! I will rip out his heart and feed it to the king!"

She spun to face Sōrél.

"I want them here! I want them to see the rape of these cities for themselves! Send Nall to them again if you must, but get the rest of the shards quickly, without further delay. Tell Cwen and Talin I want no excuses."

With a tilt of his head he indicated his agreement and leapt to Fáedre's withers, urging the war dragon into the air.

Within Cwen's camp, the King sipped luke-warm tea and passed on the Queen's message.

"We can no longer concern ourselves over the secrecy of your quest. The destruction has now grown to include Telsar and Nold in the kingdom of Æshulmæ, Fardin and Merid in the kingdom of Æcumbræ and Cridian in the kingdom of Æwmarshæ. The Guardians have been sent in force to the three kingdoms and alerted in the other four kingdoms as well. It is no longer a matter of secrecy, but the need for Guardians to patrol and maintain the security of Ædracmoræ that keeps you on this quest. Do not fail us," Sōrél commanded.

"Domangart," Cwen hissed. "He runs the trolls beneath Æwmarshæ and sends the poachers who slaughter the Equus and the dragons. He is responsible for these attacks. I am sure of it."

Sōrél looked hard at Cwen.

"Do not attempt to engage the wizard, Cwen. You do not have the skill or the strength. Just collect the shards as quickly as possible and deliver them to Nall. If we are to believe the Scroll of the G'lm, there are thirteen wyrm shards. You have collected eight; one was stolen and used against us at Calá, and another was used against us in the attacks last night. That leaves four to be found. Brengven will take you through to Merid. Yáviё waits for you there. She wishes to speak to you before you continue."

Sōrél handed Talin a tiny crystal. "This will summon Nall to you when you have need of him. Brengven, call the rift to Merid."

Bobbing his compliance, Brengven quickly summoned the rift with a sweep of his hand, allowing his companions to step through into the carnage and stench of death that was now the city of Merid.

Gagging, they lifted cloaks to cover their noses and mouths as they looked around, wide-eyed. Nothing could have prepared them for the deep, mind-numbing death surrounding them. The color was washed from the city by the ashes and the vicious storm that still raged above. Its dark clouds hung heavy above them, crackling with electricity and sending long fingers of red-gold lightning. A sudden drum roll of thunder startled them, causing them to draw weapons and crouch in alarm.

Yáviё stood before them surveying the damage. The remaining winds swept her long raven hair around her face and her violet eyes looked as fierce as Cwen had ever seen them.

"The storm will not abate as long as a single G'lm remains alive. Right now they lie hidden beneath the earth, waiting only for the night before they strike us again," Yáviё shouted over a clap of thunder.

Calling them forward she swept her hand in front her. "This is what awaits all of Ædracmoræ if you are not swift in your appointed charge. I cannot spare the Guardians to take over the quest for the four remaining shards. We must be ready to stop any further attack; I can spare no man. The moons will rise full above southern Æcumbræ tonight showing you the pathway to the Cavern of the Moons. Do not miss the chance to claim this shard. More citizens of Ædracmoræ will die if you fail." She sighed deeply and looked directly at Cwen.

"I know that my words sound harsh and demanding," she shrugged, "but by your birthright you are bound to serve the Dragon Queen. Do not fail me, Cwen of Aaradan."

Shifting her gaze to Talin, she asked, "Did Sōrél give you the crystal to summon Nall?"

"He did. I will summon him as soon as the shard is in our possession."

"And can you guarantee that his daughter will not kill him?" Yáviё smiled, easing the tension among them.

"Nay, I would not be willing to make that promise," Talin said.

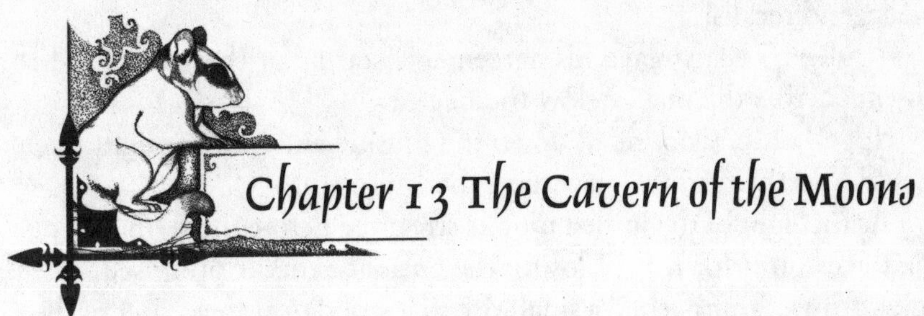

Chapter 13 The Cavern of the Moons

The five of them sat on a knoll, watching as the twin moons Ēun and Ēuné rose slowly above the horizon. Each cast a pale pathway of light across the land, creeping toward one another as the moons ascended in the direction of their zeniths.

"There are no caverns known to exist within this land. The Cavern of the Moons is merely a legend," Cwen sighed, glancing north at the storm that still raged over the borderlands.

Caen glanced at her. "I was told that long ago when the moons first rose, Ēun saw the lovely Ēuné walking before him and hurried to catch her that he might take her for his wife. At their first touch, Ēuné's glowing light merged with that of Ēun, joining them and painting the pathway to the mountain of their earthly home. The Topaz Star raged with jealousy and struck the mountain, crushing it into the earth and creating the Cavern of the Moons. Now, when we do not see the moons, it is said they meet secretly in the darkness of the cave created beneath the fallen mountain."

Cwen's eyes widened.

"Who told you this?"

"My mother," he said, glancing away as the rare memory flooded his mind.

Reaching out, Cwen touched his hand. "Then perhaps it is more than just a legend," she whispered.

"I think you are right, Cwen – look below us," Talin pointed.

Brengven leapt to his feet, shouting, "There, there is the pathway the legend recalls!"

"Indeed." Klaed gave his agreement, staring at the golden light flowing across the plain below them.

Together they pounded down the hillside and into the light that would lead them to the Cavern of the Moons.

As the light of the joined moons streamed before them, they kept their eyes on it for fear of losing the entrance that it promised. The pale pathway approached a small rise that stood near the center of the shallow valley. Gently caressing the swaying grasses, the moons' light suddenly bounced back, blinding them as if it had struck a surface of polished brass. It moved no further, but hovered and glowed brightly just above the base of the low mount.

Stepping forward, Talin extended the blade of his axe into the light, grinning as the light shimmered. He allowed the blade to slip through the glowing surface of the hill.

Withdrawing the blade, he gestured to Cwen, "I offer the legendary Cavern of the Moons to you, milady. Do you wish to enter first?"

"Nay, it was Caen's legend; let us allow him that honor."

Caen stepped forward into the Cavern of the Moons with his companions close on his heels.

By the light of their torches the travelers moved deep underground, keeping to the wide pathway. Occasionally they were forced to edge around slides of earth that nearly closed off the corridor, or crawl over them to continue on their way.

At last they came upon a large cavern, not of stone or crystal but of earth. Tangled roots created an intricate design along the ceiling that trailed across the walls and curled out onto the floor of the cave. Within the grasp of the roots lay a piece of bright white stone with a woman drawn on its face. Cwen knelt and rubbed away the generations of grime that covered the beautiful painting. The woman was tall and slender, her chestnut hair curled about her fair face. Her gowns were golden, touched here and there with royal blues and scarlet – the robes of a noblewoman. Taking her flask, Cwen wet a piece of soft cloth and washed away the bits of dirt that hid the woman's eyes.

With a gasp, Cwen called, "Talin! She has Nall's eyes. Amber eyes with no darkness at their center. See?"

Talin crouched beside her and peered curiously at the woman

depicted on the ancient stone.

He gave Cwen a puzzled look and answered, "She does look like your father. I have never seen another with eyes like Nall's. Who do you think she was?"

Cwen shrugged. "He has never spoken of his people. They were lost long ago when Ædracmoræ fell to Aléria's armies, before the shattering of the seven kingdoms. I know nothing of them."

Shaking her head, she whispered, "I wonder if he knows of this place."

Klaed and Caen came to stand behind them, lending their light and staring at the vision of the noble woman lost beneath the mountain in the Cavern of the Moons.

"She is very beautiful. Like you, Cwen. Her hair is not as rich in color, though it may have been in life," Klaed said.

Cwen slapped his arm and laughed. "I look nothing like her. Except for the golden color of my eyes I look nothing like Nall either."

Talin howled with laughter. "Nay, everything of Nall that you have is wrapped up in your uncontrolled fury and brutality. You do not look like him. You look like Näeré."

"I do not," Cwen said, adding her laughter. "I look like me. Like Cwen. Not like any other."

"You are the most beautiful woman I have ever seen," Caen murmured, leaning forward to trace the line of her jaw with just the whisper of a touch.

Cwen looked up at him with warm, golden eyes, "You know I do not believe your lies."

"I have still never lied to you, Cwen," he answered, extending his hand and pulling her to her feet.

Laughing to cover her sudden unease, she withdrew her hand and headed through a gap in the side wall of the cavern.

"We do not have time for serious conversation or tender moments, Caen. There is a wyrm shard to find before the Dragon Queen and her irritating husband descend on us, crying that we move to slowly and do not accept the graveness of our charge."

Behind her she heard his silent question, "*When will there be time, Cwen?*"

Spinning, she stared at Caen in undisguised confusion.

"What?" he asked. "Did you find something?"

"Nay, but I have never heard your thoughts before," she answered, still staring.

"Did you hear him, Talin? Klaed?" she asked, looking at each of them in turn.

Talin shrugged. "Nay, I have never heard Caen's thoughts because I have never wanted to hear Caen's thoughts."

"Perhaps it is simply the first time you have listened, Cwen," Klaed said, "for I do not hear his thoughts either."

"Think," she said, gazing at Caen intently.

"I am thinking. I am wondering what it is you are talking about," he answered with an easy grin.

"You asked me when…" Pausing, she looked at Klaed and Talin, who were listening with great interest.

"He asked you when what?" Talin cocked his head.

Klaed looked at Caen. "Just what did you ask her?"

"I asked her nothing," Caen shrugged.

Cwen pointed at him. "You did too. Do not deny it."

A rakish grin slid across his face. "Just what did I ask you?"

Turning away from them to hide a smile she called back, "I have forgotten."

Within the chamber adjacent to the room that held the painting of the woman who looked like Nall they found a clutch of eggs. Each was large enough to hold a grown man, and the mottled skin, once leathery and supple, was now stone-like and gray as death. Around the walls of the cavern coiled the ancient ribcage of the wyrm mother.

Cwen stepped to the wall and examined the bones that lay half-buried beneath the stone. With her dagger she eased out an enormous indigo shard and held it out before her. The shadow within wriggled violently in the flickering firelight of their torches.

Tapping the side of the egg closest to him, Talin leapt back as the sides crumbled away, revealing a coiled, serpent-like creature with the head of a dragon. Taking his axe, Talin crushed another egg, and then another, bashing the long dead creatures into dust. Together the four of them destroyed the remnants of the ancient clutch and sought the tiny wyrm shards from within the soft powdered stone.

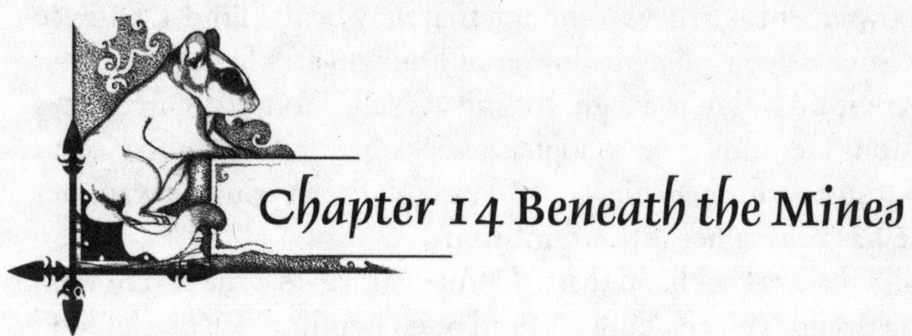

Chapter 14 Beneath the Mines

As Cwen and her companions were recovering the wyrm shards within the Cavern of the Moons a frenzied battle was being waged beneath Domangart's mines.

Guardians mounted on war dragons searched the wide corridors of the mines, slaying all that crossed their paths with fiery breath, bow and sword. The terrified screams of slaves locked deep below the mines drew the Guardians. It was here they discovered the remnants of the G'lm army that Laoghaire had released into the kingdoms of Æwmarshæ, Æcumbræ and Æshulmæ.

Thundering dragons roared as deathshades and demons screamed and wailed. Guardians fortified with the strength of Näeré's sorcery and Grumbl's wizardry met the remaining members of Laoghaire's army with a vengeance. The crash of swords and the hissing of arrows filled the caverns as the soulless soldiers of the abyss met their final death.

The retribution of the Dragon Queen was swift. Domangart was captured as he attempted to flee to Ælmondæ. Locked in the magick manacles of the wizard Grumblton, Domangart begged for mercy, swearing that while he had done nothing to stop Laoghaire's evil; he was in no way responsible for the release of the G'lm.

Nall's fist slammed into Domangart's jaw, throwing the wizard to the ground.

"My daughter seeks you, Domangart. She holds you responsible for the slaughter of the Equus and the dragons of Æstaffordæ. Her favorite punishment for poachers and those who hire them is disembowelment, I believe – though that may be too kind a sentence for one such as you," Nall bellowed in Domangart's face.

The wizard began to laugh, hissing at Nall, "Your daughter's days of freedom are numbered. Laoghaire seeks her and has promised to mete out justice for her thievery and lies. Not even you will want her after he has beaten her into submission."

Nall's furious backhand threw Domangart against the cavern wall, splitting his lips and cracking his head open, sending rich black blood over the wizard's face and soaking his hair.

"We shall keep you alive and available, Domangart. If any harm comes to Cwen I will punish you myself. You may recall my wife, the sorceress Näeré. She is quite skilled and can keep you alive for many years while I mete out the punishment you deserve."

Turning on his heel, Nall ran into Yáviё. Her eyes were dark, her jaws clinched as she stared past him at Domangart. Her heavy sword hung loosely from her left hand.

"You dare to threaten the Crown?" her voice hissed like burning oil striking hot iron. "You enslave my citizens and feed them to your trolls. You lay waste to my kingdoms. And yet even though you hang in manacles you still have the courage to threaten my niece, the daughter of Nall, with defilement at the hands of the wizard Laoghaire? You must think yourself great indeed. Cut off his legs below the knee and burn the stumps so that he does not bleed out."

As she swung back to face Nall she heard the wizard's high-pitched scream. Turning back to him she gave a deadly smile.

"Now you fear me, wizard?" she asked.

Four of her Guardians held him, manacled arms above his head with his face crushed into the filth-covered floor of his own mines. She watched as the Guardian Zeth raised an axe above his head, looking to her for the order. With a sharp nod she gave it and watched the axe cleave Domangart's right leg, sending it rolling away into the darkness of the pit. The stench of burning flesh filled the air as Zeth fired the stump to stop the bleeding.

As his wordless keening turned to muffled sobs and gagging, the Queen offered Domangart a reprieve.

"If you tell me where to find Laoghaire I shall allow you to keep your left leg," she said, kneeling next to him. "I shall offer it only once. What is your answer?"

Gasping in pain, Domangart squealed, "He has returned to his lair near the ruins of Sylwervyn's tower, though you will never find him there if he does not wish it."

"If I do not find him, I shall return for your other leg. Place the wizard in the oubliette, the deep one beneath the keep at the fortress in Æcumbræ. Water every other day. Bread four times a week until I return. Then we shall decide how much of his body will remain his own." She leapt to the dragon Aero's back and headed back toward the surface behind Nall.

Looking overhead, Yáviё breathed a sigh of relief. "The last of the horde is dead. The storm clears."

Nall said, "Do not kill Domangart, Yáviё; if Cwen is harmed it is my right to take his life."

Yáviё pointed at Nall. "It is your right to heal the harm that has already been done her. Until you do she is a danger to herself and those around her, for her fear causes recklessness in battle. Do not wait, Nall; make your peace with her soon."

"Talin summons me," Nall said abruptly, urging Ardor skyward as he waved his acknowledgement to the Queen.

"Do not be a fool," she called after him, watching him again lift his hand in silent response.

Shaking her head, Yáviё spoke over her shoulder to Näeré, who was dragging a dead demon toward the flaming pyre.

"I do not care how you accomplish it, but I will have peace in my house. Bewitch them, soothe them, put both of them to sleep or boil them in oil – I truly do not care, Näeré, but put an end to their foolishness. Sōrél and I have grown weary of it, as I know you have. End it. I know that it is in your power."

Whirling Aero around, Yáviё urged him into the air and hastened him toward her fortress and Sōrél.

Näeré watched Yáviё go, a sad smile touching her beautiful features as she answered the disappearing Queen, "Aye, I do grow weary; but peace may only come with the death of one of them, and this I cannot allow."

Exiting the Cavern of the Moons in darkness, the travelers discovered the moons had fled, taking the golden path with them. Looking back over his shoulder, Talin found the entrance once again sealed, with nothing left but a hillock of gently swaying grasses.

Rejoining Brengven in the cold camp he had pitched, they feasted on dried stag and cold tea, telling the little Feie the tale of the eggs and the shard. At Cwen's request they did not speak of the beautiful woman with amber eyes who looked so much like Nall.

Talin summoned Nall, meeting him at the edge of the grassy plain, away from Cwen as she had asked.

Nall held the wyrm shard out before him, watching the shadow squirm within.

"It is the largest you have recovered and carries the color of the joined houses. I do not like it. Not at all."

"There was a clutch within the cavern as well," Talin added, holding out the small bag containing the thirty small heart shards they had collected. "I do not know if they carry any threat, but it did not seem wise to leave them there."

Nall took the bag, looking past Talin's shoulder and searching the distance for a glimpse of Cwen.

"Now she hides from me?" he asked.

"Nay, she merely asked that I summon you away from our camp. She is not ready to speak to you again."

"Speak to me? That is what you call it?" Nall inquired. "As I recall, she screamed and ranted and waved weapons the entire time I was last in your camp."

"That is an accurate description. She did not like the pompous way you spoke to her." Talin grinned.

"I was speaking to you, not her," Nall grinned back.

"Still, she did not like it." Talin's smile faded.

"Tell her… I do not know what to say to her," Nall admitted, the lines around his mouth tightening.

"Each time we speak of you she asks only if you have spoken her name," Talin said, his gaze still solemn.

Nall's expression lost its harshness as he shook his head and asked, "How is Cwen, Talin? How is my daughter?"

"She is well, though she rants at the Queen's policies and fumes at our foolishness," Talin answered, turning back toward the camp.

"I shall tell her you asked after her," he called back.

Cwen held her breath as she watched Talin and Nall from her

hiding place behind a fall of ancient stones.

She felt Nall touch the barriers she had constructed against him in her mind, and saw his eyes searching the camp. She bit her lip and tried to force herself toward them, but her feet remained frozen to the ground.

"*You will have to go sometime*," Caen's gentle voice caressed her mind. "*You will never heal until you do.*"

She felt him step closer, but he did not attempt to touch her.

"Why can I not just go to him?" she asked aloud.

Sighing, Caen placed his cloak around her shoulders, feeling her tense for a moment before she relaxed in its warmth.

"*Because you have been afraid so long*," he whispered silently.

She watched as Talin returned and Nall strode back to Ardor, leaping deftly to the dragon's withers and heading back toward Æwmarshæ. The sky had begun to clear, the angry storm clouds falling away to leave bright starlight behind him.

"Father." Cwen spoke the word out loud.

Talin grinned.

"He asked after you," he told Cwen.

She looked up at him, prepared for the hurt she always felt.

"Did he speak my name?" she asked, drawing a deep breath.

"Aye. He did," Talin answered. "Indeed he did."

Her eyes searched his face for deception, but she found only truth.

A small smile touched her eyes and Talin saw the young girl he had once known linger there for a moment before falling back into the darkness.

Chapter 15 Indigo's Inferno

Cwen called the Equus of Æcumbræ to carry them to Æshulmæ and Indigo's tavern, where Caen felt sure they would gain the information they needed to recover the tenth shard.

As they broke camp, Talin asked Caen, "Just how wicked is this Indigo?"

"Do not be caught alone with her," Caen said without humor. "She is an expert with a blade and carries several, though you will not see them until it is far too late."

"Do you speak from experience?" Klaed joked.

"Aye," Caen answered, the chill of the word frosting the air. "Do not take what I say lightly, Klaed; it could cost you your life to disbelieve me."

A series of long whinnies announced the arrival of the Equus and Cwen went forward to soothe them. Nevin, Valckyr, Bruudwyg and Kaiper calmed within the sanctuary of her presence, making muted snorts and gentle nickers as they danced and tossed their heads.

Patting Valckyr, she reminded Bruudwyg of his rider's inexperience and laughed at the Equus' wheeze when he recalled Caen's heavy mounting. "He did promise to do better," Cwen reminded them, registering the silent Equus' laughter in her mind.

Klaed approached, watching the gentle woman Cwen became around the Equus.

"Have you ever considered treating us with such compassion?" he asked.

"Nay, never – not even for an instant," she said. "You are armed and a constant threat to all that I hold dear."

"And what is it that you hold so dear?" he asked, tilting his head and squinting against the bright morning light.

"My freedom," came her whispered answer.

"Kaiper will carry you," she said, changing the subject to something less personal. "He is gentle and will simply hear your wishes and obey. Try not to run him off a cliff."

"Caen," she called, watching as he picked up his pack and swung it over his shoulder.

"I have assured Bruudwyg that you will have improved your mount, but he seems doubtful. Though he has agreed to carry you regardless," she chuckled.

Leaping to Valckyr's back as lightly as a field sprite, she turned to watch Caen.

While the mount was not perfect, and Bruudwyg cringed in anticipation, it was far better than the first had been, and earned Caen a bright smile from Cwen and a soft nicker of gratitude from his mount.

Brengven headed off at a steady pace, assuring them as he passed that he would much rather carry himself.

Talin mounted Nevin and swung him around with a silent command, heading off after the Feie. An easy trot kept them abreast of Brengven and within speaking distance of one another.

"The last of the horde must have been discovered and slain," Talin said, staring up at the brilliant day star and warm sky.

"It is a beautiful world, Ædracmoræ," Cwen said, as if she had just noticed. "I wonder what it was like before."

"When it was shattered and the seven kingdoms separated?" Klaed asked.

"Aye, and before that – when Yáviё's mother and Sōrél's father ruled," Cwen wondered aloud.

"You could ask the Queen," Caen said.

"I could ask Yáviё – or you could, Talin. She has always liked you." Cwen laughed at Talin's grimace.

"It was my father she admired. It is not me," Talin frowned.

"Maybe Rosie would tell us," Klaed shrugged. "Or Grumblton."

"Hah! Would you really risk a beating to ask Grumbl? He is always angry. Every time I have seen him he has been angry," Cwen said, wrinkling her nose at the thought.

Laughing, she admitted, "Perhaps we do not need to know after all."

Again her companions watched Cwen as she released the Equus. Resting her face against each neck and rubbing each mane, she whispered her gratitude for their service and her wish for their safe journey.

"Use the veil," she whispered to Valckyr.

"*The one called Caen. His thoughts are all of you,*" Bruudwyg shared, making Cwen smile and glance back at Caen.

Seeing his questioning look, she called back to him, "Bruudwyg says you have improved greatly, but that your mind is rarely on the road."

Caen grinned guiltily and looked away before answering, "Even the beasts can hear my thoughts. Perhaps you could teach me to block them."

"Oh, I think I am far safer if I can hear them."

With a last touch for each Equus, Cwen released them and felt her heart swell at the sight of their shimmering veil and the fading sound of their hoof beats.

Lagoth was not a beautiful town; in fact, it was not a town at all and it made the decaying flavor of Ælmondæ appear palace-like. The tavern they sought lay beneath the settlement; its entrance was the carved opening of an ancient Gaianite mine. Above the door hung a sign of caution to all who entered, "Live Entrance into Indigo's Inferno does not Promise Live Exit".

Talin raised his brows and gave Caen a probing glance.

"You do know the most unusual people, Caen."

Caen gave each of them an intense look before stating, "Do not make note of it. She will slay you where you stand if you do."

"Make note of what?" Klaed asked.

"Anything," Caen cursed. "This is the most treacherous tavern you will ever enter. Our lives will be in jeopardy the entire time that we remain. Cwen, while you are not so much at risk, Indigo will kill you if you offend her. Do not allow your gaze to linger on anything for too long."

Brengven had remained beyond the walls since Caen had told him he was nothing more than "fodder for the wicked."

The room was filled with smoke from the un-vented fire at its center. Crude tables and chairs were arranged in tight groups around its warmth and a long, coarsely hewn bar stretched along the far end of the tavern. Caen headed for the bar, followed reluctantly by his companions.

As they neared, a woman broke away from the crowd at the bar. She was not human. Her luminous skin was a deep grayish blue-purple and on her shoulder the handprint of the man she had been talking to was fading away as it warmed. No hair covered her head; instead, leafy scales similar to those of the emerald sea dragons lay tightly closed around her face and coursed down her back. They shimmered in the firelight, as iridescent as the wings of the buttermoth. Her breasts were almost bare, with each nipple covered by a gold coin, leaving Cwen wondering what kept them in place. From low on her waist hung a scarlet loincloth held in place by a slender golden thread that circled her narrow hips. Her bright crimson eyes took in the approaching group, measuring each individually and assessing their possibilities and level of threat. She reached out as they grew close, touching Caen's chest with a delicate, long-fingered hand that ended in sharp, metallic nails.

"Ná jun bokgol vet Caen? Vi ná jai kaigol mord jevi darcor." The woman's words covered them with intense and alarming warmth.

"Speak the language of Men, Indigo. My companions do not speak Maraenian.

Her lips drew back in what they assumed to be a smile, exposing sharp white teeth and a pale blue cleft tongue.

"Why do you travel with the uneducated, Caen? It is beneath you as my acolyte," Indigo repeated in the language of Men, her eyes sweeping over Cwen and Talin without interest before settling on Klaed.

"Because we do not speak your language does not mean we are uneducated," Cwen argued.

Shifting her gaze back to Cwen, Indigo gave her a cursory

examination, dismissing her as unattractive and fragile. Ignoring the red-haired woman's remark, she returned her eyes to Caen.

"The language of Men carries no fire," she whispered, pulling Caen nearer and sniffing him.

Gripping her wrist, he removed her hand from his chest and saw her eyes deepen in color, turning the black scarlet of spilled blood. She examined her wrist as the mark of his touch changed from white-hot to yellow before fading to red and finally returning to the deep blue purple color of her skin.

"I am not your servant, Indigo, and I bear the scars to prove it," Caen snapped. "We are here on business."

Indigo's eyes slid back to Cwen, looking her up and down as one would a side of stag.

"She is worth very little, Caen. The men of Lagoth prefer the more exotic. But this one…" She reached out to stroke Klaed's chest with a long nail. "This one I will pay you handsomely for. Say, ten lule?"

Reaching around to the small of her back, Indigo withdrew a soft leather collar attached to a short golden leash.

"If we are agreed I will pay you now and take him to begin his training." Her eyes flashed, sending a wave of heat across them.

Talin coughed to hide his laugh and Cwen snickered softly with the awareness that she was not the object of the sale.

"He belongs to the woman," Caen spoke sharply, "and he is not for sale."

Another wave of heat, this one more intense, flew over them with the flashing of Indigo's eyes.

"If he is not for sale I shall just take him," she said, making a snatching gesture with her clawed hand.

"Unless you wish to fight for him," she added, her flaming eyes focused on Cwen's face.

Seeing Cwen's uncertainty, Indigo gave a soft chuckle.

"Perhaps he is worth more to me than to you?" she tilted her head in query.

Cwen raised her chin defiantly and grabbed Klaed's arm, jerking him toward her. She snatched the hair on both sides of his head and pulled his face down to hers, watching the surprise fill his eyes. She leaned into him and kissed him deeply before drawing away.

She whispered to Indigo, "Oh, I will fight for him. Indeed, I will fight for him."

Running her tongue across her teeth, Indigo nodded her agreement.

"One shadow's passing should allow you to prepare. We shall meet in the arena where I shall kill you and take your servant, human."

Walking away from them, Indigo returned to the bar, glancing back briefly as she spoke to the barkeep.

Caen grabbed Cwen by the shoulders, hissing through clenched teeth, "What are you doing? She will kill you before the blood in your heart can reach your mind."

Giving a short laugh, Cwen asked, "What was I supposed to do? Let her take Klaed?"

"Aye," Caen said softly. "I would have preferred it to losing you."

"Why did she give me time to prepare? Prepare for what?" Cwen asked.

"To make arrangements for your death and the disposal of your property. To arrange for the ashes of your body once your soul has left it. Cwen, she will kill you, horribly and painfully – she will kill you." Caen shook his head.

Talin glared at Cwen and Caen then fixed his gaze on Klaed.

"Perhaps it is not too late to sell Klaed," Talin muttered.

"I prefer not to be sold or end up in her possession after she kills Cwen. Perhaps we should just leave," Klaed suggested.

"The city is sealed. It is always closed for a contest. There is no way to leave without meeting her now that Cwen has challenged her." Laughing harshly, Caen added under his breath, "To attempt to leave would only bring death more swiftly. I warned you."

He dragged Cwen to an empty table and forced her into a chair.

"Remain here with Talin and Klaed. Try to look confident. I shall seek an advocate; hopefully I can find one with the power to make Indigo allow a surrogate, a lex, to fight in your place."

"Why is it you are so certain I cannot win, Caen?" Cwen asked.

Shaking his head, he knelt before her and took her hands in his. "She will burn you, Cwen. Reduce you to a pile of ash not even your mother would recognize. She will lead you on with her daggers, giving you false confidence, and then she will burn you. Indigo is Maraen; a woman of fire. With a thought she can send heat so fierce it can melt the shard of a dragon. You cannot win against her. Stay here and do not wander. Will you promise it?" His eyes pleaded with her to follow his direction.

Nodding slowly, she looked up at Talin and Klaed.

"I only sought to save Klaed," she whispered, feeling foolish.

"I shall order heavy ale. If you are going to be burned alive you will probably wish to be drunk. And if Klaed is about to be trained by the fire woman…" Talin shrugged, making his way toward the bar.

The male Maraen, Tujun, shook his heavy head violently. "She will not allow it, Caen. I am sorry you will lose your woman and a friend, but Indigo would only offer the use of a lex if she feared her opponent."

Allowing his eyes to drift to Cwen, he said sadly, "That woman is not fearsome enough to frighten a downy flier."

Caen could not stop the laugh that exploded from his chest.

"Tujun, do not say that where she can hear you. She will, with one swift cut, spill your guts onto the floor and walk through them with complete disregard."

"The shadow passes quickly and you have little time. Spend it with the woman. Yimi can cast a spell of emptiness so that she does not suffer at her death. Beyond that I can offer you nothing." Tujun shrugged hopelessly.

"Unless…" he added in afterthought, "you can get Jūdan to intercede on your woman's behalf."

"It has been long since she interfered in Indigo's business, but she always liked you, Caen. Perhaps with sufficient payment?" the advocate shrugged again.

"Where can I find her?" Caen asked, glancing at the shadow clock and wincing to see how little time remained.

"Above, in her chamber. Above the bar," Tujun said with certainty. "She trains a concubine and may not welcome your interruption, but I have no other thoughts."

Leaping to his feet, Caen raced up the stairs at the end of the bar three at a time and pounded on the door of Jūdan's room. Waiting a moment, he began beating the door again and was rewarded as it opened a crack to reveal Jūdan's crimson eye peering out.

"Caen," the Maraen sighed. "I should have known it would be a human."

Pulling the door open wider, she beckoned him in. A man lay on her bed, his hands and feet manacled to the posts, his flesh already welting from her heat. Flipping the coverlet over him, she spoke harshly in Maraen, warning him against speaking. Then she returned her gaze to Caen.

"What? What is it, Caen?" she reached out and ran the tip of her finger across his forehead and tasted his sweat.

"You are fearful." She tilted her head and burned him with a light flash of her heat.

"The woman I travel with has challenged Indigo. She did not know." Caen spoke the truth.

Jūdan said, "And you want my intercession to save your woman?"

Laughter bubbled from deep within the Maraen, sending a deep wave of heat over Caen.

"I have never understood your passion for human women, Caen; they offer so little."

"This is different. She is the niece of the Queen. If she is harmed the entire House of Ædracmoræ and all its Guardians will descend upon you. The Maraen will be exterminated." Caen's voice was flat and direct.

"Why do you not simply tell Indigo? She would understand the threat."

"She would not care and you know it. For her it is an act against me. She does not care what she brings upon your people," Caen said sharply.

Nodding, Jūdan leaned toward Caen.

"You will have to pledge your service."

Seeing his hesitation and his glance at the concubine on her bed she chuckled.

"I will not ask more than you can bear, Caen. You are useless if you are dead."

"No manacles, no collars. I remain free at all times during the indenture," he bargained. "And the service is only to you."

"Two days," Jūdan said decisively, "and you promise compliance."

Taking a deep breath, Caen nodded his acceptance.

"I will return to you at the end of my present charge. You have my word as a thief," Caen said spitting into his hand and extending it to Jūdan.

She wagged her finger at him, "Mere salt moisture will not suffice. This requires your pledge in blood."

Nodding again, he withdrew his dagger and dragged it across his palm, offering the Maraen his blood. Accepting it she stood looking down on her manacled servant.

"Rest. I shall return shortly," she said, stroking the man's cheek.

"I also seek a shard – the heart shard of an ancient wyrm. It is rumored that it is held within the Inferno," Caen said.

"It will cost you an extra half day's service," Jūdan said, shaking her head at his attempt to gain the shard outside of his payment.

Sensing Caen's reluctant agreement, she gave her promise in return: "I will deliver it this night. Camp beyond the flaming ridge and leave a small fire burning. I will come to you."

Standing tall, she preceded Caen from her rooms and went to challenge Indigo's authority as Cwen's newly purchased advocate.

Klaed slept with his head on his crossed arms, a single draught of heavy ale leaving him in a stupor. Cwen's eyes revealed belligerence and Talin pulled her mug from her hand.

"Caen told you to wait here. Sit. Stay – until he returns with your savior." Talin glared at her.

"Look at her! She is no larger than I. I can best her with a sword or a bow. I can dip my sword in pitch and hack her to death with its flaming blade," Cwen slurred.

"You have either had too much ale or not enough," Caen's voice whispered in her ear.

Shaking her mane of copper hair she tilted her head back and gazed upside down at him through drowsy eyes.

"I have struck a bargain. We can leave," Caen sighed.

"Did you find someone stronger and braver than me to fight the wicked fire woman?" Cwen's golden laughter gurgled.

"Nay, Cwen. I bought your freedom, for there is no one stronger and braver than you. Now, let us go before Indigo has time to reconsider the threat of your advocate."

Without further conversation he scooped Cwen up against him, leaving Talin to drag Klaed along behind.

Brengven fumed at the necessity of a flame in their camp so close to the evil tavern, but finally built the signal fire and retreated a league, telling them that he would report their deaths to the Queen on the morrow.

Klaed and Cwen snored in their drunken sleep as Talin sat cross-legged near the fire watching the silent Caen.

A sound like the rattle of dry leaves drew him to his feet, axe drawn, but Caen held out his hand in warning and watched Talin sink back to the ground.

The Maraen entered the light of the fire, her scales flashing with its reflected colors. Seeing Talin, she bowed her acknowledgement before pulling out the bag containing the wyrm shard.

"It is as black as the abyss and as clear as lightning glass," she said, drawing it from the cloth and holding it out to Caen. "There is a small dark seed within. Is this what you seek, concubine?"

"Aye, Jūdan. I am grateful…"

"Your gratitude is not necessary. Your payment is sufficient. Indigo is distressed that our agreement does not include her." Jūdan's crimson eyes met Caen's pale green.

"I will not change our bargain, Jūdan."

The Maraen nodded. "I told her you would not. Two and a half days indenture to me, unbound as long as you comply – that will remain the charge. You are bound by your blood to fulfill it. I have never known you not to execute your oath. You are an honorable man, Caen."

"May I see the woman I have saved?"

Caen led her to stand above the sleeping Cwen.

A low chuckle erupted from Jūdan's thin lips.

"Explain to me," she asked Caen in puzzlement, "why it is you gave your oath to set her free?"

A flash of heat rushed from her, burning Caen's lungs as he inhaled.

"You really should learn to control that before someone gets burned seriously," he encouraged, thinking of his coming servitude.

"It is controlled, Caen. Were it not, you would be a pile of ash. Now, tell me," Jūdan asked again.

"She is a warrior, a noblewoman of fire and ice. I can offer no more explanation than that," Caen said softly as he gazed on the sleeping Cwen.

Extending her hand, Jūdan placed it over Caen's heart.

"Be careful, hero. She will burn you far worse than I."

Bowing again to Talin, Jūdan took her leave.

The crash of a dragon landing beyond the camp brought Talin to his feet. Nall walked cautiously into the camp looking for the screaming banshee he called 'daughter'. Talin grinned and watched as Nall stood next to Caen, staring down at Cwen.

"What is it you want from her?" Nall asked Caen.

Caen met Nall's eyes and smiled. "Nothing that I would discuss with her father."

Nall frowned as Caen left him and went to the far side of the fire where he wrapped himself in his cloak and settled down for the night.

"He purchased her freedom today," Talin spoke quietly as he stepped up beside Nall.

"Freedom from whom?" Nall asked, thinking of Domangart's threat.

"A Maraen woman named Indigo. Cwen challenged her and Caen paid for her release from the challenge."

"Why would Cwen challenge a Maraen?" Nall asked, shaking his head in disbelief.

"To save Klaed," Talin shrugged. "She thought it was the right thing to do. Cwen did not know she could not win."

"Caen also bargained to recover the wyrm shard," he added, handing it to Nall. "And with his help Sidon is dead."

Nall gazed across at Caen.

"He is braver than I believed… or a greater fool."

"Aye, he is more than I thought him to be." Talin agreed.

"You go on to Æwmarshæ on the morrow?" Nall asked, turning back to Talin.

"Aye, Morg told Cwen the embers burned hot below Vissenmire, though we are not certain exactly where," Talin observed.

"Why is it everything hidden seems to lie below the ground or in a fen?" Nall muttered. "Ask Borrolon when you arrive."

Kneeling next to Cwen, Nall gently brushed the hair away from her face and whispered as he had when she was very small, "Sleep well, Cwen."

As he walked away Cwen's eyes opened and she stared after him.

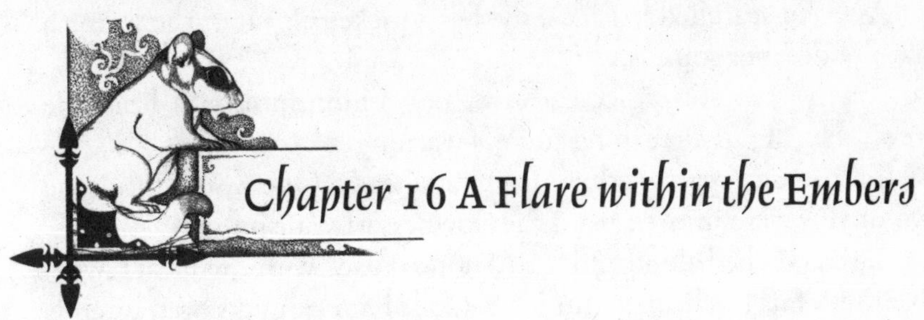

Chapter 16 A Flare within the Embers

Deep beneath Æwmarshæ they discovered an ancient altar empty of the wyrm shard it had once held.

Talin gave a deep sigh. "The wizards must have used this one to drive the armies that destroyed the cities here and in Æshulmæ and Æcumbræ."

"It is not surprising that Domangart's trolls found this shard. The mines are a giant maze and their long tendrils of corridors extend even below the mire," Talin continued, indicating a dark passage dropping steeply from the cavern where they stood.

"It might have been us lying in the ashes amid the rubble if we had arrived a day earlier to seek the Cavern of the Moons," Klaed mused as he led the way back toward the surface.

With a long sigh, Cwen headed upward after them, calling, "We will spend the night at Vissenmire and leave at daybreak for Ælmondæ. I wish to speak with the elder, Borrolon, regarding the mirror mentioned on the Scroll of the G'lm."

She felt Caen's thoughts as they swirled into her mind, bringing a shy smile to her face.

"*At last there will be time for us.*"

He took her hand and held it momentarily, eyebrows raised in a silent question.

"Aye," Cwen whispered very softly, blocking her thoughts so that she would not be overheard by Talin or Klaed. "*There will be time – but there is no 'us'.*"

As Caen searched her face, she felt a flicker of fear at the warmth that flooded her soul.

"Caen," her soft voice caressed him, filling him with heat. He drew away slightly, recalling Jūdan's warning.

Talin's voice reached them from far ahead. "One would think the two of you were injured from the slowness of your progress."

Cwen laughed aloud and Caen shouted back with a wink at Cwen, "Neither of us has been wounded yet, but I am certain Cwen intends to do me harm soon enough."

The Ancient Borrolon lifted his shoulders in dismissal, staring at Cwen as they stood outside his hovel in the mire.

"A mirror? Talks to the Feie," the elder Ancient shrugged.

"The Feie?" Cwen questioned.

"Aye, it is no mirror here. So it must be there." Borrolon nodded as if he made perfect sense.

Full bellies and the comfort of the mire left all in good humor. Brengven remained at the fire until long after dark, making Talin retell the tales of their adventures and retelling an even more embellished tale of their encounter with the dragon and the poachers.

Cwen's laughter floated lightly on the breeze, causing Klaed to encourage Talin and the Feie in appreciation of the sound. Caen had grown more sober as the evening wore on, finally standing to announce that he was going for a walk to clear his mind.

Talin looked toward Cwen and watched her eyes follow Caen as he headed through the training field toward the meadow beyond.

Silently Klaed spoke to Cwen, "*He requires your counsel, Cwen, for you are the cloud within his mind.*"

"*And he is the storm within mine.*"

Excusing herself, she stood and followed Caen.

She found him lying in the longgrass of the meadow, staring up at the night sky filled with the flickering brightness of ten thousand souls.

"Many have been driven to the heavens by the G'lm," she whispered, lying down beside him just beyond his reach.

He merely nodded without speaking.

Side by side they lay silent watching the darkness deepen.

"Have you ever paused to wonder why I have followed you for so long, Cwen? A thief like me following a noblewoman as chaste and pure as the sacred pools." His words were grave, a faint whisper in the silence of the night.

"It is not true. I am not..." Cwen's laugh was short and harsh, wrenched from her by her recollections of Aidan and Sidon.

"Aye, it is true. It is the greatest truth that I have ever spoken," Caen answered even more softly, turning his head to meet her eyes.

"I can promise you nothing, make no pledge of future vows. I have no cache of treasure and I bear the name of no House. But my desire to serve you is as indisputable as Klaed's."

"And if I asked you for your kiss?" she asked, closing her eyes against the intensity of his gaze.

"I would give it gladly," he said, drawing near enough that she could feel his warmth, even though he made no move to touch her.

"My kiss? Is that your desire, Cwen?"

The warmth of his breath touched her hair, causing her to shiver.

Opening sad eyes she admitted, "I fear where it will lead."

"It will lead nowhere Cwen, if you do not wish it. I am not Aidan." Rolling away from her, he stood and held out his hand. "I will escort you to your hovel, or back to the fire if you prefer."

She took his hand and allowed him to pull her to her feet.

The fire had cooled and its warm embers had faded. Talin and Klaed were gone and the hovels were dark. Caen walked with Cwen to the door of her hovel and pushed it open.

"Good night, Cwen," he whispered, leaning forward and touching his warm lips to her forehead before stepping back and turning to go.

"Do not leave me alone," she murmured, touching his arm, the power of her voice drawing him back to her.

Her golden eyes were bright, her lips trembled with uncertainty and her breath caught in her throat.

"Come," he said, stepping past her into her hovel.

He threw the bolt and looked at her. "That is to keep others out, not to keep you in."

Cwen's look told him she had indeed thought otherwise.

He sat down at her table and lit a candle. Looking up at her he gestured to the other chair. She sat and folded her hands in her lap, fixing her eyes on them.

Her voice was tiny and child-like when she asked, "What do you want me to do?"

"Cwen," he whispered, leaving his chair and kneeling before her, "I do not want you to do anything."

Reaching up and pushing the hair back from her face, he tilted her chin up to make her look at him.

"That is not true," he admitted. "I want you to sleep in my arms without worry or fear. I want you to let me kiss away the wickedness that still haunts you in the darkness of your dreams, and most of all I want you to allow me to wake and see your beauty before I face the day."

A tear spilled down her cheek and he whispered, "It would grieve me greatly if I were the cause of your tears."

"You are not," she said, pushing him back and standing.

Taking her nightdress from the hook next to the chair she drew it over her head, undressing beneath it while her eyes remained locked on Caen's. Going to her bed she lay down, her eyes never leaving his face.

"Show me. Show me what it is like to be held by a man who does not threaten and punish." Her voice was soft as velvet, her eyes still shimmering with unshed tears.

He sat beside her on the bed and drew the covers over her, gently stroking her hair. Lying back, he pulled her to him, nestling her head in the hollow of his shoulder and kissing the top of her head. As she shifted slightly she felt his arms loosen, allowing her freedom. He lifted her chin seeking her eyes and she placed her hand against his heart, feeling its steady beat.

As the glow of the candle flickered and died he left her side, the sudden absence of his warmth leaving her chilled. But he returned quickly, his skin warming her once again.

His kisses were soft and his touch gentle as he replaced her fearful night terrors with new memories of tender passion, and in the faint glow of the day star's rising, Caen woke to Cwen's beauty as he had often done in his dreams.

Talin and Klaed watched as Caen stepped from Cwen's hovel. He bore no smile of conquest, only the shadow in his eyes that showed he loved a woman to whom he felt he had no right to pledge.

Klaed shook his head and whispered, "And so his torment begins."

Talin gave Klaed a lop-sided grin. "Make no misstep that he will see as a threat, for he will protect her honor fiercely."

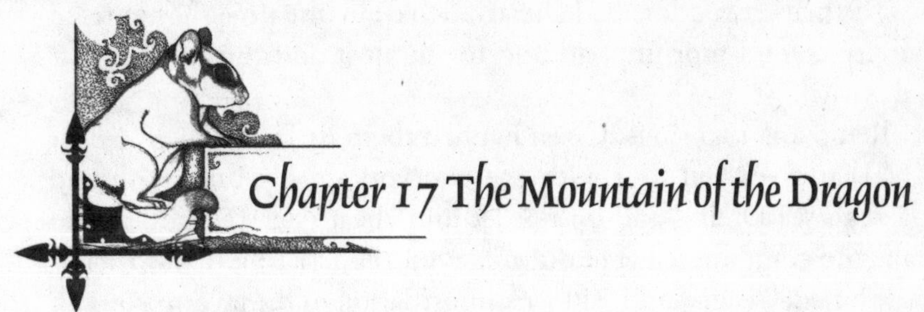

Chapter 17 The Mountain of the Dragon

Brengven took them through the rift, placing them in a dense wooded area a little less than three leagues from the city of Ezon in the kingdom of Ælmondæ.

"I will camp here while you provision and seek information," Brengven grunted, giving Cwen an odd sideways glance.

"What is it, little man?" she questioned.

Shaking his head, he muttered, "You do not seem as… hostile. Still fierce, yes; but somehow changed."

Tilting her head, she said, "I slept well and my dreams were pleasant. A night in the mire always improves my disposition."

"I shall never understand your attachment to the mire or how a mere dream can affect your disposition," the Feie grumbled, looking toward Talin, who shrugged and grinned.

"Perhaps her dreams were especially vivid," Klaed offered good-naturedly.

"Perhaps," Cwen shot him a warning glance, "we should depart before I am forced to hurt someone."

Wheeling away from them she ran off in the direction of Ezon beneath Caen's lingering gaze.

"I withdraw my observation. She is as foul as ever," Brengven fumed.

Laughing, the three men headed off after Cwen, leaving the Feie as mystified as ever by the behavior of mere mortals.

The market vendors had already arrived by the time they entered the city at mid-morning, adding to the dust and din of the city's daily ritual.

Removing two rings, Cwen handed them to Talin.

"That gives you four with the two you already carry. You and Klaed go see Drell – and do not let him cheat you. Tell him not to make me come myself. He did miss you the last time I was there," she grinned, "Caen and I will seek information in the tavern; you can meet us there after you gather our provisions."

"Use caution. There is an ill wind brewing in Ezon today," Klaed said as his eyes searched the narrow street filled with vendors.

"Klaed, it is Ælmondæ, an ill wind blows over the entire kingdom. It is the stench of poachers and slavers. Talin will keep you safe," Cwen laughed in dismissal.

Drell examined the four rings Talin placed before him.

"And where is the lovely Cwen?" the shopkeeper asked, looking up as he palmed the loose stone from the third ring.

Talin grinned and shook his head. "She is drinking in the tavern, but sends you greetings and a hope that she will not have to visit you herself."

"The stone in this ring is loose; I shall replace it for you," Drell said, quickly returning the stone he had removed to plain sight upon the counter.

"Did she kill these men herself?" he asked, glancing up again.

"Aye, and many more," Talin tossed out. "I think she looks forward to the day she adds your name to the souls she has helped find the night sky."

"Eight lule," Drell spoke quickly, "two each. That is a good price for rings of such poor quality."

Stepping forward, Klaed picked up the rings one by one, examining each with an experienced eye.

"As a nobleman I know that such rings will bring you closer to eight lule each. I do not believe the Lady Cwen will be satisfied with your offer. Perhaps we should seek her approval, Talin." Klaed looked up expectantly.

"Eight lule each!" Drell gasped. "But I must make a profit. I will offer six lule each and not a coin more."

"Done," Talin said, grinning and slapping Klaed on the back.

Caen paused and drew Cwen to him as they approached the tavern.

"What I feel for you is as foreign to me as a blue 'Taur," he said, blowing out a deep breath.

With a wan smile she reminded him, "You have made no promise Caen, nor have I."

"There are women in this tavern who… know me." He shrugged, sighing again. "And I want you to know that I no longer desire them. I do not want you hurt."

"Shall I kill them all?" Cwen asked, her face void of expression.

"Well, that might be imprudent and draw unwanted attention."

"Trust me," she said, her eyes sparkling with mischief.

With a doubtful look, he led the way into the tavern.

"Caen!" The squeal of the woman's voice was sharp as she rushed forward with her arms outstretched.

Cwen stepped in front of Caen and said brightly, her eyes flashing a warning, "I do not believe we have met. I am Lady Cwen of Aaradan."

The woman's eyes widened and she curtsied, bringing a nervous chuckle from Caen.

"We shall be sitting there." Cwen pointed, indicating an empty table. "And we require draughts of heavy ale – nay – a pitcher, for friends will be joining us. We are also seeking information on the Mountain of the Dragon. If there is anyone present with such information I am willing to pay him handsomely for it."

Sputtering her understanding, the wench backed away and rushed off to do Lady Cwen's bidding.

"You found that amusing?" Cwen asked.

"Aye, more than you can imagine." Caen laughed loudly.

Drawing her dagger from her boot Cwen placed it on the table before her, eliciting a frightened look from the bar wench who served their ale.

"Now, watch as a woman does her work," she whispered to Caen as she took a deep drink of ale, peering at the approaching poacher over the rim of the mug.

"The wench says you will pay for information." The poacher addressed Caen.

"It is I who seek the information," Cwen said in a voice barely loud enough to be heard, gaining the man's attention.

The man leered and leaned toward her.

"And what are you willing to give for it milady?"

She leapt up from her chair and slammed the dagger up under his chin, watching as his eyes grew large and a tiny sound escaped his throat.

"Today, I am willing to let you live, provided the information you have satisfies me," she answered sharply. "If it does not… well, we shall see."

Talin's voice came from behind her. "I would advise you to make the correct response. This woman has been known to remove rather important pieces of flesh when she does not get her way."

He and Klaed sat in the remaining chairs and poured ale for themselves while Cwen glared from beneath a deep frown at the poacher seated across from her. One of her knees was on the table and her other foot remained in her chair as she leaned forward with her blade across the sweating man's pale throat.

"Just where is this mountain?" Cwen asked, continuing to stare as the man blinked, trying to channel the stinging sweat away from his eyes.

"It can be seen on the horizon," the man choked out.

"If I wanted to look for it on the horizon I would not be in a tavern now, would I?" Cwen asked, pushing the blade deeper into his rolls of flesh. "And quit sweating; it is beginning to annoy me."

"By all that is holy, tell the woman what she wants to know before she cuts you and I get blood on my clothes," Klaed whined in his best impression of a dandy.

Cwen turned away from the poacher to hide her amusement before scowling back at him again.

"I am weary and I do grow hungry as well." Sighing, she rolled her eyes toward the ceiling and pushed the poacher away from her, wiping his sweat from her blade onto Klaed's shirt.

"Bring the man. There is something else I want to ask him," Cwen said to Talin.

"I regret to inform you that this request never ends well," Talin shrugged, dragging the man to his feet and pushing him toward the door.

In the shadows behind the tavern, Cwen placed her sword against the poacher's chest.

"Which horizon, you filthy son of a bane boar?" she snarled at him.

With a shaking hand he pointed to the south.

"Have you killed the Equus?"

"What?" the man asked, drawing knowing looks from her companions.

"I asked if you have killed the Equus?" she whispered again.

"Not often," the man sputtered.

Leaning forward on the handle of her sword, Cwen drove it through his heart. Pulling it out and letting him fall, she watched as the dark stain of his blood flooded his chest and the ground around him.

"Do not wipe it on me," Klaed said, frowning at her.

"Why not? You are finally beginning to look the part you choose to play, nobleman." She laughed, wiping the blade across the dry grass at his feet.

Sidon gazed out the window of the room he shared with Daedra and watched as Cwen threw back her head and laughed.

"You will not laugh long, Cwen; not long at all," he growled, causing Daedra to cower.

Glancing toward her, Sidon snapped, "Gather our things. We need to track them and obtain the next shard."

Eyes averted, she quickly followed his instructions.

As Talin, Klaed, Cwen and Caen rejoined Brengven he seemed quite uneasy.

"I sense something – and it concerns me. I cannot focus on it. It just keeps slipping away," he muttered, shaking his head.

"Danger at the mountain?" Talin asked.

"Someone following us?" Cwen asked.

Sighing, Brengven looked perplexed and went to sit near the fire with his cup of tea.

"Pack," Cwen ordered. "I want to leave now. We will travel by darkness and approach the mountain by daylight tomorrow. I prefer to search by the light of day if Brengven is this worried."

Together they quickly gathered their belongings, breaking camp and heading south toward the great black mountain looming on the horizon.

Not long after star rise they reached the barren earth surrounding the base of the mount. It resembled an enormous pile of rock, black as ebony stone and rough as dragon scales. There were huge, jagged slabs piled one upon the other ten dragon lengths high and as wide across its base.

"There is something unnatural here," Brengven whispered with a shiver.

"It is a pile of rocks, Brengven," Cwen glared. "And somewhere there is a way into the interior.

"I shall wait beyond the barren earth, on the grass beneath the far trees," Brengven stated, backing away from them.

"That little man is afraid of everything," Cwen muttered.

"But not usually without reason," Klaed reminded her.

"Aye," agreed Talin, "and he has been right more oft than not."

"He has an uncanny attachment to the enchantress Faervyn," Caen mumbled, "that we have seen first hand."

Scouring the base of the mountain they found no entrance so began to work their way upward, bit-by-bit, searching among the tumbled slabs of stone. Nearing the summit, Klaed felt a sudden surge of air as it rose from the pile of rocks at his feet.

Lifting a stone and sliding it down the side of the mountain causing a small landside, he yelled, "Air rises here, from below the earth."

Scrambling up toward him, they helped move several more rocks away from the opening. The air was cool, carrying no threat of fire. Lying on her stomach and putting her head into the hole, Cwen called for a torch. Holding it before her, she dropped it and waited for it to strike the ground below. It hit the floor of the mountain's interior with a sprinkle of sparks and a faint, faded glow.

"We may not be able to enter here," Cwen said. "Our ropes may not be long enough."

"We can dangle you from the end and see what you can see," Talin teased, drawing a glare from Caen and a grin from Klaed.

"Aye, I could use a torch to at least scan the walls and see what lies beneath this pile of rubble." Cwen shrugged, reaching out to touch Caen's shoulder as she accepted the task.

Under Cwen's careful scrutiny, Talin tied his rope to Klaed's and they pulled back against the knot to test its strength and tighten it.

Wrapping the rope around her waist, she turned to allow Caen to tie it, causing Talin's eyes to soften at her newfound trust.

With the three of them holding the rope she edged backward into the opening, leaving her dazzling smile behind, etched into Caen's mind.

As her weight drew the rope they allowed it to slip, little by little, into the depths of the mountain.

Cwen's startled scream caused them to draw her back up quickly until they heard her laughter and she called, "'Tis the skull of a wyrm – the entire mountain peak is the skull of a wyrm! You have lowered me into another eye socket. This one is far larger than the last; its teeth stand as tall as five or six men. Send me more rope and I will stand on the floor of the jaw."

Slowly playing out the rope until they no longer felt her weight, they listened for her call.

"I am free," she shouted up to them, her voice echoing within the massive skull.

Caen leaned into the hole with a torch held out before him and sought her with worried eyes.

She waved her torch and yelled, "Tie off the rope and the three of you can climb down."

"Stay where you are and wait for us!" Caen called to her.

She waited a moment then began to look for a way out of the skull.

At the base of the wyrm's skull she found that a passage followed the vertebrae and rib cage, leading down to the mountain's distant base.

"Cwen!" Caen called from the bottom of the rope.

Talin growled from his spot on the rope, "Get used to it Caen. You will rarely find her where you left her."

"Aye, I am here," Cwen shouted back, returning toward Caen and the descending Talin and Klaed.

"There is a passage leading downward from the base of the skull," she explained. "It seems to have been formed by the body of the beast and remains now, long after the bones have turned to stone."

As they began the descent through the massive passageway formed by the ribcage of the ancient wyrm, they discovered the truth of Cwen's theory.

The great bones, long turned to stone, wove throughout the mountain's interior in a tangle of switchbacks and serpentines traveling nearly half a league.

"A wyrm this great…" Cwen whispered, as if to speak aloud might wake the long dead enemy.

"It would take many stag or bane boar to fill its great belly," Klaed said only slightly louder.

"Or men – a great many men. Brengven said men were the fodder of the wyrms," Talin recalled, a tremor of unease chilling his words.

"But surely they must no longer live. Something so large could not remain hidden for long," Cwen added.

The corridor continued downward, twisting and turning with no evidence of side chambers or an altar with a shard.

"If it is the shard of this beast we seek, it will be grand indeed," Caen said, shaking his head in disbelief.

Halfway to the bottom of the mountain they found a door fashioned between two giant ribs. It was cast from the scales of a dragon – or perhaps from the wyrm itself – and was held with a large lock carved of bone.

With the butt of his axe, Talin crushed the bone lock and together he and Caen forced the door inward, releasing stale air as the squeaky hinges moaned.

Holding his torch inside, Talin scanned the room that lay beyond for danger or evidence of traps.

Calling to Caen, he asked, "If you were going to hide your treasure here, thief, just how would you do it?"

Laughing, Caen peered into the room and said, "Look up."

Talin held the torch higher and saw a ceiling of jumbled stones.

"When you lift the shard from its nook within the far wall, the ceiling will collapse and kill all who stand with you. Even if you live you will still remain trapped and merely die a slower death of suffocation," Caen explained.

"Though it is not without hope, if I were creating such a trap I would leave a second exit just in case I was the one who became trapped. Remain here while I look." Caen stepped forward, pausing at the touch of Cwen's fingers.

"Do not die, thief," she whispered, her eyes lowered. "I do not wish nightmares to reclaim my sleep."

Running his finger along her jaw he promised, "I will touch nothing, assuring my safety."

Tossing a stone onto the floor before he entered, Caen turned back and gave Cwen a wink. He walked step by cautious step to the center of the room, raising his torch to check the ceiling again before proceeding to the far wall. The giant shard lay inside a carved niche, resting on a dense pad of dried willow leaves. In the torchlight it swirled with many colors, like a droplet of water kissed by the sun.

"It must weigh two stone," he whispered loudly over his shoulder.

Systematically, he walked the torch along the back wall, seeking the breath of air that would expose a hidden exit. Near the floor, in the deepest corner of the room and behind a cascade of rock, he found what he was seeking. Pushing against the wall behind the pile he felt it shift as the seal broke and the dark corridor it hid became visible.

"Cross the room slowly, one at a time. I will have you wait behind the fall of stones while I remove the shard." He beckoned his companions forward.

Each crossed the room, walking as if on the fragile shells of a magpie's eggs and hoping not to crush them. As they gathered behind the fall of stones, Caen looked over Cwen's head at Talin and Klaed, his eyes clearly telling them not to wait for him.

Looking down at Cwen, he kissed her tenderly and whispered, "I shall see you soon, Lady Cwen."

Going to the shard he stood before it and looked over his shoulder, nodding to Talin's waiting eyes.

He heard Cwen cry out as Klaed forced her into the passage,

pushing her ahead of him while Talin followed, blocking her should she attempt to return.

With a final release of his deeply held breath, Caen looked up a last time at the ceiling he knew would fall, then back toward the safety of the passage that had already swallowed his companions. It seemed too far, but he knew that the one who had built the trap had not intended to die. He reached out and placed one hand on either side of the heavy heart shard, edging his body as far toward the exit as possible.

"Do not let me die now that I finally have a reason to live," he muttered as he jerked the shard from the niche and rolled away toward the tumble of stones that hid the way to safety.

The roar of the rock collapsing and the sudden explosion of dust left him deaf and blind. A large stone struck his shoulder, throwing him forward and cracking his head against the wall of the cavern. Shaking away the dizziness that threatened to take his consciousness, he grabbed the edge of the stone barrier and pulled himself out of harm's way. Falling to his knees as blood clouded his vision and the shard fell from his grip, he thought he heard the pounding of footsteps as the light faded and his mind drifted in and out of blackness.

"She would have killed me if I had left you." Caen heard Talin's words as he finally let go of consciousness.

He awoke to Brengven's murmured healing and Cwen's angry, golden eyes.

Seeing his eyes open, she knelt and stabbed him in the chest with her finger.

"Do not ever do that again!" she shouted, receiving a frown from Brengven as Caen winced in pain.

"I probably will not, for it goes against my nature to put my life in jeopardy. I knew I could make it, Cwen. I did," he assured her. "There was really no danger."

"Then why were you bleeding and unconscious?" she asked with raised eyebrows.

"The shard was heavier than I thought, and I was a bit slower, but I am not dead, nor are you," he whispered, lifting a hand to stroke her cheek.

Staring at him through narrowed eyes, she suddenly leaned

forward and kissed him, allowing him to draw her to him and hold her close before she pulled away.

"Nall comes. I shall return once he has gone with the shard," she said, rising to her feet.

To Talin she said, "I am going to bathe at the pool. I shall return soon. Keep these mongrels here." She winked at Brengven, causing him to grow red and fume.

"I am not a mongrel," he snapped at her.

As she reached the pool, Cwen heard the crash of her father's beastly dragon striking the earth and laughed. Why Nall loved that mangy creature she would never understand.

Washing her hair and allowing the cool water to soothe away the terror she had felt for Caen, she dried herself and wrapped a blanket around her. Then she washed her clothes and spread them out to dry.

"Well, now I recall why Aidan hated to share you." Sidon's voice scorched Cwen as if she had been struck with the breath of a dragon.

Whirling, she looked into his eyes, gasping in disbelief.

"You were dead." Her words were choked with fear.

"Obviously not, but you will soon wish you were." Sidon low sadistic laugh sounded loud in the still air. "The enchantress Faervyn has sent me for the shard."

"Come, do not make me wade in the water to claim you, for it will only make the punishment more severe."

"No," Cwen said, voice low, her chin raised in defiance, "I will never come to you, Sidon. Never again. I would rather die by my own hand."

Wordlessly Cwen screamed for help.

Cwen's silent cry ripped through the peace of Nall's mind as an axe cleaves the haunch of a simplestag.

"Cwen," he bellowed as he raced toward the pool.

Caen rose to his feet and fumbled for his sword, staggering after Nall as Talin and Klaed pounded after them.

Nall burst from the thicket and into the sandy clearing directly behind Sidon. His long double-bladed sword swung in a wide arc, catching Sidon on the side of the neck and severing his head cleanly as the man turned to meet the Guardian's headlong rush. It dropped to the ground only a heartbeat ahead of the dead man's body.

Striding through the water until he stood before Cwen, Nall asked, "Did you call for help?"

"Aye," she whispered.

Her eyes shifted to the men behind him and Nall swung around, his sword ready.

Lowering the blade, he said to Caen, "Next time you kill someone who threatens my daughter, be sure that he is dead."

Caen waded into the water and covered Cwen with his cloak, looking soberly at Nall. "I do not know how it is he survived death, but I shall indeed be more cautious in the future."

"Faervyn must have healed him. He said the enchantress sent him for the shard," Cwen said, frowning at the flicker of color she saw amid the bushes.

Striding forward, she pushed the shrubs out of the way and looked into Daedra's wide and frightened eyes. With a soft smile she held out her hand and Daedra hesitantly accepted it.

"You are free, Daedra. Go with Nall. He will take you to the fortress of the Queen. Tell her that Cwen of Aaradan requests that she give you honest work and a place to stay," Cwen spoke, looking back toward her father.

Leading Daedra to Nall, she asked, "Will you accept the charge of taking Daedra to the fortress where she will be safe from men like Sidon and Aidan?"

"Aye, Cwen, I shall see that this young woman is cared for properly."

Cwen leaned forward and hugged Nall briefly.

"It will be as if you did it for me," she whispered.

"And who will care for you, Cwen?" Nall asked, staring at Caen.

"Talin, Klaed and Caen protect me far more than I should like," Cwen admitted, watching her father frown.

Gathering her wet clothes and heading toward camp, Cwen called back over her shoulder, "Tell Mother I shall visit you in New Xavian City upon the completion of our final quest."

Nall could not stop the lopsided grin that spread over his face.

Caen said quietly, “It is good I left Sidon to die a second time if it has drawn a daughter to her father.”

Excusing themselves to Nall and Daedra, Caen, Talin and Klaed followed after Cwen.

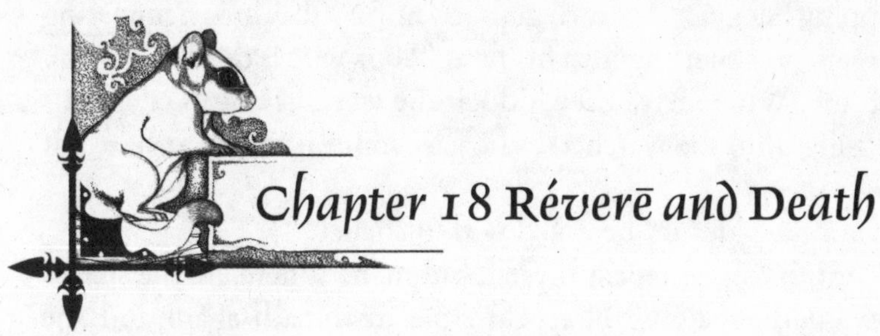

Chapter 18 Révere̅ and Death

It might be in the palace." Brengven shrugged his shoulders in ignorance.

"I have never been within the walls of Ileana's fortress."

"Ileana has a fortress?" Klaed asked curiously.

"Aye, in the days long past during Alandon's threat and the shattering of Ædracmoræ, King Aaradan hid her there. It is not a great fortress, but it is indeed a place of safety. Once she left us she went to hide among the Xavians, as she does now."

"Ileana does not hide, Feie. She is a member of the Queen's Council. I visited the palace as a child."

Brengven mumbled. "It is a good disguise."

"She is my granddame, Brengven," Cwen reminded. "She is a Sojourner, a being above reproach."

A shadow crossed the Feie's face and he nodded without further remark, though his brow remained furrowed.

Shaking her head at his foolishness, Cwen directed him to call the rift.

Beneath the Galenite fortress, Faervyn screamed her rage as she watched Nall decapitate Sidon and take Daedra away with him.

She stormed up the steps to Galen's offices and burst through the door.

"Kayann?" Galen asked, seeing his wife's flushed face and angry expression.

Dropping her guise, Faervyn grabbed him by the throat, squeezing off his breath and snarling into his face, "Your wife is dead. Now you deal with me. Where have they hidden the wyrm shards, Galen?"

Releasing him, she watched as he gasped for breath and stared at her in horror.

"Kayann is… dead?" he asked with disbelief.

"Do not make me repeat myself, old man. Where are the shards kept? I want them now." Her grip stole his breath again and she slammed his head down on his desk, dazing him and leaving blood flowing into his eyes.

"The shards. The Queen keeps the shards." Galen shook his head to clear it. "You cannot reach them, no matter what you do."

Laughing, Faervyn flung Galen into the wall behind him, breaking his neck. She waited for his soul to attempt its escape then pulled it from the air as it squirmed and twisted, trying to free itself. Dragging it toward her, she quickly inhaled it and claimed Galen's body for her own.

With a swift incantation and a flash of her hands, she was in the woods adjacent to the Fortress of the Dragon Queen. Announcing herself to the Guardians posted at the gates, Faervyn, disguised as Galen, entered the fortress in search of the shards that would activate the armies of the G'lm.

While the palace on Réverē was not nearly as impressive as the House of Aaradan, where the queen resided, it was elegant with its brilliant white exterior. It had been furnished with love for the Sojourner Ileana by King Aaradan.

Sighing, Cwen shook her head. "I recall no mirror here that appeared to be anything more than polished brass, no hidden rooms – nothing sinister or frightening. This has always been a place of peace and freedom for members of the House of Aaradan. It is where Sōrél brought Yáviё after the coronation and wedding."

Brengven tiptoed by her, sticking his head around a corner and drawing back quickly.

"Brengven, what are you doing? There is no one here except us," Cwen stated in exasperation.

"Seeking a mirror," he muttered, offended by her rudeness. "Did

I not sense Sidon's threat at the falls?"

"Oh, indeed you sensed a threat, but could not for the life of you tell us what it was. I shall show you every mirror. There are many, but that is all they are – mirrors – not doors to some hidden realm," she answered with a toss of her head.

Starting up the grand staircase, she called down, "Come, let us look in the mirrors and satisfy the Feie."

Caen rushed up the stairs to grab her hand. "Did you truly live here?" he asked in wonder.

"Aye, Caen. As a guest of the Queen I screamed and fought with my father in every room of this palace. You will probably hear the echoes of our fearsome quarrels if you listen closely." She smiled at him.

At the top of the stairs Cwen opened the doors along the corridor, gesturing that Brengven should enter and look at the mirror prominently displayed in each room.

The Feie muttered under his breath as he looked into and touched each mirror, shaking his head after each examination.

"There is nothing here," he said with a disappointed sigh.

"I told you there was not," Cwen mumbled.

"Where else are there mirrors?"

"There are two in the servants' rooms and one in each tower room. I know of no others."

"What of the lower level?" Talin asked.

"There is nothing there but furniture not in use. I loved to hide from Nall amid the covered pieces. He would shout my name so loudly that the dust coverlets would sway." She giggled at the memory of her father's fury.

"She was not an easy child," Talin grinned.

Laughing, she pointed to a long low bench along the corridor. "Talin used to hide beneath that bench, hanging on with his arms and legs thinking that no one would see his body dangling from below."

The mirrors in the towers and those in the servants' quarters were clouded with age, were firm to the touch, nothing more than polished brass – they led nowhere.

The narrow stairs to the storage rooms in the lower levels were dark, so Klaed and Talin lit the torches along the walls as they moved deeper beneath the palace.

Three rooms filled to overflowing with tables and chairs, beds and dressers opened off the bottom of the stairs. Pulling off the coverlets as they moved forward, they looked for mirrors.

"Here," Caen called from against the far wall. "There is a mirror here. It is polished brass like all the others."

"Nay, not quite like the others." Brengven pointed at his image in the reflective surface.

Around him swirled a darkness, long tendrils of dark, heavy atmosphere shifting over his image in the mirror.

"This is more than just a looking glass," he whispered, reaching forward to touch its surface and snatching back his hand as the mirror shimmered and warped his reflection.

Within the empty halls of the Queen's fortress Faervyn the enchantress slipped into Grumblton's chambers, listening as the little wizard's footsteps faded up the stairs toward the king's office. A heavy lockbox sat within his cabinet. With whispered words and a flick of her wrist she cast the spell to open the lock and lifted the lid, revealing the sapphire shard she sought. It carried the power to unleash the army lying below the Northern Mountains, just south of the Guardian garrison that protected the sacred Well of Viileshga and New Xavian City. As she slipped the shard beneath Galen's waistcoat and secured the cabinet door, she heard Yávië's voice approaching the wizard's workshop.

Opening the door, Faervyn stepped into the hall, smiling at the Queen through Galen's eyes.

"Galen?" Yávië asked with surprise.

"Yávië, I was looking for Grumblton, but it seems he has already departed."

"Aye, he is with Sōrél. Was there some special need? Is Kayann well?" Yávië asked.

"Kayann has been having some sort of spell – headaches and sleeplessness. I had hoped to get Grumbl's help."

"I shall summon him. He can give you an elixir or healing potion to restore her," Yávië said.

While they waited for Grumbl's return, Nall approached them, nodding respectfully to Yávië and extending his grip in greeting to Galen.

"Your Guardians return, Yávië. There is no news of the wizard Laoghaire near the remains of Sylwervyn's Tower. They have searched the surrounding woods thoroughly but found no entrance to any caverns. Questioning of the townsfolk brings only rumors of missing women."

"He must be found. His threat to Cwen remains very real," she replied.

Grumblton arrived and prepared an elixir for Kayann. He guaranteed that her headaches would fade in minutes and her night's sleep would be long.

"I am sure you are correct on both counts," Faervyn replied through Galen's lips, taking leave of the fortress.

In the dense forest along the back wall, Faervyn shed Galen's body and headed for the cavern in the Northern Mountains where her new army awaited.

"We should wait," Brengven cautioned his companions. "Call Nall and wait until he arrives before venturing through the mirror, for there is great evil waiting there."

"What evil, Brengven? We must get the last shard and deliver it safely to Nall," Cwen insisted. "The last shard, Brengven, and then we shall be released of this charge and free of one another."

Brengven shook his head. "It is not safe."

"Then remain here, Feie, and if we do not return by the rising of the morrow's day star, send for the Guardians." Cwen looked to her friends for their agreement.

"We can slip through and quickly search the area beyond." Talin tried to soothe Brengven's anxiousness. "Surely the evil can be no worse than what we have already seen released upon the earth."

"I will call for Nall on the morrow as you ask, but it will be too late. If no one comes for you, I fear you will all be dead, save one, and that one will no longer wish to live."

"Your gloom is giving me a headache, Feie," Cwen snapped. "We shall return with the shard before the next star rise. And then we will be rid of your constant tales of threat and doom."

With a last glower at Brengven, Cwen stepped through the ancient mirror into a lush tropical garden that appeared to be growing in a cavern beneath the earth. Caen stepped through behind her, followed by Klaed and Talin.

"What is this place?" Cwen asked in a hushed voice.

Running his fingers through his long, dark hair, the wizard Laoghaire examined his features within the polished surface of the ancient mirror. Leaning forward with eyes narrowed, he glimpsed those standing on the other side and his lips curled into a malicious grin. Cwen of Aaradan, daughter of Nall, would soon be brave enough to step into Laoghaire's lair, a labyrinth of subterranean rooms, including a chasm so deep he had never found its floor. It was into this chasm her companions would be tossed, ending any possible threat from their puny weapons.

Moving into a smaller cavern off the main chamber the wizard began to prepare for Cwen's arrival. Dressing in his finest robes and murmuring the ancient words within his mind he created an illusion of beauty for his guest – magnificent gardens filled with the scents of a thousand flowers, towering falls and pools filled with ghostfish and seagrass.

Shooing away the young demons that haunted his workshop he approached the mirror and looked again at his features. He knew that women found him handsome, for many had said so before they died. He had felt the need for a woman since consigning the last into the depths below – but now one sought him out. Sometimes one was not required to hunt for one's pleasure; it simply arrived at the door, or in this case, through the looking glass.

"Fair lady, do you wander lost within the caverns?" spoke a smooth and soothing voice.

With hands on the hilts of their swords the travelers looked for the speaker. Emerging from the corridor on their right stepped the most striking man Cwen had ever seen. His features were fine and fair and his rich sable hair fell well below his shoulders. He was even more handsome than her mother's brother and she had always thought the king to be the fairest being on the face of Ædracmoræ. He appeared to be mortal, and his robes reflected no particular kingdom. His smile was benign. He bore no aura of strength and carried no hint of threat.

She assured him she and her companions were not lost as Caen bristled with jealousy and Klaed and Talin stared with open suspicion.

"Nay, we are not lost. We come seeking a wyrm shard of great strength and importance. Perhaps you have heard of it?" Cwen returned the man's smile.

"I am sorry milady, but I have never heard it mentioned. I do not often come in contact with magickal beasts. I am the keeper of these stone gardens," stated the man as his gaze cast a spell of obedience over the three men who stood behind Cwen.

Shrugging, the man continued, "And none of it matters to me, for I have no interest in or understanding of the art of magick."

"Would you like to see the gardens?" the stranger continued, excitement lighting his face. "They are truly wondrous and it would not take much of your time. It would honor me greatly, for I take enormous pleasure in sharing them with others."

He allowed the scent of flowers to touch Cwen's mind and knew that she would join him. Soon she would speak her name and give him the power to completely dominate her soul.

Cwen hesitated, knowing that they should continue their search for the shard; but the day had been long and fruitless, and a few moments' respite amidst the beauty of the gardens would serve to soothe their weariness and feelings of failure.

"Aye, we would love to see your gardens if you are willing to share your name," she smiled, realizing he had not spoken it.

"I am simply called Dybbuk, the keeper of the gardens."

It annoyed him that she had asked for a name first, but if it resulted in her revealing her own, the flicker of annoyance would be worthwhile.

"And you, milady, what might I call you?"

"I am Cwen of Aaradan," she said, noting his bow of respect and the way he kept his eyes downcast in deference. "These are my companions, Talin, Klaed, and Caen."

Acknowledging each of them he repeated their names, watching as the light faded from their eyes to be replaced by an even heavier shadow of his magick.

"Follow me, milady," he requested, smiling as she complied without a backward glance at her protectors, unaware that they followed at his command.

She wondered at the soft tones of his voice, for they reminded her of someone. As she followed him along the path she marveled at the luxurious foliage and blossoming flowers, for the time of rest was rapidly approaching and most plants were preparing for their sleep.

There before them lay the entrance to a pool within the gardens. The opening was surrounded by trailing vines covered in the brilliant flowers of the season of the topaz star's greatest warmth and Cwen wondered if it was the heat from within Ædracmoræ rather than the star that gave warmth to these gardens.

At the entrance, the one calling himself Dybbuk turned and offered his hand.

"The pathway is uneven, milady. Would you allow me to lead you?"

Looking down, Cwen saw that the stones were steep and sharp, in contrast to the floral beauty around them. Nodding, she reached out to take his hand.

As his fingers closed around hers he whispered her name.

A flicker of unease passed through Cwen's mind, and in that instant she knew that Brengven had been right to caution her, for this man was not at all what he seemed. Laoghaire watched the realization of her error flash across her eyes and chuckled at Cwen's costly folly.

With a wave of his hand he built a wall around her companions, leaving them behind. Then he reached out and allowed his fingers to trail along Cwen's face and down her throat, pausing at the pale swell of her breast.

"Let us remove your cloak, for it hides your beauty."

She slipped it from her shoulders and handed it to him.

"Oh you are very fine, daughter of Nall. You are very fine indeed. Come, I have prepared a meal and laid out an array of dresses from which you may choose, though my favorite is the white silk. Later we have games to play," he teased, knowing that she would choose anything he suggested while in her state of bewitchment.

As he led her to his table he was awed at the change in her. No longer dressed in drab leathers, she sparkled in the shimmering white silk gown; her hair was swept up and piled high upon her head, revealing the slender beauty of her neck and the fair unmarked loveliness of her shoulders.

"Have you heard the legends of the Gryphon King? It is your golden eyes that are foretold among the legends of the rise of a great and powerful third House, though you do not seem as fierce and strong as the legends foretell. I do intend to rule that house, Cwen, and sooner than you might believe."

"Your eyes are very beautiful, Cwen," he flattered her, the repeated use of her name ever deepening her enchantment. Laoghaire felt a moment's fleeting sorrow that the bewitchment kept her silent – her voice had had a pleasant quality that he had found quite stimulating.

Stroking her face and sighing, he murmured to her, "I should like to hear the softness of your voice, but it is not necessary for the games I play. Anyway, it is probably best that you remain silent. Let us enjoy the meal before I share my secrets with you."

Cwen shouted and pounded against the walls of her bewitchment, but she knew none could hear her. Beyond the room she could see Talin, Klaed and Caen shadowed behind a shimmering barrier. Why had she not listened to the Feie?

As she sat at Laoghaire's table and listened to him speak of his plans, she grew nauseous knowing she could not stop him. Her father would come for her, but not soon enough to stay Laoghaire's wicked hand, for Brengven would not call him until the morrow's rising of the day star.

Laoghaire whispered his plans to his captive, reveling in her anguish. It was the fear that fed his hunger, and he could feel his blood warming to the task ahead.

In a distant cavern, eyes glowing in anticipation of her victory, Faervyn spoke to her army. From deathshade to demon and on to each dragon, her voice filled the void with commands.

"Together we will bring down the joined Houses and rise to rule Ædracmoræ. You will be my army, ridding the world of humans and sending the Queen and her Guardians back into the depths of darkness. I shall reclaim Ædracmoræ in the name of Abaddon, ruler of the abyss, keeper of the ancient secrets."

Below her stood the obedient G'lm, raised from the depths by the power of the Wreken within the wyrm shard. The snarls and roars were melodious to Faervyn's ears – a legion of evil to loose upon the earth, bringing death and shadow to the realm of the Dragon Queen. The sapphire shard of their resurrection lay within its receptacle, pulsing and filling the cavern with its powerful glow, touching the thousand and once more giving them life.

"Marske, the sacred well, the Verdant Forest and the New Xavian City – all will fall beneath your feet this day. The entire Council sits within the city of the Xavians; without them, the reign of light will end and with the tainting of the Well of Viileshga, darkness will flow to all the kingdoms."

The din that rose from the legion of chaos was deafening.

"Go!" Faervyn commanded. "For Ædracmoræ has been damned."

As they flooded forth, the storm of chaos grew overhead in the gloom of night, eerie red lightning gathering to charge the legion with the power of the abyss, throbbing claps of thunder growling to cover the pounding of their feet.

Faervyn's soldiers pushed west toward Marske, the great golden city built upon the Malochian ruins, and through the mountain passes leading to the fortress that guarded the precious life-giving waters of the Well of Viileshga.

The death dragons surged ahead, leading the army with fiery breath and iron talons to batter the walls of the city of Marske. The screams of the innocents broke the sleepy silence as they were dragged from their beds and devoured by the horde of deathshades and demons. No room was left unsearched, no body undefiled. Children were ripped from the arms of their mothers and tossed to the hungry dragons, while the swords of their fathers were torn away and used to murder the lamenting mothers.

Upon the back of a dragon, Faervyn howled with glee, knowing that her force was great and that the Guardians were unaware of the plague rushing toward the precious waters of the Well of Viileshga and the Queen herself as she slept in the palace in New Xavian City.

Above, the storm clouds grew, spreading out from Marske and across the Northern Mountains, stretching as far south as the Ebony Plains and pushing northward toward the Guardians' garrison on the ridge above the great valley passage leading into the heart of the Verdant Forest.

Calls of alarm rose from the southern guard towers at the sight of the raging darkness of the demonic tempest rushing toward the garrison. Signal fires were quickly lit, spreading the news that chaos had struck the mountains.

Within the fortress Nall readied the Guardians to battle the coming horde. Standing before the assembled men and women he warned of the consequences of failure.

"The G'lm come in force, hoping to destroy the Queen and her Council, but the darker plot is to taint the Well with their filth. The Well of Viileshga is the life water of Ædracmoræ, and if it is defiled by the dark horde its damage will spread to each of the Sacred Pools, sealing the fate of our world. Ædracmoræ will fall into darkness once more and chaos will reign in place of the light of peace. We must not fail to protect our Queen and the Well."

The door to the garrison flew open revealing the Dragon Queen – in all her fury.

Without a thought for decorum, Nall grabbed her arm.

"Yávië, you should not be here. The horde knows the entire Council has assembled, though I do not know how. They seek to destroy you all and taint the Well," Nall hissed under his breath.

Yávië eyes softened for a moment before flaring again.

"Galen. It was Galen, his body at least. Grumblton believes the enchantress Faervyn used his body to gain entrance to the fortress and steal the wyrm shard. Sōrél has gone to bring the Guardians from the House of Aaradan and Näeré has summoned those from the other kingdoms. Grumblton casts the spells of protection and strength upon your men even as we speak. We must not fail."

Turning to Nall's assembled troops, Yávië spoke as the ruler of the Seven Kingdoms. "On this day I remind you that you each bear the touch of the Queen and are empowered before the crown. There must be no compassion shown those who seek to harm us, for they intend to take all that we hold dear. The Well must be protected at all costs.

By the power of the Dragon Queen, I decree no mercy. Failure does not mean that tomorrow we wake as the prisoners of the victorious. If we fail it means we do not wake at all. Blessings of the Ancients on each of you."

Touching Nall's arm she bid him to follow her, and with a last command for his troops to ready themselves, he did so.

"Where are Cwen and Talin?" Yáviē asked him.

"When we last heard, they were in Réverē."

Sighing her relief, she added, "Let us hope they remain there."

Faervyn marshaled her army within sight of the garrison. It was massive, and she knew those who lived within were strong. Guardians bound by an oath to protect the Queen above all, their problem lay in the Queen's desire to lead. She would not cower within the palace; she would ride forth to meet the threat and seal her own fate in doing so. Faervyn intended to deal with Yáviē. Looking into the woman's soul as she took her life would give the enchantress great satisfaction. The signal fires told her that the Guardians had been alerted, but the horde would win against them with their sheer numbers. It would take far too long to draw the others to defend the Well.

Smiling, Faervyn lifted her arm and signaled the charge. Sweeping down the valley to meet her destiny, she urged her death dragon mount to increase its speed, dropping low to cover the Guardians coming to challenge her with a blanket of fiery breath.

A flicker of movement above her drew Faervyn's attention and she brought her mount around to face the new threat. An enormous accordant dragon loomed above her, heavily armored and belching smoke from a recent expulsion of fiery acid. The rider was a fair young man, Xavian in appearance. He cocked his head and gave a tight smile as he urged the dragon toward her, his lance at the ready. Faervyn's mount bellowed as the lance struck its chest and a sudden spasm tossed her from its back and sent her plummeting toward the ground. Snarling, she drew herself up, stopping her descent with a spell and turning to face the Xavian dragon slayer.

A second dragon, pale and ethereal, arrived. This one carried the woman she sought. The Queen's raven hair blew around her face and her violet eyes were dark with hatred.

"You seek me?" Yáviё shouted at Faervyn.

"Aye." Faervyn surged forward, launching herself in the direction of the Dragon Queen, only to be hurled away by a wizard's power.

Nay, not a wizard – a sorceress – dark-haired and sapphire-eyed, Näeré of the House of Aaradan. With a wave of her hand, Faervyn pushed Näeré away, howling her fury at the interference. Leaping from the back of her dragon, Näeré met Faervyn in mid-air, slamming a bolt of bright white light into the enchantress's chest and throwing her backward. Surging upward, Faervyn threw up a wall of flame, driving Näeré away from her as she shielded herself from the heat.

With a final scream of hatred, Faervyn flung Näeré away from her and toward the rocks below. Twisting around, she rushed toward the Dragon Queen, hands outstretched ready to draw the woman's soul.

Below them the horde scrambled up the walls of the Guardians' fortress as the death dragons pelted it with fiery breath, burning its timbers and scorching the stone. One after another the dragons crashed into the towers and parapet, finally breaking through the portcullis and arriving in the bailey. Dragon slayers armed with dragon scale shields and lances fortified by the magick of the wizard Grumblton rushed to meet the threat, pushing forward against the dragons' breath and slaying demons and deathshades as they went.

A sudden bellowing from overhead brought relief as Sōrél arrived with the battalion from the House of Aaradan. Even as he shouted his commands, his eyes searched for Yáviё. He watched in horror as Faervyn rushed toward her, screaming and howling in hatred. Sending his dragon mount racing forward to intercept the enchantress, Sōrél caught sight of Nall off to his left, intent on protecting Yáviё. Nall's dragon mount crashed into Faervyn as she was focusing on her intended target, sending her spinning away into the storm-filled sky. Racing after her, Fáedre the war dragon inhaled deeply, mixing the fiery breath that would surge forth with the force of the falls of Æstaffordæ. Fáedre roared and shot a stream of intense flame over Faervyn, leaving her writhing and wailing her rage. But as the smoke and flame cleared, the enchantress remained unscathed.

"No, Yáviё!" Nall's voice cut through Sōrél as he spun toward his wife.

Yáviё's eyes were flaming as she raised the Sword of Domesius above her head and urged Aero the wind dragon toward the enemy. Faervyn whirled to face Yáviё, poised to take the soul of the Queen of Ædracmoræ. With increasing speed, Aero charged forward, stretching out his neck to allow Yáviё a better view of her enemy. As the tip of Yáviё's scarlet blade lowered to strike Faervyn's heart, the enchantress saw the face of the wee Ancient wizard hidden among the dragon's scales and realized her battle was lost. Grumbl's finger reached out and touched the sword blade as Yáviё thrust it into Faervyn's heart, sending a surge of brilliant blue light traveling along its length and covering the enchantress as she screamed in agony and anger. A fiery shadow passed over her, setting her hair aflame and shimmering with the heat of its blaze as it played over her figure. The Guardians watched as Faervyn's body smoldered and finally burst into a great flash of fire, leaving a thousand fading embers falling toward the earth.

The thunder of dragon wings from the west brought the Guardians of Æcumbræ, Æshulmæ and Æwmarshæ shouting hails and pressing forward into the battle. Dragons swept past, lending their fire and acid to the fray below.

Näeré arrived perched primly upon her dragon, grinning at Nall and throwing him a kiss.

"I would have returned sooner, but the ground is crawling with the demon horde and the Guardians there needed a bit of magick. I trust Yáviё and Grumbl have defeated the witch?"

Nall's eyes suddenly shadowed as he looked to the north.

"The horde has broken through into the Verdant Forest!" he called, spinning his dragon mount and racing off in pursuit.

In the depths of his mind he called the Emeraldflyte of empathic dragons, urging speed and numbers to drive off the intruders.

Glancing over his shoulder, he grinned to see Näeré right behind him, followed by Yáviё and Sõrél.

"'Tis another quest to save the world," he called, urging his dragon ground-ward to intercept the horde headed for the sacred Well of Viileshga.

The storm became more violent as they approached the forest, its bolts of lightning surging and striking the tallest of the trees. Even the great Verdant Tree itself was burning in the uppermost branches.

Näeré swept forward using a spell of deluge to quench the burning limbs and leaves as Nall and the others continued downward.

The Emeraldflyte arrived with the rage only a threatened dragon flyte can bring. They swooped down in their hundreds, showering the G'lm below with their bubbling acid, sending the stench of dissolving flesh, bone and cloth and the frantic screams of demons and deathshades skyward.

The Guardians engaged the circling death dragons as Näeré ripped them from the sky by the power of her magick and tossed them toward her companions for the dragon slayers' lances.

On the ground, Sōrél battled his way to the Well of Viileshga, the Bow of Ages tearing through all who approached the precious Waters of Life. Yávië joined him, slicing through the pinned demons, separating them from their heads and watching oily black souls descend and bodies fall to ash.

Crying out in relief, Yávië pointed skyward and held Sōrél to her as she sobbed at the promise of respite the fading of the storm brought. The slowly clearing sky spoke of victory for her Guardians and at least a temporary safety for the world of Ædracmoræ.

The fortress lay in ruins, and the death brought by the G'lm had left few souls remaining in the city of Marske. Guardians had died for their Queen and now their souls drifted among the flickering lights of the night sky. The funeral pyres would burn brightly for many nights to come. The wizard Grumbl and the Ancient Rosie employed their healing hands among the wounded, as did Näeré and others with such skills. Injuries from the claws of the deathshades would cause the loss of one's life light if left untended, and many bore such wounds. Troops were deployed to Marske to take care of what remained of the city's population.

Yávië and Sōrél stopped to speak to each of their Guardians, not leaving for New Xavian City until long into the following night. They left Nall and Näeré behind to arrange for stonemasons and carpenters to begin the repairs.

Within the black wizard's caverns, Laoghaire stood and smiled at Cwen.

"It is time we retired, sweet Cwen of Aaradan." His soft voice caressed her and he saw a tear roll down her cheek.

As he stepped forward, the air before Cwen darkened and thickened, swirling with the whisper of words she did not understand. In the subtle, shifting darkness a man arrived. He was so much like her tormentor that she shuddered in revulsion, but his voice was calm and familiar, taking away her fear.

"Release her, or I shall do it for you." The words were silken, but the threat behind them was unmistakable.

Laoghaire laughed. "Do it if you think yourself able."

Cwen felt a sudden lightness as her mind was freed.

"Go with Synyon. She will free your friends," the man who had freed her from the mind witch's spell urged.

"Synyon! You have brought Synyon to me?" Laoghaire eyes burned with anticipation.

"Lohgaen brings you nothing; I am perfectly capable of arriving on my own should I wish it. Your games do not amuse me, Laoghaire; I am far too complicated to enjoy them." Synyon's wispy words floated from the shadows.

"Come, Cwen of Aaradan. We have work to do." The young woman extended her hand to Cwen, waiting for her to accept it. "I am Synyon. Do not believe anything either of these warring warlocks tells you. They are both demented – though Lohgaen is the more handsome, I do believe." She winked and drew Cwen down the corridor toward the barrier that held her companions.

Laoghaire drew back his lips in a snarl.

"How dare you enter my home and…"

"Do you forget it is also my home? Or do you no longer pretend to be my father?" Lohgaen baited.

"You have not cast your shadow here in over three summers. Why now?"

"You cannot be allowed to harm the daughter of Nall," Lohgaen sighed.

"I did not intend her harm. She must be my wife if the legends are true," Laoghaire said, brushing back his hair.

"She will not be your wife. Nor will you rule the House of the Gryphon. The artifact is lost, and without it, so are your fruitless schemes," Lohgaen replied, watching Laoghaire's color deepen at his son's disrespect.

"You have made me strong, Laoghaire. Do not make me use that strength against you," Lohgaen warned his father, the timbre of his voice deadly.

"You want her for yourself!" Laoghaire laughed, throwing Lohgaen backward with a wave of his hand. "You are jealous."

Rising toward his enemy, Lohgaen spun giving Laoghaire a vicious kick, flinging him against the far wall.

"Cwen has chosen the thief called Caen. I want nothing from her," Lohgaen said, shaking his head and staring with distaste at the one who claimed to be his father, a man he had despised for as long as he could recall.

"But I shall see her safe." He stared down at Laoghaire.

Laoghaire launched himself upward, grabbing Lohgaen by his cloak, swinging him around and slamming him into the floor. Lohgaen leapt up and flung a bolt of crackling electricity, catching Laoghaire's shoulder and throwing him off balance. Again he released a charge, leaving a smoldering hole in Laoghaire's cape as the older wizard rolled away.

"We shall see who wins the lass," Laoghaire said with a wicked laugh as he swept his cape around him and disappeared in a cloud of ash.

"She will not be harmed," Lohgaen's words fell in the empty cavern, "just to satisfy your madness."

With a wave of her hand Synyon released Cwen's companions, looking them over and shrugging.

"I suppose they will have to do. Draw your weapons gentlemen. The young demons Laoghaire calls soldiers will be here very quickly. They are small, but they are vicious and their bite is nasty," Synyon instructed.

As she completed her final sentence the small demons scampered around the corner, snarling and hissing.

"See? Right on time as always." She gave a low chuckle.

Cwen grabbed the blade Caen tossed to her and watched as he nocked a bolt in his crossbow and sent it flying into the chest of the closest demon.

Klaed strode forward, swiping demons on either side of him with the flat of his blade, stunning them before he struck a second time to behead them.

Glancing over her shoulder, Synyon smiled broadly at Talin, who stood staring at her with an eyebrow cocked.

"If you do not slay the beast behind you, you may die before we meet," she laughed, raising her chin in the direction of Talin's left shoulder.

Whirling, he swung the axe, neatly slicing the screaming demon in two before turning back to Synyon with a foolish grin on his face.

Cwen slammed into him and struck another beast as it launched itself toward his head.

"Have you lost your wits?" she hissed, elbowing him sharply in the ribs. "Gape at her when the enemies are dead. I do not wish to die because you have suddenly become interested in a woman."

Synyon crushed the head of the final demon spawn beneath her boot and swung back to gaze at Talin.

"Do you have a name?" she asked, "Or are you too dazed to speak it?"

Talin did not speak. He tossed his axe over his shoulder and frowned.

"Is he a mute?" Synyon asked Cwen.

"No, he is an idiot," Cwen snapped. "And his name is Talin."

"Talin," Synyon said softly, tilting her head as she gazed at him with eyes so dark he could not decide if they were black or brown.

Whirling at the sound of approaching footsteps, Synyon threw out her hand in readiness to defend them. Talin watched her fluid movement and wondered at her power. She was short – half a head shorter than Cwen – but strong and lithe and magickal. Her hair was rich and dark and fell to her shoulders.

"Lohgaen," Synyon whispered, "you nearly died."

The man that stood before them was not a stranger, for he had once saved Talin from Cwen's enchantment at the hands of Aléria. A smile crossed his face and he gave a small nod. "But not at your hands, I trust."

"Aye, at my hands. Why must you always sneak up on me? Shout your name when you are coming. I thought you were Laoghaire." The beauty of Synyon's low laugh sent a shiver up Talin's spine.

"So you thought I had allowed him to kill me? And come for you?" Lohgaen teased.

"So it may not have been a reasonable thought – but I did not know 'twas you," Synyon added, turning to wink at Talin and causing him to frown again.

"We must go," Lohgaen spoke to Cwen. "You should not remain here where you are at risk."

"We cannot go," Cwen said, shaking her head. "We have come for the shard of a wyrm that must be hidden in these caverns. We cannot leave without it."

"If such a shard existed, Laoghaire would have found it and used it. I believe he did use such a shard to release an army of death soldiers within the kingdoms. There is nothing here, Cwen, and to remain is foolish." The dark wizard's gaze was solemn, his voice tight with tension. "I cannot protect you if you do not listen."

Cwen drew back, staring.

"Protect me? I do not even know you. Why should I allow your protection?"

"Because your companions cannot protect you from the wizard Laoghaire." Lohgaen's forehead creased with concern. "You need not understand. Simply do as I ask."

"It is quite apparent that you are used to being obeyed. I am not obedient. I do as I choose and do not like being ordered about. You have my gratitude for freeing me from the wizard's spell, but he is gone and now you have become the threat." Cwen's voice was sharp with building anger.

"He could force you." Talin's voice came from Cwen's side, the sound of his voice drawing a smile of pleasure from Synyon.

"I could, but it is not my way. I only disarmed her to save your life," Lohgaen answered, his eyes focused on Cwen.

"*You* disarmed me?" Cwen looked disbelieving.

"Aye, he did," Klaed laughed. "He whispered in your ear and your swords dropped from your hands."

Lifting her chin in defiance, Cwen said, "But you will not bewitch me now?"

"I have no wish to bewitch you, daughter of Nall. I only wish to have you see reason. It is not logical to disobey those who seek to keep you safe." Lohgaen's voice was a velvet caress.

Talin and Klaed laughed openly, while Caen nearly choked attempting to hide his laughter.

Klaed spoke through gasps of laughter, "Cwen is not one to see reason and logic unless they lie along the road she has chosen to travel. Your time will be better spent helping us find the shard than arguing your case before Her Ladyship."

"Her Ladyship?" Cwen spun to glare at Klaed.

A sudden rumble rose from the depths of the cavern, bringing with it a great shudder that threw them all to the floor.

Rolling, Lohgaen quickly shielded Cwen with his cloak, drawing her tightly against him as Synyon cast a veil of shadow to hide herself and the others.

From the icy mist at the floor of the dark void appeared a creature's head, nearly a quarter dragon's length from snout to crown, broad and heavily armored in shimmering white and silver scales, its dark eyes gleaming as they caught sight of those who had come for the shard.

Lohgaen leapt to his feet, throwing out his arms and calling on the primordial masters to create the glowing barrier he hoped would protect them.

The thunder of the beast's voice froze them in their places as its eyes sought Cwen's.

"You seek the Wreken shard, daughter of Nall?" the wyrm's voice boomed as its great head rose above them.

Great jaws snapped a hand's breadth from Talin as he leapt forward with his axe drawn.

"Kneel!" bellowed the wyrm. "And lower your eyes."

Talin drew back and knelt down as the wyrm's eyes bored into each of those before it.

"Step forward, Cwen of Aaradan, daughter of Nall, Defender of the House of Lochlaen." The voice lowered to a deep growling purr.

Pushing herself up, Cwen started to move toward the beast, but Lohgaen's hand stayed her progress.

"Do not test us, Son of Laoghaire," the voice warned.

Releasing his grip on Cwen, Lohgaen bowed his head in acknowledgement.

"I seek only to protect her."

"As is your right," the wyrm conceded, causing Cwen to scowl at Lohgaen.

Resting its head on the floor before Cwen, the great creature locked its eyes on hers and spoke, "You, Woman of Lore, seek the remaining shard of the Wreken and wyrm. Do you know the power it wields?"

"It can wield no more than the power to destroy Ædracmoræ, and I am charged only with its collection for the Queen. I am no woman of lore or legend."

A sharp crack of laughter shook the cavern.

"If only that were true, Cwen of Aaradan. Is your Queen just and fair, a ruler above suspicion, disinterested in conquest and power? If she is not, your world is in grave danger."

Cwen's laugh was disbelieving. "Yávië rules the Houses of Ædracmoræ and Aaradan and the Seven Kingdoms. There is no greater power. She is just and fair. As for 'above suspicion', you ask the wrong source, for I distrust everyone."

"And should a House rise against her? What then? Would she not seek the power of the Wreken wyrm shards for herself?" asked the dragon-headed serpent.

"She has sworn she will destroy the shards so that none may ever use them," Cwen whispered, suddenly less certain of the crown's desire to possess such potential power.

The Wreken wyrm nodded its approval of her caution. "And if I told you they could not be destroyed by your Queen, what would your decision be, Woman of Lore?"

"She already has the shards." Cwen's voice shook and her eyes grew wide.

"But you will reclaim them," the Wreken stated.

Cwen's laughter was choked by a sudden fear. "She is the Queen. I cannot defy her command."

Behind her, she heard Talin mutter, "It would not be the first time you defied the Queen."

Ignoring his taunt, she questioned the Wreken, "And if I reclaimed them? What then? If they cannot be destroyed the danger would still remain."

"Only those empowered by the Wreken can destroy the shards, for it is we who placed them here."

Cwen's nervous laughter bubbled forth. "You are the creators of the chaos, according to the ancient tales. Wreken ruled the wyrms and the race of Man was fodder."

The Wreken sounded amused as it answered. "Tales of the Feie. Great exaggerations, I assure you. If men were fodder it was because they followed the dictates of the Sojourners to slay the wyrms that held us. The Wreken sought no rule over Men. The armies of the G'lm fought only our enemies, though in the end they were damned, twisted against us by the Sojourners, and we were forced to hide beneath the earth."

Cwen sank to the ground. "How can I know who to trust? You speak against the Houses of my birth and are naught but a beast from the depths of a fog-filled abyss, yet you ask that I believe you over Yávië. I cannot make that choice."

"Touch the shard and see the truth."

The great wyrm suddenly drew back with a shudder, gagging and retching as if a bone had become lodged in its gullet. With a final heave it spat forth a great shard, which rolled to a stop before Cwen as the wyrm dropped away into the deep gorge. There was a collective gasp from her companions as they saw the shard. It pulsed and hummed, casting its deep golden glow over them. Through it ran rivers of darkness, black as ebony, and within lay a great shadow that pressed toward the surface of the shard as if straining to escape.

From the shard the voice of the Wreken spoke faintly, for it no longer held the power of the wyrm. "The power to destroy the shards is granted to you, daughter of Nall."

"No, I do not wish it." Cwen turned her face away.

"This choice is not yours," the Wreken's gentle voice continued, "for you have been granted that which you need to complete the task before you. Touch the shard, Cwen."

"No." Cwen shrank away, shaking her head against the Wreken's demand.

"Seek the counsel of those who serve you," the voice suggested.

Cwen turned and looked at Talin and watched his smile widen to a grin. "I am no servant, but a bit more adventure cannot hurt."

Her eyes shifted to Klaed.

"You are and always have been Lady Cwen. I shall serve you. Besides, I am just learning to play the part of the disgruntled nobleman well."

"Caen?" Her voice was soft and her heart swelled with feeling for him.

He stepped forward and held her, whispering, "I will stand by your decision."

Her eyes swept past Synyon and Lohgaen, but Lohgaen's voice called her eyes back to his face.

"I am bound to serve you, Cwen of Aaradan, whether you wish my service or not. But I do not speak for Synyon, for she has a strong voice of her own."

Looking toward Synyon, Cwen watched the woman wet her lips and glance toward Talin.

"I shall follow." Synyon nodded her acceptance of the charge.

Cwen's eyes settled on the shard. The sight of it chilled her.

"Woman of Lore, it is understood that the burden of the power of the Wreken is great, but you will not have to carry it alone."

With great trepidation, Cwen reached out and allowed her fingertips to touch the shard. The warm golden color covered her, wrapping her in its visions.

She no longer knelt in the cavern with her companions, but stood in the tower of a mighty fortress gazing out across fields sodden with the blood of the great wyrms. The G'lm ravished the bodies as they had done in the cities of Ædracmoræ's kingdoms, ripping and tearing at the flesh they consumed. Beside her in the tower stood two ethereal beings and a wizard she recognized as Laoghaire.

"Who are they?" she whispered.

"Sojourners," was the Wreken's soft reply.

Then a second vision swept before her: tens of thousands of G'lm screaming for blood as deathshades, demons and deadly, foul-smelling dragons fell upon the House of Aaradan and its Seven Kingdoms, relieving Ædracmoræ of every living being as neatly as the sharpened dagger trims the fat from the stag. Above, the storm of chaos darkened the sky and a sudden flashing image showed Cwen the world's dying heart. With each attack, the burning heart of Ædracmoræ cooled, leaving the earth chilled and the vegetation slowly dying. The final deadly strike of the massive army would put out the flame that warmed the world, leaving it in death and darkness for eternity.

"How can I stop this death?" Cwen's breath was ragged as she emerged from the visions, her eyes seeking Talin's.

"My granddame is a Sojourner," she whispered, shivering.

"She hides," the Wreken sighed. "Her war was won with the joining of the House of Aaradan to the House of Ædracmoræ. She guides the Queen's Council in its search for the shards to secure her future. It was she who called you. You must reclaim the shards and restore the balance of power by giving rise to the third House. Touch the shard, Cwen."

Cwen once again placed her fingers on the shard, expecting visions more fearsome than the first, but none came. Instead, a slender thread of golden light curled into the palm of her hand. Warm and comforting, it slipped within her, sliding slowly toward her heart and wrapping itself around it, seeking the rhythm of her life's blood.

Gathering the large shard from the floor she handed it to Talin and watched him place it in his satchel.

"Let us now steal some shards." Cwen's voice carried a hint of humor and a smile touched her lips and lit her eyes as she winked at Talin.

Lohgaen's soft voice stopped Cwen.

"We shall meet you at the House of Aaradan. New Xavian City does not welcome our kind."

"And what kind are you, Lohgaen?" Cwen asked.

"One who cannot hide his darkness," he murmured.

"I shall open the way for you and summon your Feie," he added, whispering the spell that caused the gardens to fade and created an exit into the fields.

"Cwen," Lohgaen called after her, "do not trust strangers."

Waving back at him she shouted, "You are a stranger, Lohgaen."

Synyon laughed at his expression, "She will make your life miserable for as long as you serve her. And just why is it you serve her?"

"I am not certain," he answered, "but I shall see her safe until her duty is ended and my House restored."

Brengven waited in the field, looking worried and pacing the grass flat. He rushed forward as they appeared, shouting, "I thought you were dead. I have summoned Nall."

"Well un-summon him," Cwen snapped. "I wish to deliver this

shard myself and I do not intend to do it on the back of a dragon."

Quickly pulling a blanket from her pack, she handed it to Talin, who raised his eyebrows in question.

"I must change. I cannot go to New Xavian City wearing this dress."

He grinned as he held out the cover. "I had not even noticed it."

"No, you were too busy gawking at the wizard's woman," Cwen grinned mischievously.

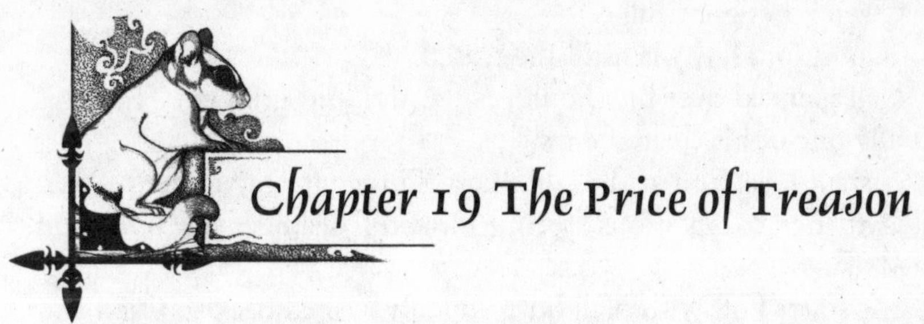

Chapter 19 The Price of Treason

The dragon appeared, sweeping in and dropping like a boulder, shaking the earth, rattling the branches of trees and scattering leaves about with a final brush of his enormous wings.

"It seems a bit too late to un-summon Nall, Cwen." Talin laughed at her expression. "Try not to chase him with a sword or stab him with your dagger."

Cwen stifled a smile as she stepped from behind the blanket, tossing the white dress to Talin before going to meet her father.

"You have found the last shard? Brengven told me you were dead." Nall glared at the Feie.

"Well they were late! And they told me to summon you if they were late. They went into a terrible place; I could sense it," Brengven fumed.

"The Feie exaggerates," Cwen said. "We do have the final shard and we are very much alive as you can see."

Nall blew a breath of relief. "Those demons attacked the city of Marske and nearly reached the Verdant Tree before we stopped them. The fortress that guards the pass was destroyed. Yávië and your mother are very concerned about you. We thought you had remained in Réverē."

"We shall arrive at New Xavian City through the rift and allow you to take the shard. I am sure Yávië will be more comfortable knowing it is safe," Cwen said.

"I could take you home," Nall mumbled.

Cwen's eyes grew huge.

"Upon that filthy beast?" she teased.

Nall glanced over his shoulder at Ardor and grinned. "Today is actually one of his cleaner days."

"I shall meet you at the city. I am riding with my father," Cwen called to her companions, seeing looks of disbelief on Talin and Klaed's faces.

She started off with Nall but suddenly rushed back to Caen and threw her arms around him.

"Do not lose your way," she whispered, allowing his soft kiss.

Waving, she raced off to catch Nall, who was now seated on Ardor and waiting for her. Leaning down, he extended his hand, eyes widening with pleasure when she leapt up to catch it as if she had done it everyday of her life, swinging up lightly behind him and wrapping her arms around him.

Ardor grumbled at Nall's silent command to behave and rose gently, banking away toward New Xavian City.

"It is not that I cannot ride a dragon," Cwen smiled, "I simply choose not to do so."

"But why did you choose not to do so?" Nall asked.

"I just prefer the warmth and intelligence of the Equus," she answered with a shrug so like her father, "rather than the rough scales and stubborn minds of dragons."

Ardor surged upward, hoping to dislodge the foul female, but Cwen maintained her seat and laughed, which only annoyed the dragon further.

When they finally settled on the grassy slope before the city, Ardor snaked his neck out and extended his scales in hopes of scaring Nall's malicious offspring.

"I do not fear you, Ardor. You are no more fierce than a downy flier. If you do not intend to eat me, do not pretend you do," Cwen teased, and watched Ardor grumble at Nall.

"He is a belligerent beast," she grinned.

"Aye, and a friend." Nall admitted.

The others waited near the gate, where Brengven fussed and muttered. "I shall camp in the safety of the forest, for I have already seen the council chambers here."

Caen reached out and took Cwen's hand, smiling at her wind-burned cheeks and wind-blown hair.

"A dragon flight is hard on a woman," she winked, leaning forward to kiss his cheek.

"I have never been in New Xavian City. It is said there is no safety here for thieves," Caen whispered to her.

"You are the Queen's thief, Caen. She will allow no harm to come to you."

"Come," Nall called. "Let us show them you are safe."

As they entered the palace Näeré looked up and tears filled her eyes.

"Cwen," she said, hugging her daughter. "Finally you have come home."

"I cannot stay, Mother. With the delivery of the final shard our duty is ended and we will be free of the Feie and free of Yávië's command – and I have accepted the request of another," Cwen said.

"And you, Talin? Will you leave us too? Klaed, do you not intend to stay?" Näeré asked them, seeing the intent in their eyes as they both shrugged evasively.

A small shiver touched Näeré's soul as she searched her daughter's face.

"Did I hear that someone wished to escape my command?" Yávië asked, entering the hall with a curious look for each of them.

Cwen grinned. "Indeed we do wish to be free. You are a harsh taskmaster, Yávië."

Eyeing Nall, Yávië asked, "Do you bring the shard?"

"Aye," Nall said, pulling the great golden shard from his pack and placing it on the table.

Yávië looked at its color and then at Cwen.

"It is the color of your eyes," she stated. "And somehow it is different; there is no darkness at its center. At last all are accounted for and we need not fear they will be used against us. Many have died because of their power. I shall deliver this last shard to the Fortress and we shall destroy them once and for all."

"What if they cannot be destroyed, Yávië?" Cwen asked the Queen, drawing looks of warning from Klaed and Caen.

"Why would you think they could not be destroyed? They appear to be crystalline like a dragon's shard. Surely they can be crushed."

"But if they cannot be destroyed? What will you do with them?" Cwen asked again.

"Lock them away where they can never be found, I suppose. They must never be used; the destruction from only three of the armies was horrendous. Had they reached the Well, Ædracmoræ would be a place of death," Yávië answered. "The G'lm must never be freed again."

Nodding her agreement, Cwen went to stand next to Caen.

"Five days forth there is a Council meeting and I would like you present," Yávië said. "I would like all of you there."

"We shall leave for the fortress on the morrow then. I look forward to seeing Sõrél," Cwen agreed.

"As do I," Klaed murmured, earning a giggle from her.

"Do you require Brengven to attend?" Cwen asked Yávië.

Recalling the Feie's discomfort, Yávië nodded, "Tell him, just this one last time."

"Let us provide you proper rooms for this night," Yávië insisted.

Smiling her gratitude, Cwen graciously declined. "That is kind, but Brengven awaits us and we have much to discuss, for we are no longer gainfully employed in the service of the Queen."

"You could be if you chose. There is room among my Guardians for each of you," Yávië offered.

"I have only begun to heal the wounds between Nall and myself. The restrictions of the Guardianship would rub them raw again," Cwen observed as she looked at Nall and Näeré.

Näeré's voice was sharp within Nall's mind. "*There is something very wrong.*"

Raising an eyebrow, he looked from his wife to his daughter and back again. "*Wrong with Cwen?*"

He saw Näeré's barely perceptible nod and heard her soft and fearful whisper. "With all of them – they hide something from us."

Returning to the camp that Brengven had prepared, Klaed stopped them and sought Cwen's eyes as he spoke. "If we are caught we will be beheaded. The full fury of the crown will be against us."

Cwen reached out and placed her hand on his chest above his heart.

"It will be far worse than beheading. If we are caught we will be charged with high treason. The three of you will be stripped and taken to your place of execution tied to a hurdle that is drawn behind an Equus. You will then be hanged and your manhood and intestines removed. They will be burned before your eyes while you still live. At some point in this agony you will die from pain or loss of your life blood. Then you will be quartered and boiled in wizard's oils to prevent the pieces from rotting too rapidly. Your remains will be displayed atop the fortress gates as a warning to others who might consider such traitorous acts. As a woman, I will fare much better. Yávië will simply have me burned at the stake for the sake of decency. So we must not be caught. Yávië will not see this as a game. It is the betrayal of the crown by those she entrusted with the safety of Ædracmoræ. Those who spoke against us will be quick to condemn.

"The three of us and Brengven will arrive at Yávië's Council meeting as we said we would. Caen will steal the shards with the help of the wizards. It will not surprise Yávië if we tell her Caen decided to disregard her request and go on his way. Brengven must not know what we intend."

Cwen's words brought the deep chill of fear to each of them.

Cwen lay with Caen, apart from the others. Tears as large and clear as flawless crystals filled her eyes.

"You have made my heart light again and swept the darkest dreams from my mind; in return, I have placed you in dreadful danger and given you the burden of responsibility for other lives as well. We may all die traitors' deaths. You must truly wish you had remained hidden beneath the leaves of the glen in days past," her voice made small by her fears.

Pulling her nearer, Caen drew his cloak tightly around them and kissed the tears away.

"Were I to die this very night of the torture you described, I would not regret a moment of the time I have spent with you." His voice caught and he glanced away to hide the tears that would soon mingle with Cwen's.

"I ask that you release Klaed, for he is far too noble for what we intend to do and too much of a hero to fail you." Caen looked back at Cwen and saw her nod of agreement.

"It seems I am surrounded by champions… or fools," she said.

Cupping her face in his hand, he kissed her tenderly and whispered, "Perhaps we are all a bit of both."

Caen fumbled with the laces of Cwen's dress.

"You did not tell me it would be so hard to fasten," he muttered, causing her to look around at him.

"I would have asked Talin, but I thought perhaps you had more experience." She winked at him and watched his color rise.

"My experience is in unfastening them, not fastening them." He shook his head and tried to insert the same lace into its hole for the third time.

"I will do that for you Cwen, if it will not cause offense." Klaed offered with a wide grin.

"No offense will be taken," Caen said, dropping his hands and deferring to the nobleman.

"Release him," Caen whispered into Cwen's ear as he stepped away to pack his knapsack.

Klaed deftly laced Cwen's dress and spun her around to face him.

"You are a beauty, Lady Cwen. And I will not lie and say that I am glad that you have chosen Caen, though he is a far better man than I thought him to be." Klaed sighed and gave her his contagious smile.

The smile turned into a frown when it was not returned, and he saw the worry and sorrow etched on Cwen's face.

She reached out and drew him to her and held him tightly.

"You have always sought to make me smile. But now I cannot, for the burden I bear is too heavy. I must release you to remain at the fortress. I cannot risk your life in open opposition to the Queen. Brengven says that Yáviё intends to offer you a position on the Council. Take it. Be my eyes within the circle of the crown."

"You believe you will be caught?" Klaed asked.

"Nay, but I do believe we will be suspect. In your position as liaison within the Council you can stand for us and send us word."

"How will I serve you if I cannot reach you?" he frowned.

"I shall send a beast to you with word of our location. Something that will not be questioned – a downy flier or a magpie. Do this for me, Klaed." She gripped his hands, intent on gaining his consent.

"I do believe you care for me, Cwen of Aaradan, and that you wish to spare my life, but I also see the wisdom of your plan and therefore accept your terms," Klaed said, leaning forward to kiss her on the cheek.

She blushed and said, "I have never forgotten your gentle kindness when I was like a wounded bird. You are indeed a nobleman and a gentleman, Klaed of Drevanmar."

As he watched her walk away, Klaed turned and spoke to Caen, who had joined him. "You know that I love your woman?"

"Aye, and you know that I must soon leave her?" Caen asked, his words breaking with his sadness.

Nodding, Klaed searched Caen's face. "She will not take it well."

"I fear that is too kind. She will turn from me. Whether she will ever forgive it I do not know."

"Why do you not tell Cwen that you gave your oath to the Maraen to save her life?"

Caen said, "She does not know the Maraen. She would not believe there was no other way. Will you keep her from pain?"

Klaed promised, "I will not let them burn her."

Caen's eyes closed at the thought and he held out his hand to Klaed. He spoke the feelings of his heart. "You have become a friend, Klaed."

Cwen looked on as Caen and Klaed exchanged the grip of friendship. "What do they talk about?" She looked up at Talin.

"You." He shrugged.

She frowned. "I feel that I have just been sold as a bullram at market."

Talin laughed. "Caen would never sell you to another, though Klaed might offer to buy you."

Cwen's eyes brightened and she whispered, "And I would never allow Caen to be sold."

Chapter 20 Theft

Nall stared at his daughter and elbowed Näeré.

"*She is beautiful*," his silent words filled his wife's mind.

Näeré chuckled aloud, "Have you never looked at her before?"

"Aye," he admitted grudgingly, "but she was never in a dress."

Cwen was speaking quietly to Talin and was startled by the sudden hand upon her arm.

"Your mother senses there is something wrong, though she does not know what it is," Nall murmured in Cwen's ear.

Cwen looked up at her father. "I believe she must be sensing the danger of the past, for I was held by the wizard Laoghaire."

Frowning, Nall looked back at Näeré, who shrugged and sighed, "Perhaps."

Yávië took Klaed aside and she spoke to him in hushed tones, smiling at his acceptance of the offered councilor's position.

As Ileana entered, Cwen tensed and stepped behind Talin where her granddame would not see her.

At Yávië's invitation the Council members took their seats at the table and their guests sat in the extra chairs placed along the wall at the foot of the table behind Sõrél.

Cwen sought each face; all were known to her as family members. Yávië, her aunt, Queen of Ædracmoræ, always strong and just; Sõrél, the King, devoted to his wife and family; Sõvië, Cwen's cousin and daughter of the Queen; Xalín, Sõvië's lover and the ruler of the Xavians; Nall and Näeré, Cwen's parents – while oft at odds with her, their loyalty was without question; and Ileana, her granddame and the Sojourner who had called her to this quest. The wizard Grumblton was absent, for he guarded the wyrm shards.

Yáviё stood and addressed those assembled.

"It is in peace we assemble this day, a peace brought to Ædracmoræ by the gathering of the ancient wyrm shards that control the G'lm. We owe this peace to Cwen, Talin, Klaed, Caen and Brengven. While great devastation has touched many cities of Ædracmoræ, we need fear no more."

Calling them to her, she continued as they stood before her.

"Cwen and Talin have accepted a new task. Caen has gone on his way to rob the rich and fill his pockets with lauds, for it is what he does. Brengven seeks only to return to the beauty of Réverē. However, Klaed has agreed to remain and serve the Crown as a councilor. He will be housed at New Xavian City and act as a liaison between the court and the people of Ædracmoræ.

"Your task has been difficult and you have served the Crown well. It will not be forgotten." Yáviё spoke her gratitude to each of them as she placed the ribbon holding the medal of service over their heads, settling each near their hearts.

Cwen felt weak, knowing the deception she intended and a small moan escaped her lips, causing Talin to grab her hand and squeeze it hard. Turning her pale face toward him, she swallowed the moment of fear.

Taking a deep breath, Cwen thanked Yáviё, noticing over her shoulder that Ileana was staring at her quite openly.

Suddenly her granddame was there, holding Cwen's hand and examining her pale, fear damp face.

"You are ill, Granddaughter?" Ileana asked.

Cwen nodded and gave a small smile. "I am exhausted, and Brengven's boiled fowl does not seem to be sitting well."

"Perhaps Näeré will give you an elixir to settle your stomach," Ileana murmured.

"Aye, I shall ask her," Cwen said gratefully, withdrawing her hand and drifting off toward Näeré.

"Cwen!" Ileana's voice was sharp and drew the looks of everyone present.

"Aye, granddame?" Cwen asked, trying to look innocent and puzzled.

"You did not see a living wyrm in your travels did you?"

Cwen laughed with feigned relief, lying deftly, "Nay, granddame. From what Brengven has told us of them and the remains we saw, we should all be dead if we had encountered a living wyrm."

Ileana nodded, her eyes narrowing as she gazed after her granddaughter.

In the stone chamber beneath the fortress, Caen crept quietly along the wall toward the vault of the crown. He knew it would be guarded and he hoped the veiling stone would provide sufficient cloaking to hide him from whoever watched the shards.

A sudden stir of air and a soft whisper caused him to freeze. Lohgaen appeared, followed by Synyon.

"You were supposed to wait for us," Lohgaen chastised. "Cwen will not trust me if I allow harm to come to you."

Caen shook his head. "She will not trust you no matter what you do or do not do. I speak from long experience. The shards are in the vault that holds the crown and jewels of the queen. There will be a guard."

Lohgaen nodded and waved Synyon forward.

"Let her see who it is and deal with them."

Synyon slipped silently down the long corridor, casting a veiling spell at the last moment before she swept into the vault room.

She cleared her mind, leaving it void of all thought. Then she saw Grumblton sitting cross-legged on the floor and quickly exited back the way she had come.

"It is the Ancient wizard Grumblton," she sighed. "He will know we are there if we so much as allow a fleeting thought to cross our minds. The thief will be defenseless. Why is it you must always serve those who cannot help themselves?" she asked Lohgaen crossly, receiving a scowl from Caen.

"I am not helpless."

"Oh, really?" Synyon said, rolling her eyes. "Not only is he helpless, but he is obstinate and the lover of the woman you desire. Lohgaen, sometimes you act with no logic at all."

"You desire Cwen?" Caen bristled with offense.

"Nay, I have no desire for your woman; she has made her choice. If we do not stop arguing we will soon draw the entire army of the Queen down upon our heads," Lohgaen snapped, glaring at Synyon. She wrinkled her nose and glared back.

"Can you clear your mind?" Lohgaen asked Caen, shaking his head at the look of confusion he received.

"We shall have to cast the spell of sleep on the old wizard," Lohgaen whispered, glancing sideways at Synyon.

"We? I suppose you mean me," she sighed with exasperation. "We are doomed in the company of your lady and her defenders."

Spinning, she cloaked and returned down the long hall, clearing her mind as she went. As she slipped into the vault room she blew the sleeping powder into Grumblton's face and evoked the spell, watching with satisfaction as the little man dropped to his side and began to snore.

Leaning out, she withdrew the veil and beckoned Lohgaen and Caen forward.

"Hurry. The sleeping spell will not work long on this one. Cute little fellow," she grinned and tapped Grumblton with the toe of her boot.

"You think everyone is cute," Lohgaen said, shaking his head.

"Nay, only small, grumpy old wizards and the one called Talin." She winked at Caen, making him frown.

"Quick," she said, poking him in the ribs. "I hope you are a good thief at least, since you seem absolutely useless otherwise. What is it the golden-eyed woman sees in you anyway?"

Drawing his lock picks, Caen began to work the lock.

"That is personal," he tossed over his shoulder.

"Oh, personal. You know what that means, Lohgaen? You will have to be very good…"

"Hush," Lohgaen whispered, sending her a fierce look.

"Well you will," she taunted. The heavy lock fell away with a snap and Synyon clapped her hands. "He really is a thief."

Together Caen and Lohgaen lifted the great stone lid and quickly counted the shards.

With a sigh, Caen nodded. "All are here."

Opening their bags they wrapped each shard in cloth and settled them at the bottom, covering them with the rest of their belongings.

"Who are you?" Grumblton's voice growled behind them.

"Oh scat!" Synyon swung toward the diminutive little wizard and knocked him on the head with her staff. Grumblton fell like a stone, a large knob rising on his forehead where he had been struck.

Shaking his head, Lohgaen muttered, "So much for magick." Leaning down he checked to see if the little man lived and sighed with relief that he did. "Not that it will matter when we are found guilty of treason," he grinned grimly. Casting a heavy veil over the three of them he urged them to run.

At her mother's home Cwen drank the nasty tasting elixir that Näeré offered while Nall leaned against the wall and talked to Talin.

"There is nothing wrong with your stomach," Näeré said, eyeing her daughter suspiciously. "But your nerves are so taut with anxiety I am surprised you are not screaming."

"I am always fraught with apprehension when I am forced into a Council meeting," Cwen snapped, her anger flaring.

"What is it you have done?" Näeré bit her lip as she eyed Cwen.

"I have done nothing. How could I possibly do anything? I have been locked away with the Council all morning. And your constant suspicions are going to make me scream," Cwen raged.

Talin placed his hand on her arm, only to have it flung away.

"What do you want?" Cwen snarled at him.

"It is time we left." His voice was a sharp command, drawing looks of surprise from both Nall and Näeré.

Apologizing to them he grabbed Cwen's arm and dragged her toward the door.

"What are you thinking?" he hissed at Cwen once they were outside.

"I cannot do it." She looked up at him. "I cannot risk your lives."

Shaking his head, he whispered, "It is already done."

Grumblton's shrieking brought Nall and Näeré racing past them, headed for the fortress with weapons drawn.

"Veil and run as if your life depended on it," Talin hissed, "for indeed it does."

Casting the veil, Cwen raced away behind Talin.

Chapter 21 Fear

They were crouched in the cold mud of the fen, dirty, damp and miserable.

"If I take them back…" Cwen said, looking up anxiously for confirmation, her eyes dark with exhaustion and fear.

"Cwen, you have done the right thing." Lohgaen knelt before her. "If we were able to steal the shards so easily, so others would be. The little wizard did not see the thief. He saw only Synyon and me. Even if they suspect the thief, there will be many who can speak for him, saying that he left a day earlier. We can pay someone to say he was in Ælmondæ if need be. And you and Talin were in the Council chambers; surely you will not be suspect."

"I cannot believe what I have done. I only hope that I am burned before I have to hear the screams of your torture." She held her head in her hands and wept.

"I am surprised that you would choose such a weak woman," Synyon mumbled under her breath, drawing a warning look from Lohgaen.

Talin glanced at her and caught her eyes, feeling his color rise as she held his gaze.

"She is not weak," he stated firmly. "She simply does not wish to cost us our lives."

"Your lives will be worth nothing if we continue to sit here in the mud and try to change what is already done by simply speaking of it. Complete the task and rid yourselves of the shards. Prove to the

Queen that your intent was only to protect her fragile empire. Then perhaps she will merely toss you into her prison for the rest of your lives instead of hanging you for high treason," Synyon spoke, looking at Talin all the while.

Lohgaen agreed. "And what we need most now is a safe, dry place to stay the night. There is an abandoned township just beyond the fen. 'Tis not a palace, but it will be far drier and warmer than the mud of this swamp."

He extended his hand to Cwen and pulled her up as she took it. Looking to Caen, he called him to them.

"Warm her and give what comfort you can. She must regain her fire or she will be lost."

"Do not speak of me as if I were not present," Cwen spat, bringing a smile to Lohgaen's face.

"I shall speak of you any way I see fit, Cwen, and there is naught that you can do about it," he mocked, watching her eyes spark. "It is better that you be angry than maudlin in the mud."

Within the abandoned buildings of the neglected township they ate a cold meal and settled down for the long and uneasy night ahead.

Caen rubbed Cwen's hands to warm them and tried to make her smile.

"You have mud on your face and leaves in your hair and you are still the most beautiful woman on Ædracmoræ."

She looked up at him and touched his face, whispering, "I am so afraid for you."

"We were not seen. Grumblton did not recognize Synyon or Lohgaen, and my back was turned to him. He was terribly cranky when he woke from the sleeping spell and will be more so when he wakes from the thump on the head he received from Synyon, but I think he will believe it was strangers who stole the shards."

Gathering some moldy hay, Caen made a bed upon the dirty floor and spread his cloak over it.

"It is the best accommodation the town has to offer," he grinned, drawing her down beside him.

Finally she smiled and eased his aching heart. "I care not for the room, only for the company."

When their passion had warmed them and exhaustion had finally claimed Cwen, Caen watched her sleep, drawing his warm cloak over her. He leant down and kissed her temple and softly whispered his good-bye. Soundlessly he gathered his pack and slipped out into the darkness to fulfill his promised service to Jūdan.

Outside the building where Cwen lay wrapped in the warmth of pleasant dreams, Lohgaen's murmured words stopped Caen.

"And so you leave her."

"Aye, I must, or bring the wrath of the Maraen down on our heads. It seems there is enough threat without that," Caen nodded. "You will keep her safe?"

"It is my intent, though it will be more difficult without you. I sense that Cwen does not choose easily and your abandonment will bring pain and anger. Many men have not survived servitude to the Maraen; their heat damages the heart, though I sense that yours was healed by one with knowledge of the damage. It will be interesting to see if you recover a second time."

Caen laughed softly, "Aye, the healer was Maraen. If I please her perhaps she will see fit to heal me again."

"Good journey," Lohgaen said. "I shall see your lady safe."

Without a backward glance, Caen headed for the road.

Cwen stepped from the side of the road to stand before Caen. Her feet were bare and her eyes still soft with sleep. In her hands she held his cloak.

"You intend to leave me?"

Reaching out he gently touched her face.

"I cannot take you where I must go, Cwen."

He saw her eyes cloud over with hurt as she slapped his hand away.

"Go, you have promised nothing. Just go," she whispered, tossing his cloak to him and turning away so that he would not see her eyes fill with the tears of loss.

She listened until his footfalls faded then fell to her knees as her tears mingled with the dust.

Strong hands drew her up, and she looked up into Lohgaen's dark eyes.

"Come, Cwen, and I will help you sleep without dreams. He will return for you when he can."

"I shall kill him if he returns," she murmured sleepily as Lohgaen's gift of dreamless sleep began to make its claim.

"I do not want him," she sniffed, wiping her nose on Lohgaen's soft shirt.

"Aye, you do, more than anything," he said, lifting her and carrying her back to the nest of hay Caen had built for her.

Grumbl's screams of rage were unprecedented; Nall had never seen the little wizard so angry.

"She cast a spell on *me*! The witch cast a spell on *me*!" he wailed angrily. "And then she struck me with her staff!"

"And somewhere during her attack on you she managed to steal the shards," Yáviё scowled at him. "Who was with her? Who were they, Grumblton? They must be caught quickly before they can use the shards against us."

Grumblton looked up at her crossly and pointed a finger at her. "One was the thief you hired to hunts for them in the first place. I recognized his boots and cloak, though his back was turned and his head was in the vault."

"Caen stole the shards?" Yáviё asked with disbelief.

"Aye." Grumbl's voice was positive.

"And the others? You had never seen them?" she prodded.

"Nay, but the darkness was heavy on them. They know the magick of the abyss."

Yáviё looked up at Nall.

"Your daughter has betrayed me, just as you said she would. I do not believe the thief would have acted without her direction. He does not have the backbone for it."

Nall froze, physically forcing the denial from his mind.

"I do not know," he said tersely.

"Nay," Näeré said. "Cwen would not betray us. I know that she would not."

"Then call her to us and let us ask." Yáviё's chin rose, her eyes glittered with anger. "Just where are our heroes at the moment?"

"Yáviё," Sōrél cautioned, his hand on her shoulder. "Let us discover the truth before we hire the lynch man."

"I am the lynch man. And if I find they have betrayed me I will execute them myself," Yáviё snarled.

"Nall, send Guardians to find Cwen and Talin. I want the thief brought to me alive. She will come for him."

Seeing his hesitation Yáviё slapped him.

"Do it. Or you will find yourself guilty of treason as well. You command my Guardians. Are you no longer capable of the task?"

Nall's mind was racing with thoughts of Cwen and the danger to her. If he did not keep control of the Guardians he could not protect her at all.

"Aye, I can do the job better than any other," he answered briskly and turned on his heel, heading to the garrison to gather a detail of men to search for Cwen and Talin.

"Nall!" Näeré raced after him, grabbing his arm and swinging him toward her. "You cannot do this!"

"If I do not, who will?" He searched his wife's face. "If I am removed from command, if Yáviё has any reason to distrust us, Cwen will be dead within a fortnight. She and Talin do not have the skill to keep ahead of the Guardians who will hunt them."

He pulled Näeré to him and hugged her to his chest.

"I have never been a skilled liar, but I am about to become one. I will find her and keep her safe, Näeré. I promise I will. I shall need small items that will be recognized as Cwen's or Talin's, as many as you can find."

Näeré nodded.

"Why would she do this?" She asked in confusion. "I sensed the turmoil in her; she was filled with doubt and despair over it."

"I do not know," Nall shrugged. "Perhaps she will tell me when I find her. Just remember, we must remain above suspicion."

Yáviё stormed into the throne room and swept the articles from the table.

"My most trusted allies – and their offspring brings treachery against my House," she ranted.

"Why did I not listen when Nall said the girl would betray us?" she asked, glaring at Sōrél.

"You do not know that she has betrayed you, Yáviё."

"Your mother says it is Cwen's doing! She felt it during the Council meeting, but could not filter out the reason for Cwen's sudden guilt and fear. Now it is evident, is it not? The girl is a harlot, murderer and a thief."

"She is Näeré and Nall's daughter, Yávië. Do not treat them with such disrespect. My blood runs through her veins as well."

Yávië whirled on Sōrél, her dagger pressed against the throbbing pulse at the side of his throat. "I suggest you choose your loyalty now, husband, remembering that there is only the Crown or those guilty of treason to select from. You cannot stand for both. I do not care whose blood runs through their veins, their treachery will not go unpunished."

Sōrél reached up and wrapped his hand around his wife's where it held the blade, feeling it prick him and make his blood run.

"You forget I am one half of the crown, Yávië," he reminded.

"Nay, it is you who forget where your loyalties must lie." She snatched the blade away, returning it to the scabbard at her waist.

"If they have betrayed us, I will be the first to condemn them. But I will not condemn them without justice, and I do not believe you wish to either." Sōrél's voice offered soft reason.

"Grumblton saw the thief. Recognized him," Yávië whispered in hurt and disbelief. "And Ileana is positive Cwen is involved. We have always trusted her insight; she is a Sojourner and far more sensitive to deception than even Näeré."

"Then we shall start with the thief. If Talin and Cwen have nothing to hide they will come willingly when summoned," Sōrél assured her. "Nall has already sent men to search. They will begin in the vicinity of the fortress and continue until all are found and brought before us. Surely you can ask for no more?"

Yávië stared at Sōrél for a moment before reluctantly giving her agreement.

The morning found Cwen red-eyed and fierce, snapping at everyone and belligerent towards every suggestion they made.

Synyon stood in front of Cwen, looking up at the fiery-haired, golden-eyed woman that Lohgaen insisted on protecting.

"I do not like you very much. You have the voice of a harpy and the manners of a troll. If I find you too intolerable, I shall cast a spell and reduce you to unconsciousness. Then Lohgaen can simply tote you wherever it is we must go. Are we clear about this?" Synyon's voice was honeyed, but her eyes were sparkling with irritation.

Cwen blinked her disbelief and drew her sword.

"Oh my." Synyon shook her head. "Do you intend to slay me with that?"

Cwen drew back the sword and slashed at Synyon with a fierce forehand, but she was stunned as the sword bounced off the barrier surrounding its intended target. The force of the blow sent a shudder up Cwen's arm and the sword dropped from her aching fingers.

Lohgaen stepped between the two women with fire in his eyes.

He grabbed Cwen's arm and shook her.

"When Synyon tires of your nonsense she will merely turn you into something small and scaly, or send you to sleep for endless days, or kill you in the event she forgets you serve a purpose. Do not annoy her."

"She called me a troll," Cwen frowned, rubbing her arm.

Talin watched with a brittle smile on his face.

"For someone sworn to protect Cwen, you do go about it in a most peculiar manner," he called to Lohgaen.

Lohgaen gave a low chuckle, "If I do not intercede she will not last long enough to worry about the charge of treason."

"You travel with me because I serve your purpose?" Cwen's voice was filled with fury.

Turning back to her, Lohgaen looked into the fire of her eyes with amusement.

"Aye, you do have a purpose. And it is very evident you have not spent much time with wizards. Come, and I shall explain it to you." Lohgaen offered his hand and Cwen drew back.

Grinning, he beckoned her to him and her eyes widened as she stepped forward against her will.

"I do not wish to use magick to gain your trust and obedience, but I fear we do not have time to waste on your foolishness. Now, come." Again he held out his hand, releasing her of his control and nodding his approval as she reached for his hand.

"Do not bewitch me." Her voice held a faint quiver.

"Cwen, I have no wish to bewitch you or harm you in any way. I am here only to serve as your protector. If you could just believe that, our time together would be much more pleasant," he said, releasing her hand and leading her toward a small wooded area.

Gesturing to a fallen log he offered her a seat.

She started to refuse, but recalled her forced steps and reconsidered.

Once he saw her seated he dropped cross-legged to the grass before her.

"You are what legends are made of, Lady Cwen of Aaradan. The golden-eyed woman legends foretold many lifetimes ago, long before the shattering of Ædracmoræ. Do you know your history, Cwen? Have you listened to the stories of the past? They are not mere tales of the Feie."

Seeing her frown, he laughed, "Nay, I did not think so."

"I do not understand…" Cwen began, but Lohgaen touched his fingertips to her lips to silence her.

"I am going to help you, Cwen; help you destroy the wyrm shards and make peace with your Queen. And then you are going to help me restore the House of Lochlaen. After that?" he said pleasantly. "We shall see what you choose to do."

"Just who are you?" Cwen asked.

"I am just a traveler who knows a bit of magick and a great deal of history." His smile touched his eyes, lighting his face and sweeping away the darkness. "And I am your servant, Lady Cwen."

Sighing, she smiled back at him, "For a servant you are very disrespectful."

"I shall try to improve." He bowed and lifted her hand, kissing it gently.

"I am not sure I liked that." Cwen's words were tense as she drew her hand away.

He nodded his acknowledgement and replied, "Then I shall not do it again. Do try not to annoy Synyon."

A faint sound reached his ears and he threw Cwen down, covering her with his body and incanting the spell of shadow as he rolled beneath the fallen log.

"Shhhh," he cautioned, whispering, "Dragons approach.

Guardians already seek you."

She squirmed, trying to free herself of him. "Talin!" she hissed.

"Synyon will not allow anything to harm him."

Talin watched Cwen walk away with Lohgaen and considered following, but Synyon's silken voice stopped him.

"He would not like your interference – and he will not harm her in any way. He is celibate, you know."

Talin looked startled, causing effervescent laughter to bubble up from deep inside Synyon. "Though he does not like me to tell it."

"It is rather personal," Talin admitted.

"Well, we are alone at last. What do you think we should do?" Synyon cocked her head and smiled fetchingly.

"Are we required to do something?" Talin asked, feeling the warmth of her gaze.

She shrugged and slid toward him with the grace of a dancer.

"Nay, I do not believe it is a requirement, but I do get bored very easily. Do you?"

"You are a wizard?" he asked.

"Are you changing the subject?" she questioned, standing very close to him.

"What was the subject?" Talin asked, suddenly confused.

"Boredom," Synyon whispered, her warm breath caressing his cheek.

"I am not bored," Talin said, shaking his head.

"No," she answered, leaving Talin lost and uneasy.

She gurgled with laughter at his bewilderment, allowing the golden sound to flow over Talin like cool water.

"I am not a wizard. It is what you asked," she said.

"It is very hard to have a conversation with you," Talin frowned.

"Really? I thought I was making it very easy," she said, licking her lips and drawing Talin's gaze to her mouth. It was beautiful. Her lips were shiny with the moisture of her tongue and they tilted up at the corners as if she were always smiling.

Talin felt warm and leaned forward slightly, hearing her teasing laughter as she placed her hand against his chest.

"It is not that easy."

Together they looked up at the far off sound of dragons' wings and she drew him quickly to her as she dropped to the ground, enfolding him in the magick of her shadow spell.

"You are quite handsome," she whispered. "It would be a shame to see you hanged for treason."

"If you are not a wizard, what are you?" Talin asked, bringing more lilting laughter.

"I am a thaumaturge. Do not try to say that too quickly or you might hurt yourself," she giggled. "Perhaps you would prefer to call me Synyon?"

"Synyon," Talin said, her name wending its way in his mind.

"I am a great fighter, and though not nearly so many dweomers resonate within my mind as within Lohgaen's, I have very strong offensive magick and that can be quite useful," Synyon explained.

Suddenly she noticed Talin's arms were wrapped around her. "Are you comfortable?" she asked.

"Aye, quite," he answered, giving her a crooked grin.

Drawing away from him, she stood and shed the shadow she had cast before reaching down to offer him her hand.

Lohgaen and Cwen were entering from the glen; Lohgaen's face was dark with annoyance.

"Already they seek you. We must move quickly and find safety. Bael is a good place to begin. I am accepted there and none will ask questions about my traveling companions. We shall leave at dark fall. Rest while you can."

Cwen watched Talin's eyes follow Synyon and shook her head.

"What does she offer, Talin?" Cwen whispered at his side.

Grinning, Talin shrugged and laughed, "I do not even know what she is."

Cwen poked him and grinned, "Oh, she is very much a woman. But do not offend her, for Lohgaen says she could turn us into small scaly creatures."

Cwen wandered beneath the tall braid tree and called to the tiny downy flier hunting butter moths above her.

"Aye, mistress? How may I serve you? " the wee creature asked, sitting on its haunches and wrapping its fluffy black-tipped tail around its legs. Its bright black eyes looked down at her, and as she held out her hand, palm up, the little flier launched himself toward her, spreading his legs and gliding slowly down to sit in her hand.

"I must ask that you travel to the New Xavian City and see one called Klaed. He is a Councilor there and will be awaiting your arrival. Tell him we go to Bael. Will you do that, little one?"

"Aye, and shall I seek you in Bael?" asked the flier.

"If he has news for me, aye." Cwen held the little beast close and breathed her scent onto him, binding him to her and giving him comfort.

"Safe travel, flier," she whispered.

"I am Bastien," the flier spoke, giving a small bark and racing away in the direction of the distant city.

Chapter 22 The Thirteen

As Cwen lay down to rest, the soft voice of the Wreken filled her mind.

"*Cwen, you do not have the remaining shards. Until you do, you cannot journey to the Well of Flames and destroy them. Gather the shards beneath the earth. Two of Faervyn and one of Domangart.*"

Standing quickly, she looked for Lohgaen and found him felling trees within the wood. With a mere wave of his hand trees leapt from the earth and fell a dragon's length away.

Feeling her presence, he halted his practice and swung toward her.

"How may I help you, Cwen?"

"We must claim the missing shards – the ones that remain in the receptacles in the caverns of the G'lm. The Wreken has told me." She looked ready to cry and he touched her shoulder to ease her tension.

"Before we go to Bael we shall have them all. I assure it." He seemed so positive that she could not help but smile.

"Are you always so sure of yourself?" she asked.

Smiling in return he answered, "I have no reason to be otherwise."

"Tell me where we need to go," he continued. "I shall take you there under cover of darkness. I cannot create a rift during daylight, for the Guardians are very good at detecting the changes rifts create."

"Two are in Æstretfordæ. One near Calá and the other at the

southern edge of the Northern Mountains; the third is the one used by Laoghaire in Æwmarshæ. Do you think we can find them?" Cwen asked doubtfully.

"I am quite good at divining. Let us seek the waters of the pool and see what they will share."

Once again Lohgaen held out his hand to Cwen and was pleased when she accepted it without hesitation. He led her nearly a league to a small pool amid a fall of rocks. Its water shimmered with the glow of the moons in the growing darkness; it was clear and free of any living thing – no water plants or fish marred its surface. Leaning over the water, Cwen clearly saw her reflection with Lohgaen peering over her shoulder.

"We are quite beautiful, are we not?" he laughed.

Cwen laughed with him then looked up at him more seriously. "Synyon is right, you are very handsome."

"Synyon thinks me handsome? I was unaware. She treats me as if I were a bane boar carrying the slitherwort poison. She is often foul. Much like you." His smile was almost shy, surprising Cwen.

"I am sometimes quite difficult," she shrugged. "Have you made me forget Caen?"

He turned and looked at her sharply. "Nay, nor would I ever. Have you forgotten Caen?" he asked.

She sighed deeply, "No, not really, but it does not hurt so much when you talk to me."

"Then I shall have to talk continuously, for I promised him I would watch over you in his absence."

"He will not return. He only wanted…" The hurt flared and she could not speak the words.

"What you believe of Caen is not true. No more than what the Queen believes is true of you."

Lohgaen's voice was low and soothed her, though she doubted he knew Caen well enough to judge.

"Show me what you see in the pool," she asked, as much to change the subject as out of real interest.

"Much magick flows through you, Cwen. I can feel it when I touch you, your very being hums with it. Why do you not practice it?"

"I wish only to be me. I do not want to be a sorceress or a Guardian or a member of the Queen's Council. I want only to be Cwen," she whispered, wondering if he would understand.

"Then you probably do not enjoy being the Woman of Lore," he chuckled, the sound deep and pleasant.

"Nay, but I do not believe I am anyone who would be called wise, so that title probably belongs to another Cwen of Aaradan, daughter of Nall." Her laugh was abrupt and without humor.

"Now show me what you see in the pool," she nudged him.

He knelt, drawing her down next to him and speaking the words she did not know. With his hands he called the image forth, asking if she knew it.

"Aye, it is very near Calá, just a few leagues away," she nodded.

"And this?" he questioned, pulling another image into the richness of the water.

"An entrance to the caverns beneath the Northern Mountains," Cwen grinned. "Will you show me how to do this?"

"Perhaps when we have time to teach you the words you must know. Now look – is this the third place you seek?" The water lapped restlessly, erasing the old image and settling to reveal another.

Cwen drew back in fear. "It is the troll mines, Domangart's troll mines. He had the second half of the cipher stone. I stole it from him."

"So you truly are a thief?" Lohgaen asked, raising an eyebrow.

"When I must be. I am also a murderer and, according to some, a woman of loose morals and no honor." Her voice had grown harsh and he sensed that she was recalling old memories that left her raw.

"If you have stolen something of great value from Domangart you should be quite proud, for he is not an easy target," Lohgaen said honestly.

She shrugged and smiled shamelessly. "I wore a dress; he was no match for it."

Lohgaen laughed loudly and looked at her with genuine amazement.

"You are remarkable, Cwen. You truly are." He started to touch her face, but drew his hand away.

Instead, Lohgaen stood and called the rift that would lead them to the missing shard near Calá. In the darkness he knew that it would go unnoticed by those who sought Cwen and Talin.

Sending a silent command to Synyon and the whisper, "*We shall return with the shards. Take care of Talin.*" He felt her smile and had a tug of sympathy for Talin.

"They have gone," Synyon said, holding up her hand to ward off Talin's frustration and concern.

"He has taken her to recover the three missing shards used to raise the G'lm armies. Apparently we cannot destroy the shards until we have them all. You need not worry about her. She is safer with him than any other man on Ædracmoræ. He is Lohgaen of the House of Lochlaen." She saw Talin's look of confusion.

"Just trust that what I say is true. She is safe. He will kill anyone who attempts to harm her. Anyone." Synyon nodded her own agreement at her statement.

"Now what shall we do while they are gone?" Her gaze had become mischievous and Talin suddenly felt as if it were he who needed protection.

"You could teach me how to wield your axe," she grinned. "I would like that."

"You are too…" Talin hesitated.

"Small?" she offered.

"Aye. The axe is heavy and requires great strength."

"Let me see it." She held out her hands and cocked her head, waiting for him to draw it and hand it to her.

Slowly Talin slid the heavy axe over his shoulder and laid it across her palms, still supporting most of its weight in his own hands.

"Let go," she said, looking up at him.

Releasing the axe, he stepped back and watched her with astonishment.

The length of the axe crackled with light and she lifted it as if it weighed nothing.

"You see? Strength can come from many sources. For you, it comes from a broad chest and strong arms; for me, it comes from the mind." She tossed the axe back to Talin and grinned.

"Do not ever underestimate me, Talin. Come, let us take a walk and breathe the air of freedom – in case on the morrow we are imprisoned."

She held out her small hand and Talin accepted it, turning it over and smiling at its softness.

"Are you always so fascinated by women's hands?"

He blushed. "I do not often hold them."

Her smile grew and she tugged his hand, leading him off toward the divining pool.

Cwen stared at the emerald shard resting in its receptacle and tried to imagine the soldiers she had seen below Révere̅ coming to life. It was a horrible thought, and now that she had seen first hand the devastation that they caused, she could feel nothing but fear at the sight of a shard.

Lohgaen stood beside her and held open her bag. "We cannot waste time, Cwen. The day star will soon rise and we must return to Talin and Synyon before it does. I must get you to Bael and to safety."

Cwen lifted the shard, wondering how a thing of such beauty could bring such horror.

Placing it in the pack, she looked up at Lohgaen, and murmured, "I am grateful for your company and your kindness."

"I offer both freely," he said, and opened a rift that would lead to the caverns below the Northern Mountains.

They stood in a large cavern, one of many in the warren below the mountains. Each cavern had held many soldiers, and the sapphire shard before them had allowed Faervyn to send death toward the Well of Viileshga, the source of Ædracmoræ's life waters.

Cwen shook her head, recalling her father's words of how close the horde had come to tainting the well and darkening all the earth.

A footfall on the rocks below drew Lohgaen's attention and he raised his hand in preparation to slay the intruder.

Cwen grabbed his arm, staring at the man below them, a Guardian, his amber aura pulsing with strength and purity. It was Yávië's Guardian, come to deliver the charge of treason.

"Stay here," Cwen whispered.

Touching her arm, Lohgaen warned, "I will not let him take you."

With a deep sigh she nodded she understood.

She went to the steps and slowly made her way down them toward her father.

"I did it. The others would not have done it if not for me," she said in a small, strangled voice.

Nall's brow creased. "Why?"

"Yáviё cannot destroy them and I can." She shrugged, too tired to explain. "I could not risk leaving them with her, where they might be stolen."

"They were stolen, Cwen. Yáviё knows that it was Caen, for Grumbl recognized his clothes. The Guardians hunt for you and all who travel with you. I do not know how long I can keep you safe."

"You are not here to charge me with treason?" Cwen asked, her surprise evident.

"Cwen, you are my daughter." Nall breathed a deep shuddering sigh. "I am only here for the shard, but it appears I am too late. How is it that you can destroy what Yáviё and Grumbl cannot?"

"I do not really know. One called a Wreken has given me the power. He said it was the Wreken that placed the armies on the earth in the first place, to fight against their enemies the Sojourners. He showed me a battle from long ago; the Sojourners were slaughtering the wyrms that bore the Wreken. He has given me the power to destroy the shards and end the threat to all of us. I must do it, but I am so afraid for Caen and Talin."

"Are they traveling with you?" Nall asked, glancing up toward the man who remained in the shadows above them.

"Nay. Well, Talin does, but Caen has gone." Her voice revealed her hurt and Nall swallowed the words of contempt that threatened to erupt, instead asking, "Then who is that?"

"Just a friend who has sworn to protect me – and he can Nall, he is a wizard of great power."

Nall snorted. "Powerful enough to put Grumblton to sleep?"

"Nay, that was another, but she also travels with us." Cwen looked away, her heart heavy.

"Where will you hide? Ælmondæ will not be safe. Guardians have already been dispatched to search the city there. They will descend on any who know you with the fury of the Crown." Nall blew out a deep breath. "I must be able to tell your mother you are safe. I promised her."

Cwen stood on her tiptoes and hugged her father. "I will be safe." She whispered in his ear, "Lohgaen will not let harm come to me."

Nall stared at the man in the shadows and held Cwen tightly.

"I will need something of yours that I can use to mislead the troops. I will send them as far away as possible if you will tell me where you are going."

"Use my signet to distract them. Bael. We go to Bael. After that, I do not know, but Klaed can tell you. I will send word to him. I must seek the Well of Flames." Cwen said quickly. "I must go. We cannot use the rift during the day because the Guardians… I am sorry." She hung her head. "I have truly brought great shame on you."

"And I on you, unjustly. I did not know, but I should have." Nall put his hand under Cwen's chin and lifted it until her eyes met his. "I am sorry I did not know you better."

Looking up at the man in the shadows, Nall called, "Keep my daughter safe."

With a last hug Cwen spun and raced back to Lohgaen, who grabbed her hand and pulled her through the rift into the caverns of the troll mines.

Nall watched them go and then headed back to his waiting dragon.

The trolls' eyes glittered in the flickering torchlight. The scratching of nails and shuffling of feet reached Cwen and Lohgaen from all around.

Lohgaen pulled Cwen close and whispered, "Do not fear them; they will not attack as long as I am with you, for they fear the curse of the wizard above all else. It was a wizard's curse that made them the hideous horrors they are."

Keeping her close, Lohgaen began the descent to the caverns where the army of the G'lm had been discovered by Domangart.

The rumble of troll growls followed them, causing Cwen to cling tightly to Lohgaen.

"They want to eat me," she shuddered.

"Aye, the scent of you does bring the thought of a meal to their tiny minds. Far too many women have been offered up to them when Domangart and Laoghaire tired of their games."

Cwen cringed and pressed closer to Lohgaen, trying to bury herself beneath his cloak.

"Finally I see reason rise to your surface," his warm laughter teased.

"Here." He slipped off his cloak and wrapped her in it, chuckling at the sight of her small frame lost within its folds. He raised the hood and tucked her hair beneath it.

"Now to a troll you are naught but another wizard. My scent will protect you and drive them back."

He pushed her gently in the direction of the troll who had crept up behind them and watched her eyes grow wide as the troll hissed and shrank away.

"Why are they so fearful of you?" she asked.

"They fear the scent of death," Lohgaen murmured, looking away. "It clings to me like a vine to the braid tree."

Cwen looked up at him from under the heavy hood of his cloak. "You have killed many?"

He reached out and pulled her closer to him.

"Nay, but I have lived with the scent of it for so long that it is part of me."

Within the great cave where the army had stood they found the dust of the G'lm that had been destroyed by the Guardians and the smoky wyrm shard that had activated them. Lifting it, Lohgaen wrapped it and added it to his pack with the others; then, looking at Cwen, he called the final rift that would take them back to Talin and Synyon.

The camp lay empty and Cwen called out to Talin in alarm.

The pounding of boots was soon heard and Talin burst into the clearing with his axe drawn, glaring at Lohgaen.

"I was told no harm would come to… "

Looking around at Cwen, Talin asked, "Why did you call me?"

"I was afraid the Guardians had taken you. We ran into Nall in the caverns near the Northern Mountains. He says he will try to keep the Guardians looking in the wrong direction. The dawn will come quickly. If we are going to Bael we should do so now."

Nodding his understanding, Talin looked back and saw Synyon coming at a more leisurely pace.

"I told you she was not harmed. She merely calls for you out of habit." Synyon glared at Cwen.

"Enough," Lohgaen said, seeing Cwen's mouth opening for a retort.

With a sweep of his hand the air shimmered and pulsed, revealing the port city of Bael beyond it.

"Say nothing. I shall speak for all of us," Lohgaen ordered, reclaiming his cloak from Cwen before stepping through to the city.

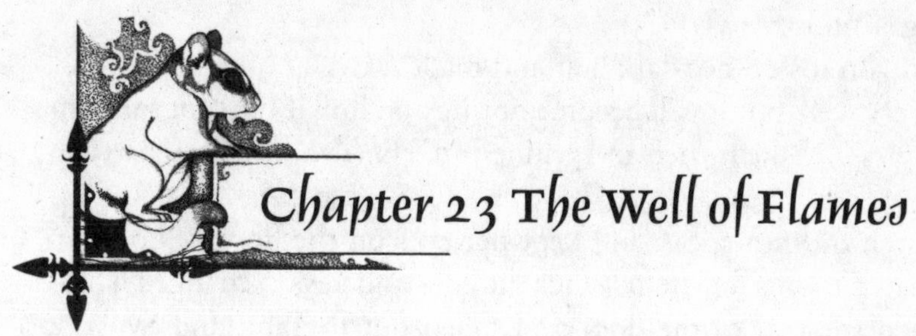

Chapter 23 The Well of Flames

Talin watched Bael's citizens react as Lohgaen passed by. They drew back or turned away; none approached him and none made eye contact.

At a drab inn on a narrow back street, Lohgaen turned to them and asked them to remain outside while he spoke to the proprietor. Cwen immediately shook her head.

"I will not be left in the street with her." She stuck out her chin to indicate Synyon and received a smile from Lohgaen.

"You are being left in Talin's care. Is that better?" he asked.

"Nay, you said he could not protect me, and I know she will not," Cwen said crossly.

"Actually, Synyon would protect you with her life if it were necessary, even though she pretends she would not. Of course, she could protect you just as well if you were a scarlet lizard or a downy flier." Lohgaen chuckled and Synyon smirked.

"Very well, you will come inside, but you will not speak or look up at the proprietor. Will you obey those rules?"

"Why should I not look at the man?"

"Because, he will remember your eyes."

"Oh," Cwen answered with a shrug, "I can do nothing to hide them."

"I could," Synyon said. "If I turned you into a scarlet lizard or a downy flier your eyes would be black."

"Synyon!" Lohgaen snapped, "I grow tired of this bickering and baiting. End it now."

Synyon tossed her dark hair and made a face at him.

"Very well, but it will become boring and dull if I do not torment her. Unless…" she turned and grinned at Talin, "you wish to entertain me."

Cwen did not speak and kept her eyes on the floor as Lohgaen negotiated rooms for them. Once the coin and keys exchanged hands Lohgaen stepped to the door and called out to Talin and Synyon, drawing them into the inn.

"Next to each other," the innkeeper called as they started up the stairs. "Last two rooms on the left."

Lohgaen led the way.

Opening the door to the first room, Lohgaen gestured to Talin and Synyon.

"Your accommodations."

Talin raised an eyebrow, causing Lohgaen to laugh.

"The ladies have made it abundantly clear that it is necessary for you and me to guard against the danger of their feud. It is not possible that they be left alone together, therefore Synyon will protect you and I shall protect Cwen. I assure you that Cwen will be safe. I can also guarantee that you will be well protected against the threat of others, though Synyon may pose a threat to your heart if you do not keep it well armored."

"Cwen?" Talin asked, still scowling.

"I prefer the threat of Lohgaen over what that witch may bring. At least I am familiar with the treachery of men."

"I am not a witch," Synyon fumed, raising her hand threateningly.

Cwen drew back behind Lohgaen as she saw the bright sparkles of light grow around Synyon's fingertips and drift slowly across the space between them.

Shaking his head in exasperation Lohgaen blew the trailing magick back toward Synyon and pointed toward the open doorway.

"In," he ordered. "Rest while you can. Cwen and I shall seek information about the Well of Flames. We will bring a meal when we return."

Talin and Synyon entered the room, but Synyon grabbed

Lohgaen's hand as he tried to draw the door closed, asking, "How will you hide her eyes?"

Smiling at her earnest concern, he murmured, "Cwen is about to become a holy woman."

Synyon burst out laughing and ducked back into the room as Lohgaen pulled the door shut.

"Come," he said, shepherding Cwen before him into the adjacent room.

Seeing doubt clouding her eyes at the presence of the single cot, he gestured to the chair.

"I shall make myself comfortable at the table when the time to rest comes. You need not fear me, Cwen. I have chosen to avoid the gifts of women."

Cwen stared openly. "You are a holy man?"

"Nay, only a wise one," he said. "Women are a weakness of my father's, but I have preferred to avoid the temptation."

"I do not believe you," Cwen whispered, seeking his eyes. "I have seen the way you look at me."

Laughing his soft laugh, he answered, "I did not say I did not look at women. I do not believe there is a man who would not seek to fill his mind with beauty. Now, you need to change from Cwen to a holy woman from the cloister of Belasis. It will not only hide you, but give you the unfailing respect of all you meet."

He drew clothing from his pack and handed it to Cwen, watching her face as she realized she would be fully veiled beneath the soft scarlet fabric woven of rich satin and spider silk.

"How did you steal the clothing of a holy woman?" she asked.

"I did not. Synyon did," he replied.

"You will have to turn your back," she sighed, "I am too modest to change with you watching me."

He tilted his head and looked at her with renewed interest. "That does not seem in accord with someone described as having loose morals and no honor."

With a nod he pulled out a chair and faced the wall, giving her the privacy she requested.

Lohgaen chastised himself for his thoughts as he listened to the soft rustle of fabric behind him.

"You may look at me now," Cwen said finally.

"You are a thaumaturge. No one will ever know that you are not. They will fear your power and honor you for your skill." Lohgaen took a deep breath. "I will provide any magick you may need; they will not realize it does not come from you."

Cwen wrinkled her forehead and said, "I am a what?"

"A high prophetess, trained at Belasis, as was Synyon, though she never took the vows. She is far too caustic to be a holy woman. You will need to keep you voice even and soft. A holy woman never raises her voice, only her magick. Do you believe you can do that, Cwen?" Lohgaen asked, stepping to her and lifting the long veil that hid her face.

"I do not practice magick," she replied.

"I was not speaking of magick, Cwen, for I have all the magick you will need. Your voice must be one that seduces, lulls and calms, hypnotizing those to whom you speak. Imagine that you are attempting to make them do your bidding just by using your voice."

Cwen started to shake her head, but suddenly felt held in his gaze.

"Do you bewitch me, Lohgaen?" Her voice was soft and low.

"Nay, Cwen, it is you who attempt to bewitch."

His eyes grew darker, drawing her gaze deeper, where she thought she saw a faint flicker of golden light in their depths. She placed her hands on his chest and gently pushed him away.

"I think you are a danger to me," she whispered breathlessly.

Smiling, he pointed, "That is the voice, Cwen. None will resist it and we shall gather the information we need from those who do not wish to give it."

Opening the door he pointed to her, "Veil down."

She raised her hands and drew the veil over her face, hiding her golden eyes and becoming a Prophetess of Belasis.

A sudden scratching at the windowsill drew their attention and a tiny downy flier scrambled in, bounding across the bed and onto Cwen's shoulder.

"The one called Klaed says the father, Nall, seeks to help you, but he must know where you go," the flier squeaked.

"Wait here. I shall give you a message for Klaed when we return,"

Cwen replied in beast speech.

Then, turning back to Lohgaen she preceded him out the door.

In the Fortress of the Dragon Queen Yávië stood before Nall, her eyes bright with anger.

"Why have the traitors not been brought to me?"

"Because they have not been located by the Guardians," Nall answered. "They have searched Ælmondæ, leaving no tavern or inn outside their scrutiny. Horsfal's has been searched in Æcumbræ, and he swears he has not seen Cwen since she sought the cipher stone at the beginning of her quest. None have reported sight of them."

Yávië shook her head. "It is not good enough, Nall. Hire the independents. Put a bounty on the head of the thief. Offer more if he is brought to me alive. One hundred lule paid to anyone who leads me to him. I want him found, Nall, and I want him punished. He broke into my vault and took the most dangerous artifacts I have ever seen. What if he is selling them about the kingdom to those who will use them against us? Find him and bring him to me."

Zeth entered the throne room and bowed respectfully to Yávië before reporting to Nall.

"We have located Cwen's signet in a tavern in Æshardæ. It is believed she may have sold it for traveling money."

"Send a battalion to Æshardæ. Search every city and township, every tavern and inn. They must be somewhere. Check the port cities; they may have hired a boat to take them to Ælmondæ, thinking it safe since we have already searched it," Nall commanded.

Ileana's voice came from the doorway, "Bael. They have gone to Bael. I have seen it in a vision. She is traveling with Lohgaen of Lochlaen; he seeks to use the shards to restore the House of the Gryphon to power. Send the battalion to Bael, not Æshardæ."

Zeth's eyes met Nall's and Nall nodded slowly, bile rising in his throat. "Search Bael."

Watching Zeth leave, Nall felt his heart pounding against his ribs and prayed to the Ancients that Cwen had moved on.

Lohgaen followed Cwen into the tavern and allowed her to choose a table. He sat next to her, alert to any danger, though he did not expect any unless her disguise failed. He smiled at the low, mellow tones of her voice. She had practiced all the way from the inn and indeed she did sound very much like a prophetess. He knew that she had certainly had an effect on his tattered soul.

As he had directed, she sent forth her silent call for knowledge of the Well of Flames.

"Prophetess," the bar wench lowered her eyes, "may I offer you tea?"

Nodding her scarlet covered head, Cwen spoke in silken tones. "Tea, and nourishment for the wizard. You bear a scar that aches, allow me to take its pain."

The wench fell to her knees before Cwen and wept into her lap. Laying her hands on the girl's head, Cwen took the pain as she had taken Talin's for so many years.

Food and tea arrived and no one else attempted to speak to them. Cwen carefully lifted the veil to the level of her mouth and sipped her tea, watching as Lohgaen ate like a starving man, which she was sure he was.

"Do not forget to save some for Talin and Synyon," she whispered into his mind, causing him to cough and look up at her.

Her voice was like a sacrament, salving his tormented soul. He knew in that instant that she truly was the woman of legend he sought. He reminded himself that she had chosen Caen and whispered back, "And for you, my lady? Are you not hungry also?"

"My hunger is deep and cannot be satisfied by bread and jam." Her smile beneath the veil was soft and sad, bringing an ache to Lohgaen's empty heart.

"You seek the Well of Flames, Prophetess?" The approaching man's voice was hushed in reverence.

"I do. Have you knowledge of it?" Cwen's mellifluous voice caressed.

"Aye, I have heard that it lies within Fireend, amid the steep crags and deep fissures. It is said to be guarded by the mistral dragons, hideous beasts of wind and fire. The well itself leads into the very heart of Ædracmoræ's flaming center," the stranger explained.

Crossing the table with coin, Cwen murmured her gratitude and blessed the man's life and the lives of his ancestors and heirs.

Gathering the remaining meal of bread, jam and meat, Lohgaen rose and waited for Cwen to stand and lead him back to the inn where she sent the downy flier on his way with a message for her father.

Sitting on the floor in Talin's room they ate their meal and talked about traveling to Fireend.

"It will require warm clothes, for it holds an ice field much like the Halcyon, though I have heard tales of warm areas on the western coastline where smoke and ash have been seen in the sky above by passengers of passing ships," Synyon stated, licking her fingers and grinning at Talin.

"I have never known anyone to go there. It is barren; the home of mistral dragons and not much else," Talin answered, his eyes fixed on Synyon's lips.

Cwen felt like gagging at their nonsense. She was positive that Synyon must have bewitched Talin, for his behavior was unlike any she had seen in all the years she had known him.

"Talin," she whispered into his mind. She was rewarded with a blank stare. *"Are you bewitched?"*

She saw him shake his head slightly, but the foolish smile remained plastered across his face.

"*I think you are*!" she hissed into his thoughts.

She felt Lohgaen's thoughts even before she was aware of their meaning.

"*He is not bewitched, exactly. She has simply caught his fancy and he is not quite sure what to do about it. She will not harm him, Cwen, and if his heart is broken, it will mend.*"

She looked at Lohgaen, feeling her heart quicken as she saw his smile.

"*I do not believe he has ever had his heart broken by a woman.*" She caressed the wizard's mind with the voice he had taught her to use.

"We shall leave with the darkness, so it is wise that we rest. I shall seek provisions once I know that Cwen is safely asleep," he said aloud. Silently he reminded Synyon to be alert, for Cwen would be alone.

Seeing the thaumaturge nod, he stood and offered Cwen his hand, pulling her to her feet and leading her out the door.

She stood in their room, as if uncertain what to do.

"Sleep," he whispered. "You are weary and our journey will be cold and unpleasant. I will obtain what supplies we need and return before darkness falls. You will be safe; Synyon listens."

"She hates me," Cwen shrugged.

"Nay, she simply finds you foolish. As you grow wiser she will like you better," Lohgaen said.

"And you believe I shall grow wiser?" Cwen looked doubtful.

"I believe you do already, Cwen of Aaradan."

She lowered her voice. "It is my fear of you that makes me wiser. I fear that if I am disobedient you will bewitch me as she has done Talin."

She gathered her scarlet robes around her and lay down on the small cot, drawing the coverlet up over her.

Lohgaen drew a small leather bag from his pocket and dumped its contents on the table. Sitting up, Cwen saw that he was counting lauds and quickly drew the remaining two rings from her fingers. Standing, she crossed to the table and placed them before him.

"They will fetch a good price if you are wise in the ways of dealers and thieves. If you are not, I shall have to go with you and see that you are not cheated," she grinned down at him.

"And how is it that you have the rings of poachers on your fingers, Lady Cwen?" he asked, examining the rings.

"I stole them from the dead." She answered and returned to the cot.

He counted his money and placed the rings within the bag beside the coins. When he looked up she was sleeping, a tiny frown creasing her forehead.

As he stood to leave he gave himself a solemn reminder, "She has chosen Caen."

Six Guardians entered Indigo's Inferno and fanned out, all searching for the thief, Caen.

Indigo approached the woman who appeared to lead them, the heat of her Maraen anger flaring around her and distorting the air.

"It is unwise to bring threat to the Maraen, Guardian." Indigo's voice was low and furious.

A wave of heat struck the Guardian Rydén, scorching the air she drew into her lungs and causing her skin to redden.

"We do not come to threaten the Maraen," Rydén answered. "We seek only the one called Caen, by order of the Queen. He has been charged with high treason."

"Your queen does not rule the Maraen. This is by her own agreement with the Deviant," Indigo reminded her.

"Nay, but she does rule over the thief known as Caen. You will gain her favor if you release him to us, Indigo."

"He is no longer here. Jūdan granted him healing when his service ended. I assume he seeks the woman, Cwen. He cared enough for her to bind himself to the Maraen in order to save her life when she foolishly challenged my authority," Indigo responded.

Rydén gazed into the Maraen woman's fiery eyes, recalling Sōrél's warning against angering Indigo to her flash point. The Maraen's full flare would leave the tavern a hollow cave filled only with ash if she failed to control her heat in a moment of fury.

Indigo smiled, revealing her sharp teeth. "Your king remains wise. He has given you good advice, Guardian. Take your soldiers and go. Tell Sōrél that the Maraen send the sanction of the Deviant."

With a deliberate flare of heat that left Rydén's face blistered, Indigo turned her back on the Guardian with a rattling of scales and a shimmering wave of rising temperature.

"Caen," Cwen murmured as she woke to a hand on her shoulder.

It was not the pale green of Caen's eyes that met hers, but Lohgaen's dark, intense gaze.

"Nay, Cwen, not Caen. We must go. The night is at its deepest and there is less risk of detection from the Queen's hunters."

Lohgaen placed a heavy, furred cloak on the bed. "You will be warmer and more comfortable in your leathers. I will wake Synyon and Talin while you change."

Cwen stood and retrieved her leathers from the hook behind the cot.

"I could feel Caen's suffering in my dreams, the heat of his burning." Her chin quivered and her voice shook with emotion, her eyes glistening with pooling tears.

Lohgaen nodded his understanding and whispered, "Caen's suffering has ended, Cwen."

He watched the first tear form and slowly make its way down her cheek. He hated himself for denying her the truth, but he could not make himself speak the words that would release her from the sorrow his statement brought. By this simple act of omission he would bind her to him in the pain of her imagined loss.

As he left the room, he admitted silently, "*I am sorry, Caen, but my needs outweigh yours, and hers.*"

"I am coming in," he spoke outside Synyon and Talin's closed door. Entering, he was relieved to find them nearly ready to travel.

"Cwen is dressing, and then we shall leave. Her heart is very tender this hour," he said, "so do not goad her, Synyon."

Her lips opened to give a sharp response, but the words remained unspoken as she sensed what he had done.

Silently she questioned him, "*Why, if you do not intend to take her for yourself?*"

His silent reply was curt in her mind, "*Because I cannot afford her the distraction of searching for him. If she believes him dead her sorrow will make her less challenging.*"

"It is not your finest hour, Lohgaen," Synyon snapped aloud, causing Talin to look up from tying his bedroll to his satchel.

He rose and shouldered his pack.

"I hope that Cwen is not harmed," he stated, stepping aggressively toward Lohgaen.

"She is not harmed, but her dreams have foretold the death of Caen at the hands of the Maraen. She aches with sorrow and our gentleness will make it easier to bear," Lohgaen replied with a warning look at Synyon.

Synyon placed her hand on Talin's arm. "If Lohgaen causes her harm I shall help you kill him."

Lohgaen gave a short laugh and opened the door, gesturing them out.

"You do not believe Talin and I can kill you, Lohgaen?" Synyon asked.

"I think it would be very foolish of you to try," he snapped back, opening the door to the room where Cwen waited.

She remained as he had left her, standing in the middle of the room holding her leathers, her tears dampening the scarlet robes she still wore.

"Out," he snapped at Talin and Synyon, pushing them out and slamming the door after them.

"Cwen," Lohgaen said hoarsely, shaking his head at his own stupidity.

She looked up at him and whispered, "I told him to go. I did not even tell him I cared for him. Why did the Maraen burn him?"

Lohgaen took a step back as the desire to comfort her consumed him. He watched as her knees buckled and she sank to the floor, the guilt and sorrow more than she could bear.

Lifting her, he sat on the cot and held her while he drew her pain away and took her memory of the nightmares and Caen. Placing her sleeping form on the bed, he called to Synyon.

Seeing Cwen, Synyon glared at Lohgaen. "You told her you would not take her memories of Caen. What happened to that 'goodness' you professed to be practicing?"

"We suddenly have no time for it. Guardians have arrived; I can hear their shouting at the gates. If we do not leave now they will discover us. Dress her, and do it swiftly. I will carry her through the rift," he snarled, looking up to see Talin's angry face.

Pointing at Talin, Lohgaen growled, "I do not have time for any foolishness. If you insist on being stupid I will leave you behind and let your Queen deal with you. Do you understand?"

Eyes narrowing, Talin replied, "You will give her memories back when there is no longer need for her strength."

"I will," Lohgaen agreed, stepping into the hall and listening for the clomping of Guardians' boots on the stairs.

Synyon tossed the scarlet robes to Talin. "Put them in my pack. She will need them at the well."

"Lohgaen, come call the rift!" she shouted.

Lohgaen scooped Cwen up and summoned the rift to Fireend, allowing Talin and Synyon to step through first before he swiftly followed.

Chapter 24 The Wrekening

Näeré looked at Nall in unconcealed horror.

"What do you mean you are going to 'take' Yáviё?"

"You are going to cast the spell of deep sleep over her and I am going to take her to Fireend," Nall said.

"Näeré placed her hand over his heart and whispered, "It is treason. Sōrél will hunt you to the ends of the earth."

"Sōrél will not know I have taken her. He has gone to New Xavian City to organize the search for Caen. If all goes well, Yáviё will see reason and we shall return long before he is even aware she is gone."

"And if all does not go well?"

"Then I will be executed and my soul imprisoned to ensure it is never again summoned."

His expression was grim as he pulled Näeré to him, taking comfort in her softness and the scent of her freshly washed hair.

Drawing back he gave a tight smile. "It is the only way. Yáviё will never believe what she does not witness first hand. Cwen will destroy the shards at the Well of Flames and Yáviё must be there to see her do it."

"Yáviё will kill you if she is given the chance," Näeré whispered in fear.

"Then she must not have the chance. I shall bind her and keep her bound until I see reason in her eyes."

Näeré could not halt a smile. "It is rare to see reason in Yáviё when she is in full fury."

"Aye," Nall laughed, "but I will see it. I know her better than any save Sōrél, and I will convince her she is wrong about Cwen."

"Ileana feeds Yáviё's suspicions, though I am uncertain why. I do not believe that the wizard Lohgaen of Lochlaen intends to overthrow Yáviё's rule. Cwen says the Sojourners were somehow involved in the original destruction of Ædracmoræ by the G'lm armies," he added, his voice filled with unease. "It was Ileana who directed me to send the Guardians to Bael in search of Cwen."

Näeré looked up at him in confusion.

"Cwen suspects Ileana of some treachery?" she asked in disbelief. "She is my mother, Cwen's granddame. What can Cwen think she has done?"

"It was unclear and there was little time to talk, they were so intent on getting the shards and arriving in Bael under cover of darkness. She mentioned the Wreken. I have never heard them mentioned outside of legends. She said a Wreken had given her the power to destroy the wyrm shards, something she says Yáviё and Grumblton cannot do," Nall answered with a shrug. "I only know that regardless of what else she has done Cwen would not commit treason, nor do something that made her look guilty of it, without good cause."

Näeré wept and hugged Nall tightly.

"Let us abduct the Queen," she whispered at last, shaking her head at their idiocy.

They entered the throne room to find Yáviё at the table, poring over an ancient book.

Looking up at the sound of their footfalls, she beckoned them to her.

"There is something not quite right about all of this G'lm business," she spoke softly. "I have been seeking the answer, but as yet I have not found it. Ileana is nervous, almost fearful, and I have never seen her show a glimmer of fear before. Have you?" she asked, looking up at Näeré.

"Nay, Yáviё, I have not," Näeré answered, watching for Nall's signal that she should cast a spell of sleep over the Queen.

"In the lore of the Ancients, there is mention of a race called the Wreken and reference to the War of the Wreken, though there are no details, nothing that explains who they were or what they did. I shall consult with Grumbl when he returns with Sōrél," she sighed.

Nall squeezed Näeré's shoulder and watched as she whispered the words that would take Yáviё's consciousness.

"Sleep, Yáviё." Näeré's words soothed her and Yáviё fell forward onto the pages of her book.

"It is good the pages cushioned the blow, or I would also be held responsible for the knot on her forehead," Nall hissed, lifting the Queen and throwing her over his shoulder.

Pulling Näeré close with his other arm, he kissed her and said, "Return to our rooms and act as if you know nothing."

"Bind her, or she will kill you," Näeré reminded, pulling Yáviё's sword from its scabbard and the dagger from her boot.

Smiling, she recalled the one Yáviё concealed in her bodice and quickly had Nall lift her so that she could retrieve it as well.

"I think that is all, but with Yáviё you never know. Be very careful, Nall."

"Go," Nall fussed, pushing Näeré away, "you must not be seen with me if I am caught."

With one last kiss, Näeré ran back toward their rooms.

Silently Nall summoned the dragon Ardor to the field beyond the prickleberry thicket at the seldom used side entrance to the fortress.

Ardor scowled at the sight of Nall carrying the unconscious Queen of Ædracmoræ.

"Who has done this?" the dragon boomed.

"I have done this and if you do not stop your bellowing the whole kingdom of Æstaffordæ will know," Nall chuckled.

Laying Yáviё on the grass, he drew soft strips of spider cloth from his satchel and bound her hands and feet. Reluctantly, he added a gag to stay the screams of rage he knew she would issue as soon as she awoke. Tossing her back over his shoulder, he leapt to Ardor's withers and urged the mighty dragon skyward, casting a glance behind them to see if there was any evidence of alarm. Seeing none, he breathed a deep sigh and directed Ardor toward the northwest and Fireend.

The bitter cold was brutal after the warmth of the inn. Lohgaen drew the fur cloak tightly around Cwen and cast the spell to awaken her.

Smiling at her confusion, Lohgaen whispered, “I carried you while you slept.”

Frowning, she pushed against him, glaring as he placed her on her feet before him. “I do not like to be touched,” Cwen fumed, straightening her cloak around her.

Ignoring her complaint, Lohgaen pierced Talin and Synyon with his gaze.

“We shall need a place to spend the night, someplace not so exposed, where we can build a fire. I do not wish to approach the well in darkness, for there are tales that it is guarded by the mistral dragons. If we must fight them I prefer to do it in the light of day. There, above us in the rocks, we may find cover,” Lohgaen stated, pointing to the craggy black outline of the mountainous rock formations.

Taking Cwen’s hand he led the way up a narrow, winding path leading into the towering rocks.

Talin held out his hand and was rewarded with Synyon’s warm hand in his. Following after Lohgaen and Cwen, they began the trek upwards.

While no caverns were apparent, the rock formations often twisted and circled, forming natural walls around small sheltered clearings, and it was in one of these that Lohgaen chose to set up camp for the remainder of the darkness.

From his pack Lohgaen drew small logs to build a fire, using the dried vegetation that grew against the onyx-like walls as kindling. Once the fire flickered to life he cast a spell of heat and watched it blaze and warm the area.

Hot tea was quickly prepared and welcomed by all, for while there was no brutal wind as in the Halcyon Ice Fields, the chill of Fireend was deep enough to make the bones ache and slow the fingers. The meal was bannock, but with the pappleberry jam Lohgaen had thoughtfully provisioned – not as dry and dull as it could have been.

Cwen warmed herself at the fire, watching Talin and Synyon share some secret tale that brought Talin’s deep laugh and Synyon’s low, throaty one. Smiling, Cwen felt a tiny pang of jealousy, not wicked and green-eyed, but just a twinge at the easy way Talin spoke with Synyon. Since Lohgaen had begun traveling with them she had not spent time with Talin, and she suddenly missed his friendship.

"He feels the same." Lohgaen's voice came from her side as he sat down with his tea. "He misses the camaraderie of your days before I arrived. Soon you will have those days again, Cwen."

"She takes his heart," Cwen shrugged, turning to look up into Lohgaen's eyes. "What must I do at the well?"

"I do not know, Cwen," Lohgaen answered. "I know only that I must see you safely there. The Wreken will guide you. You should disguise yourself as a prophetess, for it will confuse the mistral dragons and any who may have followed."

"And you will protect me?" She had never felt so helpless and alone, so dependent on another for strength. "I am not accustomed to being protected by others. It makes me feel useless."

Lohgaen chuckled and refreshed her tea. "You are the only reason we are here; you are the strength of the legends. Do not see my protection as a weakness. You are becoming a great woman, Cwen. The legends of the future will sing your praise for what you do on the morrow."

A thunderous crashing alerted them to the arrival of a heavy dragon somewhere beyond the towering walls to the west, closer to the Well of Flames.

A few minutes later, Synyon's voice floated across the fire, "Others arrive, for I can see the glow of a fire to the west, near the well."

Stepping to her side, Lohgaen peered through the crack in the wall. "*Nall,*" he whispered wordlessly.

"*And he brings the Queen,*" Synyon added. "*Treachery or salvation, I do not know.*"

"I would hate to have to kill the Queen of Ædracmoræ," Lohgaen whispered aloud, staring intently into the distance at the faint glow of firelight.

"And the father of your woman," Synyon added, a bitter smile once again reminding Lohgaen of his broken promise.

"She is not my woman. She is Caen's. I have not forgotten that, even though her memory is gone," he said, his heart constricting at the unwanted recollection.

Yávië slowly opened her eyes to find herself lying near a small, well set fire. She was warm and covered by heavy cloaks. She tried to rise, but found it impossible due to the bindings on her wrists and ankles. Screaming in fury, her voice pushed against the soft cloth that rested against her lips.

She rolled away from the fire until her back touched a wall. Struggling to bring herself upright, she finally managed to get her back against the stone and draw up her knees. Pushing with all her might, she inched her way upward until she stood. A sudden shadow cast on the far rock wall caused her to freeze and listen for footsteps or the voice of her captor.

As she saw the man step forward she launched herself at him, slamming into his midsection with her head and receiving a satisfying "ummph" for her effort. The man fell backward with her on top of him. She drew back her head and butted him sharply on the chin.

Strong arms enveloped her and swung her away. He dusted himself off before speaking to her.

"Do not struggle, for you will only hurt yourself," Nall's familiar voice spoke.

"*Nall?*" Yáviё's silent fury mounted and she thrashed against the bindings until the edge of the cloak fell across the fire, bringing Nall to her.

Pulling off the cloak and stamping out the burning corner, he muttered, "I told you not to struggle."

Lifting her to a sitting position, he wrapped the cloak around her shoulders and knelt before her. His eyes were tired and sober, but his voice was calm and held no fear. "I will remove the gag if you wish to talk to me aloud, but you must not scream and frighten others who camp nearby."

"*Cwen?*" her voice hissed in his mind.

Nodding, he stared into the fury of her violet eyes, her heavy, raven-colored hair was tangled and her cheek was scraped where she had tried to rise from the ground.

"*Sōrél will…*" Her thoughts pierced.

"He does not know, and will not until he returns from the city with Grumbl. And your thoughts have been blocked from him, so he will not be coming to your aid." Nall stopped her threat. "I did not do this without thought, Yáviё. None saw me take you and no one knows where we are, not even Näeré," he lied.

Yávië shook her head and looked back at him. "*You would not harm me.*"

"Nay, I would never harm you, Yávië," Nall answered with a shrug. "I would like to offer you tea and sit and talk with you through the darkness of the night while we await the destruction of the shards."

He searched her eyes for any hint of reason, but saw only the truth. She would try to fight him and flee if he were to release her bonds.

"Those who travel with Cwen are strong enough to overpower Grumbl. They care only for Cwen's safety and I do not believe they would allow you to take her. To draw their attention to our presence would not be wise. If I remove the gag will you promise not to scream?"

He saw her hesitation and grinned. "If you scream, I will have to see that you sleep again."

Her eyes narrowed in threat, but she finally nodded her acceptance of his terms.

Slipping behind her he untied the gag, loosened the soft fabric from her mouth and drew it away.

Her voice was low and threatening. "I cannot allow you to live after what you have done. Your entire family has become traitorous."

Laughing softly he reminded her, "Yávië, you are my family."

He saw her scowl and knew she was thinking about the death she intended to mete out.

"Who travels with Cwen? The thief? Talin?" she asked suddenly.

"Talin and two wizards who feel she requires their protection. When last I saw her, I felt that the one with her would have slain me if I had attempted to take her with me."

"And when did you last see her, Nall? While you were supposed to be serving the charge of treason and bringing her as ordered?" Yávië glared.

He brought a cup of tea and held it out, watching warily as she reached forward to take it in the fingers of her bound hands. As she took the cup he stood up and out of range of the hot liquid.

She smiled a tight smile. "It is unfortunate that you have chosen death."

"Drink your tea," he said. "And think about what you were doing when last we spoke."

She glared as she sipped the steaming willow bark tea.

The day star rose and cast deep shadows among the soaring rocks.

Cwen was once again dressed in scarlet and hidden beneath her guise of Prophetess of Belasis. They made their way west, continuing along the narrow trails, which grew warm as the black rock became saturated with the heat of the topaz star.

Lohgaen paused, listening for any hint of threat. Hearing none, he encouraged them forward.

Against her complaints, Nall lifted Yávië and climbed to a ledge above the Well of Flames. Hidden at the center of a clearing within the crags of standing rock lay a deep opening, and from its depths rose a thin column of heat and ash. It appeared that the only entrance to the well lay along a narrow trail that opened into the clearing. It was here Nall was sure Cwen and her companions would arrive.

Lowering Yávië, he looked into her eyes and saw only fierce anger.

"It is important that you remain quiet, Yávië. There are mistral dragons said to guard the well and those approaching will not stop to ask our intent before striking us."

With a sigh of exasperation she gave a fiery look and nodded her understanding.

"Why do you do this, Nall? Throw your life away for a daughter you have never cared for, one you spoke only ill of even before she turned to treason."

Nall looked at Yávië and nodded. "It was true. I did not take the time to know her and so I misjudged her. She is honorable and fiercely guards Ædracmoræ from all she sees as a threat – even you, Yávië."

Yávië's laugh was bitter. "What possible threat could she believe I pose to this world? Does she forget it was I who brought about its rebirth?"

"Nay, Yávië, she knows your love for Ædracmoræ is great, so great you might unwittingly harm it in an attempt to defend it. She knows you cannot destroy the shards, and so she must, for the power to do so has been granted her by the very Wreken of which you spoke." Nall raised his hand against her questions. "I do not know the how or why, Yáviё. I only know that Cwen seeks to follow the truth."

Nall looked down at her with a smile she recalled from very long ago, the smile of a friend who was bound by a blood oath and shared all she held important.

"Long ago, Yáviё, you asked me to make a choice, a choice between the truth and the law. It is all I ask of you – the same choice. Has the truth come to have no meaning for you, Yáviё?"

Without thinking, Yáviё reached up to touch Nall, but quickly drew back her hands as she remembered they were bound.

"Have I become so callous that I no longer seek the truth?" she asked, her eyes suddenly sad.

"Nay, you are merely you. Often you strike quickly, before the truth is fully revealed. All I ask, Yáviё, is that you see what happens here before you charge Cwen and Talin with treason. They do not seek to harm Ædracmoræ or the Crown."

Looking away from him, Yáviё peered over the ledge at the Well of Flames. A sudden flash of scarlet caught her eye and she pointed with her bound hands as a tall, dark man in a cloak the color of ash and a holy woman entered the clearing below. Behind them came a small, slender woman and Talin.

Lohgaen raised his hand to halt them and gazed at the surrounding area, taking in every crag and shadowed corner, his eyes stopping briefly on the ledge where Nall and Yáviё lay hidden from view.

Holding out his hand to the prophetess and guiding her toward the deep hole at the clearing's center, he silently alerted Synyon to the presences on the ledge above before continuing forward with Cwen.

They knelt and began to withdraw the shards one by one, unwrapping them and laying them around the edge of the Well of Flames. There were thirteen great wyrm shards, all but one containing the life of a Wreken waiting to be freed from the prospect of serving the evil of the Sojourners and the G'lm army.

A sudden stirring of the air within the depths of the well

announced the arrival of the mistral dragons. They swept upward, trailing ash and heat, their windy scales the color of storm clouds and their bellows deep and threatening. Six in all, they rose into the glaring light, scattering burning cinders over those below.

"Prophetess," the elder dragon called, hovering before them, flanked by the others, "you have come to fulfill the legend of the Wreken?"

Cwen's voice was commanding in its softness, a song seducing all before her into obedience.

"You, Guardians of the Well of Flame, are released. Today the Wreken find liberation from the cruel judgment passed so long ago by dictate of the Sojourners. Never again will they be forced to lend their great power to the armies of darkness, the horde of the abyss. They will be free to seek the safety of the new host."

The great dragon's head bowed, showering all with ash and embers.

"And you stand sheltered by the power of the dark wizard?" The dragon's booming voice shook the stones around them, bringing cascades of dirt and rock down over the ledges.

Cwen's hand rose toward the dragon, drawing him forward.

"Nay, I stand sheltered by the power of the Wreken. It is they who guide my hand." She sent her silken voice in a caress, causing the dragon to lower its eyes in respect.

Turning his flaming eyes toward the ledge where Nall and Yávië lay, the great dragon roared, "Treachery awaits you, Prophetess. Shall I sting them with my breath?"

"Nay, I shall mete out judgment as it is commanded," Cwen soothed him.

With a final growl the mistral dragon rose and called the shifting, ethereal, smoky bodies of his companions to follow, sweeping away toward the south.

Cwen kneeled and took the first of the wyrm shards in her hands. Words she had never heard and did not recognize flowed freely in her mesmerizing voice, covering the emerald shard that held the Wreken whose power had destroyed Calá, granting its prisoner freedom within the Well of Flames. Leaning forward, she allowed the shard to fall, watching as it entered the darkness, dropping into the rising heat and billowing ash and smoke of Ædracmoræ's heart. Silently it fell, its power already taken by the army of the G'lm

The second shard was smoky, its power used to release the G'lm on the five cities within the kingdoms of Æwmarshæ, Æcumbræ and Æshulmæ. She lifted it and held it tenderly as she repeated the words that would release the Wreken from its center. As the shard fell, Cwen felt the joy of the Wreken within and smiled beneath her veil.

Sapphire came next, a Wreken wielding the power of an army that nearly reached the Well of Viileshga under Faervyn's command. Cwen's soft words granted it a safe journey to Ædracmoræ's fiery heart.

As Cwen whispered the Wreken's words of freedom to the amber shard it began to pulse brightly, its fiery light sweeping across them like the light that guides the ships by night. Releasing it, Cwen observed its drop toward the molten center of Ædracmoræ.

Far away, in a cavern beneath the ruins of the Fortress of the Dragon Queen, five hundred stone soldiers awaited the call of a new master.

The amber shard struck the molten stone at the bottom of the well and the shard burned away, releasing the captive Wreken. In its cavern the G'lm army slowly crumbled into dust.

As it was granted freedom by Cwen's words, each shard in turn burned away, freeing a captive Wreken and destroying the remaining stone soldiers in hidden caverns deep within the ground. Four hundred fell with the crimson shard's destruction, eight hundred crumbled with the violet. With the rose, azure and pale yellow shard's release, nine hundred soldiers collapsed into harmless powder in the caverns where they stood. The black shard burned away to release five thousand beneath Ælmondæ and the shard whose colors swirled as brightly as the rainbow caused another thousand's fall. Unknown to those above, the indigo shard laid waste to the largest army of them all, for twenty thousand deadly soldiers awaited their master's call amid the labyrinth of caves deep beneath the Valley of Shadows.

When only the empty golden shard lay before her, Cwen felt the Wreken's movement as it released its gentle hold upon her heart and slipped out into the palm of her hand. There it lay for a moment, issuing mercurial golden threads of light before returning to the golden wyrm shard to seek its own release.

Cwen gently stroked the shard and whispered, "I shall miss your company, Wreken."

The shard pulsed once, brilliantly, before falling into a peaceful rhythm, the rhythm of Cwen's heart.

"We are bound, you and I," came the Wreken's calming words, "for those who host the Wreken gain a power that remains. Always I shall counsel, always I shall care."

With a soft, tearful smile, Cwen lifted the final Wreken's shard and let it go, sending it plunging into the burning heart of Ædracmoræ. A sudden trembling threw those around the well to the ground. On the ledge, Yávië and Nall were flung backward into the wall behind them. The rumbling continued and the well belched a great tower of smoke and ash into the sky, followed by blue-white flames and the thirteen Wreken. They shot into the sky, eyes ablaze with the joy of freedom. Above the well they sparkled with the pure, fiery light of life, the dark shadow of captivity driven away with their release. Each bore the color of its shard and pulsed in a slow, serene rhythm. They melded together and drew apart repeatedly, as if in greeting, colors swirling into and out of one another as the Shining Ones moved together. The golden Wreken descended and hovered before Cwen, featureless at first, but quickly mirroring her face in recognition and gratefulness.

"We are Wreken, bound to the new host, the heart of Ædracmoræ," the smooth voice caressed her before sweeping away to rejoin the others.

Cwen slowly raised the veil from her face and looked up at the ledge where her father stood with Yávië.

"I shall go willingly to face my fate." Her voice was strong and fearless. "What is done is done, and by its doing Ædracmoræ is safe from eternal darkness, its heart restored. My fate is of no importance. I ask only that you spare Talin."

Talin looked at Cwen and then hard at Lohgaen before he shouted up to Yávië, "And the thief called Caen."

Yávië opened her mouth to reply, but was stopped as the amber Wreken suddenly broke away from the others and soared upward to drift before Nall and Yávië. Yávië reached out to touch it, causing it to shimmer with amusement.

They watched as the Wreken's image shifted from formlessness into that of a man – tall and handsome, broad shouldered and well muscled, a man of strength and purpose, a councilor of old.

"Do you know this host?" the Wreken asked.

Yáviė shook her head in confusion, turning to look at Nall as a small sound escaped him.

"Nall?" she looked at his pale face and saw his shaking hands.

Reaching out, she clutched him with her bound hands and slid with him to the ground.

His voice was hoarse with emotion and he shuddered as he spoke. "Father?"

The Wreken shifted forward, enveloping Nall and sharing his memories of its former host, an Eunean councilor called Valadrin.

"You knew him?" Nall asked in disbelief.

"I shared his heart; he gave me life," the Wreken replied, continuing to envelop Nall and fill him with recollections of his birth father.

Still grasping Nall's arm, Yáviė shared the images of his childhood, memories of a nearly forgotten father's care and love.

When the Wreken finally withdrew, it paused before Yáviė and whispered, "The choice you make is yours alone; do not falter on your path to the truth."

Yáviė's nod was barely visible, but her acknowledgement gave Nall hope. He turned to her and slashed the bindings on her wrists and ankles before pulling her up to stand beside him.

As the Wreken of Valadrin floated back toward the others, Nall led Yáviė downward along the path toward Cwen and her companions.

Above, the Wreken eddied one last time before disappearing one by one into the depths of Ædracmoræ.

When he entered the clearing, Nall left Yáviė and started toward Cwen, only to be stopped as Lohgaen stepped before him.

"I cannot allow you to take her." Lohgaen's voice was quiet with the strength of his conviction and his eyes slid from Nall to Yáviė and back.

"She is my daughter," Nall said, feeling anger rise.

Cwen stepped forward and slipped in between them, facing Lohgaen.

She placed her hand on his heart and looked up at him, drawing his eyes to her face.

"I cannot let them take you, Cwen," his whispered words were choked with emotion.

"Perhaps they no longer wish to take me," she smiled, reaching up to touch his face as her voice poured over him.

He looked up and over her head toward the Queen of Ædracmoræ.

Yáviё came forward to stand with Nall, a small flicker of recognition in her eyes.

"Lohgaen," she spoke and watched as he nodded, confirming her recognition.

Cwen turned back to face her father and Yáviё, but Yáviё was not looking at Cwen; she was still staring at Lohgaen.

"She is bound to the House of Lochlaen," Lohgaen stated firmly.

"What I have seen of her would indicate that she is pledged to none. A young woman of fierce determination and great honor, bound to no one save the world that she protects," Yáviё replied, her words aimed at Cwen.

Lohgaen bowed and returned Yáviё's chilly smile.

"We have an agreement," he explained.

Nall scowled and stared at Cwen.

Laughing, she leaned forward, pulling her father to her and hugging him tightly.

"Without his help I could not have made it to the Well of Flames." She looked back at Lohgaen, her eyes soft with gratitude. "Without his help I would have been lost to the wizard Laoghaire and Talin would be dead."

"Without Lohgaen you could not have stolen the wyrm shards from my vault," Yáviё added, looking to Lohgaen for confirmation.

"Aye," he admitted, "though it was Synyon who outwitted your wizard."

Yáviё and Nall looked toward Talin and the small woman next to him. Talin lifted a hand in greeting, while Synyon merely shrugged and grinned impishly.

Yáviё placed her hand on Cwen's shoulder and saw the strength of conviction within her niece's golden eyes.

"I wish you could have simply come to me and told me what you needed, but since your father assures me I would not have listened, perhaps your hand was forced. I hold you blameless, Cwen, as I do Talin and the thief. Whether Lohgaen presents a threat is unclear."

Synyon's chuckle caused Yávië to glance in her direction, frowning.

"You find humor in my words?" the Queen asked.

Synyon shook her head. "Nay, I merely find it amusing that the Queen of Ædracmoræ and I are in agreement. Lohgaen's intentions are always shadowed. Talin and I are agreed to kill him if he causes harm."

She poked Talin with her elbow and watched with pleasure as his color rose and a scowl crept across his face.

"Just know, Queen of Ædracmoræ, that we shall watch him closely," Synyon added with a wink.

Raising an eyebrow, Yávië tilted her head and gazed at Talin.

"Shall I trust the fate of my kingdom to one so obviously besotted by another?" she asked.

Talin's frown deepened. "Aye, we shall guard Ædracmoræ with the same fierceness that we protect the golden-eyed girl."

Cwen's smile lit up her face and she spun and raced to hug Talin. He hugged her back with a lop-sided grin and whispered in her ear, "I could never find a better friend, and I am too old to seek one."

An unexpected shift in the air made all draw their weapons as before them a rift opened, depositing Näeré and Sōrél.

Looking around at the weapons directed against them, Sōrél asked Yávië bluntly, "Where does my loyalty lie?"

Her laughter flowed like the water from the falls of Æstaffordæ and she seized him with her free arm as she sheathed her sword with the other.

"Am I to assume no one here is charged with treason?" he asked, kissing her quickly as her 'aye' bubbled forth.

Näeré went to Nall and said, "I could not bear that Yávië might kill you."

Nall looked at Yávië and watched as she held up her hands in surrender and said to Näeré, "He reminded me of who I am."

Lohgaen looked down as Cwen slid her hand into his. Her gaze was steady and her voice calm as she asked, "What do you ask of me, Lohgaen?"

He looked up at those around them and saw the same question

in their eyes.

"Yes, Lohgaen, what do you ask of her?" Synyon's voice teased.

"I seek the restoration of my father's house," he stated. "It is told in the lore that Cwen of Aaradan will return power to the House of the Gryphon."

"Lohgaen," Yávië said, hair flying as she violently shook her head, "it is folly. The House of Lochlaen fell to evil long before the destruction of Ædracmoræ."

"Fell to Laoghaire's evil, Yávië, through my true father's misguided trust of the wizard. If I do not seek to rule my own house, Laoghaire will rise to power against you."

"Laoghaire seeks the power of the House of Lochlaen? By what right? You are heir to its throne as decreed by Lord Lochlaen before his death," Yávië said.

"The path to the throne of Lochlaen has become twisted," Lohgaen shrugged, giving Synyon a warning glance as he saw her lips parting to speak. "The artifact was stolen and the gryphons fled. Legend says Cwen of Aaradan, the Woman of Lore, must seek to restore a balance of power to Ædracmoræ."

"Is it true you seek to overthrow the Crown, Lohgaen?" Yávië's voice was tense and her eyes flared a warning.

"Nay, I seek to save it." He returned her gaze. "The House of Lochlaen was always allied with the Crown. That will change if Laoghaire is allowed to rise to power."

"And do you profess to be the Woman of Lore, Cwen?" Yávië asked.

"I profess nothing. I agreed to help Lohgaen once he had helped me steal… destroy the threat to Ædracmoræ posed by the Wreken bound within shards. The Wreken called me Woman of Lore, but I have no knowledge of such legends."

"She did not listen to the history that was taught," Synyon said brightly, drawing glares from Yávië, Lohgaen and Cwen. "Well, obviously she did not."

Walking away, Cwen went to Nall and Näeré, hugging her mother briefly before asking, "Who are your people, Nall?"

"A people long dead. Someday we will speak of it – at a time when no other seeks your counsel," he said.

"The Wreken who sought you, was your father his host?"

Nall answered in a hushed voice, "He said my father gave him life, bore him in his heart."

"I saw a woman painted on a stone within the Cavern of the Moons. She was a noblewoman, beautiful and fair. Her eyes were just like yours."

"Rylarre. My mother's name was Rylarre. Perhaps it was she." Nall said.

"When I return I should like to know about the past," Cwen said, placing her hand on her father's cheek.

He pulled her close and hugged her fiercely, kissing the top of her head as he had when she was a girl.

"Go," he whispered hoarsely. "Seek Lohgaen's lost past and fulfill your destiny, Cwen."

With a last hug for her mother, Cwen turned back to take Lohgaen's hand. Together they went to Talin and Synyon. A wave of Lohgaen's hand summoned a rift, leaving a shimmering tell in the bright midday light.

"Wait," called Sōrél, drawing a scroll from inside his shirt. Handing it to Yáviё, he watched her smile as she read.

Taking the signet from her finger and the dagger he offered, she pricked her finger and allowed her blood to flow across her seal. She then placed the mark of the Crown on the parchment that recalled the charge of treason against Cwen, Talin, two unidentified wizards, and a thief called Caen.

Stepping forward, Yáviё handed it to Cwen. She leaned forward to kiss her niece's cheek and whispered, "Safe journey."

Cwen drew the scarlet robes of the prophetess around her and bowed to the Queen before slipping through the glistening rift and disappearing after her companions.

Epilogue

Upon and eyrie woven of golden thread and chale branches hidden from the eyes of Man, the female gryphon raised her head and sought her mate's cold, gold eyes.

"The woman comes," she clicked. "She brings the heir to the throne of Lochlaen as foretold."

Rising to his full height, the male gryphon nodded to Nesika, his life bond, as he stretched his mighty wings and lifted from the nest. Soaring in the light of the silent sun, he banked away toward the Isle of Grave on Ælarggessæ to call the others from their slumber.

Preview

Coming Winter 2007

The Damselfly's Daughter
A new Ancient Mirrors Tale
from the author of
The Dragon Queen
and
The Wrekening

"ON A DAY in the Age That Comes, when the Damselfly's kiss no longer grants magick to Man, a halfling woman shall rise to return light unto darkness and darkness unto light. In the days when wickedness wends its way upward wearing a shimmering shield, then shall she stand beside the man of meager magick and together they shall reunite the races."

From the Legend of the Age That Comes

Reserve your author signed copy at www.ancientmirrors.com.
Turn the page for the exciting preview.

Hunters and Healers

Dismounting the gryphons, the hunters slowly approached the scorched remains of the settlement. Here and there flames still flared briefly as the dried wood of the hovels was exhausted. A light spring wind sent cinders scurrying and hissing in the last remnants of snow.

"Harpies," Nilus spat, kicking at a smoldering body with disgust.

"Nay, I do not think so. They do not bear the talons of the harpies. See? The feet appear human," Ilerion disagreed, examining the charred remains. "And the harpies do not build hovels, only stick eyries."

Squatting next to another burned corpse, Ilerion reached out and touched it, testing for heat. Finding it cool enough to handle he reached under and turned it over, examining the vestiges of the amputated wings. The blackened flesh came away in his hands and delicate bones crumbled beneath his touch. Moving on to another he lifted it and discovered the wings severed.

"Check the bodies beyond you," Ilerion called to Nilus. "It appears that the wings were severed from each body."

After lifting several bodies with the toe of his boot, Nilus shouted back, "Aye, I have not found a single one with wings attached."

Wandering from corpse to corpse, Ilerion checked each of them; none had escaped the blade of the butcher. It was impossible to tell if the wings had been cut before or after death and silently he muttered the hope that they had been cut from the dead.

A high keening wail shattered the silence of death bringing Ilerion to his feet, sword drawn, eyes searching for the creator of the terrifying sound. Atop a small knoll stood a figure so covered in gore and ash that it was impossible to determine the identity. A second scream echoed through the smoke filled glen as the figure crumpled backward to the earth.

Leaping forward, Ilerion raced toward the fallen individual and dropped to his knees beside it.

It was a woman, naked and blood-smeared. Her features distorted by swelling and dark bruises. Pulling the cloak from his shoulders, Ilerion covered her before placing his fingertips below her jaw, feeling for the life beat. Slow and faint, but there.

"Out of mercy finish it," Nilus spoke behind him. "It will not live long, if indeed it lives at all."

"She lives." Ilerion said, gathering the woman and lifting her to his chest. "If we can reach the healer before the life fades away there is hope that she may continue to live."

"Ilerion," Nilus' face crumpled in concern, "it is not a woman, for there are great bloody wounds in its back where wings grew. It is… a beast. Ananta will chase us away if we bring her such a creature."

"Not a beast, Nilus. Without the wings she is only a badly beaten woman, the healer will help us." Ilerion's eyes warned against speaking further of beasts.

Squatting, Ilerion laid the woman across his knees to examine the wounds high on her shoulders. Pulling a shirt from his pack, he tore it and stuffed the pieces into the gaping holes to slow the bleeding. Lifting the unconscious woman over his shoulder he whistled for Grundl, his gryphon mount.

Shaking his head at his partner's foolish risk, Nilus leapt to his mount and urged it skyward, banking toward the outskirts of Lamaas and the healer, Ananta.

As he mounted, Ilerion heard the gryphon's question in his mind, *"Whose life do we save today, Hunter?"*

"I do not know her name." Ilerion answered.

Ancient Mirrors Glossary

A

Aaradan [AIR uh dan] – mortal father of Sōrél and Näeré

Abaddon [AB uh don] – a Sojourner, leader of the dark horde, brother of Alandon

Abyss – group of caverns deep below the earth inhabited by Abaddon and the dark horde

Accordant dragon – dragons with the ability to soothe the minds of Ancients, Men and Guardians

Alandon [AL an don] – a Sojourner, Yávië's father, brother of Abaddon

Aléria [uh LAIR ee uh] – Yávië's twin sister, competitor for the throne of the Dragon Queen

Ancients – A group of ancient wizards created by the Tree of Creation to reconstruct the seven worlds and call the Guardians. They are also responsible for all law and prophecy.

Animus dragon – dragons with the ability to create pain and chaos within the minds of Ancients, Men and Guardians

Æ

Æcumbræ [CUM ber] – second of the seven worlds reconstructed by the Ancients

Ædracmoræ [DRAC mor] – world of Yávië's birth

Ælmondæ [la MOND] – sixth of seven worlds reconstructed by the Ancients; prison for those damned by Alandon

Æwmarshæ [wah MARSH] – fourth of the seven worlds reconstructed by the Ancients
Æshardæ [SHARD] – first of the seven worlds reconstructed by the Ancients
Æshulmæ [SHULM] – third of the seven worlds reconstructed by the Ancients
Æstaffordæ [STAF ford] – fifth of the seven worlds reconstructed by the Ancients; the ancestral home of Sōrél and Näeré
Æstretfordæ [STRET ford] – seventh of the seven worlds reconstructed by the Ancients; place of calling for the Guardians Nall, Rydén and Yáviē

B

Bane boar – inedible beast, often infected with the poison of the slitherwort, which can cause death in Guardians and Men
Bannock – flat bread, also called morning buns
Beast speech or speak – language shared by Guardians and Ancients with the animals of their worlds
Blood oath – an oath of consequence that is the result of sharing one's blood for the purpose of healing
Bloodren – small reptilian creature with venomous claws and teeth; causes blood rages in its victims
Bow of Ages – wielded by Sōrél, a gift given to him by Ya'vanna
Brake – a thicket
Bullram – massive animals with wooly coats of long hair, often domesticated and used as beasts of burden or mounts; wild bullram are hunted for their meat and hides
Butterpillar – larval stage of the butter moth, favorite food of downy fliers

C

Chale tree – hardwood tree used for construction and burning
Creation crystal – crystals used to hold souls
Crimson grass – deep scarlet longgrass

D

Darkness – often used in reference to the dark horde, used interchangeably with shadow beings

Day dove – small bird with a soft, comforting song; also called a lonely lark
Deathawk – A large black and gold bird of prey, occasionally seen with scavengers; one called Hawk is bonded to Nall
Death dragon - cleanses the world of the dead and dying; usually have particles of decaying flesh and ash clinging to them. They are occasionally seen soaring with the deathawks and klenzingkytes above the Crimson Fields and Wastelands
Downy flier – small winsome creature covered in soft gray fur, known for their keen night vision and sense of smell; the one called Xander is bonded to Yáviё
Dragon Queen – Female ruler of Ædracmoræ and the Seven Kingdoms, Yáviё's birthright
Dramm bush – short leafy bush often used as a source of shade by the Ancients
Dweomers [DWO meers] – memorized lines of ancient spells held within the mind of a thaumaturge or wizard.

E

Emerald flower – brilliant green flower of the crimson longgrass
Empath – one with the ability to feel and soothe the sorrow and misery of others
Equus – magickal steeds bound to the House of Aaradan

F

Fallowass – small furry beast of burden, often owned by Ancients
Feie [fay] – a race of short, stout, fiery haired enchanted wizards
Firedrake – large fire-breathing lizard
Fire imp – elemental fire demons usually found in the company of a mothering haruspex
Flyte – a family group, blood clan, of dragons led by a Matriarch

G

Gaianite crystal – energy crystal used to provide light and power for Maloch's machines during the machine wars
Galen [GAY len] – human leader of the Galenites; swore a life debt to Yáviё and became the seventh Guardian
Galenites – tribe of men created by Yáviё and assigned to Galen Gall

wasp – stinging insect found within the gall of the chale tree Giant Stones – twelve standing stones erected by an unknown source before the time of remembering
G'lm [glim] – great Army of Darkness, composed of deathshades, demons and locked beneath the earth of Ædracmoræ following its reunification
Golden thread – magickal thread or rope used in binding spells
Gorn – a Dark Guardian; follower of Aléria
Grass cat – mid-sized feline, Valia is the hunting and companion animal to Rydén
Grosshare – small mammal hunted and eaten when larger prey cannot be found; often hunted to teach children the use of the bow
Guardian – one called into service to protect and defend a person or world; Guardians are given conditional immortality by the Ancients who call them into service.

H
Hand – measurement of length or height based on the average width of a man's palm
Haruspex – a veneficia or diviner of entrails; the birthmother of fire imps
Heart shard – contains the soul of a dragon; collected and protected by dragon Matriarchs and Guardians. Only by the crushing of the heart shard can a dragon be destroyed. Also referred to as the shard
Herbs of truth – ingredients gathered and prepared by Ancients when calling Guardians or casting binding spells
Hirudinea [high ru DIN ee uh] – the leeches of Fever Fen
Horde – group of evil shadow beings consisting of demons and the damned, often referred to as the darkness or dark horde
House of Aaradan – ruling house of the Kingdom of the Serpent, believed destroyed in the time beyond remembering
House of Ædracmoræ – ruling house of the Dragon Queen
Hovel – a small cottage constructed of chale wood and longgrass, used as housing for both Ancients and Guardians

I
Iaito – legendary sword; origin unknown, but suspected to have been brought by the Sojourners from their dying home world. It is now

possessed by the Guardian Rydén
Ice beast – invisible creature found living deep within the Halcyon Ice Fields
Ice dragon – glacial dragons formed by the crystal structure of frozen water

K

Kingdom of the Dragon – House of Alandon and Yáviё's birthright
Kingdom of the Serpent – House of Aaradan and Sōrél's birthright
Klenzingkyte – large scavenging bird frequently found in the company of death dragons

L

Lake of Lost Memories – ancient lake with the ability to remove and store memories
Laoghaire [LEER ee] – dark wizard who claims to be the father of Lohgaen
Life debt – an oath of service given by one being to another in gratitude of a life saved
Lohgaen [LOW gan] – dark wizard, legal heir to the House of Lochlaen, the gryphon king
Lonely lark – small bird with a soft comforting song; also called a day dove
Longgrass – indigenous grass of the seven worlds; often crimson, but can be green or yellow

M

Maelstrom – violent elemental wind being accidentally created by the entanglement of the winds during their creation and release
Magick – the art of conjuration and spell casting practiced by witches, wizards, and sorcerers
Matriarch – female ruler of a specific race, blood clan or flyte
Meremire – home of the Æstretfordæ Ancients
Mind crawler – colloquialism for an empath
Mirror – the eyes in which a summoner sees himself; also refers to

the ancient mirrors used to move back and forth between the seven kingdoms
Mistral dragon – dragons of the seven winds, malicious and evil tempered
Mock dragons – flying war machines created by Maloch; also referred to as the soulless
Morning bun – flat bread, also called bannock
Mountain blackthorn – indigenous flowering plant with deep violet-colored blossoms

N
Näeré [nair UH] – a Guardian, twin sister of Sōrél
Nall – a Guardian, first life brother to Rydén

O
Oubliette – a windowless cylindrical chamber entered through a trap door in its ceiling that opens into the floor of the tower above. Näeré and Sōrél were hidden in the oubliette during Alandon's attack on their fortress.
Oils of wisdom – gathered and prepared by the Ancients for use during the calling of the Guardians and for binding spells
Oystereggs – fruit of the prickleberry bush

P
Pearl of Perception – a jewel held by the sea dragons said to bring knowledge of a person's foolish mistakes when they lay their hands on it
Pledge – an oath of protection given by one being to another. Guardians are pledged to their charges and to their dragon flytes
Plumquats – fruit of the chale tree eaten during celebratory dinners
Prickleberry – a thorny bush that produces oystereggs; its flat, pad-like leaves are used for stone forging
Promise – given by a man to the woman he intends to wed

Q
Quest – to perform a prescribed feat within the constraints of a prophecy

R

Reclamation of Souls – cleansing and rebinding of minds. This action was performed on Maloch's people before their reassignment to the Xavians and the Galenites
Root of the Verdant Tree – the last remaining vestige of the ancient verdant tree given to Nall within the chamber of the Sojourners
Rydén [ry DEN] – a Guardian and first life sister to Nall

S

Sacred Sword of Domesius [doe MEE see us] – wielded by Yáviё; given as a gift by Faera the war dragon
Sea dragon – dragon evolved for life within the waters
Seven pools – sacred waters of the seven kingdoms used to cleanse Yáviё's sorrows
Shab-ot – a gyre used between the pages of the Book of Trolls to keep evil from entering the world through the dust within the pages
Shadow – to veil oneself; also used when referring to the dark horde or shadow beings
Shield of Viileshga [vee LESH ga] – dragon scale shield given to Nall by Adra at the Well of Viileshga
Simplestag – a common herd animal found on all the seven worlds, it is hunted for both meat and hides
Siren – female trickster with the power to sing beasts, men and Guardians to sleep
Slitherwort – a poisonous plant with toxins that can cause death to a Guardian or Man
Span – measurement of length or height based on the average width from outstretched thumb to tip of fourth finger of a man's hand
Sōrél [soe RELL] – Captain of the Guardians, twin brother to Näeré, future king of the House of Aaradan
Soulless – Maloch's flying machines built in the image of dragons
Sōviё [so VEE uh]– daughter of Yáviё and Sōrél, future queen of Ædracmoræ and the Seven Kingdoms
Spider grass tea – a cold tea used as a daytime beverage
Spider cloth – strong fabric woven of spiders' silk and used for lightweight clothing
Staff of Souls – created for each Guardian from the roots of the

willow, it is used in the summoning ceremony when one Guardian summons another and in the ceremony to reunite the seven kingdoms into a single world
Stone sprites – tiny enchanted beings released from the Giant Stones by Yávië

T

Talisman – artifact of a Guardian
Talonmet – a Dark Guardian, follower of Aléria
Thaumaturge [THOM a turj] – scholars of the arcane, users of dark offensive magick
Thralax [THRAY laks] – giant fur-covered man-shaped beast found in Spire Canyon, feeds primarily on the flesh of men
Tree of Creation – willow tree and last remaining life from the world of Ædracmoræ in the time beyond remembering; creator of the Ancients; an instrument of Ædracmoræ's rebirth

U

Urn of Pledges – stone urn used to catch the Guardians' blood at the Ceremony of the Pledges

V

Veil of mist – gift given to the Guardians by their Ancients; it enables them to travel without being seen or heard
Veneficia – a haruspex or diviner of entrails; the birthmother of fire imps
Verdant Tree – tree guardian of the world; an instrument of Ædracmoræ's rebirth
Vows of promise – words spoken under the direction of a wizard that bind a man and a woman as husband and wife

W

Waffle root – root of the chale tree used to make matches and torches, burns very hot and very bright
War dragon – massive fire dragon obedient to the Guardians and bound to Yávië by pledge
Wastelands – the vast desert home of the remains of the Fortress of

the Dragon Queen
Well of Viileshga [vee LESH ga] – life-giving water of Æstretfordæ, home of the verdant tree that holds Adra and Ardane's heart shards.
Willow bark tea – a hot tea made of willow bark and used for its medicinal properties
Willow tree – the Tree of Creation
Wind dragon – ethereal dragons of the seven winds bound to Yávië by pledge
Witches and Wizards – those experienced in the art of conjuration and spell casting, both good and evil

X

Xalín [ZAHL in] – son of Kayann, adopted by Galen, birth father was an unknown Sojourner
Xavier [ZAY vee ur] – empathic leader of the Xavian people
Xavian City – city created and held in place by the minds of the Xavian people

Y

Ya'vanna [YAH van ah] – mortal wife to Alandon, Yávië's and Aléria's birthmother, past Queen of Ædracmoræ; a Dragon Queen
Yávië [YAH vee uh] – first born of Alandon, future Queen of Ædracmoræ; a Dragon Queen and Guardian

Z

Zeth – a Guardian, young and inexperienced